DATE DUE		

THE HAMILTONS OF BALLYDOWN

Recent Titles by Anne Doughty from Severn House

ON A CLEAR DAY
BEYOND THE GREEN HILLS
THE WOMAN FROM KERRY

THE HAMILTONS OF BALLYDOWN

Anne Doughty

This first world edition published in Great Britain 2004 by
SEVERN HOUSE PUBLISHERS LTD of
9–15 High Street, Sutton, Surrey SM1 1DF.
This first world edition published in the USA 2004 by
SEVERN HOUSE PUBLISHERS INC of
595 Madison Avenue, New York, N.Y. 10022.

British Library Cataloguing in Publication Data

Doughty, Anne, 1939-
The Hamiltons of Ballydown
1. Ireland - Social conditions - 19th century - Fiction
2. Historical fiction
I. Title
823.9'14 [F]

ISBN 0-7278-6084-4

Typeset by Palimpsest Book Production Ltd.,
Polmont, Stirlingshire, Scotland.
Printed and bound in Great Britain by
MPG Books Ltd., Bodmin, Cornwall.

Acknowledgements

I am once again indebted to family, friends and complete strangers, who have spared me their time, told me their stories, allowed me to climb on their field-gates with my camera, or tramp across their land to explore some long-abandoned house.

I am also grateful to librarians and the keepers of archives, particularly at the Irish Studies Centre and the Robinson Library in Armagh, and at the Banbridge Heritage Centre in County Down.

Even more encouraging than these generous people are the readers who put their names on library waiting lists as soon as they know there is a new novel due. When the work is difficult or demanding, these are the people who keep me going, both by their numbers and their comments.

It is to them that I dedicate this seventh novel: *The Hamiltons of Ballydown*.

Anne Doughty
Belfast, 2004

One

Ballydown, June 1896

The rain came in the night, sweeping in from the south, pattering softly on the bedroom windows. Rose stirred briefly and listened to the gentle, persistent beat on the thatch and the steady drip into the stone gutters below. The garden needed it and the neighbouring farmers would be grateful, she thought, as she drifted back into sleep.

It was still raining when Rose knelt to rouse the banked-up fire and boil the kettle for breakfast. Great swags of low cloud made the kitchen dim and the stove sulky, even with the front door propped open to improve the draught.

'That was a good drop we had in the night,' John said, as he tramped downstairs and paused in the doorway, his tall, broad-shouldered frame cutting off the misty light.

'You'll all get wet on the way to work,' Rose laughed, as she moved back and forth across the low-ceilinged room bringing the teapot from the dresser and fresh bread and butter from the small, chilly outshot beyond the kitchen, an addition to the house when it had been a farmhouse with enough cattle to need a dairy.

'Well, Sam and I might get wet, but I think it'll clear,' said John thoughtfully. 'There's a bit of a lightness out to the west. Give it another hour,' he advised, as he dropped into his armchair by the stove and pulled on his boots. 'Will I give Sam another shout?' he asked, as the kettle began to sing and she reached up to the mantelpiece for the tea caddy.

Rose paused and listened. After a moment or two they heard the heavy tread of stockinged feet on the wooden stairs. A robust figure, already as tall as his father, Sam glanced silently out at the rain, disappeared into the cupboard on the window side of the stove and emerged clutching his own well-polished boots.

'Boiled egg, Sam?' Rose asked, as he drew up his chair to the table.

He nodded, half asleep, the soft skin of his face shining from the touch of cold water. He'd washed so quickly there were still traces of soap behind his ear. He looked younger than his almost sixteen years.

'Are you for town today, love?' John asked, as she poured tea and cut them thick slices of the previous day's baking.

'No,' she said, looking out at the rain and shaking her head gently. 'I might have gone in, but I want to get on with Sarah's dress. Only a week now to her birthday,' she added, smiling.

There was no danger whatever of anyone forgetting Sarah's birthday. At thirteen, she was quite capable of reminding them all of the event, but she never failed to point out that her day was also her mother's day. She'd been born on Rose's thirtieth birthday in the house in County Armagh when they'd lived with John's mother, Granny Sarah.

Rose dropped the eggs neatly into John and Sam's waiting egg cups, filled up their mugs and went to the foot of the stairs.

'Hannah. Sarah,' she called firmly. 'Time to get up.'

The voice that replied was Hannah's. It usually was. Hannah was often awake long before anyone else. She would lie and listen to the familiar morning sounds, enjoying the quiet and the warmth of her own bed with her own special quilt, the one she'd designed when her mother and her mother's friend, Elizabeth Sinton, had offered to make it for her.

Rose turned away from the steep, twisty staircase. If Hannah was awake she'd make sure Sarah got up. Not always an easy job, but Hannah had the measure of it. She listened for another moment to the footsteps overhead, then, satisfied, she turned to Sam.

'I have cheese or cold bacon and baker's loaf,' she began. 'Or you could have some of each.'

He smiled sheepishly and nodded. Sam always had a good appetite. When his lunch box came back in the evening there wasn't so much as a crumb to throw to the birds. She watched him scrape out the very last morsel of his egg, invert the empty shell in his egg cup and stab it with his spoon before she turned away to the dairy.

'Well, the fairies never sail far in your eggshells,' John laughed, as he looked across the table. 'But I'm afraid we've left it too late. They're gone. That's the fault of those that neglected their eggshells.'

'Is there any more tea in the pot?' Sam asked, hopefully.

'Aye, there is. Plenty.'

'Are ye still workin' on the stenters?' he asked, glancing up at the clock, as his father refilled both their mugs.

'No, we got them sorted out. I'm not sure what Hugh has in mind the day. We might even get lookin' at those drawin's I told you about. Ivery time he goes to lay a hand on them doesn't someone arrive with trouble at one mill or t'other.'

'Here you are, Sam, and a big piece of cake too.'

He got up from the table, bent down and kissed her and took the lunch box from her hands.

'You've got a grey hair, Ma,' he said suddenly, as he straightened up.

'Only one, Sam?' she said, throwing her soft morning plait of dark hair back over her shoulder and laughing up at him. 'I'm glad you can't count. I've had to stop pulling them out or I'd have no hair left.'

'Ach sure what's a few grey hairs between friends,' said John, stroking the crown of his head as he stood up and reached for his cap on the row of hooks by the door. 'Better grey than nay. I'm beginnin' to feel the draught rightly wi'out m' cap these days.'

He moved across to the foot of the staircase, stepped up the two bottom treads, his head bent in the low stairwell. 'Cheerio, Hannah. Cheerio, Sarah. See you tonight.'

A small chorus returned his greeting.

'Will I see you midday?' Rose asked, as she handed him his jacket.

He slipped an arm round her waist and kissed her.

'All bein' well,' he said cheerfully over his shoulder as he and Sam stepped out into the swirling mist and tramped down the garden path.

John was right about the rain. By the time Hannah and Sarah finished their breakfast, collected what they needed for school and wheeled their bicycles round to the front of the house, the fine drizzle had stopped. As she followed them to the gate, Rose caught the first glimpse of the sun gleaming sporadically through cloud from which only the finest beading of moisture swirled around them as they freewheeled down the steep hill.

She stood at the garden gate, watching them go, Hannah's slim, composed figure following more cautiously as Sarah wove her way expertly between the potholes on the unmade road. Dark haired, with startling blue eyes and pale skin, her chin jutting forward as she pedalled, Sarah was always in the lead. Hannah might be four years older and almost ready to leave school, but these days it was Sarah who led the way, just as James had done when he and Sam went everywhere together.

Rose cleared the remains of breakfast, washed up in the deep Belfast sink in the dairy, cleaned the Modern Mistress stove with black lead and emery paper and scrubbed the long wooden table. She swept the floor and added the crumbs from the bread board to those she'd flicked on to the garden path where the small birds could carry them off to the fledglings that chirped and squeaked in the nearby bushes and trees.

She paused a moment and drew back in the doorway, floorbrush in hand, to watch a blackbird, a robin and a thrush swoop down one after another and disappear with full beaks. Though it was only the first week of June, their bright summer plumage looked worn and faded already, so hard did they work raising their broods.

By mid-morning, the first beam of sunlight glanced across the large, white-washed room. It threw reflections of the south-facing windows across the floor, lit up the solid legs of the table and caught the fine motes of flour dust hanging in the air as she slid cakes of wheaten and soda bread into the oven. She wiped her hands on her apron, moved lightly across the flagged floor and leant against the doorpost, her eyes half closed in the brightness. She turned sideways to let the sunlight play on her shoulders, always stiff and sometimes sore after the effort of cleaning the stove and kneading the bread. The deep warmth was like an embrace, reassuring and comforting.

The last of the mistiness had gone and the sky was patched with blue. She drew in a deep breath of the rain-washed air, full of the mixed scents of summer. Cut grass from their own meadow behind the house, pollen carried on the light breeze from the mature lime trees in the avenue of Rathdrum, the handsome gentleman's residence at the top of the hill, and the mixed perfumes from the deep herbaceous border that followed the line of her own garden path.

Almost seven years now since they'd moved, the best of their old furniture carefully loaded on Sinton's dray. There was Granny Sarah's sideboard, the dresser they'd bought when she died and they'd had to sell the rest of her well-loved pieces because their landlord was able to turn them out of the house at Annacramp. There'd been no space for fine pieces in the abandoned two-room cottage opposite Thomas Scott's forge.

What excitement there'd been that day, driving fifteen miles into unknown country and a new home only John had seen. A new place with new neighbours. For the four children, it was the longest journey any of them had ever made. Once she'd settled them in, she'd begun planting her garden, trusting her cherished cuttings to a different soil, a changed aspect and a slightly different climate. As she walked the length of the path, nipping off dead leaves and the odd faded bloom from the flourishing border, she nodded to the old friends who'd come with her, tiny fragments when they arrived, now vigorous plants or thriving bushes.

Down by the gate she leant over a clump of foxgloves and dropped her handful of bits into the old bucket carefully hidden amongst the luxuriant growth. Everything she'd planted had grown and flourished.

'And so have we all, thank God,' she whispered.

She rested against the gate and gazed out across the broad lane that ran up and over Rathdrum Hill. The fields they owned on the southern slopes below the lane were rented out to a neighbouring farmer, but John himself made sure the hawthorn hedges were cut low each autumn so that nothing interrupted her outlook over the rich lowlands of the Bann valley.

The low hills here were steeper than those in Armagh, but they had just the same gently curving shape. One behind another, like eggs lying in a basket, they ran away into the distance as far as she could see, until the now familiar outline of the Mourne mountains rose on the horizon, sharp and clearly drawn against the sky, the miles between so reduced in the clear light, she felt she could stretch out her hand and touch them.

The bright sunlight bathed the richness of the new growth, the hedgerows and trees fully leafed but not yet quite mature, the whole countryside a sea of green, rippled and dimpled. No wonder the people who came in their carriages to visit Banbridge said that only now did they understand why Ireland was called the Emerald Isle.

'All this and mountains too,' she said aloud.

Until she'd married John and travelled north to Ulster, there'd always been mountains in her life. As a child, born in Donegal, she'd lived with the Derryveagh mountains all around her. She could still remember setting off one day to climb the long ridge that ran along their valley, because she'd so wanted to see what was on the other side. Later, when she and her mother lived in Kerry, she never tired of climbing the lowest of the mountains near Currane Lake so she could stand under the vast expanse of the sky, the mountains around her, the Atlantic beyond.

She still thought of her mother so often. At times, she wrote letters in her head, telling her all the news, just as she'd done after she and John were married in the little estate church close to Currane Lodge and he'd taken her away to a new life in a far country. Hannah and Rose had served the Molyneux family for so many years, Sir Capel had made her wedding day a holiday. She'd had gifts from servants and family alike and been seen off with her John in a cloud of good wishes. That she'd never see her mother again was the last thing she'd ever imagined.

Over the years, she often saw herself back in the housekeeper's quarters, drinking tea and sharing her news. Even now that Hannah had long lain in the shadow of the church tower, she did it still, calling up her mother's steady gaze as she listened so carefully to all she had to say and responded with the shrewd, kindly wisdom so much a part of her.

Could she or Hannah have foreseen that Rose would own a two-storey house with ten acres of land, the gift of a wealthy man, James Sinton, because she'd saved his life and those of his wife and children?

Night after night, after the rail disaster outside Armagh, from which the Sintons, Rose and the children had all escaped unscathed, she'd woken up gasping for breath, struggling to get back to them, running and running and making no headway, calling to them and they never hearing. It was only when she tried to find words to tell her mother what had happened that Rose found comfort. The more she let her mind move back into that room where they'd shared so much of their daily life, the more she was sure Hannah would have said that some good may come from even the most heartbreaking events, if only you have the courage to accept what has happened.

Events had proved how right Hannah would have been. That event, the cruel and bitter disaster that tore the heart out of a community and left no one free from grief or anxiety, had, in fact, lifted Rose and John out of a hard and limiting life and set them down in a brighter world, full of hope and possibility for them and their children.

She smiled to herself, thinking how pleased her mother would be if she knew John was too busy repairing and inventing textile machinery to shoe horses. Not only did his employer pay him handsomely, but he'd encouraged him to put down his first patents. Already, they'd yielded more than his year's earnings when he'd worked in Drumcairn mill.

Hannah might have smiled with pleasure at their good fortune, but John's own mother would have laughed out loud.

'Aren't you the lucky one?' she'd have said.

She could still hear Granny Sarah's voice. Arriving in her home, a new bride, weary from a long journey, her mind full of images of countryside she'd never seen before, Sarah made her laugh the moment she crossed the threshold, welcoming her son with an irreverent gaiety.

'Sure he always lands on his feet.'

And indeed, it was true. Although they'd had hardship enough before they came to Ballydown, John had certainly landed on his feet once again. She'd never known him happier in his work.

And what about the children, Rose?

She saw again the closely written pages in the flowing copperplate which Hannah had perfected to record the accounts of Currane Lodge.

The last letter she'd written to her mother was the week before she died. Sarah had just started school, Hannah was able to sew the babies' dresses Rose had made for years to boost their income. James was eleven years old, taller than Rose, and he and Sam were mad about engines.

'Your grandson James is apprenticed in Belfast now, Ma. He's with Harland and Wolff, the biggest shipbuilder in the world,' Rose said aloud. 'He's taller than John, but not as broad. And he likes to be called Jamie.'

Rose turned her head and glanced up the hill to where Rathdrum House lay hidden behind its avenue of limes. Sometimes when the air was very still, or the wind in the right direction, she could hear the ring of a hammer from the workshop attached to the stable block. She could always tell whether it was John or Hugh Sinton at the anvil. John's stroke was steady and strong, but punctuated with the small, dancing rhythm all blacksmiths use. Hugh's stroke was rapid, persistent and unvaried in pace, full of a pent-up energy, just like the man himself.

This morning all was silent. She could imagine the pair of them peering at some model they'd made, a design for an improved system of energy transfer, a more efficient method of performing some process in one of the linen mills.

Hugh had inherited four of them. Millbrook spun the linen thread, Lenaderg wove the cloth, Seapatrick specialized in hemstitching and the largest mill of all, nearby Ballievy, right on the River Bann itself, did the bleaching and finishing.

Since they'd come to County Down, she'd learnt a whole new language. She knew all about the spinning and the weaving and the finishing of linen, but she had to admit she wasn't always sure exactly how the machines worked.

No doubt she could have found out more, but, unlike Sarah, she was reluctant to interrupt Hugh, or his sister, Elizabeth, when they came to Ballydown and talked about the everyday business of the mills and their work people. If Sarah wanted to know something she'd ask and go on asking until she understood. Rose shook her head wryly. Sarah's first meeting with Elizabeth the day they arrived was one she'd never forget.

'Good day and welcome, Rose and John. I'm Elizabeth Sinton. I'm sorry Hugh couldn't be here. He had to go over to Millbrook.'

The tall, angular woman who emerged from the front door of their new home was dressed rather severely in a dark skirt and a plain white blouse that accentuated her height, her already greying hair and her rather forbidding countenance. She shook hands with Rose and John warmly enough, ran her eyes over the children, a slight frown on her face, and then greeted each one correctly by name as she shook hands with them.

'Good day, James. Good day, Sam. I've heard a lot about you. You must come up and see the workshop as soon as you've settled in. I hear you are both keen on engines. Good day, Hannah. Good day, Sarah. And who is this?' she asked, kneeling down unexpectedly on the garden path where she was face to face with Ganny, Sarah's constant companion.

'This is Ganny,' said Sarah, promptly. 'My granny made her for me. She was grey like you, but you're *much* bigger.'

'You mean taller, Sarah, don't you?' said Rose awkwardly.

'No, I said bigger,' retorted Sarah shortly.

Rose felt herself blush, but Elizabeth Sinton didn't appear

to be in the slightest offended. Entirely focused on Sarah, she smiled warmly, her strong, plain face suddenly transformed, her grey eyes sparkling.

'I hope you'll bring Ganny when you and Hannah come to visit me. I'll show you a doll my grandmother made for me,' she said, her rather formal way of speaking softening as she laid a finger on Ganny's grey woollen hair.

'I've taken the liberty, Rose, of making up the two new beds that arrived earlier in the week, in case any of you needed to lie down,' she said, as she stood up. 'Please don't trouble to return the sheets. Hugh brings me so many to try out for him I could furnish one of Miss Nightingale's wards,' she added with a little laugh. 'Now I shall leave you in peace. The dray will probably take at least another hour, but I've left some refreshments ready. Good day to you all.'

'Funny lady,' said Sarah, before Elizabeth Sinton had even closed the garden gate behind her. 'I like her,' she added decisively, as she yawned hugely and marched towards the open front door.

But if Sarah's reaction to Elizabeth Sinton had embarrassed Rose, worse was to come. While Hannah admitted she was tired out after being up so early and having had such a busy morning, even before the journey, Sarah refused to make use of the other bed. She tramped round the house, looked into every room, opened built in cupboards, turned the tap on and off in the room beyond the kitchen, explored the garden and climbed up on the fence to look over into the field where her father said they could keep a mare if they decided to have a trap.

When she heard an unfamiliar voice in the big kitchen, she shot back inside and stood staring at Hugh Sinton as he welcomed her parents and shook hands with James and Sam.

'Good day, Sarah,' he said, as soon as his eye lighted upon her.

He moved forward to shake hands with her, his body awkward and ungainly as he hunched his left shoulder to enable him to swing his left leg forward. He held out his hand and smiled at her, his handsome, tanned face marred by a white scar that ran diagonally across one cheek, reappeared on his forehead and disappeared into his thick, dark hair.

'Did a horse kick you?' Sarah enquired. 'Our friend Thomas has a scar like yours. He nearly died, only Ma and George Robinson took him to the Infirmary in Armagh. Did you nearly die too?'

Before Rose had time to draw breath, Hugh had released Sarah's hand and nodded.

'Yes. I was ill a long time. Elizabeth nursed me for months. But the horse didn't kick me. It fell and threw me in our own yard. There was a piece of metal lying on the ground and it cut off the front of my knee, so it doesn't work very well.'

'Does it hurt?'

'Yes, it does sometimes,' he said easily. 'But I'm still here, God be praised,' he added strongly, as he straightened himself up again.

'I think it's time Sarah was in bed,' said Rose apologetically.

Hugh had given her a smile she would never forget. Sudden and full of an unexpected warmth, it showed her what a handsome young man he still was. John had been quite right. Hugh was just as kind and as considerate as his older brother James, even if he lacked James's graciousness.

'You've all had a long day and need your rest,' he said gently, as Rose picked her up. 'Sleep well, Sarah.'

He swung his bad leg into action over the stone floor. 'God bless you all,' he added, pausing in the doorway, before disappearing at speed down the garden path with a strange rocking motion.

The sun had risen towards its zenith and the mountains were now less clear as the heat shimmered on their rocky slopes. Rose shut the garden gate behind her, crossed the lane and leant on the five-barred gate in the low hawthorn hedge opposite. Michael MacMurray's cattle had retreated to a patch of shadow where a well grown ash tree raised its leafy crown above the line of the eastern boundary of the rich, sloping meadow. She studied the familiar countryside from this new perspective, delighting in the richness of full leaf. In as little as a week's time, though still beautiful, the foliage would no longer be translucent.

She listened to the familiar sounds of a summer's day. The distant rush of water from the tail race of the bleach mill, the sudden scream of the swallows swooping low over the field in front of her, the creak of a cart on the road below and the bark of a dog somewhere across the river.

Sometimes the days were so full she could pass a whole week without ever having time to stand here and give thanks for the good fortune that had brought them to this place where they'd settled so happily. So many of her worries for the family were 'a thing of the past', as John would say. The children were growing up, they were well and healthy, and there was money in the bank to help them on their way. What woman could ask for more?

On the still air, she caught a sound that was not familiar. To begin with she couldn't even describe it to herself. Persistent and throbbing, a little like the distant thud of beetling hammers. No, not hammers, a rougher sound. More erratic and more turbulent. As she listened it seemed to be getting louder and coming closer all the time.

'Missus Hamilton . . . Missus Hamilton . . .'

She spun round as she heard her name called and found a young lad running up the hill towards her. Without pausing for breath, he jerked his head towards the top of the hill. 'C'mon quick, it's Sam,' he called over his shoulder, as he ran past her.

'Sam?' she gasped, as she turned to follow him, her breath caught with sudden anxiety. What could possibly be wrong? And how could Sam be up the hill when his workplace was down in Tullyconnaught, not far from the mill itself?

She'd never seen this lad before, yet he knew who she was and had obviously been sent to look for her. She followed as quickly as she could, anxious lest the retreating figure disappear from sight. As she reached the less steep gradient beyond the crest of the hill, she saw the slight figure swerve through the open gate into the avenue leading to Rathmore House.

By the time she reached the driveway, gasping for breath, perspiration trickling down her face, she could see Elizabeth directing the lad to the workshop and hurrying after him. Rose struggled on and arrived at the gable of the house just in time to see the young lad, a rolled red flag clutched in his right hand, spill out his message to John and Hugh.

'Ach, good man yourself,' said John, clapping him on the shoulder.

She slowed down, a stitch in her side, and walked as quickly as she could towards them. John turned and caught sight of her. He was smiling. She felt such a relief. It must be all right if he was smiling.

The throbbing noise had grown louder, louder even than the pounding of her own heart.

'Down to the stable wall, Elizabeth,' called Hugh, as he jerked his bad leg into action and hurried away from them.

John came towards her and slipped an arm round her waist.

'Yer all outa breath,' he said quietly.

'I'm all right now,' she said, drawing a great gasp of air into her small chest. 'I thought there was something wrong. What's happening?'

'D'ye not hear?'

'I hear a noise, but I don't know what it is.'

'C'mon. Hugh's right. The stable wall's the best place.'

Hugh had fetched a ladder to make it easy for Rose and Elizabeth to climb up. They stood in a line on top of the solid wall and looked down on the stretch of main road that ran along the foot of the hill towards Corbet and Katesbridge. The road was empty, its rough surface a pale gash through the green countryside.

'Will you not get into trouble, Billy, for leaving him without a flagman?' asked Hugh coolly, addressing the boy who stood beside him, shading his eyes against the light.

'Ach no. Wait till ye see. There's no need for me.'

It was only when she caught the smell of smoke on the clear air that Rose guessed what they were waiting for.

'Can ye feel the vibrations?' John asked her quietly.

Rose wasn't sure. She was still hot and shaking after the effort she'd made, but before she had time to answer, a man waving a red flag appeared. Yards behind him, with a cloud of smoke and steam swirling round them, not one, but three, highly polished road engines steamed steadily along the highway below, each one hauling three loaded wagons.

'Is that the new Fowler then?' asked Hugh, leaning forward, his eyes pinned to the foremost engine. 'I think your da's going to have to walk a bit faster, Billy,' he added, as the flagman leading the procession caught sight of them and waved his red flag up at them.

'D'you see who's up front, Rose?'

It was some moments before the smoke parted and Rose saw a familiar figure. For a moment he appeared to be quite unaware of his audience, but then the flagman checked the road ahead, turned back and called up to him. With a great beaming smile, young Sam Hamilton wiped his brow with the back of his arm and raised it in salute to the little group of spectators on the hillside above.

They waved back and stood watching till the last engine had passed and the only movement below was Billy taking a shortcut to catch up with the convoy when it paused to take on more water at Corbet Lough.

'Well, Rose, what do you think of that?' asked Hugh, his voice barely concealing his excitement. 'The new engine and him not turned sixteen. Are you not proud of him?'

'I am, Hugh, I am,' she nodded, tears springing to her eyes. 'I can hardly believe he's grown up so quickly,' she said, trying to blink them away. 'It's just the smoke,' she said feebly. 'It makes my eyes water.'

'Just wait till young Jamie launches his first ship,' he said, nodding sympathetically and turning his head away to give her time to recover. 'We'll have to do better than a wall to stand on that day.'

Two

'What about a cup of tea or a glass of lemonade by way of celebration?' Elizabeth asked, as she climbed down from the wall and turned to watch John swing Rose lightly to the ground beside her.

Hugh ignored the ladder and slithered from the wall to land on his good leg. He smiled sheepishly across at his sister. 'Sounds good, Elizabeth,' he began, 'but we've only just got to those drawings.'

Elizabeth waved a hand in the air. 'Well, it's always polite to ask,' she said, looking from Hugh to John. 'A refusal never offends.'

They all laughed. Almost every shop in Banbridge had a notice, handwritten or printed and clearly displayed behind the main counter, which said: *Please do not ask for credit, as a refusal often offends.*

'What about you, Rose?'

'You know I love your lemonade,' Rose replied, still laughing, 'but I dashed off with the front door wide open and my baking things all over the table.'

'And who do you think would steal your baking things, Rose?' Hugh asked, his tone light and teasing.

'No one at all, Hugh,' she agreed, shaking her head. 'I'm sure there hasn't been a soul past the house all morning, but there was a jug of milk should've gone back to the dairy. And there's bread in the oven,' she added, finally remembering what was prompting her to go straight home. 'But I'll be up tomorrow, as we planned,' she called over her shoulder, as she turned on her heel. 'If I don't have to bake more bread, that is.'

She walked steadily along the lime avenue, grateful for the cool shade and the soothing murmur of myriads of insects at work in the green canopy above her head. The light dazzled her as she emerged from the leafy tunnel, but as she turned down the hill a whisper of breeze threw tendrils of hair gently across her perspiring forehead.

She was grateful for the movement of air. She still hadn't quite recovered from trying to run uphill after Billy, her heart in her mouth, sure that something dreadful had happened to Sam. It ought to teach her a lesson not to assume the worst. Not to worry so much about her children, particularly when they weren't children any more.

They'd certainly seemed like children when they arrived at Ballydown. But each year since had brought such changes. James was a young man now, set out upon his own life in Belfast. 'Little' six-year-old Sarah was thirteen, a full two years older than the boys and girls who left school as soon as the law permitted to go and work in the mills.

Perhaps all mothers worried about their children. Was it a habit that grew up when children were young and vulnerable and stayed with you when they became sons and daughters, well grown and with every appearance of good health? Or was it the knowledge that life is perilous, that loss is part of life and simply has to be borne?

So many children died young, not just stillborn infants, or babies who didn't thrive, but lively young toddlers who caught whooping cough or diphtheria. Older children who died of tuberculosis. She'd heard of plenty of those, as well as her own friend's child. She would never forget Jane Wylie, only nine years old.

She walked faster, her stride increasing with the thrust of her thoughts, her eyes searching the fields and hedgerows as if they had the answer to her questions. There were carpets of buttercups in the meadows, a creamy froth of cow parsley lining the sides of the road, dusky pink spikes of valerian sprouting from the tops of the stone walls.

She took in the colour and the light. What a pity to spoil such a lovely day with such anxious thoughts. Yet she sensed it was the day itself that made her so uneasy. Life had been so good since they'd come to Ballydown. Just like a summer day. But summer is a short season. Like the challenge of winter, the years ahead might make a demand upon her she'd be hard pressed to meet.

'Come on, Rose,' she said aloud, 'you must do better than this.'

Rather than worrying herself about the future, she ought to be giving thanks for all the good things the last seven years had brought. How silly to let such sad thoughts cloud Sam's big day.

The smile he'd sent winging up the hill had so delighted her. It was that same slow, warm smile he'd give her when he came back from the Tullyconnaught Haulage Company while he was still at school, his eyes bright, his forearms streaked with axle oil. He'd spent as many Saturdays and holidays as he could down at their maintenance sheds. Since he was a little boy, he'd wanted to drive an engine, a railway engine or a road engine, he didn't mind which, and he made himself so useful down at the sheds, a job was waiting for him the moment he left school.

It was their good friend James Sinton who'd persuaded him he needed to stay at school till he was thirteen, however, and then do a proper apprenticeship. Now, three years later, he'd done it. He was not just a young man who could *drive* an engine, he understood them. He could service them and maintain them, coax and persuade them to work to their greatest capacity without strain. That's how he came to be trusted with the precious new Fowler this morning. No wonder William Auld, the senior flagman, sent his son to tell them all to look out for Sam.

A few minutes later Rose was back in her kitchen, giving her full attention to the bread. She tapped the soda and wheaten with a practised finger. The dull, hollow sound told her they'd taken no harm. The bread might be a touch drier than usual, but that was no great mischief when there was plenty of butter to spread on it.

She set the cakes to cool in the dairy, wiped the kitchen

table and washed up her mixing bowl and measure. Although the stove was still alight, it was pleasantly cool in the big kitchen, the shadows on the floor visibly shortened now the sun had reached its highest point. If the weather settled in as warm as this, she could leave the stove unlit and do her cooking on the gas rings at the far end of the dairy.

The gas had been laid on when the house belonged to the manager at Ballievy Mill, piped all the way down from Hugh's own gas plant at Rathdrum. He'd set it up as an experiment while he was still in his teens and it had been such a success he'd been encouraged to introduce gaslight in all his mills.

She thought back to the days when they'd lived in the cottage opposite the forge. It hadn't even got a stove. There were times she'd come home from shopping in Armagh and find the banked-up fire on the hearth had burnt itself out. If the children were home before her, they'd have to sit in the dark because she couldn't let them light the Tilley lamp. She couldn't even make a cup of tea till she'd coaxed the turf back to life, just when she was tired and aching to sit down. If the stove was really slow these days there was the gas to fall back on, and after dark there'd be the soft glow of the lamps on either side of the mantelpiece.

The lamps were the first thing Hannah noticed on the day they arrived. While Sarah was fascinated by the tap in the dairy, turning it on and off and watching the water gurgle down the plughole in the deep white sink, Hannah was examining the delicately engraved shades and the fine wire chains that hung below them. They were so easy and safe to set going even Sarah had been allowed to take her turn lighting them.

But then, she thought, any gas lamp Hugh chose would be simple and safe.

'Simplicity and safety, those are the most important things with anything new,' she'd heard him insist a dozen times. 'When you've hundreds of work people, most of them quite unfamiliar with any kind of technology, some of them very young, it has to be within their grasp, otherwise it's simply a source of danger.'

Nevertheless, accidents there were, for all his awareness of danger and his efforts to protect his workers. Hardly a week passed without some report in the *Banbridge Chronicle* of a serious injury or death.

Rose looked up at the clock. After the excitements of the morning and the need to study the new drawings, it would probably be another hour before John appeared for a bite of lunch. She carried her small sewing table over to the window, fetched the bodice of Sarah's dress from the cupboard and spread it out on her knee. The machining had been done on Elizabeth's new Singer, the delicate shirring and decorating of the bodice was left for her own practised hand.

She ran her eye over the pretty patterned fabric and threaded her needle. She so hoped Sarah would like it. The trouble was, she was often unpredictable. It was one of the many contradictions in her character that, though she loved colour and texture, she paid not the slightest attention to fashion and was usually totally indifferent to what she was wearing. The only dress she'd ever said she liked was Rose's best silk. She'd insisted that one day she would have one just like it.

Shopping together in Robinson Cleaver's new store in Belfast for material to make the birthday dress, it was Elizabeth who put her hand out to the fine lawn fabric draped on a display stand.

'Do you think she might like this one, Rose?' she said, smiling broadly. 'It's not exactly silk,' she went on, 'but the feel of it is so soft and the little flowers are so pretty.'

'Yes, I think you're right. It is soft, isn't it? Let's go and look at patterns and see how many yards I'll need.'

She smiled to herself, recalling the moment. Elizabeth was kind to all the children, but Rose had always known that Sarah was her favourite. Whenever she heard of her latest enthusiasm and the difficulties into which it had inevitably led her, the warmth of the response, the hint of a smile in the voice, so regularly gave her away.

Though Sarah was not given to expressing her feelings very obviously towards those closest to her, Rose knew the feeling was mutual. She'd accepted Elizabeth and Hugh from their very first meeting, making up her mind in an instant, whereas Hannah had taken her time. Polite and responsive as Hannah always was, it was weeks before Rose could be sure she was completely at ease with them.

For herself, it had been a pleasure getting to know Elizabeth. She was one of those women who spoke her mind readily enough, but seldom said anything sharp or unpleasant. They had slipped easily into what had rapidly become a very close intimacy, each openly grateful for the presence of a like-minded woman friend so close by. While Elizabeth had aunts and cousins aplenty, they were widely dispersed around the countryside and she seldom visited away from home, for although she had a competent and trusted housekeeper who would see to her brother's needs, she knew how often Hugh could be overcome with loneliness or discouragement. Despite his firm convictions that he must always do his best for his fellow creatures, he didn't apply his convictions to himself. He took little thought for his own comfort or peace of mind and allowed himself little leisure or pleasure.

Sitting side by side in the conservatory of Rathdrum House one pleasant October morning some months after they'd become close friends, a pile of quilting pieces between them, Elizabeth had put down her work and looked thoughtfully at Rose.

'I've never really told you about that evening you arrived, have I?' she said, peering at her over the top of her spectacles.

'How do you mean?' Rose asked, as she finished off the square she was working on. 'Do you mean the shock you got when we all arrived and you found out who you'd have for neighbours?' she asked, teasing her, simply for the pleasure of seeing her smile.

'No, I wasn't too concerned about that,' Elizabeth replied laughing. 'Your dear John talked about you and the children the day James brought him to meet Hugh. I had a fairly good idea from the man himself that you and I would be friends. What didn't occur to me was what a happy thing your coming would be for Hugh. Having you and the family has made such a difference to him.'

'Has it?' asked Rose, genuinely puzzled.

Hugh had always been a kind neighbour, thoughtful and helpful, somewhat hasty at times and occasionally rather short tempered, but Rose had certainly not observed any difference in his behaviour over the months since their first meeting.

'That evening you arrived I kept supper late, so he could go down and see you,' Elizabeth began. 'When he came back he was in such good spirits I couldn't quite believe it. Usually in the evening he's so tired and his knee aches so persistently I can hardly get a word out of him, but that night I could see he was full of something he couldn't wait to tell me. To tell you the truth, Rose,' she went on, with a slight, wry laugh, ' I was expecting to hear about a piston or a drive shaft, or something I hadn't even heard of before. But no. He dropped into a chair and said, "I've found the daughter I might have had. She has beauty like Florence had, but she has my own mother's candour. It's a rare quality."'

Elizabeth smiled sadly before she went on.

'Hugh was about to be married when he had his accident. Florence was a very attractive girl, well educated and from a Quaker family like ourselves. Our local meeting had been only too delighted to grant them permission to marry. But after the accident she visited Hugh just once. Within months, while he was still struggling to be able to walk again, she married out of unity.'

'Out of unity?' Rose repeated quietly.

'She married a man who wasn't a Quaker,' Elizabeth explained. 'It was an awful blow to her family. They were fond of Hugh and very strict about such matters, but she showed no more feeling for her family than compassion for Hugh.'

Rose was overcome by a sudden sadness. She liked Hugh, enjoyed his company, appreciated his easy relationship with John and his pleasure in the activities of the children. Despite his disability, at twenty-four he was a lively and attractive man. She wondered often enough why he hadn't married and why he appeared to have no thoughts of doing so.

'To be honest, Rose, though I've not said this to anyone,' Elizabeth confided, her work lying idle in her lap, 'I've often thought what she did hurt Hugh far more than the edge of metal lying on the cobbles.'

Rose nodded. 'Being let down would be hard at any time,' she began, 'but when he was lying there wondering if he would walk again . . .'

Her voice trailed away into silence, as she shook her head. 'If you really love a man, you don't let a misfortune like Hugh's get in the way, do you?'

'No, *you* don't. You wouldn't and I wouldn't,' agreed Elizabeth quickly. 'Hugh was alive and would have mended. All the quicker, had he had her wishing him well and encouraging him to be better. I love Hugh dearly, but the love of a half-sister doesn't compare with the love of a sweetheart. I often think he would have willingly died, but he thought it a sin not to struggle for life when he had so many responsibilities.'

'Responsibilities?' Rose asked, surprised.

Surely Hugh didn't think of Elizabeth as a responsibility when she was so capable of running her own life as well as his. From her very first meeting with them, she'd seen how much Hugh admired his older sister. He always treated her as an equal and regularly asked for her opinion.

'My father married twice, Rose. My own mother, Hester Pearson, died shortly after I was born, when James was only five. Father didn't want us brought up by nannies, so he married Agnes Barbour. It wasn't a love match, but she and Father seemed happy enough together and she was good to James and me. There was nothing of the wicked stepmother about Agnes, but when Hugh was born she absolutely adored him. She wanted another child to be closer to him in age than we were, but for many years she didn't conceive. Hugh was twelve when she became pregnant again. She was in her forties then and a rather delicate woman. Her little girl was born dead and a week later Agnes died too.'

Rose put down her work and looked at Elizabeth's sad face. In her mid-thirties, some years younger than herself, she had the smooth skin of a young woman, but her fair hair was already threaded with grey. Only when she smiled was Rose aware of a young woman with sparkling grey eyes who must certainly have seemed beautiful to some young man. But that was not the story Elizabeth wanted to tell. Not yet.

'Agnes had just inherited the Banbridge mills from her father and uncle,' Elizabeth went on. 'Of course, when her will was read she'd left everything she possessed to Hugh. Poor boy, he'd been taught from childhood that those who have been given privileges, like wealth or intellect, have the greatest responsibility. So, as a boy of twelve, he faced up to the responsibilities of being a mill owner.'

Elizabeth paused, smiling.

'When he left school, he went into the manager's office at Seapatrick to learn the business. He hated it.' She shook her head. 'He had a perfectly good grasp of mathematics, but he had no feel for buying and selling. He loathed being shut up indoors. He couldn't bear the noise of the machines, but he couldn't admit it, could he? He was the boss. Poor Hugh, if he could have given it all away he would, but, as he and the family saw it, it was God's will he do his best for the people who depended on him. James and I knew he was unhappy. We tried to get him to talk to Father, but Hugh felt that wouldn't be right. It was his burden. He had to learn how best to carry it.'

'So what happened? How did he get out of the office?'

'Well, it was Father who found the way in the end. He knew as well as we did Hugh wasn't happy. He was sorry for it, but to begin with he could see no way to help him. Then, one Sunday morning in the silence of the Meeting House he asked for guidance. It wasn't the first time he'd asked, but, as he said afterwards, his faith had not been strong enough.'

She paused and glanced at her friend over her spectacles.

'You remember, Rose, that Quakers don't sing or pray aloud?'

'Yes, I remember. You explained about the Inner Light and trying to find it for yourself.'

'Well, as Father sat in the deep silence, he became aware of the tick of his own fob watch. It seemed to get louder and louder. He tried to ignore it, because it was distracting him from opening his mind to God. As the minutes passed, he became convinced the ticking was so loud it was surely disturbing the other worshippers. "Something must be wrong with it, I'll have to give it to Hugh to fix," he said to himself. And the moment he thought of Hugh, the ticking faded to a murmur.'

Elizabeth beamed at her. 'Father told the story against himself, time and time again, to make the point that we're so busy asking for answers, we don't hear them when they come. But that was the turning point for Hugh. You see, Father knew Hugh could never bear to see things left broken. First, he'd do his best to mend them, then while he was about it he'd see if he could get them to work better.'

'So what happened after that?'

'Well, usually after a sign the person involved has to consult their conscience to see how the answer fits with the situation. Father admitted it all fell into place by the time they'd eaten the midday meal, but he waited a few days to see if further enlightenment might be given. Then he sent for Hugh and made some suggestions. He told Hugh that, as he was not well fitted to the office, he should develop his talent for repairing and improving machinery. Then it would be proper to leave the buying and selling and the running of the mills to men who had the talent and the experience to do it much better than he could.

'Father said that when God lays a burden on one of his servants he also gives them the strength and the wisdom to carry it,' Elizabeth explained, taking up her work again. 'If a burden seems too heavy, that's because there's something to be learnt to help you carry it. You need to ask for insight. From your friends, from your conscience, from God.'

'And so Hugh was able to use his talent and not feel guilty about running the mills.'

'Well, not quite,' said Elizabeth quietly. 'Hugh is hard on himself, too hard. But I know he gives thanks every day when he steps out into the workshop with John for company.'

She paused thoughtfully for a few moments before she went on.

'When Father died, he left his drapery business to James, with the provision of an income for me. Hugh already owned the Banbridge mills. Four hundred workers, Rose, nearer five with the new bleach works. And no wife to support him,' she ended sadly. 'Perhaps now you see why I'm so grateful for you and for your dear John,' she added, smiling warmly. 'Hugh's been so much happier since we've had Hamiltons at Ballydown.'

It was well after one o'clock before Rose heard the click of the garden gate and the tramp of John's boots on the flagged path.

'Did ye think I'd fell and forgot?' he said cheerfully.

'No, I guessed you'd be late,' she said, putting her sewing into its linen wrapper. 'Hugh had a look about him. He wasn't going to leave off till he'd made a start on those drawings.'

'Aye, ye're right there. If Elizabeth hadn't come out to him, he'd have clean forgot about a bite of lunch.'

'Are you starving?' she asked, smiling at him as she took away the cloth she'd draped over the bread and the cheese. 'Buttermilk or tea?'

'A mug of tea would go down well. It's got very warm,' he replied, wiping his forehead with a bare arm, his shirt-sleeves rolled up above his elbows. 'The workshop's cool enough, but it fairly hits you when you come out from under the trees.'

'There was a wee breeze earlier, but it's gone very still now. Not the sound of a bird,' she said softly. 'I think they're all hiding from the heat.'

'Was your bread all right?' he asked, as he cut himself a slice of cheese and added it to his plate.

'Well, you're about to eat it,' she replied, bringing the

teapot to the table and pouring for them both. 'You might need a bit more butter. But we have plenty.'

There was something in the tone of her voice made him look up from his plate. She'd laughed when she'd told him he was about to eat the morning's bread, but now, as she sat down opposite him, her face looked sad, her eyes downcast.

'Did ye fright yerself over Sam this mornin'?' he asked cautiously.

She nodded and said nothing.

'Sure it's only a week now,' he said gently. 'Don't you always think the worst about things this time o' year?'

'Not just this time of year, John,' she replied quickly. 'I could understand it if it was just this week, or even this month. I'll never forget how hot it was up on that railway bank and walking back across the fields. But I can worry now *any* month of the year. I thought something awful had happened to Sam when that wee lad came running up the hill.'

John looked down at the crumbs on his plate and reached for another slice of wheaten. He had an idea women worried more than men and it wasn't a good thing. But what could you do about it? What did you say?

'Ach, I'm sorry ye were upset. Were ye not pleased at the cut of him?'

'Yes, I was,' she said warmly. 'It was just great. I'm more annoyed with myself. I have a kind of feeling we've been too lucky, too blessed, that maybe we've hard times ahead of us.'

'And why shou'd that be?'

'It's just a feeling, John. I wish I could put it away from me.'

She smiled across at him, knowing in her heart he couldn't help her. There was nothing he wouldn't do for her, but on the few occasions she'd seen him depressed he'd been unable to do anything for himself, so she could hardly expect him to help her now.

'Maybe you're right about it being June,' she said with an effort. 'I try every year not to go over it all in my mind, but what might have happened if our carriage door had been locked still haunts me, or if James hadn't spoken up and told me there were no brakes to stop us.'

She got up abruptly and went to the stove for the teapot.

'Aye, ye might all be dead like poor Mary Wylie an' the boys,' he said baldly. 'An' sure what kind of a way wou'd I be alive if ye were? But ye're not lyin' there in the churchyard wi' the children and the rest of them. Ye're alive an' well with one son just finished his apprenticeship an' another one well on his way at Harland's. Would any o' that have come about but for what happened that day? Wou'd we be sittin' here with plenty o' butter on your good bread, an' money in the bank?'

He paused and gathered himself for several minutes before he went on in an unexpectedly solemn voice.

'Rose, the workin' o' these things is beyond me. Aye, an' I think they're beyond James, an' Elizabeth, an' Hugh, for all they're educated people and thinks about suchlike things. None of us knows what's roun' the corner. We just have to enjoy what we have an' be strong to face the future when it comes.'

He paused, surprised at himself, and sat looking rather sheepish.

'You're right, love,' Rose said, getting to her feet and bending down to kiss him. 'You've got it worked out as well as any of our educated friends might have. I know you're right. "Develop strength of spirit to shield you in adversity." Wasn't that one of the lines in that copybook we used to talk about? And you can't strengthen your spirit if you don't make use of all the good things. And we have so many.'

Three

The summer that followed Sam's first day as leading driver for the Tullyconnaught Haulage Company turned out to be a long and happy one with Rose and Sarah's joint birthday the overture to a season full of new and unexpected pleasures.

Back in the spring of 1890 James Sinton himself had suggested to Rose that the two families should join together on the nearest Saturday to their special day in happy remembrance of their miraculous escape. Seven meetings had come and gone, the annual event was now looked forward to as much as Christmas. Even Jamie Hamilton, who preferred to spend most weekends in Belfast, made the effort to catch the first train to Armagh at the end of his Saturday morning's work to be present at the celebration lunch.

The eighth family party was one of the happiest days Rose had ever spent. She loved the spacious house in Armagh, the well-planted garden Mary had created, the rich green of the tree-lined Mall spread out beyond the sitting-room windows. Each time she visited that elegant room, with its high ceilings and tall windows, she marvelled at the good fortune which had come to them out of the darkest of days.

This year she felt it more than ever as she caught John sheepishly eyeing his two pretty daughters, Hannah, cool and slim, full of a gentle grace, Sarah, in her new flowered lawn dress, as tall as her sister and as dark as Hannah was fair, her eyes sparkling with excitement, totally absorbed in all that was going on around her.

She couldn't help but smile when she saw how comfortably John now stood beside James Sinton, their backs to the marble fireplace, the hearth glowing only with the bright colours of summer flowers. Now in his mid-forties, with grey hair at his temples, he carried himself as well as when he'd bought a coat in Dublin to wear at his wedding in Kerry.

She looked from John to Sam. He was more like his father than Jamie, broad-shouldered and fuller in the body. He preferred to listen rather than talk. Red-headed and lighter in build, Jamie was much more ready to put himself forward, always talkative with people who could answer his questions. He was busy telling James about the recent big orders at the yard, which were sure to lead to further expansion. The chance of a manager's job when he finished his time in the drawing office was looking better than ever. Sam smiled, pleased his brother would succeed in getting what he so much wanted, but content enough himself. He already had what he'd wanted since ever he could remember.

A perfect day, in every way, Rose and Mary agreed, their family party strung out ahead of them, as they strolled under the shade of the trees on the Mall. Sunlight poured down on the dazzling white figures moving back and forth over the smooth turf of the cricket pitch and the groups of men and boys watching from the long grass by the boundary.

In front, Hannah and her particular friend, Helen, a year older and more than a head taller, had their arms round each other's waist, their heads close together in talk while they pushed Mary and James's longed for young son in his elegant perambulator. Sam was strolling shyly with Susie Sinton, just turned thirteen and clearly impressed by Sam's broad shoulders and smart turnout. Behind them, she heard Jamie's voice once again deep in conversation with James Sinton. Sarah and little Mary, the youngest of the Sinton girls, were standing on the low wall that divided the shady walk from the road beyond, so that John could point out the library where Rose had borrowed books for him when they lived at Salter's Grange.

Sarah and Mary knew the library perfectly well. It was John who'd never noticed that whenever they happened to pass the small, elegant building Sarah always asked the same question: "Was that where Ma used to go for the books?" She knew perfectly well he'd happily tell the story of how her mother had met James Sinton in the reading room one day, after the disaster, and how he'd found them all a new home and a new job with Uncle Hugh and how they'd all become friends and had a party every year ever after to celebrate their escape.

The fine weather that blessed them on the 'big day' continued all through July and August with only a handful of cool, showery days to interrupt it. When Elizabeth and Hugh went off to Manchester for an important Quaker conference, John had two weeks holiday. Jamie, who now got quite upset if anyone called him James, had his annual holiday at the same time. The first week, he went on a cycling tour with his friends from work, the second, he came home. He and John cut the meadow behind the house, repaired the unused stable and visited the Armagh Horse Fair. They arrived home well pleased, having bought a good-natured chestnut mare called Dolly for the new trap. It was all very well, said John, for Hugh to go and order a motor carriage while he was in Manchester, but for the moment a pony and trap would do very nicely at Ballydown.

At weekends and on the long summer evenings the new trap took them further afield than they'd been before. While John was at work, Rose drove Hannah and Sarah to picnic by the little loughs set amid the green hills. They walked round the old church at Magherally and tried to read the oldest of the weathered tombstones. They went down to their own parish church of Holy Trinity and studied the memorials and monuments in its cool interior. After visiting Dromore cathedral, they stared up at the viaduct nearby marvelling at the graceful soaring arches that carried the railway from Belfast southwards. After a long moment, Sarah declared it was too difficult to sketch. What she wanted was a photographic camera like Mr. Blennerhasset's, the guest at Currane Lodge who'd sent her parents an album of photographs of their wedding.

The fine weather faded gently into a mild autumn, the leaves lingering in tones of gold and russet with neither wind nor frost to loosen them and send them drifting under hedgerows. The mornings were misty and the evenings shorter, but there was no cold, no challenge from rain or wind to make the daily tasks a burden.

When Hannah and Sarah went back to school and Dolly was left to lean over the five-barred gate and wonder where they'd gone, Rose felt it strange to be alone again. For a few days she missed Sarah's bright ideas and enthusiasms and the liveliness of her two daughters, but then she realized quite suddenly she was grateful for the quiet.

'Well, what's new in the world today,' she asked with a smile as John settled himself for a bite of lunch on a pleasant September day.

'Oh, nothing good, according to Hugh,' he said wryly. 'He says he'd three copies of *The Times* to read last night full of the trouble in South Africa. The Boers are determined to have their way and rule themselves and our government is just as determined not to let them. He thinks there'll be a war out of it if someone doesn't talk sense to both sides.'

'Do you think the Quakers will intervene?' she asked, as she fetched bowls from the dresser and took them to the stove.

'Like when they went to the Czar to try to stop the war in the Crimea,' he replied, nodding to himself. 'They're certainly thinkin' about it from what I hear. All the Monthly Meetings in Ireland are charged to consider what to do an' they've written letters to Friends in America and in Europe forby. There's not all that many of them, I know, but most of them's educated people. You'd admire them for the trouble they put themselves to,' he added, as she put a bowl of soup in front of him.

'But you don't think it'll do much good?' she said, looking over her shoulder as she filled her own bowl.

'Ach, when one's as bad as the other, there's no come and go,' he said shortly. 'The Boers say they've the right to their own country after the trek they made to get away from the

British. The British say they have no right to run against the law, keeping slaves and suchlike. But sure it all boils down to who's goin' to benefit from the diamond mines. Whoever comes out top it won't be the ordinary Africans,' he said, sadly.

Rose shook her head and buttered a slice of wheaten bread. James and Hugh Sinton read their newspapers assiduously. So for that matter did Elizabeth. She'd been surprised to find how much attention they paid to events on the other side of the globe.

'You can't run a business anymore as if it were a local matter,' Hugh had explained one evening when Rose asked him why he read the London papers so carefully. 'Take what happened in the sixties, during the American Civil War. No raw cotton coming in to Lancashire, so the mills had to close. Mill owners were ruined and thousands of workers turned off. There were whole families where every one of them worked at the mill, so there wasn't the price of a loaf coming in. There must have been poor souls who starved, though we'll never know the extent of it. You don't just get famine when the potato crop fails,' he said shortly. 'And while they suffered in Lancashire, we benefited here in Banbridge.'

'Why was that?'

Sarah had been sitting so quietly on a low stool by her father's chair that Rose hadn't noticed it was well past her bedtime.

'How could *we* benefit?' she demanded, her dark eyes wide as she stared at Hugh and waited.

'Manufacturers needed cloth, Sarah,' he said, looking at her calmly. 'They always need cloth. When they couldn't get cotton they came to us for linen. The mills here were overwhelmed with orders, they couldn't expand fast enough. They were so desperate for labour that even children of ten were taken on without too many questions being asked.'

'Hannah's ten and Sam's nearly ten,' she said, glancing at her brother and sister. 'Would they have had to work in the mills?'

'If their family was poor and encouraged them to,' he said honestly.

'Are we poor?' she asked abruptly, looking at Hannah and Sam. 'Ma, are we poor?' she went on, her voice rising ominously.

Rose had got to her feet and picked her up, feeling her small body stiffen as she twisted in her arms and turned back to stare at Hugh and Elizabeth sitting with her father by the stove.

'No, Sarah dear, we're not poor,' she said soothingly. 'You needn't worry about that,' she went on, as she carried her upstairs to bed.

Hugh had come down the next day as soon as the children had gone to school to ask if Sarah had slept properly.

'It was thoughtless of me to mention the children working in the mills, Rose,' he said with a sigh. 'You know we Quakers favour plain speaking even with children, and I know you think it a good thing yourself, but I should have been more careful. She's too young to have to face the truth about such hardship. She'll learn all about it soon enough.'

'She's fine this morning, Hugh,' she had replied warmly, touched by his concern. 'She was chattering away at breakfast about a nativity play they're rehearsing at school. But it's a warning to me,' she added ruefully. 'I know she listens to everything that goes on, but sometimes I forget, because she always looks as if she's not paying the slightest attention. No harm done, Hugh, but I'll make sure I have the fire lit in the parlour next time you come down and we'll leave the children the kitchen table for their games till bedtime.'

'Lovely drop of soup, Rose,' John said enthusiastically as he tipped his bowl to spoon up the last of it.

'Would you like some more,' she said, beaming. 'There's plenty.'

He smiled and shook his head. He always ate lightly at lunch-time even when he was very hungry. Bending over a model or working at the anvil in the afternoon could give you bad wind if you'd eaten too well.

'D'you remember, Rose,' he said thoughtfully, as he munched the rest of his wheaten bread, 'yer ma once told you that when she thought of yer father, God rest him, she always said to herself how pleased he'd be to know you were all well, that you'd enough to eat and weren't in want?'

'I'd forgotten that,' Rose admitted, shaking her head. 'You've a great memory. I never know what you're going to come out with next.'

'Ach, I forget plenty,' he said, laughing quietly. 'But I often think of what yer Ma said when I see you put out more bread or more butter. I know how your father musta felt. He lived through desperit hard times,' he said, shaking his head at the thought of it. 'We've had our share, I know, but nothin' as bad as your ma and da. We've had great luck.'

'Some might call it luck,' she said sharply, as she stood up and pulled the kettle forward on the stove to make them a pot of tea. 'You've worked for your luck. If you hadn't studied so hard those years when you were with Thomas and then at the mill, you'd not be much use to Hugh.'

'An' what about all the wee dresses that kept us alive when the Orangemen took their work away from Thomas an' me because we wouldn't go out drillin' with them?' he retorted promptly.

Rose smiled across at him and raised her eyebrows as she reached a hand up to the mantelpiece for the tea caddy. She heard the scrape of his chair as he moved from the table to his comfortable armchair.

'Goodness, I forgot,' she said suddenly, as she put the tea caddy back. 'You've a letter. It came yesterday and I forgot all about it. I'm amazed Sarah didn't spot it,' she added, as she handed it down from its place by the clock. 'At least we know it's not the landlord putting us out.'

John turned the envelope over, read the return address and smiled.

'No, indeed it is not,' he said firmly. 'I know what this is and it might be the price of a new dress,' he said, beaming at her. 'It's the Patent Office in London,' he said, ripping open the envelope.

She watched his face as he unfolded a stiff sheet of notepaper and extracted a slip of paper. She felt a sudden stab of anxiety as his eyes scanned whatever message it bore, his lips moving soundlessly.

'What is it, John?' she said urgently.

He looked up at her, his eyes dilated, his mouth open. He handed her the slip of paper and sat back in his chair, the letter still in his hand.

'What d'you say to that then?' he asked, the first glimmer of a smile touching his lips.

She set the teapot down again, came across to his chair, put her arms round him and kissed him.

'I'd say, "Congratulations, John Hamilton,"' she said softly, the cheque he'd passed across to her still clutched in her hand. 'I just wish your mother were alive to see this,' she added, aware that tears were now streaming down her face.

Rose was sure she'd never forget that moment when John showed her his royalty cheque. Even when he'd explained why the amount was so high, she'd had difficulty grasping it. A simple enough wee thing, he'd said, but it helped stop the threads from breaking, and the greatest time waster of all was when a machine stopped for one thread.

It was only when she went to the bank and was persuaded to open a deposit account with a shiny, gold-embossed pass book that she really believed what had happened. With this amount of money in the bank there'd no longer be any question of supporting Hannah and Sarah, as well as Jamie, in whatever career they might wish to follow. She put the pass book in Granny Sarah's old handbag at the back of the sideboard and peeped at it now and again to reassure herself it wasn't a pleasant dream.

It seemed the Hamiltons were not the only ones to have had good fortune this year. In November and December, letters came to Ballydown from her sister Mary Doherty in Donegal, her older brothers in Scotland and Nova Scotia and her younger brother Sam in Pennsylvania, full of good news, new jobs, new houses, marriages and babies. From Gloucestershire, her former charge, Lady Anne, still lamented the move from Sligo, but she was heartily glad no one was now likely to shoot her husband simply because he was a landlord. She was hard at work refurbishing the draughty mansion he'd inherited from a distant cousin and encouraging him to take up his seat in the House of Lords and continue the work he'd begun as an Irish MP.

There was good news too from their old home at Salter's Grange. Their former neighbour, Mary-Anne Scott, once such a thorn in the flesh, had taken ill and died about eighteen months after their move. To their delight, their old friend Thomas had remarried, a widow with a grown-up son and daughter. Now, he and Selina had a little daughter of their own. But the news that delighted Rose most of all was of his eldest daughter, Annie. Bullied unmercifully by her mother, she'd been a poor downtrodden creature whom Rose had pitied but hadn't dared to help. Thomas insisted that Rose would find her 'well improved'. She and her new stepmother were the best of friends and Selina had helped her find a job in a dress shop in Armagh. Now she was walking out with a young farmer from Ballyards. 'A right sort of a fella,' Thomas said approvingly.

Rose was delighted to count up all these items of good news, but as she did so she felt troubled that her horizons seemed so narrow compared to Elizabeth. While her friend was concerned about the fate of Boers and Africans, she herself was more involved with the fate of an unhappy child, the victim of a mother so obsessed with the wrath of God she had neither time, love nor kindness for her own child, or for her neighbours.

She did read the local newspapers and the *Illustrated London News*, which Lady Anne sent her each week, but were it not for Elizabeth's searching questions she doubted she would give much attention to world events. Elizabeth always wanted to know what she thought about things, a local matter like a recent anti-Parnellite rally in Newry, or the latest bill going through Parliament, or the current crisis in South Africa.

It was part of their commitment as Quakers to pursue peace and goodwill by all possible means, Elizabeth had once explained, and you couldn't do that unless you were well informed.

'But can you really know the truth about what's going on, Elizabeth? Don't you remember that story about the mill in Ballygawley, burnt down by disaffected workers? Then we found out it was a spark from a traction engine catching a thatched roof that had started it. Newspapers can only print the reports they get. How can you rely on them?'

'Mostly we don't. That's why we write letters and set up committees of our own. It's not perfect, but at least we can trust other Friends to try and see things as clearly as possible. One has to try, even if one fails.'

Rose was impressed by her friend's commitment, but she wondered what could ever be achieved in South Africa when you had two groups of people so determined to treat each other as enemies. She remembered well enough the Land League's struggle and her brother Sam's hard work for the people who were being exploited and evicted. True, much had been achieved, but the bitterness generated between landlords and tenants and between strong farmers and their tenants had never gone away.

Sam was now a successful land agent in Pennsylvania and a leading Trade Unionist. When she read his long letters she was made so sharply aware of the disappointments he'd suffered. Even when he put a brave face on it, she knew he despaired of social justice as often in his new world as he'd once done in the old.

She often wondered how Sam would get on with people like Hugh and Elizabeth, people as privileged as the Molyneux, yet, like them, no more wishing to exploit their fellow creatures than they had been. The Land Leaguers would have condemned Sintons and Molyneux alike simply because they were owners or employers.

She remembered Old Thomas, the coachman at Currane Lodge. Sam said Old Thomas was probably the founding father of all manner of protest in that part of Kerry. Until she'd heard him hold forth about The Great Famine, she'd never even heard of Quakers.

'Sure the Quakers kept whole villages alive. Did ye not know? And they diden ask what ye believed, they only asked what ye needed. Would it be food or clothes, or the both?'

Thomas was unambiguous in his praise. The Quakers had raised money, he said, in Britain and America. They'd manned soup kitchens and distributed aid. They'd supplied vegetable seeds to plant and taught people who lived near the coast how to fish. Even if they could save so few, at least they'd tried. Thomas would never forget them for that.

When Christmas came and the Hamiltons went to Holy Trinity for the Watch Night service, Rose wondered if 'goodwill to all men' could ever be anything other than a pious hope. One more of those things you expressed regularly on Sunday and forgot as regularly on Monday.

In the chill spaces of the newly enlarged church where she'd stood with Hannah and Sarah on a hot August day studying the marble carving of a ship trapped in ice, the memorial to a local man who had given his life looking for the Northwest Passage, Rose thought of her friends, Elizabeth and Hugh, sitting in a small, plain meeting house, waiting upon inspiration to guide them in their service to others.

She had never thought of extending 'friendship' to all people, wherever they were and whatever their need. She wondered if there was more she herself could do, she who had so much, and was so very happy with her family all around her. She looked up at the ship locked in the ice and thought of the surviving crew setting out to walk to safety, the message they'd left for the benefit of others who might follow. Crozier had failed, for he'd not achieved what he'd set out to achieve. Nevertheless, his efforts had not been in vain.

She felt sure trying and failing and accepting failure as a part of her life was the only way. There was such joy in success, and she'd had her share, but you can't go through life without failing, however hard you try. The important thing would be to learn to accept failure when it came and never to let it defeat you.

Four

The mildness of late autumn carried on into the early weeks of the new year, but towards the end of January stormy weather gathered itself with much more than its usual force. On a night of wild wind that whined and moaned and lashed rain furiously against the small-paned windows of Ballydown, the corrugated iron roof of the turf store was ripped off and thrown halfway across Dolly's sodden meadow. At the top of the hill, branches were torn from the limes in the avenue at Rathdrum and an old tree fell, narrowly missing one end of the workshop.

By the time John picked his way through the litter of broken branches, an early messenger, breathless from his struggle with the wind, had already arrived to report a damaged roof at Millbrook, two miles north of Banbridge. A little later, another young lad climbed through the shattered branches with a message warning Hugh that the Bann looked as if it might burst its banks and flood the bleach works at Ballievy.

Before they could set off to view the damage, John and Hugh spent a cold, gust-blown hour pulling aside the torn branches so they could drive out in the brougham. The mill manager at Millbrook would have sent for their builder, but Hugh himself would have to give the orders for the work needed to secure the roof. He would then have to go to Ballievy, where the danger of flooding would increase hourly with the run-off from the mountains and the surrounding countryside.

It was a difficult week for everyone, bringing the first real cold of winter. Rose didn't go into Banbridge as she usually did. Apart from her walks to the foot of the hill when she heard the bread man's bugle, she stayed indoors, making sure there was a good fire for Hannah and Sarah coming in from school and a tasty and satisfying evening meal for the huge appetites the bitter cold always generated.

It was a relief to everyone when the storms died away. The quiet weather that followed was just as cold, but very still. Every blade of grass, every twig was coated with a glistening rime that seldom melted even when the sun reached its highest point in a translucent blue sky. The light was so clear the mountains moved dramatically closer, their outline as sharp as a freshly made pen sketch.

By the middle of February the ground was frozen hard after continuous frosts. Each morning, Rose took a kettle of hot water outside to fill the dish for her little birds. Each morning, she had to loosen and tip out the glistening disc left over from the previous day. As she threw it into the flower bed, she noticed the lopsided sculpture of ice the individual discs now made, joined together by the slight melt in the noonday sun.

She poured the boiling water into the shallow stone dish John had bought her to replace the old frying pan she'd once used. The steam rose in clouds around her. Even so, by the time she'd gone back into the house and refilled the kettle, the water would have cooled. Within the hour, its surface would have silvered over and she'd have to walk out and poke it open again. She never grudged the task, for in weather like this there wasn't a drop of water to be had between here and the river.

With the clear, quiet weather continuing through February, the lengthening evenings were more apparent, but the mornings were still dark when John and Sam set off for work, the light growing weakly as Hannah and Sarah got ready for school. What didn't change was the cold. On the last day of the short month the sky was still dark as they wheeled their bicycles out on to the hill. The heavy cloud that had masked the pale sunrise thickened through the morning. When John came in for lunch he looked up at the leaden sky and said he was sure they'd have snow.

An hour later, Rose watched anxiously as the first flakes swirled round the windows. She looked at the clock. Hannah had a choir practice, so she'd be later than usual. She went to the door and watched the fine flakes swirl towards her. The tiny fragments were more like ash from a bonfire than proper snow. She spoke severely to herself. It might well be evening before there was any amount lying. She shut the door, lit the gas lamp, took out her sewing and settled down to wait for Sarah.

'Are you frozen?' she asked, when she came in by the back door.

'Bits of me are,' she replied, putting an icy cheek against Rose's warm one. 'And I'm starving,' she went on, depositing her satchel on one kitchen chair and dropping her short, heavy cape on to another.

Rose decided not to remind her there were hooks for satchel and cape. Not today.

'Go and cut yourself some bread and jam while I make us a pot of tea,' she said, as Sarah stood in front of the stove, shivering, her dark eyes reflecting the leaping flames beyond its open doors. 'I've put out some new damson,' she added, as Sarah turned away and headed for the dairy.

'Oh good. Damson's my very favourite,' she said, beaming.

Rose had just poured their tea and was waiting for Sarah to reappear when she heard a scrabbling sound outside the front door, so tentative she wondered if it could be a knock at all. To be sure, she went to the door and opened it. A bitter, chill wind poured into the warm kitchen.

'Wou'd this be Rathdrum?'

Rose stared at the woman on her doorstep, so out of breath her words were barely audible. A woman younger than herself, but shorter and bent over, a great bundle in one arm, her face seamed with lines of weariness and anxiety.

'No, I'm afraid it's not,' replied Rose honestly. 'Was it Rathdrum you wanted?' she added, quite unable to think what the woman might want there at this hour on such a day.

'I've ta get a ticket fer the dispensry,' she explained, gasping as she humped her bundle higher in her arms.

The bundle began to cry, more like a kitten than a child.

'Come in and rest yourself for a minute or two,' said Rose quickly. 'It's quite a bit up the hill yet. The steepest bit as well. I've just made a cup of tea,' she added encouragingly.

'Can't stop,' she said abruptly. 'The chile's bin sick since the morn. It's tha' weak it can har'ly cry.'

'I'll go for the ticket,' said Sarah firmly as she swung her cape over her shoulders and pushed her way past them. 'Go in out of the cold, I won't be long,' she said quickly to the hunched figure and set off at a run before Rose could say a word.

'Come and sit by the fire,' she urged, as the woman stepped reluctantly into the kitchen. 'Sarah's a good runner but it'll be at least ten minutes till she's back. Here, have some tea. It's only just poured.'

The woman sank down in John's armchair and hoisted the child on to her knee. She sat awkwardly balanced on its edge, looking around her uneasily, her eyes moving curiously over the stove, the pool of light from the gas lamp and the rows of plates and dishes on the dresser. The thin shawl she'd wrapped round her child fell away from its face, a small pale face but for two bright spots of colour on its cheeks.

'Could you eat a bite? It would give you strength,' Rose said gently as she saw the listless eyes rest on Sarah's plate of bread and jam. 'Here, give me the little one and have this with your tea,' she went on, 'I'll drink mine later.'

She reached out for the close-wrapped bundle and found it much lighter than she'd expected. But then, the poor woman had been carrying it against the force of wind and snow. No wonder she'd been hunched over. The child barely moved when she took it in her arms. The small, pathetic cries continued as she walked it up and down the kitchen shushing it and rocking it, trying to soothe its agitation.

She paused at the edge of the lamplight to study the screwed-up face that lay against her shoulder.

'What age is the baby?' Rose asked easily, trying to make the woman feel more comfortable.

The woman threw a glance towards her but couldn't speak,

her mouth was so full of bread and jam. She went on pushing food hurriedly into her mouth as if the plate would be taken from her at any moment.

'Two in April,' she replied in her flat, exhausted tone, as she swallowed the last morsel and drank deep from her mug of tea.

Rose was shocked. If she'd said a year, it might have fitted the weight in her arms, but at nearly two the child must be pathetically thin.

'Had you no one at home to send for the ticket?' she enquired sympathetically.

'They're all in the mill till seven. My man and the two boys,' she said matter-of-factly. 'I had a girl, but she got the cough and died last year. She was eight,' she added, with a falling tone that somehow suggested it was her being eight had caused her to get a cough and die.

'Can I pour you some more tea?' Rose asked, as her visitor drained the very last drop in her mug by tipping her head so far back the light from gas lamp above shone down full upon her.

Under its soft, luminous glow, the woman's face was sharply lit. Tight-stretched over protruding cheek bones, her skin had a brownish, muddy look, her dark, wispy hair, already showing streaks of grey, was drawn back from her face and tied with a bit of rag. Her eyes were small, deep set and listless, all light gone out of them. They glistened with moisture. Whether with the bite of the cold or with tears of frustration and exhaustion Rose simply could not tell.

The woman shook her head, clearly on edge, listening for any sign of Sarah's return.

The baby had grown quieter in Rose's arms, though the two red spots of colour on its cheeks had not abated. She continued to walk up and down the kitchen rocking it in her arms, glad when she saw her visitor stretch her bony hands towards the comforting flames.

She offered her own name and was given one in return. Not a name she knew, but she recognized the name of the scattered hamlet where the woman lived, a mere half a mile away as the crow flew. The children used to run down from their own meadow to play by the small stream that marked the boundary with Lisnaree, but by the road from where she lived it was nearer two miles to Ballydown. No wonder she was hunched with carrying and ravenous with the effort and the cold.

Rose was about to ask Maisie McKinley which of the mills her husband and sons worked in when they heard the sound of a vehicle on the road outside. A horse whinnied above the crunch of wheels and was answered by Dolly in her warm stable.

Maisie got up immediately and held out her arms for her child as Sarah burst into the kitchen, her cheeks pink, large, soft snowflakes caught in her dark curls.

'Hugh's brought the brougham down to take them to the dispensary. I'll go too, there's room for three,' she added before Rose could protest.

'What about your homework, Sarah?'

Sarah cast a glance at the slight figure clutching the silent child and shook her head dismissively.

'Have you another blanket, Ma?'

Rose ran upstairs and fetched one and simply stood watching as Sarah threw it round Maisie's shoulders, gathering the fullness at the front for her to clutch in her free hand. When Sarah wore that particular determined look, she knew better than to try to stop her.

'Come on,' Sarah said, turning to Maisie, 'the path's slippy. Walk on the grass, it's safer,' she insisted, as she drew her out into the snow. 'Back later, Ma,' she said over her shoulder, as Rose hovered in the doorway. 'Don't come out in the cold.'

She did as she was bid, shutting the door before the brougham began its cautious descent of the hill. She shivered fiercely as she came back to the stove. She knew nothing would have stopped Sarah from going with Maisie to the dispensary, yet she felt she ought to have tried.

Hugh would take care of her, of course, and make sure she didn't sit around in the cold. She did her best to reassure herself, but she knew it was not the cold or the icy roads she now feared. Between coming in from school and going off with Maisie, Sarah had grown up. With the others the change had come almost imperceptibly. Even now, there were moments when she looked at Sam and still saw the child she'd nursed. Hannah had always seemed older than her years and seldom needed her as much as Sarah had. But now her littlest love was striding into womanhood and nothing she could do would stop her. Nor should she stop her. But she could not hide from herself the fact that, more than for any of the others, she feared for Sarah's happiness.

'Where's Sarah?' John asked, as he sat down in his armchair and pulled off his wet boots, his glance flickering from Hannah to Rose as they moved about the kitchen, setting up the evening meal.

'She went with Hugh to the dispensary,' Rose replied coolly.

'A bad night for her to be out,' he said slowly. 'Maybe ye should've said no.

'Da, you can't say no to Sarah when she takes a notion,' said Hannah promptly. 'You know what she's like.'

'Aye, ye have a point,' he said quietly. 'She came up to us in the workshop like a whirlwind and told Hugh he'd need the brougham,' he began. 'She didn't ask him,' he went on, 'she told him. An' I hafta say he just laid down his work and went straight out for the mare and I helped him harness her up. An' she just stood there watchin' us an' niver a word to either till she jumped up beside him. "There's a poor woman with a sick child down home with Ma," says she to him. "She was comin' up here for a dispensary ticket. The least we can do is drive her there." He never said a word, just looks at her an' gets up an' takes the reins, an' off they go.'

'Was he annoyed with her, do you think?' asked Hannah, as she finished her job and drew over a chair to sit down beside him.

'I cou'den tell ye, Hannah,' he said, honestly, looking her full in the face. 'The daylight was near gone and he was in a hurry. And ye know the faster Hugh moves the more he holds his head down. He might not've been annoyed, but he was powerful quiet.'

Rose smiled ruefully at John as he sat back in his chair and looked up at the clock. Sam should be in any moment now, desperate for his supper. She'd expected Sarah and Hugh back long before this.

'What was wrong with the we'an, Rose? Had ye anythin' in the house to give it?' John asked, as they all settled down to wait.

'No, I couldn't give it anything for I'd no idea what was wrong. It certainly wasn't wind and it had no cough. But then it was so weak it might not have had the energy to cough. Poor thing, it was so thin I could feel its ribs through the shawl she'd wrapped it in. She looked half starved herself,' she said sadly, her eyes leaving him and focusing on the corner of the stove where Sarah's plate of bread and jam had sat.

'I wonder what's keeping them,' she said, with a sigh, at last putting into words the tension they were all feeling. 'They were here about half four and it's after six now. It's only fifteen minutes to the dispensary.'

'It's not far, right enough,' said John agreeably. 'But maybe the doctor was away out an' they hadta wait till he was back.'

'And maybe Hugh drove them back up to Lisnaree after they saw the doctor,' said Hannah reassuringly. 'It would be very slow on the hill with the brougham,' she went on, 'and the new mare is perhaps not used to snow. She's quite young, isn't she, Da?'

John agreed that she was, but after that they all fell silent. John went to the door, stepped outside, closed it behind him and listened. Usually in the stillness of the night the noise of a vehicle could be heard a mile or more away, but by now the snow was lying thickly enough to muffle the sound. The air was close to freezing again, which would put a light crust on the snow and make it even more difficult for driving. He sighed, went back in, and sat silently by the fire attempting to read the newspaper. Rose took up her sewing and Hannah started her homework.

They were all startled when the door opened without warning, an icy blast swirled round their legs and Sam came into the room. Sarah was at his back, her face white, her hair dusted with flakes of melting snow.

Rose fetched a towel and Hannah undid the fastening on her sister's cape. Sarah protested, but her own fingers were too numb to release the firm catch. She let Rose rub her hair in stubborn silence.

'Where's Hugh?' John asked, puzzled, as he rose from his chair to draw Sarah close to the stove.

'He's comin' in a minit,' said Sam, tramping into the room. 'He's tying the reins to the gatepost. But he's not stoppin'. The mare's near done an' he says Elizabeth'll be anxious. I overtook them on the hill an' led the mare,' he explained, as he stood, his coat collar still turned up, his cap pulled down over his eyes, his trousers now dripping gently on the hearth. 'I'll go up the hill with him an' see him over the worst bit.'

'God bless all here,' said Hugh wearily, as he closed the door and looked across at Sarah, now sitting with her hands spread to the flames.

She did not turn round.

'Ah, man dear, that was a long hour. Did ye get the doctor?'

'Yes, we did. But we had to wait in the queue.'

'And when Maisie got in the child was dead,' said Sarah, fiercely, turning to stare at Hugh, who stood awkwardly by the door, one arm braced against the wall for support.

'Ach dear,' said John, dropping his eyes and glancing sideways at her. 'Did he say what was wrong with it?'

'It wasn't an it, Da,' she said calmly, looking him in the eyes. 'Her name was Sophie and she would have been two in April. But she was only a weaver's daughter,' she went on bitterly. ' Maisie says he took one look at her face, said "dead" and then asked her what name to put on the death certificate. She showed it to me. It says croup. Maisie says that's what they always put when they don't know, and don't much care anyway,' she ended furiously.

'I must go,' said Hugh sharply, breaking the silence that

greeted her outburst. 'We did what we could, little as it was,' he added, more quietly.

'I'll come with you an' lead the mare,' said Sam, as Hugh's hand touched the latch. 'I'll not be long, Ma,' he said, glancing over his shoulder to where his mother stood, bracing herself for what was to come.

'I think you should change your skirt, Sarah, that hem is soaking. Go and do it while Hannah and I start serving the meal.'

'I'm all right as I am, and I don't want any supper.'

'Thank you,' prompted John automatically.

'Thank you,' repeated Sarah icily.

Hannah came over to Sarah's chair, knelt down and put her arms round her. She said nothing. Just stroked the still damp curls.

'It's all his fault,' Sarah burst out. 'Those stupid tickets. Why couldn't Maisie just have gone to the dispensary? If she'd gone this morning, Sophie might still be alive,' she cried, staring at her parents as if they were personally responsible.

'Sarah, there's mill owners that makes no provision at all for their workers,' John began, a warning note in his voice. 'All Hugh's people and their families can go to a doctor. But I grant you, it was hard on Maisie she had to come to Rathdrum. Normally there's some neighbour's chile able to run and get a ticket when it's needed. That was bad luck.'

'And then he gave her money,' she spat out, ignoring what John had just said. 'Sophie's dead and *he* gives her money. How can he do such a thing?' she shouted, her voice cracking as she burst into floods of tears.

Hannah tucked a clean hanky into her hand. When Sarah ignored it, she took it up again and wiped Sarah's tears herself.

'Sarah love,' Rose began quietly, 'it's very sad about poor little Sophie, but think how Maisie would feel if she couldn't afford to bury her in the churchyard. Hugh knows there are fees even for children, and the McKinleys won't have a family plot.'

'The McKinleys haven't got anything. You should see the

cabin they live in. One candle on the table and a pot of potatoes over the fire,' Sarah said, grabbing the handkerchief from Hannah to blow her dripping nose.

'But how is that Hugh's fault, Sarah?' Rose persisted gently. 'Not many men would have left their work and harnessed the mare to take her into Banbridge and then up to Lisnaree afterwards. How is it his fault?'

'It's what he pays his weavers. Three of them working and they're all half starved like little Sophie.'

John shook his head and looked at Rose. He had no idea what to say and she knew from experience that offering bare facts would do no good, even if she had any facts to offer.

'Perhaps Maisie's husband doesn't bring her all his money home,' said Hannah calmly.

Sarah stared at her in amazement, her face red and swollen, her mouth still quivering.

'What do you mean? I don't understand you,' she said crossly, shaking her head violently as Hannah got up from the hard stone floor where she'd been kneeling.

'Sarah, many of the weavers go out and get drunk on pay night,' Hannah began. 'Some go to the cock fights and lay wagers they can't afford. I'm not saying Maisie's husband is one of those,' she added quickly, 'but he might be. It might not all be about wages.'

'Hannah's right,' said John promptly, grateful for his daughter's intervention. He'd been going to point out that the two boys might only be winders and they'd earn very little, but he'd thought better of it.

Rose saw the tempest was slowly dying down. It was time to move everyone towards supper.

'Sarah, I know you're upset, but we can't do anything tonight to help Maisie. If you'll dry your eyes and eat your supper we'll go over and see her as soon as the snow melts.'

'And take her some clothes and food?' she asked sullenly.

'No,' said Rose firmly. 'We'll go and ask her what we can do to help.'

'Why? Why not take food and clothes when we know she has nothing?' she threw back.

'Because even the poorest people have their pride, even if it's the only thing they have,' Rose insisted quietly. 'Do you want to offend her?'

'No. I don't. She has enough to bear,' she muttered, her tears now reduced to a miserable sniff.

And there are plenty more like her, Rose thought, as the door opened and Sam's large, snow-covered figure slipped in and latched it behind him as quickly as he could.

'It wou'd skin you out there,' he announced, his back to them all as he hung up his coat and cap and brushed fresh snow from the knees of his boiler suit. 'You shouldn't have held back fer me,' he said cheerfully, looking at the waiting table. 'Ye must be starvin'. I could eat a horse.'

'That's amazin', Sam,' said John, turning towards him. 'I've niver known you to be hungry of an evenin'. Has the snow given you an appetite?'

As she bent to open the oven door, Rose sent up a prayer of thanks for Sam's timely arrival. Sarah had actually laughed at the idea of Sam not being hungry. It was the first small thaw in the ice she'd generated in the warm room. Dear Sam. Even if he'd not been busy with the snow he'd brought in, he wouldn't have noticed anything amiss. A situation would have to be dire indeed for him not to greet them with his usual smile and an easy comment about the events of the day. A rare gift perhaps, but she was not entirely sure it was a good thing, given all life could throw at you.

Five

'Can we go and see Maisie when I get home from school?' asked Sarah next morning, as soon as she came downstairs to breakfast.

'We'll see,' said Rose absently, distracted by the headache she'd woken up with.

She paused, her hand on the latch of the door to the dairy and tried to remember what she was doing when Sarah spoke.

'Do you mean "no"?' Sarah threw back at her.

'No, I don't,' she replied, as the whatever-it-was she was about to remember slipped away from her like a mouse disappearing down a hole.

She came back to the breakfast table and stood looking down at it until Hannah got to her feet. 'We need some more milk, Ma. You sit down. I'll get it.'

Rose did as she was bid and poured three cups of tea, aware that Sarah was still staring at her.

'When I say "we'll see", I mean just that,' she said, making an effort to sound firm, though she didn't feel remotely firm. 'It depends how much light is left when you get in and whether it has snowed again. If the weather's bad, we'll have to leave it till tomorrow morning.'

'And what if it's still bad then?' Sarah persisted.

'We'll meet that when we come to it.'

'You always say that, doesn't she, Hannah?'

Hannah paused, milk jug in hand, looked at Sarah and bent towards Rose. 'Say when,' she said quietly, as she added milk very slowly to her mother's cup of tea.

'Thanks, love,' she nodded, thankful for the small, loving

gesture. It was so like Hannah to make putting the milk in her tea a way of comforting her without antagonizing Sarah further.

'Yes, she does often say that,' Hannah agreed, sitting down and looking across the table at her sister. She helped herself to wheaten bread and reached across for the damson jam when Sarah forgot to pass it over. 'You can't always plan what you're going to do, not even in summer. Look how often we changed our plans in the holidays when it got too hot, or when we remembered it was Fair Day in Banbridge, or when Dolly threw her shoe. That's what "we'll meet that when we come to it" means. You know that perfectly well, Sarah.'

Rose drank her tea gratefully, but wasn't sure she could face eating anything. She'd had a restless night, full of confused dreams about the past. They'd left her feeling down-hearted and oppressed and her head was beginning to throb. As soon as she'd got them off to school, she'd take a headache powder and sit down for a little while till it went away.

Sarah had subsided for the moment. She was spreading damson jam liberally on another piece of wheaten bread.

'Are you going up to see Elizabeth this morning, Ma?' Hannah asked lightly, one eye resting on Sarah as she munched.

'Yes, I'll go,' Rose said, brightening a little at the thought of Elizabeth's company, 'unless the snow comes on again.'

Friday was their usual day, the heavy work of the week behind them. Elizabeth had a housekeeper who did most of the cooking, but she didn't spare herself on what needed to be done. The house was large and full of good furniture, books and family mementos. She had plenty to do to keep it in order, for she regularly entertained visiting Friends who came to minister, or to report to their Monthly Meeting.

As she thought of walking up the hill to see Elizabeth, she remembered John's parting words.

'Da said to tell you it had thawed a bit and you'd be all right if you kept to the middle of the road,' Rose began. 'It'll still be solid ice at the sides and you're to take good care and walk down the hill with your bicycles . . . and probably up again as well. Sam says the main road should stay open with the road engines moving. They're not bothered by the snow till it gets quite deep.'

'Don't worry, Ma,' said Hannah reassuringly. 'We're out early today. We'll be home well before dark.'

Rose was even more grateful when they left. She poured the last of the tea and sat by the fire to drink it and collect her thoughts, but her thoughts did not want to be collected. She went and took her headache powder, put together a basket with her sewing things and a pot of the new damson for Elizabeth and set about clearing the breakfast table.

By the time she'd done that, and even before she'd washed up, she had to sit down again, she was feeling so shaky and shivery. She hoped she wasn't starting a cold. Jamie was coming home on Saturday afternoon and would be staying over till Sunday, the first time in five weeks he'd been to see them. She missed Jamie. The last thing she wanted was to be sniffing and blowing and red in the nose when he came so seldom and had so much news to tell them.

She sat by the fire gathering her energy to wash the dishes, make up the fire and leave all tidy. An hour later she woke with a start, amazed she should have fallen asleep. Her cheeks were burning and her head still throbbed, though she was sure she'd taken the headache powder.

'Oh dear,' she said aloud. 'I think I am getting the cold. I can't go to Elizabeth like this.'

She walked to the window and looked out. Large, heavy flakes were falling from a uniformly leaden sky. Not a great day to be out at Millbrook. The sky had been clear when she'd heard John and Hugh go past in the brougham, but it certainly wasn't turning into a very good day for inspecting the new roof. They'd probably have to content themselves checking out the looms instead.

It was two months now since they'd set going again the old looms they'd modified themselves. The production figures would tell them whether they should modify the rest, or whether the only way was to install something more up to date. It was a big decision, John said. An awful lot of money was involved.

She moved round the kitchen feeling slightly dazed, trying to decide what to cook for the evening. John and Hugh would have something to eat at Millbrook, but it would be a long, cold day for them, even if they did try to get back with the last of the light.

She went out into the dairy, always cool in summer, now full of an icy chill. She saw her breath stream around her as she filled a glass of water from the tap. She gulped it down and felt sweat break on her body as if she'd gone out into the blazing sun. She gripped the solid edge of the Belfast sink and closed her eyes. She was forty-three now and her monthly bleeding had stopped. Was this the change her mother had told her about, the sweats that came unexpectedly by day and by night, bad enough at their worst to soak a nightgown?

She staggered back to her chair by the stove, closed her eyes and prayed that the throbbing in her head would go away.

Even as she lit the sitting-room fire after breakfast, to have it warm and welcoming when Rose arrived, it occurred to Elizabeth that the hill might prove to be too slippery. When it began to snow and showed no signs of stopping she sighed, looked around the empty room and told herself Rose was being sensible. There would be other mornings, she knew, but she felt a sudden sharp disappointment, for today she'd needed to talk to her.

'Oh well, it can wait,' she said briskly, as she carried a small, finely made writing table from under the window to sit facing the fireplace. 'May as well make a virtue out of an extra morning,' she added. 'Besides, it's a pity not to enjoy such a lovely fire.'

It was a good opportunity to catch up on overdue correspondence. It was not that she disliked writing letters, personal ones or those she wrote as secretary to one of the committees run by the Monthly Meeting, it was more a case of such tasks being left aside when more pressing ones presented themselves.

She worked steadily, grateful for the warmth of the fire on her knees, ignoring as best she could the backs of her legs, which were growing colder and colder. As the morning hours passed slowly, the small pile of sealed envelopes grew. A little after noon she got to her feet, the backs of her legs now quite numb, her shoulders aching from concentration. She walked round the room briskly, replaced her table under the window and stood with her back to the fire, her skirts hitched up. When her legs thawed out she crossed to one of the tall, large-paned windows and ran her eyes over the white blanket spread out over the familiar features of the cobbled yard, the outbuildings and the garden beyond.

Snow always made ordinary things extraordinary, she reflected. The wall beyond the stable, topped last night with the ragged remnants of grass and weeds, was now smoothed to uniformity, not a trace of the fragments of campanula escaped from the flower beds or the ragwort blown in from the nearby meadows. The stable itself had a hefty covering, the tracks of the brougham long since covered. The snow still fell, creating a vast silence, a silence which drove humans indoors to seek warmth and shelter like the wild creatures themselves.

She turned to the fire, thrust into its orange heart a well-seasoned log from the basket on the hearth. It crackled immediately, as the tinder dry outer skin caught fire. The smell of applewood rose towards her, overwhelming the hour and the day in a flood of unbidden memory.

The lines of apple trees marched up and down the hills of her grandfather's farm. On the slopes of Fruit Hill near Loughgall, in the midst of the Armagh apple-country, trimmings were burnt in autumn bonfires and seasoned logs from previous years were saved for the sitting-room fire at Christmas. Long ago now, but the memories of her grandfather had never faded, the old man who had made her and James so welcome throughout their childhood.

He had lost both wife and daughter. Sons he had, both

near and far, well-loved enough, but of his only daughter, his beloved Hester, her children were all that was left to him. Both James Sinton and their stepmother understood his need and the Pearson farm was always a part of young James and Elizabeth's life, a happy place, still active and busy, despite the old man's loss.

His bristly moustache and thick mass of white hair often intimidated those who didn't know him, children and adults alike, but his brown face and sunburnt hands were what Elizabeth remembered most vividly. She and James had never feared him, though, being much younger, Hugh had found him a formidable figure. He loved them all, cherishing them as he did the apple trees he had planted with his own hands, row upon row of them, throwing well-ordered orchards like a woven mantle across the swelling folds of the little hills on which his farmland lay.

It was at Grandfather Pearson's bedside that Elizabeth had met Charles Cooper, a young man from Armagh, newly qualified at medical school in Edinburgh.

She sat down abruptly and stared at the blazing log. She was twenty-two when he'd been able to ask her to marry him. Now she was thirty-seven. How could it be she still felt such grief after all this time? So many wise words had been poured over her. So many kindnesses offered. But nothing had touched the hurt of the sudden, unexpected loss. Time had not healed the pain, it had only made the pain a familiar thing, like a physical pain that sometimes faded to a shadow and at other times leapt up, sharp and undiminished, like today.

He had been so unsure of himself. She'd found it hard to grasp how confident he was in his medical practice, yet so awkward with her. As the weeks of her grandfather's last illness progressed, he grew easier, able to talk to her about his work and his hopes for the future. He'd showed her how to watch for the early signs of distress and how to treat them before they became a trouble to the old man. They were watching together when he died, slipping away so peacefully that they embraced each other, dry eyed and thankful, before setting about what had to be done.

A year later, on a hot summer day, when she was working in the garden at Rathdrum, a message had arrived to say Charles had been taken ill in a village near Armagh where he'd gone to help the local doctor with an outbreak of cholera. Later that day, while she was making preparations to go and take care of him, a letter was delivered telling her he had died.

She had taken care of others since. First her father, then Hugh. At one time, she'd thought of training to be a doctor, now that some medical schools were open to women, but it always seemed there was some more pressing need in her immediate surroundings. Now, surely, she had left it too long. Her place was here at Rathdrum, her consolation her friends and family, her dear friend Rose and her four young people.

She picked up her morning's letters and looked at them. An elderly aunt and uncle now living in the farm at Fruit Hill, a cousin in England, another in Canada, a brother of Charles who practised in Manchester and still wrote to her about his work and his family. A web of loving thoughts, spanning distance, weaving the past to the present. It was something to give thanks for. Something to set against the ache of loss, of what might have been if Charles had lived to be her cherished husband.

The snow had stopped and a pale sun glinted feebly on the horizon as Hannah and Sarah cycled out of Banbridge on the wet and muddy strip of main road where the road engines had passed, their back wheel strakes scraping the fresh snow and leaving it to melt as they hauled in loads of coal for the mills and carried off webs of cloth to Newry and Belfast.

Rathdrum Hill was a different matter. Stopping at the junction of their own road with the main road, Hannah looked at the deep, unmarked surface dubiously.

'I think we'll have to leave our bicycles at MacMurray's,' she said, testing the depth with her front wheel.

'We can carry them,' said Sarah. 'They're not heavy.'

'You're quite right,' Hannah agreed.

If you wanted to get anywhere with Sarah it was best to begin by agreeing with her.

'They're not heavy at all, but if we slipped when we're carrying them we could hurt ourselves quite badly. If we have our hands free we might be able to save ourselves. Ma would be so upset if one of us had a bad fall, don't you think?'

Sarah nodded briskly and Hannah breathed a sigh of relief.

'Then we'll just have to be extra careful as far as MacMurray's,' she said briskly, lifting her bicycle clear of the snow and stepping cautiously towards the nearby farm entrance.

The MacMurrays had cleared their yard and one of their barns stood wide open. They parked the bicycles and greeted Michael MacMurray, who was pitching fodder into the byre.

'I expect the brougham will be back soon,' he said, walking with them across the yard. 'Don't think Mr Sinton an' yer da could do any better on the hill than you. I've a space cleared ready for them.'

The sun had disappeared behind the trees that sheltered the MacMurrays' farm from the westerly winds and the light was beginning to fade as they tackled the hill. The snow lay much deeper than usual and Hannah soon began to tire.

'I shall be glad to get home,' she said breathlessly, as she stopped again to rest.

'I'll make you some toast,' Sarah replied quickly, turning round and tramping back to encourage her sister with a warm smile. There's baker's bread from yesterday. And *damson* jam,' she added, rolling her eyes.

Hannah laughed and moved forward again, using the tracks Sarah had made.

'Here, give me your hand,' said Sarah, grabbing at her. 'I'll give you a tow up. It's not very far now.'

Despite Sarah's vigorous efforts, Hannah was even more breathless by the time they got to the garden gate. Her creamy skin looked paler than usual, while Sarah was bright eyed, her cheeks rosy from exertion. She pushed open the gate as far as it would go against the snow and left Hannah to close it as she clumped down the path to the front door. She threw it open and stopped dead. The kitchen was empty, dark and cold.

'What's wrong, Sarah?' Hannah asked sharply, as she caught up with her. She peered past her and took in the empty room. 'Where's Ma?'

'She's not here. And the fire's out,' Sarah replied hastily, a note of alarm in her voice.

'Perhaps she's still up with Elizabeth,' said Hannah soothingly.

'But she knows we're early today,' Sarah protested. 'Anyway, we're not early anymore. It must be way after four by now,' she went on, stepping over to the stove to peer up at the clock on the mantelpiece, its face just visible in the pale light reflected from the snow.

Hannah followed her gaze and registered sooner than she did that the clock had stopped. A bad sign, for she knew her mother wound it regularly every morning after they went to school. She scanned the room desperately for some explanation.

There was no note on the table, but in the dim light she recognized a familiar shape. Her mother's basket was still sitting there, the corner of her well-wrapped sewing poking out. She took a deep breath and stopped herself from hurrying upstairs.

'She had a bit of a headache this morning. Maybe she's having a lie down,' she said calmly. 'I'll go up and have a look while you light the lamps, Sarah.'

But Sarah wasn't listening, she was flying upstairs and along the short landing to the largest bedroom. Hannah followed hastily and they arrived at the open door together.

Rose lay face down on the bedside rug, her everyday boots lying beside her. The bedspread had been thrown back and the covers opened, but she'd not succeeded in getting into bed. She'd caught at the bedspread as she fell and it was twisted round her slim body like a winding sheet.

It was almost completely dark by the time Hannah and Sarah managed to take off Rose's dress and get her into bed. Her body was stone cold and only her hoarse breathing convinced them she was alive, for her eyes were shut and she seemed unaware of being moved.

'Go and boil water on the gas, Sarah, and fill the stone jars while I get more blankets,' Hannah said, the pallor of Rose's face reducing her voice to a whisper.

'Can I not go for the doctor?' Sarah whispered back.

'No,' Hannah said firmly, desperately looking round for a reason to stop Sarah racing off into the night. 'I need you to help me. We must get her warm again. Go on, get the kettle on, quickly.'

Hannah paused long enough to light the gas lamp before she brought extra blankets from the chest in Jamie's room. She covered the still figure and tucked them well in at her sides, then put her warm hands against her mother's face. It felt colder than snow.

At the foot of the hill, John and Hugh manoeuvred the young mare out of the shafts of the brougham and noted the two bicycles parked against the wall of the barn.

'I see the girls did the sensible thing,' said John easily, as Michael MacMurray came up to join them.

'Aye, the hill's as bad as I've known it, but they're safe home maybe an hour ago,'

'A good night to be indoors,' said Hugh agreeably, as Michael walked with them across the well-swept yard to the snowy road beyond.

'*Da, Da.*'

John turned away to stare up the hill. Against the smooth dim surface a small figure raced headlong towards him, tripping and recovering itself by turns.

'Sarah, what are ye doin' out? What's wrong at all?'

'Ma's sick. She was lying on the floor,' she gasped, leaning against the gate for support. 'We have to get the doctor.'

John stared at her, his eyes large in the light of Michael's lantern. Distress written all over her, her chest heaving, her cape was covered in snow where she'd fallen in her haste to get help once Hannah let her go.

'It'll be quicker to ride the mare,' Hugh said. 'Can you lend me a saddle, Michael, and get me up on her?' he said urgently. 'You go up home, John. I'll be as quick as I can,'

He urged John away with a gesture as Michael threw a saddle over the mare's back and bent to tighten the girths.

Sarah followed John upstairs and saw him look at her mother's inert figure. When she heard him speak to Hannah, his voice breaking with distress, she slipped downstairs and out into the night. Even if the doctor was in his dispensary and even if he came on his horse right away, she didn't think he'd be much use. It was fully dark now and the wind was getting up, blowing fallen snow from the hedgerows in her face. It didn't matter about the snow. It didn't matter how many times she fell over, she would just keep going till she got there. The only person who might be any good was Elizabeth and she must fetch her.

Six

Rose felt cold. Icy cold. Even in the barn where she slept curled in a blanket in the hay it was cold, but outside it was even colder.

When she heard her mother call, she ran across the farmyard to the tall, whitewashed pillars that supported the gate into the Ross farm. Ma was standing there with her friend Emily, and Emily's husband, Walter. They were all looking up the road from Ramelton and waiting, the January sky a monotonous grey, the wind catching at Emily's wispy hair.

Back in the barn she'd been holding the sheepdog pups in her arms, small helpless creatures, their eyes not yet open, but their bodies fat and warm, well fed and well licked by their mother, a bright-eyed border collie, Walter's best servant when he was working with the sheep. She longed to feel their warmth again.

'Look, Rose, they're coming.'

Rose stared into the distance and listened. The tramping feet made a strange, rhythmic roar. As the straggling procession of figures drew closer she began to recognize faces. Friends and neighbours from Ardtur, children she'd been at school with before Adair turned them out of their home. She waved at Owen Friel and Danny Lawn, who were walking side by side carrying a big bundle between them. As they passed, she saw it was a child, all hopped up in an old cloak. It was crying, but it made no sound. The rhythmic roar grew louder.

'Come, we'll go part of the way with them,' Hannah said to Rose, taking her by the hand. 'We'll never lay eyes on them again,' she added, turning to Emily, a bent old woman who leant wearily against one of the great white pillars with their conical tops. There was a stone sticking out of each pointed top to stop the fairies dancing on them and bringing bad luck to the house.

Walter stood under the other pillar. He didn't believe in fairies. He read to them every night from his Bible. Some nights he read from King James's Bible, some nights from the Gaelic Bible Ma had given him when they'd come to shelter in his barn. She could understand both. What she couldn't understand was how Walter came to have King James's Bible in the first place.

Even more puzzling now was the roar these people were making. They didn't look as if they were making a noise. Their lips weren't moving. They weren't speaking to each other, or shouting, or cheering, they just moved silently past. But the noise went on. It drowned out the sound of their tramping feet and it went on just as loudly even after they'd passed by.

'They're going to Gartan to say goodbye, explained Hannah. 'We'll follow them there and wish them luck.'

Gartan was their own lough, grey and still in the morning light. But she knew it wasn't to the lough itself they were going. They would be following the track well above the shore to the old ruined church with its graveyard and the Holy Well. The hill up to the church was steep and she was out of breath. If she hadn't held on to her mother's hand she'd never have got up that hill at all.

There were crowds and crowds of people everywhere, all round the church, most of them were crying. Men and women and young girls and boys. They knelt by graves and kissed the crosses that marked their family burying grounds. Many of them plucked grass and put it in their bundles or in their clothes. Some of the women wore only a shift. They didn't even have a bundle. They wiped their tears on bare arms.

Rose stood listening to the roar they made as they lined up outside the tiny stone chapel Saint Columbkille had built. She watched as one by one the figures went inside and lay down on a big flat tombstone.

'What are they doing that for?' she asked.

'For forgetfulness.'

She stared at her mother, baffled, her mouth open.

'They say that lying on the saint's stone will spare you memories,' Hannah began. 'If you're going to Australia and may never come back, it would be best to forget the happiness and joy there was with the friends and family you'll never see again. It would be a small mercy for the poor souls if it were so.'

'Ma, what's that noise?' she asked, at last, as she watched the company forming up to take to the road again.

'That's a lament, the caoine, they call it.'

But whatever it was called, she still didn't grasp how people could make such a noise if their lips never moved.

Sarah felt no cold at all as she struggled up the hill to Rathdrum, her face prickling with heat, her breath streaming round her in the frosty air. The breeze was strengthening. When it caught up snow from the hedgerows and threw small flurries in her face, she was glad of its cooling touch, wiping the moisture from her face with the back of one gloved hand.

She'd told herself as she set out that it didn't matter if she fell in her haste to get to Rathdrum, but the first time her foot skidded on ice below the snow and she fell sprawling, she changed her mind. It wouldn't be much use to Ma if she twisted her ankle and couldn't get there. Better to slow down a bit however much she wanted to get there quickly.

'Keep to the middle,' she said aloud, as she picked herself up hurriedly and shook out her skirts.

Hugh's mare would have left its tracks before the morning's fall. If she could find them, there'd be only eight or nine inches of crisp undisturbed snow above them, while at the edges of the road in the shadow of the hedge there'd be double that amount. What she had to avoid at all costs was blundering into the ditch, invisible where the faded grasses of winter masked the deep channel, freshly cleared and deepened to drain away the heavy rains of autumn.

There was no moon and the starlight was dimmed by

fleeting wisps of low cloud. Only from the snow itself came a feeble gleam in the enveloping darkness. She knew the hill so well she could hardly believe it went on for so long. She was gasping for breath by the time the gradient evened out and she peered around for any sign of the square stone pillars that marked the entrance to Rathdrum.

She stood breathing heavily, unable to pierce the darkness. It had never occurred to her she might arrive at the top of the hill and not be able to find the entrance. It had to be to her right, but where exactly was it? If she were to leave the road at the wrong place, she'd be sure to end up in the ditch. Tears of anxiety and frustration sprang to her eyes.

Think, Sarah, think. Ask for help.

She sent up a quick, incoherent prayer and stood quite still. Elizabeth always said there was no point asking God for help and not waiting for an answer. She stood and listened as intently as she knew how. Now she'd stopped struggling through the snow, the night was completely still. Far away, she heard a dog bark in the silence. Suddenly, unexpectedly, and very close at hand, she heard a soft, rushing noise. A tree had shed part of its burden of snow only a few yards away, and she knew the limes of the avenue were the only trees on this part of the hill.

She ran towards the sound and almost fell over again. As she straightened up, she saw the faint outline of a gatepost and, much further away, the misty gleam of light spilling from the fanlight above the front door of Rathdrum. Between her and it, partly sheltered by the trees, the avenue had only half the snow she'd ploughed through on the hill.

She picked up her skirt, raced to the front door and banged the knocker vigorously. She'd never before knocked at the front door, but the light spilling from the sitting room showed her the piled-up snow at the side of the house. Besides, it was nearer.

'You must come quickly,' she gasped breathlessly, as a startled Elizabeth opened the door.

'What's wrong, Sarah?' Elizabeth asked, as calmly as she could, having taken one brief look at her distraught face.

'Ma's ill,' she said, choking on the words. 'Hugh's gone for the doctor, but if he's that man I saw yesterday he's no use. Please hurry,' she pleaded. 'Get your cape quickly. I'm so afraid she'll die.'

'All right, Sarah, I'll come this minute,' Elizabeth said reassuringly, 'but I need to know what to bring. Now tell me quickly what happened.'

'We came in from school and it was dark and the clock was stopped and her basket still on the table with her sewing,' Sarah began hastily. 'We thought she was here, but she was lying on the bedroom floor. She was as cold as ice.'

'And what did you do?'

'We put her in bed with stone bottles and blankets.'

Elizabeth nodded as she reached for her outdoor boots and sat down in the hallway to put them on. She swung her cape round her shoulders and fastened it, then reached for a shopping basket.

'What was her breathing like?' she asked, as Sarah edged her towards the door. 'Soft and whispery?' she suggested, stopping firmly by the closed door.

'No, it was loud, like when Da snores sometimes. It made a horrible noise in her chest. That was how we knew she wasn't dead,' she threw out, tears now streaming down her face.

'Now then, don't cry, there's a good girl,' Elizabeth said, hugging her. 'We haven't time to be upset. Go up to my bedroom. There's a bottle of lavender water on my table. Bring it to me in the kitchen. On the way there, go to the sitting-room cupboard. Bring me a bottle of elderflower wine and the brandy. Have you got Friar's Balsam at home?'

'I don't know,' said Sarah, shaking her head in despair.

'Never mind. I've got plenty. Now go on. Hurry.'

The long procession marched down the road. Letterkenny, Dublin, Southampton, Abyssinian. That's where people said they were going. *Abyssinian* was a ship. People in Australia had sent them money to buy tickets and they were going there where it was warm. Even without a shawl Australia was warm. So she'd heard. She wondered if she would ever be warm, even if she was in Australia.

The sun had come out now. It was shining in a clear blue sky. But it was still winter. There was snow on the ground and there was another procession of people coming towards her. They were making the same strange noise, a kind of rhythmic roar, up and down, up and down. But their lips didn't move either.

She looked around her at this unknown place. Beside her, crowds of people had gathered to watch the procession. The people who approached were barefoot. They carried bundles and small children, their faces were reddish-brown and deeply lined by sun and wind. She looked carefully for a familiar face but she knew no one among these people.

Suddenly, she remembered who these people were.

'Cherokee,' she said aloud.

'Good riddance,' said a man in the watching crowd.

'Look around you, Rose,' said a soft, familiar voice at her elbow. 'Look at the faces around you. Irish, English and Scots,' he went on. 'All the dispossessed who came to America to make a new life. Look at what they've done, greedy for gold and land. They've evicted the Cherokee.'

'Sam,' she cried, whirling round, longing to see her brother's familiar face, his red hair and kindly eyes.

But there was no one there.

She turned back to the dejected column tramping onwards to new land far away. Many of them wouldn't get there. Sam had told her four thousand died on that winter march to Indian Territory. Now she was seeing them herself. Individual men and women. Men carrying bundles of possessions, women with babies and children clinging to their skirts.

Great cold drops of water fell from the clear sky and burnt her chest and shoulders. Others dropped at her feet. As she watched, the ground moved and flowers pressed through and bloomed on the surface of the dead land.

Most of the Cherokee moved silently with their eyes on the ground ahead of them, stony ground, cold and hard on bare feet, but, suddenly, one woman looked straight at her,

her eyes like two black coals sunk in her withered face. She held out a hand as if begging for help.

'Is there nothin' at all ye can do fer the poor woman?'

Rose heard the voice, a man's voice, somehow familiar among all these strangers asking her to help, but she knew she could do nothing to help the woman. She might die. Or her children might. Sam had told her the only memorial to this long, bitter journey was a flower, a rose with white petals and a gold centre. Everywhere these people had passed on their way to Oklahoma, the white rose had sprung up to mark the Vale of Tears. The Cherokee Rose, he'd called it.

She looked down at her feet. The little roses were springing up all around her.

It took no more than five minutes for Elizabeth to collect up what she needed from the shelves and cupboards in her kitchen, but the few moments it took to wrap the bottles from bedroom and sitting room in clean, spoilt cloth seemed interminable to Sarah. She'd flown through the familiar house, found what was asked for immediately and could think of nothing but getting back again to Ballydown. Every minute seemed like an hour, a delay she could not bear.

Elizabeth moved quickly enough on the avenue, but she couldn't match Sarah's speed on the hill. Nor could she risk dropping the basket full of the precious remedies she'd gathered together.

'No sign of the doctor,' Sarah said sharply, as they slithered in the well-tramped snow by the garden gate.

'We'll do what we can till he comes,' Elizabeth said reassuringly as she used the gatepost to steady herself.

Sarah ran ahead and opened the door. The kitchen was still stone cold, but both gas lamps were now lit. Sam rose from his knees by the stove, a box of matches in his hand, his face pale, a dirty streak across his forehead. He stood staring silently, his body stiff with tension as he watched them take off their capes.

'Could you make a pot of tea, Sam?' Elizabeth asked gently, as she cast a long glance at him.

'Aye, surely,' he said, grateful to have something to do. He picked up a kettle from the newly lit stove and went towards the dairy.

Elizabeth heard Rose before she saw her. The harsh breathing vibrated as far as the small landing outside the bedroom door. It confirmed her worst fears.

She came to the bedside where John sat, his head bowed, his face tear stained, holding one of Rose's hands. Hannah held the other.

'Rose might do better sitting up,' Elizabeth said quietly. 'We'll need all the pillows you can find,' she added, nodding at Hannah and Sarah. 'While there's life there's hope, John,' she said softly. 'Can you lift her right up for me.'

He put his arms round her and lifted her as if she'd been a child, her face against his shoulder, her long, dark hair clinging to his jacket as they piled up the pillows, settled her back against them and tucked a blanket over her shoulders.

When she heard sounds outside, Sarah stuck her head out of the window.

'It's him. The one we saw yesterday. Hugh's with him.'

They stood back from the bed as they heard the heavy tread of feet on the stairs and the doctor appeared, his riding cape still in place.

A small, squarish man in his late fifties, he nodded curtly to John and ignored Elizabeth and Hannah. Sarah had stepped behind the door to let him pass. Re-emerging, she stood watching him with a fixed, steely glint in her eyes as he parked his leather bag and took out his stethoscope.

He examined Rose's chest, pressing the cold metal against her warm skin and listening, his lips pressed tightly together. He looked at her and shook his head.

'Do you have other family nearby?'

John stared at him uncomprehendingly and said nothing.

'My brother works in Belfast,' said Hannah quietly.

'Better send for him right away. The chest is filling up. There's nothing I can do,' he said abruptly, folding up the stethoscope, dropping it in the bag and snapping it shut.

'Is there nothin' at all ye can do fer the poor woman?' John asked desperately, jumping to his feet, his eyes dilated, his face tight with anxiety.

'No, I fear not,' he said coolly. 'There is an infection for which we have no treatment. She might be more comfortable lying down,' he added, with a slight backward glance as he picked up his bag and made his way downstairs.

Hugh had ensured that his fee awaited him on the table.

'I did warn you the journey might be wasted,' he said, as he picked up the coins and put them in his trouser pocket. 'Good evening, Mr Sinton,' he added politely, as he let himself out.

Hugh had been standing awkwardly in front of the stove, fidgeting restlessly and casting his eyes round the empty kitchen. At the doctor's words he dropped down into John's armchair and buried his head in his hands, unable to fend off the weariness of the day and the strain of these last hours any longer. His body ached from the effort of riding, mounting and dismounting in snow with one leg always liable to give way under him. Being civil to a man whom he'd found it hard not to dislike and trying desperately to set aside his own anxiety for Rose and the family had left him spent and discouraged.

His situation he now acknowledged. He was exhausted. But exhaustion was no cause for despair. Not only had he been taught that despair was a sin, but long ago he'd proved to his own satisfaction that despair leads nowhere. Even sitting on a chair, too tired to move, there must be some way he could help his friends. It was up to him to find it.

'Tea, Hugh?'

He looked up into Sam's face and saw someone he hardly recognized, his face ash white, his voice little above a whisper. Sam, the carefree one, the lad who always had a smile and an easy word, had disappeared. It had probably happened the moment he'd stepped over the threshold of his parents' room and seen his mother laid out on the bed.

'Is the doctor still with her?' Sam asked, as he poured tea awkwardly from a very large pot.

'No, he's gone.'

'What did he say?'

'Nothing to help us, Sam,' replied Hugh, honestly. He took a long drink from his mug of tea, made up his mind and got to his feet. 'I'm going up the hill to get Elizabeth. If there's anything to be done, she'll do it. Will you give me a hand up on the mare?'

'Elizabeth's here,' said Sam shortly. 'Sarah went for her. She's been upstairs since just before the doctor came.'

'Thank God for that, Sam,' he said, with a huge sigh of relief, as he subsided again gratefully. 'I'll wait and see what she wants me to do. Stay or go, or fetch something, whatever would help, before I see to the mare. Now, come on, Sam, pour some of that tea for yourself and sit down with me here till we're called for. Elizabeth knows what she's about. I'm the living proof of that,' he added encouragingly.

Rose was tired. Very tired. She'd spent all day scrubbing and cleaning and now it was nearly dark. She couldn't go and leave it all behind, the garden Granny Sarah had cherished for so many years. Perhaps, if she made the effort to go out into the fresh night air she might feel less exhausted. The air in the house was unpleasant, moist and humid. There was a smell, too, like what you got in hot weather when you had to boil towels, or working clothes stained with grease or oil. Not a very pleasant smell at all.

'Come on now, Rose, another breath or two and you'll feel better.'

She didn't recognize the voice and she didn't feel better. She would just lie back in her chair for a minute and close her eyes.

Granny Sarah was making lavender bags. Rose watched her. She'd laid out the stems to dry on the sideboard in the parlour and now she'd brought them back into the kitchen to draw the dry blooms from the shrivelled stems. The whole room was full of the spicy smell as she freed the purple flowers into a bowl ready to dish them out into the little bags she'd made. The pieces of ribbon to tie them were cut and waiting.

'Lavender lifts the spirits,' she said, looking across at her, her eyes twinkling.

Rose smiled to herself. If only that noisy machine outside would stop its thumping she probably would feel better. It must be Robinson's thresher. If it was, it would go on till darkness fell. But then she'd sleep. All she wanted to do was sleep.

Elizabeth looked from Rose's colourless face to John's gaunt and tear-stained one. Then she glanced at Hannah and Sarah. Above the harsh, effortful rhythm of Rose's breathing, she could hear the murmur of voices downstairs, but not what was being said. The front door closed, feet tramped the churned-up path. The high-pitched whinny was most certainly the doctor's horse. He was gone and with him what hope he might have brought. She was in little doubt now that whatever she herself might do the outcome was between Rose and her Maker.

'Hannah,' she said softly, 'I need a bowl of hot water, a towel and the Friar's Balsam from my basket. I also need you to start making a hot meal. I had some supper with Mrs Lappin, but no one else here has had a proper meal all day. Can you manage that?'

Hannah nodded silently and was out of the room in moments.

'What can I do?' demanded Sarah.

'Go and tell Hugh to make up some brandy and hot water for your father. And then see what you can do to help Hannah. There'll be vegetables to prepare.'

John opened his mouth to protest and then closed it again. One look at Elizabeth's face told him she'd not give up hope till all was lost. He gathered himself and waited to see what part she had for him.

'I'll need you to help me when the balsam is ready,' she said steadily, 'but please go down and speak a word to Hugh. He'll be exhausted by now and maybe not able to keep up heart. Encourage him,' she said, as she put her hand on Rose's forehead and smoothed back her tangled hair.

In the few moments when she was alone with Rose, Elizabeth prayed. Once, in her schooldays, in an account of the English Civil War, she'd read the prayer one of the commanders was supposed to have offered up before a major battle. She'd never forgotten the simple words. 'Lord, if I forget You this day, do not Thou forget me.' Her own prayer was not much longer, but there was a difference. She was in no danger of forgetting God, for she was sure that He was Rose's only hope. Her own part was simply to do His will. So she asked for guidance at all times through the evening and through the long night which might lie ahead.

When she opened her eyes, Hannah was coming through the door with a steaming bowl of water, a towel over her arm. Sarah followed behind with the bottle of Friar's Balsam.

'Da wants to know what you think we should do about Jamie?' Hannah began, as she set the bowl down on Rose's dressing table. 'Hugh says he'll go up to Belfast on the train and bring him back. Sam says he'll go. He heard this afternoon there's no snow in Belfast. They could be back together on the last train.'

Elizabeth stood up and counted drops into the boiling water.

'Tell your father I'd rather Sam went. I might need Hugh here. And I need one of them now, while you girls make the meal. See you give Sam something he can eat on the train,' she said quickly, as she stirred her mixture. 'Hurry now, I need John or Hugh. Either of them.'

The hours passed. In the bedroom Elizabeth worked out a routine that she hoped might ease the rough, noisy breathing. Friar's Balsam to keep the upper chest moist and open. Lavender to comfort her distress. It was Charles who had given her the idea of using lavender. He'd insisted that a body was much more likely to give up its struggle if it felt there was no comfort to be had. For want of it, he'd seen unhappy women die in a difficult labour where others in greater straits had pulled through. Even on the battlefield, he'd read, a man with a sweetheart, a wife or a family could often sustain a wound that brought death to another, but he did need support and comfort.

By ten o'clock the heat from the gas lamps and the steam from bowls of boiling water had made the bedroom moist and warm. Elizabeth was pleased that Rose was warmer to the touch, but she herself found the damp warmth was making her sleepy.

'John, I need a breath of fresh air,' she said quietly, as she stood up. 'I'll only be gone a few minutes. Is that all right?'

'Aye. She seems steady enough, even if she's no better,' he said calmly.

'It's a long journey, John, if she can make it. Every hour is an achievement.'

She closed the door gently behind her and went downstairs. Hugh was sitting by the blazing fire, his hands folded in his lap, his eyes fixed on the carved American clock on the wall by the dairy door. Hannah was in her mother's chair opposite him, sewing. Only the set of her shoulders told her she was making an effort for the sake of Sarah, who was sitting on a low chair, staring into the fire and yawning hugely.

Hugh was praying, of course. That was how he always prayed when he had a need and there were people present.

She went out through the dairy and across the back of the house to the privy. From the stable she heard the small movements of Dolly and Hugh's mare, Bess. Black as night was Bess, hence her name. And tonight *was* black. No moon, the stars lost beyond thick cloud.

She stood for a moment in the cold, frosty air, drawing the freshness into her lungs, relaxing the tension in her shoulders and stretching her legs, cramped with sitting for so long, so close to the bed. She had no way of knowing if fluid was still gathering in Rose's lungs and she knew no way of stopping it if it was. Only one more remedy still sat in her basket. A large jar of sprigs of dried rosemary.

'Rose and Mary,' she said aloud, suddenly seeing the familiar name as two names. The herb that grew so prolifically in the sunniest part of the garden at Rathdrum was named for Rose herself and for her dear friend Mary Wylie, who had died in the Armagh disaster.

'Life and death, such close companions,' she whispered to herself, as she stared up at the starless sky. As they would be tonight. She wondered if John, or Hannah, or Sam, knew how significant the later small hours would be, the hours when the body's reserves were at their lowest and the spirit most likely to slip away.

Across the valley beyond Dolly's field she saw a point of light in the deep darkness. Somewhere in the hamlet of Lisnaree, there were people not yet abed. Perhaps the family of that child Hugh had told her about, the one he'd driven to the dispensary when Sarah came running to fetch him. Poor child. Whatever ailed it, it stood small chance of living, so frail its little body. So Sarah had said. Wide eyed and angry she'd been, Hugh had told her later that evening. She'd blamed him for the woman's need to walk to Rathdrum to fetch a ticket.

Poor Hugh, it had vexed him to see Sarah so upset. She'd meant to talk to Rose about it this morning. Ask her what best to do. How they could explain things to Sarah and comfort Hugh. All that was irrelevant now. Their hurt would be as nothing if they were both to lose Rose.

She took one more deep breath to clear her head of sleep, shivered, and went back to meet whatever the night might bring.

Seven

Elizabeth didn't know what time the last train left Belfast for Banbridge, but it stopped at all the stations on the way and there was a two-mile walk at the end of it, so it might well be midnight before Sam and Jamie arrived back at Ballydown. With the main road icy and the snow cover on the hill now freezing it could be even later. She sighed and went back into the house.

After the deep darkness of the night, it took some moments to adjust to the dazzle of light from the gas lamps. Three pairs of eyes looked up expectantly as she came into the kitchen. She paused by the table, looked around and saw her basket had been placed carefully on a chair by the door. She stepped across and brought it into the light.

'Hannah dear, I'd like you to make up a mixture of elderflower wine and honey. It needs to be warm but not hot, sweet but not sickly. A cupful would do to begin with. And a small teaspoon. Good girl,' she added encouragingly, as Hannah rolled up her sewing, got to her feet and took the bottle and jar from her hands.

Poor girl. She saw how pale and immobile Hannah's face had become, but Sarah looked even worse. Even paler than her sister, she had great dark circles under her eyes. She had jumped up from her chair the moment Elizabeth had appeared, ready to do whatever she might ask.

'Sarah, I need two people to sit with me all night. Your father will be one, for I know he won't leave your mother, but it may be a long night, so I shall ask Hannah to sit with us until Sam and Jamie get back. I'll send Hannah to rest then. I'll need you about two o'clock. Then we'll start all over again,' she explained quietly. 'What I want you to do now is go to bed and sleep, so you'll be fresh when everyone else is tired. If Ma gets worse I'll call you immediately. You're only a step away.'

To her great surprise, Sarah came and hugged her, kissed her sleepily and went upstairs without another word.

Hannah had taken the elderflower and honey out to the dairy, where the mixture would be easier to make on the gas ring. Through the open door, Elizabeth could hear her small movements as she fetched a saucepan and struck a match. There was a tiny chink from a spoon as she measured the liquid from the bottle and jar.

'And what of me, Elizabeth?' said Hugh softly, his eyes upon her, full of all the questions he would not put into words.

She smiled warmly and touched his cheek, grateful to share her burden if only for a single moment.

'You've been doing just what I wanted,' she said, softer still. 'Pray for me too, that my strength will serve.'

'Is there *any* hope?'

'Just what we make for her, for the moment,' she said quickly, moving away from him and sorting items from her basket as Hannah came back into the room.

'Hugh, I want you to make up a rub,' she said, in as normal a voice as she could manage, taking out a large jar full of tiny, dried sprigs. 'Put the rosemary in the oven till its well warm, but not hot. Then crush it in a dish with the back of a spoon. Mix it with this,' she added, producing a small jar of goose fat. 'It's the oil you need, not the little spikes themselves, so pick out as many as you can after you've mixed it. One of us will come down for it later when we've tried the elderflower and honey,' she added, as he pushed himself awkwardly to his feet.

Sam had been in Belfast a number of times, both with his father and with Hugh, but he'd never travelled to the city on his own, nor visited his brother at his recently acquired lodgings. Before he left the house, he wrote down the new address carefully, even though he'd memorized it as soon as

Jamie told them about his move. He'd also extracted some battered notes from the shiny new leather wallet in the top pocket of his best jacket where he kept his savings until he felt it was worth the trouble of taking them to the bank.

The Belfast carriers had told him there was no snow in the city, and they were right, but as he came out on to the steps of the Great Northern Station he reckoned it was colder in the city than in Banbridge. A bitter wind gusted down over the edge of the Antrim Hills and poured along the empty streets like floodwater, sweeping up the fragments of straw from horses' nosebags and the torn remnants of posters once attached to walls and doors.

When he crossed Great Victoria Street from the station, to his amazement, there wasn't a soul in sight. He'd walked almost the whole way to the White Linen Hall before he met a scurrying figure who was able to tell him where he could find the nearest cab rank.

It was a long, cold wait before he heard the clatter of hooves and exchanged words with a cloaked figure hunched up on the box.

'Ye'd have been quicker taking the tram from Carlisle Circus,' said the driver, looking down at Sam.

'I might,' said Sam agreeably, grateful to see the prospect of progress at last, 'but I don't know the city well. And forby, I need ye to wait to bring my brother and me back to catch the last train for Banbridge.'

'Aye well,' said the man, not committing himself, 'it's a fair step to the place ye want. It'll cost ye a bit.'

Sam nodded. He'd been warned about cab drivers who overcharged, but he hadn't time to argue. He urged him to make speed, got into the cab and sat down.

He'd never been in a hire cab before and he was not impressed. It bumped and creaked over the rough surface of the road. Worse still, it moved so slowly he became more and more anxious, for the journey seemed to be taking an enormous length of time. Jamie had said his digs were convenient for the shipyard and the trams ran regularly from a terminus nearby. Sam could now make out the dark tracery of masts and rigging of ships towering over the shops as they crossed a bridge, but he saw no sign of tramlines.

There were rows of workers' houses, small and close together, the lights from their windows spilling out into empty, silent streets. Here and there a mill building rose like a cliff, its dark face pierced with square patches of light, the noise of looms so loud he could feel their vibration on the cold, heavy air.

Adrift in the middle of a city, travelling from one unknown place to another, with no familiar landmark anywhere to be seen, Sam felt desolate. He wished now he'd let Hugh come. Maybe there was nothing he could do for his mother at home, but he wished passionately he'd never left her. He could be standing in a corner of the bedroom where she lay, her face deathly pale, her slight shoulders moving with the harshness of her breathing, her long, dark hair falling limp around her.

When he was a little boy, he used to comb her hair. He could still remember the first day Hannah asked if she could comb Ma's hair. Ma had said yes, so he'd asked too. She'd laughed and said, 'Why not. Am I not the lucky one to have two assistants to dress my hair, when Lady Anne herself has only one?'

Sam wiped his tears absently with his sleeve and looked at his watch. It was already after nine o'clock and the cab was going yet more slowly because of the steepness of the road.

'There yar. Fifty-six. There's no lights on. I hafta charge for waitin'.'

'I'll only be a minute or two,' Sam reassured him, as he jumped down and made for the tall brick house sitting behind a privet hedge.

He knocked and waited. Then knocked again. Surely there must be someone at home. The fanlight above his head produced a faint gleam as a light went on somewhere within. The letter box rattled and from within came a thin, querulous voice.

'Who is it? Have you forgotten your key?' a woman asked.

Through the panels of roughened glass, Sam could see she was bending her mouth to the open letter box.

'My name's Sam Hamilton. I want to speak to my brother Jamie. Is he in?' he asked, bending down to the small aperture.

'No, he's not.'

'Well, where's he gone? Tell me where I can find him,' Sam went on, a note of desperation creeping into his voice.

'Sure how would I know? I mind my own business,' she said huffily. 'Why do you want him at this hour when respectable people are in bed?'

'Our mother's ill. Very ill. The doctor said to get him. If I don't get him soon, I'll miss the last train back to Banbridge.'

'Banbridge, dear save us,' she said, her careful pronunciation falling foul of her surprise at the thought of such a journey. 'Well, I'm sorry for you, young man, but I can't help. He and some of the other lads he works with have gone out. They go off regular every few Fridays, but whether it's the pub, or gaming, or what, I don't know. They don't tell me. But he'll not be back for an hour or more, I'd say.'

'Will ye give him a message?' Sam asked, suddenly aware of the minutes ticking away.

'I will.'

'Tell him Sam says get the first train home in the mornin'.'

'Is that all?'

'Aye.'

He straightened up as the letter box dropped shut, then tramped down the path to where the cab waited, the horse blowing in the cold air.

'Back to the station as fast as ye can, like a good man. I must catch that train,' he said urgently to the driver.

'Did ye not get him?'

'No, I didn't. So I must get back m'self. Do your best for me an' I'll see ye right,' he said, as he jumped in and buried his face in his hands.

It wasn't reasonable at all to be annoyed that Jamie was out with his friends and had told no one where he was going, but Sam didn't feel reasonable. He didn't know why, but for the first time in his life he felt angry with Jamie, the big brother he had always loved and admired. If he missed that train and couldn't get back home he'd be angrier still.

There was no response at all when Elizabeth tried Rose with a little of Hannah's mixture on a spoon. Her lips were stiff. She was so far away in her thoughts they responded neither to the warmth nor the sweetness. The mixture simply trickled out of the edge of her mouth to be wiped gently away with a damp cloth.

Her breathing seemed to have lost some of its harshness, but the fact that it was a little quieter was no comfort to the three who kept watch. It was also a little slower. John and Hannah could see for themselves perfectly well what Elizabeth knew already. Rose was tiring. Breathing was such an effort, it had become slower and shallower.

'I think we'll try the rosemary now,' she said steadily, when two further hourly applications of balsam and lavender appeared to have made no significant improvement.

They moved all the pillows. While John supported Rose, Hannah and Elizabeth undid her nightgown and left her back and chest exposed. There was no danger of Rose feeling cold for the room was too warm for the comfort of those who sat by the bed. John regularly wiped sweat from his forehead and Hannah's paleness was hidden by a rosy flush.

Elizabeth rolled up her sleeves, lathered her hands and began massaging shoulders and upper chest alternately. Such narrow shoulders to carry all the weight of a family's need. Not undernourished, simply lightly made, the small breasts shapely and still firm, the waist so narrow it was no more than the few handspans of the skirt she'd worn at her wedding.

She thought of the child who'd held her baby brother in the straw-lined cart when her parents walked away from the wreckage of their home in Ardtur. Rose had told her how they'd survived the bitter cold of that late-April day and the weeks that followed when their home was a kind neighbour's barn. Rose had survived that hardship, she reflected, but then the infection attacking her chest was a very different enemy.

It couldn't be escaped by taking to the road and seeking shelter elsewhere.

From downstairs the click of a door latch and the sound of voices echoed up through the stairwell. John and Hannah listened intently as Elizabeth concentrated on what she was doing, easing the tightened muscles of the shoulders, drawing her long fingers up over the rib cage and encouraging the weary chest muscles to continue their work. Neither Hannah nor John said a word till she'd wiped the remaining traces of the rub from Rose's warm skin and fastened up her nightgown.

'That's Sam back,' said Hannah, 'But I don't hear Jamie.'

'John, will you hold Rose forward till I get the pillows ready.'

He took her in his arms again. Elizabeth arranged the pillows and waited. For several minutes she stood silent, watching him, thinking he might not be able to let her go, but then, very gently, he kissed her cheeks and placed her against the mound of pillows that kept her upright.

'Go down and see Sam and stretch your legs, John,' she said quietly. 'She's all right for the moment.'

Rose couldn't think why for the life of her she'd come. Her feet were sore and bleeding and she was so out of breath there was pain in her chest with every gasp she took, but now she was here she might as well look.

'Just where Owen said it would be,' she whispered to herself.

The dark, square castle rose on a promontory jutting out into the lough, the only building in the whole long valley. A road ran close to the loughside, a dusty, beige line cutting through the greens and browns of the shore and the clumps of vegetation growing by the water's edge. Around the castle itself there were trees and a walled garden. As she watched, a carriage appeared, moving briskly along the new road until it reached the castle itself. It turned into the great open space by the main entrance and stopped. Grooms and footmen came running out to attend to horses and passengers.

'So you've come back too,' said a voice at her side.

'Owen Friel,' she gasped, startled and amazed. 'I thought you were in America with Danny Lawn.'

To her surprise, he didn't reply, he just stood looking down at the castle. Long, long ago, when they were both children, she'd climbed the mountain to see the castle, but it hadn't even been built then. She'd been so exhausted after the climb, Owen had carried her part of the way home.

'That's Her Ladyship,' he said abruptly, as a woman emerged from the coach. 'Adair's dead ten years or more and they say she loves this place. She's good to the tenants and takes care of them. Not much good to us now, Rose. Or Danny either.'

Danny was standing on her other side. He'd been a big, awkward lad, no use at school work, but physically strong and so good-natured he'd do anything for anybody. He seemed little changed since she'd last seen him more than thirty years ago, except for the strange clothes he wore. A two-piece suit of rough, beige-coloured cloth with markings on it she couldn't make out. It was a bit like a uniform, but not as well made. He stared out over the lough, apparently unaware of her presence.

'Well, you've seen it now, Rose. There's nothing more to do. We all did what we could to set it right,' Owen said. 'That's the end of it.'

She looked around at the broken rocks on the summit of the mountain where they'd stood, but they were gone. She was amazed they could have disappeared so quickly. Then, she remembered. With an awful sinking feeling as if her heart were about to stop, she saw again the rope tied round their necks where the collars of their shirts should have been.

'We'll try Rose Mary now.'

She wondered who Rose Mary was and why they were going to try her. Perhaps she was a new kitchen maid come to the servants' hall to see if she would suit. Poor girl, she'd have a lot to put up with. Mr Smithers, the butler, would be watching her every move, and when Cook's back was giving her trouble there was no pleasing her at all. Rose was glad she was a lady's maid now. However awful Lady Anne's tantrums might be, she never scolded like Cook or Mr Smithers. She'd been at Currane Lodge so long, there wasn't much about the staff or the family she and her mother hadn't talked over together while they sorted the linen or mended the gowns. At least her mother would be kind to poor little Rose Mary.

'Ach, there ye are. I was lookin' everywhere for ye.'

Rose turned round, smiled and held out her arms when she saw who it was. Mary Wylie hugged her and kissed both her cheeks.

'Sure, I'm sorry we didn't get seats together,' she said, nodding at her. 'But we'll put that right. Isn't it a shame the train's broke down and they've had to send for another one. C'mon an' we'll take a wee walk till ourselves,' she said, her blue eyes dancing, a broad smile on her face.

The train had stopped. All along its length people were climbing down from the carriages and making their way through the long grass on the railway banks to find a shady place under a hawthorn bush or in the shadow of great mounds of briar covered with bright pink roses. The sun beamed down from a flawless blue sky. It was a perfect day, even if at this moment she was very hot and felt terribly out of breath.

'Where have the children gone, Mary?' she asked, a sudden anxiety touching her.

'Ach, didn't they find wee friends from school. Yours and mine are away wi' them to see if the band is going to play. They're down at the back wi' all their instruments. They might as well play us a tune.'

Rose smiled. Dear Mary. She was looking so lovely today in the blue blouse she'd made from material she'd once given her. She slipped her arm round her soft, generous waist and felt her friend's arm tighten around hers. They strolled slowly along the broad, smooth path beside the empty train, the sound of children's voices in their ears.

'You're lookin' tired, Rose. Shall we go and sit under that nice big tree. Maybe ye'll have a wee sleep.'

'Oh yes, Mary. What a good idea. I am so very tired.'

When Hannah slipped silently downstairs a little after two o'clock for a drink of water and a breath of fresh air, she found Hugh and Sam asleep in the two chairs by the fire. Hugh woke immediately, impatient with himself for having nodded off.

'Any change?' he asked quietly, glancing at Sam's sleeping figure.

'She seems weaker,' Hannah replied with a sigh, as she drew her hands wearily down her flushed cheeks.

'Can I take your place for a few minutes?' he asked tentatively.

'Yes, if you want to. I need to go outside and Elizabeth wants more warm water,' she replied in a whisper, when Sam didn't stir.

'They were both boiling a few minutes ago,' Hugh said softly, nodding at the kettles, as he pulled himself to his feet and made for the stairs.

Narrow and wooden, they were awkward and difficult for his bad leg, but he managed without making too much noise. He straightened himself up at the open door of the bedroom and took in the scene before him. Rose's immobile face now had a little colour, but her harsh breathing had faded to an irregular roughness. John's face streamed with sweat, or tears, or both. Elizabeth, her sleeves rolled up and her blouse unbuttoned, still managed to look her unshakeable self.

'Can I do anything?' he asked abruptly.

'Yes,' she replied, rising. 'Sit with John and Rose till I come back. I'll only be a few minutes.'

She was grateful for the freshness of Sarah's bedroom as she slipped inside and shut the door carefully behind her. It wasn't worth lighting the lamp for the few minutes she would need, so she lit the bedside candle.

'Sarah,' she said softly, taking the cold hand that protruded from the bedclothes.

Sarah's eyes opened slowly and filled instantly with anxiety.

'It's all right, Sarah, she's still with us, but I shall need you soon. I want to explain what you have to do. Are you awake enough to listen?'

'Yes, of course,' she insisted, as she sat up and swung her legs out of bed. She was still wearing all her clothes, her school pinafore crumpled and creased. She pushed her feet into her shoes and tied them quickly.

Elizabeth spoke slowly and clearly, made sure she understood and then sent her downstairs to fetch Sam.

There was barely space to move in the bedroom when Sam and Hannah came back upstairs with Sarah. There was certainly nowhere for them to sit. Once Elizabeth took up her place again, Hugh offered to wait downstairs, but John stopped him. 'No, stay where ye are, man. Sam'll find ye a chair.'

Sam brought the chair from his own bedroom, settled Hugh beside his father and leant against the wardrobe door behind them where he could watch Elizabeth across the squares and diamonds of the winter quilt and observe Hannah and Sarah side by side at the bed's foot.

They sat in silence, the only noise the reluctant, laboured breathing of wife, friend and mother, the unconscious woman who lay so unnaturally still, her head thrown back against the piled-up pillows, the cloud of her dark hair spilling all around her.

The room grew quieter and yet warmer. Rose's face began to flush slightly as the minutes passed. Elizabeth made no move to mix Friar's Balsam or even to rub her chest and hands with lavender water. She sat, holding one hand, watching her face, as John also sat, his eyes never leaving her for a moment.

From downstairs they heard the chime of the American clock, a strange, muted sound, as if it measured time in some different world. It gathered itself, rang the quarters and struck the hour. One, two, three.

There was a slight movement from those gathered round the bed, an intake of breath, an easing of weary muscles, but from Rose there was no movement at all.

'Has she gone?' John asked, his eyes dilated, as he looked away from Rose for the first time and stared at Elizabeth.

'No,' replied Elizabeth, leaning forward to wipe trickles of moisture from Rose's face. 'But she's close.'

The park and gardens were familiar, but to begin with Rose could not remember where they were. The long flight of steps up to the big house and the formal gardens on either side were far too grand for Currane Lodge, but not grand enough for Lady Anne's new mansion in Gloucestershire, which had fountains and a parterre.

She and Mary walked on, along shady paths and across little clearings dappled with sunlight and full of birdsong. From time to time, through the trees, they caught sight of a lake, a bent old willow leaning over into the water, swans floating along serenely, their dazzling whiteness perfectly reflected in the unruffled water.

She felt better. And the idea of a little sleep under a shady tree was so appealing she could hardly wait to get there. There it was, out beyond a wide, sun-drenched stretch of lawn, a huge cedar, its branches spread wide, the lowest almost touching the ground. A pool of cool, dark shade softly spread with fallen fragments lay at its feet.

'Ma-a, Ma-a, Ma-a.'

She paused on the edge of the woodland, looked around and wondered where the noise had come from. There were no birds to be seen in the bright, sunlit space between her and the cedar. Perhaps it was one of the sheep in the park that lay beyond the house and gardens.

'Ma-a, we're over here.'

The voice seemed familiar. It was as if someone was calling her, but she couldn't make out the words. She looked around. Mary had gone. The place where she still stood in the shadow of the trees was completely unknown. It was growing hotter and hotter. It was so hot she could hardly breathe.

'Ma-a, we're over here.'

She struggled to wipe the dripping moisture from her face, but now it seemed it was not just her face, she felt her legs, her arms, trickle with sweat. The pressure in her chest was unbearable. She took a deep breath and felt a flash of pain, as if someone had tied a cord tightly round below her breasts. She recognized the voice now. It was Sarah and she was calling her.

Suddenly she found herself in her own bed, gasping for breath and sweating so fiercely that drips of moisture rolled down her forehead and got into her eyes, blurring her vision as she struggled to make out the shapes around her.

'Hello, Ma.'

She tried to reply but she couldn't manage a sound. Someone was wiping her face with a damp cloth. She glanced up at her and recognized Elizabeth. Her eyes moved slowly round the room, rested a moment on each member of the gathered company, and the tight immobility of her streaming face softened towards a smile.

'She's back,' said Elizabeth quietly, as her eyes closed again and she drifted into sleep. 'The fever's broken. We're not out of the woods yet, but we must give thanks.'

Eight

As soon as Elizabeth was able to reassure them the greatest danger had passed, Sarah and Sam agreed to go to bed. There would be plenty for everyone to do in the morning, she said, but now, until the fever subsided, she and Hannah needed all the space they could get for changing Rose's nightgown and the bed sheets.

Hugh returned to his seat by the stove, kept the fire going and made mugs of tea for them all at four o'clock and then again at six. Even John allowed himself to nod in his chair, though he'd not leave Rose's side until the fever was past and she no longer needed lifting and sponging.

In the early dawn, Sam woke, dressed quietly and slipped out of the house without disturbing anyone. He walked briskly down the hill, arrived at his workplace in Tullyconnaught at the usual time and explained to the foreman why he had to go straight home. He arrived just as Hannah came downstairs to begin making breakfast and Hugh stirred in his armchair by the stove.

'How is she now?' he asked, as he hung up his cap.

'Asleep,' she said, smiling wearily. 'Proper asleep, Sam. She looks different. You could sit with her while Da has his breakfast.'

'What did you say, Hannah?' Hugh said, yawning hugely. 'I must have nodded off again. Quite disgraceful of me when you've been awake all night,' he added sharply.

'I can sleep later, Hugh, now Ma's improving,' she replied gently. 'She's managed to swallow some elderflower and honey and some water. I know Elizabeth's pleased.'

'She's had no sleep either,' said Hugh thoughtfully. 'Have

you been out, Sam?' he asked suddenly, as Sam added his jacket to the row on the hooks by the door.

'Aye. I went down to work to tell them I wou'den be in. It's thawed in the night and still thawing. There's a clear strip the whole way down the hill,' he went on, looking pleased.

'Great news, Sam,' Hugh said, nodding as he pushed himself to his feet. 'I have a thought to put to John and Elizabeth. I'll need the brougham if they agree. Would you give me a hand to take Bess down to MacMurray's and get her harnessed up?'

'I will surely. Say the word. That's what I'm here for.'

They turned at the sound of feet on the stairs and waited till John had moved stiffly to the very bottom.

'How is she, John?' asked Hugh steadily.

'She's asleep, but she's like herself,' he said, with a great gusty sigh. 'Aye an' she knows us well enough, but she's that tired she can't speak or do anythin' to help herself. It's a miracle, Hugh. That's all it is, an' her that near gone,' he said, sitting down abruptly in the nearest chair and dropping his face in his hands.

'This man needs his breakfast,' said Hugh lightly, clapping John on the shoulder, as Hannah came back from the dairy with a jug of milk and a loaf of baker's bread.

'An' so does your Elizabeth,' said John, wiping away tears unashamedly and looking up. 'She's the only one of us has never closed an eye all night. An' she's still up there,' he said wearily.

'She is, and you'll not shift her till she's good and ready,' Hugh came back at him, a small smile touching his sombre face. 'But I may be able to get her some help,' he added. 'John, I have a mind to go over to Dromore to a doctor there she's spoken of. I don't know him personally, but she speaks well of him. I'll leave Bess at The Grapes and take the train and bring him back with me as soon as he's free to come. He may be able to advise us better than your man last night,' he said dismissively. 'What do you think?'

'Ach, Hugh dear, sure the two of you's been the savin' of

us. I'll say yes to whativer you think. Will I go back up and let Elizabeth come down an' talk to you.'

'No, I'll go, Da,' said Sam promptly. 'Have your breakfast. Call me when yer ready to go, Hugh, an' I'll come down the hill with ye.'

After the fierce cold of the previous day the quiet March morning seemed almost warm by contrast. By the time Sam had seen Hugh safely on his way into Banbridge, a few pale fingers of sunlight were catching the drifts of melting snow under the hedgerows, great shining drops hung like pale flowers on the saturated, bare branches, and the wide puddles by the roadside reflected the first patches of blue in the clearing sky.

Hugh was tired and his body ached from fatigue and a night spent on one chair or another, but he was in the best of spirits as he manoeuvred the brougham out of MacMurray's yard and let Bess pick her own path along the muddy road into town. He left her with the groom in the stableyard of the inn and splashed his way across The Square and up the slope to the railway station.

It was only seven miles to Dromore, by no means beyond Bess's capacity, but he was glad he'd not attempted to drive. The open country to the north-east had caught more of the snow, and where the Dromore road lay sheltered from the south its entire surface was still covered.

In the town itself there were few vehicles moving and he had some difficulty keeping his feet as he made his way to Doctor Richard Stewart's house in Dromara Street.

'Good morning,' he said, to the dark-gowned woman who opened the door and regarded him dubiously.

'I should like to see Doctor Stewart,' he went on, returning her gaze directly. 'I am quite aware how early it is but I am willing to await his convenience however long that may be,' he said firmly.

'Who shall I say is calling?' she asked, as she waved him into a waiting room full of heavy, polished furniture.

'Hugh Sinton from Banbridge,' he said, as he moved awkwardly past her and seated himself on the nearest chair.

'I'll tell him you're here,' she said, her cool, businesslike tone betraying just a hint of curiosity.

Only a few moments later, Richard Stewart himself appeared.

'Sinton, you are early indeed. I trust you are well yourself,' he said, looking at him closely, as he got to his feet.

'I am, thank God,' said Hugh warmly, as he shook the outstretched hand. 'But I have friends in great need. My sister is still there with them. I'd be grateful if you would come back with me and give us your advice.'

'Certainly, I shall,' he replied, nodding vigorously. 'But may I ask how you got here? The roads into Dromore from the south were all impassable last night, so my stableman tells me.'

'I came by train,' Hugh replied, smiling. 'But you're right enough. It's thawing now, but I doubt if Bess could have managed it. I've left the brougham at The Grapes waiting for us, if you'll be so good as to come back with me. Ballydown is about two miles out, towards Corbet.'

'What time is the next train? Do you know?' Stewart asked quickly. 'I don't often use the train myself,' he explained. 'My patients live in such awkward places I still find it easier to ride. Though maybe one day I'll acquire one of these motor carriages,' he said shyly.

'An hour from now,' Hugh told him.

'Why, that would give me time to have a little breakfast,' he said cheerfully. 'I hope you'll join me. If you'll forgive a professional comment, I think you've had a rather taxing and tiring time,' he said, glancing at Hugh again. 'Indeed, I think I must insist,' he went on. 'In fact, I positively prescribe it,' he added, beaming at Hugh.

Hugh laughed and decided it would be quite discourteous to resist such a genuine offer. Richard Stewart was still the agreeable man Elizabeth had remembered. He liked his directness and his warmth and he had a shrewd suspicion that those twinkling eyes missed nothing of what passed before them. A man in his forties, obviously unmarried, he was smooth skinned and just a little plump. His manner had a soothing and reassuring quality. What interested Hugh was that the manner was not assumed. It was simply the man himself.

They breakfasted in a small dining room at the back of the tall, Georgian house – a south-facing room with French windows giving on to a long, narrow garden, still completely enveloped in snow.

'I should perhaps admit that I will take somewhat longer than you to walk to the station,' said Hugh circumspectly, as the housekeeper removed their plates. 'I needed a good ten minutes to get here.'

Stewart consulted his watch.

'Time for another cup of coffee,' he declared and refilled their cups.

'That was a most excellent breakfast,' said Hugh gratefully. 'I must thank you for prescribing it. Would that all medicine were so pleasant,' he added smiling. 'I didn't know how hungry I was. My own fault entirely. Both my friend and his daughter tried to persuade me to eat at Ballydown.'

'Good. Good,' said Stewart, beaming with pleasure. 'A hot breakfast will stand to you as we make our way to the station.'

The journey back to Ballydown was achieved without difficulty, despite the thaw turning the road out of Banbridge into a sea of mud. Bess was never troubled by mud, or by rain, it was only ice made her nervous. They kept up a good pace, though Hugh did not press her.

He took the opportunity to tell Stewart all he knew about the circumstances of Rose's illness, both before the doctor had been sent for on Friday evening and what had happened afterwards.

In response, Stewart asked a lot of questions. Some of them surprised Hugh, for they related to the members of the family and the parts each of them had played during the long night. Particularly, he asked about 'Miss Sinton', until Hugh persuaded him to be less formal, knowing they had once been close friends.

'I must confess to knowing something of your sister's nursing ability,' he admitted, as they drove along the last stretch of the main road. 'I was at medical school in Edinburgh with Charles and I still keep in touch with another contemporary of ours, now in Manchester, who corresponds with her. He told me she'd once considered doing medical training. He finds her comments on nursing matters most pertinent.'

'Yes, I fear I have probably deprived the medical profession of a good doctor,' said Hugh honestly. 'I and other members of my family whose needs she met, one after another,' he added sadly. 'It is so easy to be wise after the event, is it not?'

Jamie had almost finished his breakfast before the housekeeper appeared from the kitchen and bent over his chair.

'There's a message for you, Mr Hamilton,' she said, in the rounded tones she used for dealing with Mrs Caldwell's young gentlemen.

'For me?' said Jamie, startled.

'Your brother came last night while you were out,' she said, underlining the *while you were out* with a note of disapproval. 'He said you were to get the first train home in the morning.'

Jamie bridled before he gave any thought to what the message might mean. What was young Sam about, leaving orders for him?

'Did he say why I was to come home?' he asked sharply.

'He may have done. I don't remember,' she said with studied vagueness. 'He came in a cab long after I was in bed. I had to come all the way down to the front door,' she went on, in an aggrieved tone.

'There must have been some good reason,' Jamie replied crossly, his first angry reaction now tempered by anxiety. 'Is someone ill? Has there been an accident?' he demanded.

'Yes, I think there *was* something amiss. Your mother, I think,' she said, her eyes glittering with unpleasantness. 'I think that's what he said,' she added, as she swept up the dirty plates and took them to the kitchen.

Jamie got to his feet and ran his eyes round the oval table where the boarders ate their meals. There were empty chairs where one or two of those with longer journeys to work had already left, but most of the others were still munching toast and marmalade.

'Harry, I have to go home early,' he said, as he leant over his closest companion, a colleague from his own drawing office. 'I think my mother is ill, but old Biddy won't tell me properly what my brother said. He came while we were out last night and she's only bothered to tell me now. Damn her,' he ended furiously. 'Can you explain to the boss for me. I've missed the first train already.'

Harry nodded, his mouth full of toast. 'We were pretty late, after all,' he said, swallowing quickly.

'She could have left a note in my room.'

'If she can write, Jamie,' he said, with a sideways look. 'Sorry about your mother. I hope you find her better. I'll tell Harding why you're absent. He can't very well call you out if it's serious,' he added, helping himself quickly to more toast before the newly arrived rack passed to the other side of the table and emptied itself completely.

Jamie thought about changing his clothes and decided not to bother, so he set off in his dark suit with his spotless stiff collar as he did every morning of the week, except Sunday, when he could sleep late so long as he was prepared to do without breakfast. Harding was a stickler for proper dress. The first thing he'd learnt in the drawing office was nothing to do with ships, but everything to do with polished shoes and trousers pressed with a knife-edge crease. It cost a fortune to send his shirts and collars to the laundry, but his new friends warned him it would be false economy not to do so. If he wanted a place at the end of his apprenticeship, he had to fork out, even if it left him with little money for the pleasures of life.

He collected his shaving things and his pyjamas, pushed them into a bag and set off briskly, catching a tram almost immediately. It was some distance from the city terminus to the Great Victoria Street Station, but although he walked briskly, he arrived to find a queue at the ticket office and the second Banbridge train just pulling out. With an hour to wait before the next one he went in search of the waiting room, picked up an abandoned copy of the *Belfast Evening Telegraph* and occupied himself reading the advertisements for ocean passages and a discussion of the new Bill that would remove the need for flagmen in attendance on road engines.

Hannah was sweeping the floor when she heard the brougham on the hill. She put away the brush, smoothed the creases from her skirt and called a warning up the stairs before she opened the door.

'Miss Hamilton, how do you do,' said Richard Stewart, smiling at her and casting a casual glance round the bright, empty kitchen. 'Mother upstairs?' he enquired gently, as Hugh propelled himself up the path behind him.

'Yes. My father and younger brother are with her,' she replied, with a gentle smile as she shook his hand. 'We persuaded Elizabeth to lie down,' she went on, addressing Hugh. 'She sat up all night with Ma,' she explained, turning back to Richard Stewart.

'And so did you, young lady,' Hugh reminded her. 'Is Sarah still asleep?'

'No. She's gone up to Rathdrum to see Mrs Lappin and tell her where you and Elizabeth both disappeared to.'

'Oh dear, I'm afraid I quite forgot poor Mrs Lappin. How remiss of me,' said Hugh ruefully.

'I rather gather you've all had a great deal to think about during the night. May I go up?'

Hannah led the way and brought him into the fresh and tidy room where Rose lay propped on her pile of pillows. Her face was pale but the harsh note in her breathing had quite gone, leaving only a roughness, a catching of air on inflamed passages that sometimes made her cough.

Richard Stewart looked at her for a brief moment, then shook hands with John and with Sam, who blushed and slipped away to leave his father alone with the doctor.

'We nearly lost her, sir. If it hadn't been for Miss Sinton,' said John, releasing Rose's hand and moving himself and his chair into a corner of the room where he'd be properly out of the way.

'So I've heard,' said Stewart quietly, taking his place by the bed. 'I doubt if I could have done as much for you last night as she did. But I'll see what I can do now,' he said as he turned to lay his bag on the dressing table behind him. His back to the door, he opened it and took out his stethoscope.

He turned when he heard a slight rustle of skirts. Elizabeth stood in the doorway, her clothes creased and crumpled, her hair newly brushed, her face fresh and alert.

'My dear Miss Sinton,' he said, bowing to her. 'I'm not sure you need me at all, but your brother asked me to come and I did so most willingly. I would appreciate your help with my examination.'

He sat down beside the bed, took Rose's hand in his and touched the pulse lightly. She didn't stir, her eyes closed, her face quite peaceful. He nodded reassuringly to John, then turned to Elizabeth.

'I want to examine her chest, but I don't want to startle her. Can you tell her what I'm going to do. Were she to wake it would be helpful, but I am reluctant to disturb her.'

She nodded and moved to Sam's empty chair.

'Rose dear, Doctor Stewart is here. Can you wake up for a little,' she said, leaning close to her and stroking her cheek.

She opened her eyes and smiled sleepily.

'Good. Good,' he said quickly, as he stood rubbing the trumpet end of his stethoscope against his hand to warm it.

'Now, Mrs Hamilton, can you take a deep breath? Good. Was that painful? Yes, I thought so. Unpleasant, I fear, but not a danger. Could you manage to take some more for me? Very tiresome when you are so tired, but we'll soon be done.'

Elizabeth observed with interest. He treated Rose as gently as a child, his ease of manner at odds with the powerful concentration she observed in his eyes and on his brow.

'Does it hurt when I press here? And here? And here?'

Rose responded with the slightest of gestures, sometimes no more than a glance towards him.

'There now, go back to sleep, Mrs Hamilton,' he said, stepping back to allow Elizabeth to adjust the bedclothes.

'If I send that charming girl of yours up to her mother, we could have a word downstairs so as not to disturb her,' he suggested, looking from John to Elizabeth.

They nodded and exchanged glances as he closed up his bag and waited for Elizabeth to go ahead on to the landing. Once downstairs, he stood comfortably in front of the fire beside Hugh until Hannah had taken John's place and he'd come down and seated himself.

'There is still some fluid in the lungs,' he said easily, without preamble, 'but it is not a threat to her. I would hope it will clear within the week. I think you are quite right to have someone sit with her day and night for a day or two, certainly while she is very weak, but after that, provided there are no setbacks, she can be left to sleep. She will need many days of rest before she can walk again, but she must get up for a few minutes every day, beginning on Tuesday.

'I congratulate you, Miss Sinton. The infection was fierce. It has caused much inflammation and might well have been fatal, but some combination of your skill and treatment and, no doubt, your prayers, have brought her through. For such a slightly built woman, she has shown amazing strength, but then, as I observe, she is fortunate in both her family and her friends.

'I think I detected both lavender and rosemary when I came into the house. I doubt if I could recommend anything better for ease and refreshment, but I'll prescribe a tonic which will encourage her to eat as soon as she's feeling less exhausted. I can give her something to ease the pain in the chest when it becomes tedious, but I fear it will remain for a long time. I hope none of you will feel discouraged when I say that it may be some months before Mrs Hamilton is able to resume her normal activities. All being well, she will recover completely. A long holiday would be of great benefit to her if it could be arranged.'

He looked from John to Elizabeth, Elizabeth to Hugh, and smiled broadly at them all.

'Oh dear. How pompous we doctors always sound when we pronounce,' he said, laughing. 'We study so long to know so little, I suppose we have to convince ourselves we're not totally ignorant. All we can do is our best. I would be very happy to come and see Mrs Hamilton again and perhaps discuss with Miss Sinton some breathing exercises to help recover the lungs. But for now I rest my case,' he said with a small flourish of his hand.

'I'm most grateful to you, sir, most grateful,' said John emphatically. 'We'll mark what you said and Elizabeth here will keep us right.'

'I have no doubt of that,' said Richard Stewart, turning towards her and holding her gaze for a few seconds.

'Well, I must be on my way,' he said, with a hint of reluctance. 'I have no surgery on a Saturday, but I do visit the more urgent cases in the afternoon. I shall look forward to coming again,' he said, as he moved towards the door. 'Call on me at any time if you have need,' he insisted, as he shook hands with Elizabeth and John and turned away to follow Hugh down the damp path to where Bess waited patiently in the sunshine.

They were almost halfway to the station when Richard Stewart finally decided to say what had been on his mind since Hugh had appeared in his waiting room some three hours previously. As one of the biggest mill owners in the district, Sinton of Rathdrum was well known, but the doctor also knew something of his personal history.

'Sinton, am I right in thinking that you Quakers put a value upon plain speaking?' he asked, as they moved along at an easy trot.

Hugh smiled at him, full of a warmth and gratitude he felt it difficult to express.

'Quite correct. Am I to hope you're going to apply for instruction?'

'No, I think not. I'm far too set in my ways – though I

admit I admire much about your Society of Friends. We must make leisure to speak of such things. I fear I grow tedious for want of conversation.'

'I had not observed that,' Hugh replied, his eyes twinkling.

'Well then,' said the older man, gathering himself visibly and then relaxing with a smile. 'I am going to indulge in some of your plain speaking. You may say the Spirit has moved me.'

'The Spirit moving is not the prerogative of the Society of Friends.'

'I heard of your accident many years ago. I knew, too, that your sister had nursed you,' he began slowly. 'But I had never laid eyes on you till this morning. There is something I must say to you. I am sure you had the best possible nursing – I can think of no one better than your dear sister – but there have been remarkable advances in the area of orthopaedics in the last ten years, particularly in Manchester, where I practised for some time before coming back to my native county. I keep in touch with some of my colleagues there and some of my fellow students from Edinburgh days. There is one I would highly recommend who could almost certainly improve your mobility and most likely reduce the pain you suffer. There now, I have done what I was called on to do and I am almost certain to catch the next train,' he said as they drove past the Crozier Monument and turned towards the station.

'Thank you,' said Hugh, looking at him squarely. 'I'd never thought of any betterment. I've tried to give thanks for the life I was given back, but I will now give some thought to what you've said,' he said soberly.

'Good,' said Richard Stewart with a beaming smile, as he climbed down from the brougham. 'Keep me informed about Mrs Hamilton. When the weather improves, I hope I might tempt you to come and dine with me. I think we would not be lost for conversation.'

'I should enjoy that very much,' Hugh replied, as he shook the reins. 'Good day to you, Stewart. We'll meet again soon.'

* * *

Jamie was unlucky. Had he not paused to refresh his memory about the Sunday Service trains for his return to Belfast next day, he would have come out of the station and seen the brougham manoeuvring away from the setting down point. But Hugh was in good spirits and in no mood to dawdle. A few moments after Richard Stewart walked into the station, he was already spinning merrily out of the town on his way home.

Jamie had no objection whatever to walking. For most of his life it had been the only means of going anywhere, and he'd always been a good walker, but today the road was thick with mud and he was wearing his best town boots. He could already imagine what a job he'd have to get them dry even before they could be brushed and polished.

The sun was now high in a clear sky, some real warmth touching him as he strode out, but the fresh greenness of fields and hedgerows newly emerged from their covering of snow did little for his depressed spirits. Whatever he might find wrong at home, he had troubles of his own. Money to begin with. No young man could possibly manage on the pittance paid to apprentices. The weekly sum barely covered his tram fares and laundry bills, and although his father paid his board and lodging, he made him no allowance.

He enquired if he was all right for money each time he came home, but his visits were now infrequent. Back in his first year, when he had spent so much time studying, he'd told his father he could manage perfectly well. Now he had friends, he saw the mistake he'd made in not being open about his changed situation. Only last week, he'd made up his mind to tell his mother his troubles this very weekend. Now it looked as if that might not be possible.

He couldn't really understand it. His mother was never ill. She got her share of coughs and colds in winter, as they all did, but he'd never known her lie in bed. So what could have brought Sam to his door last night? And in a cab. Cabs cost a fortune. But then Sam was never short of money. He paid for his keep at home, but he had a proper wage out of which to pay it. Often enough on his overnight visits, he'd seen Sam take notes from his pay envelope and put them in the wallet he kept in his best jacket, dropping only the handful of coins into his trouser pocket.

By next year it would be different. His apprenticeship would be over and he would get a Manager's job. He was quite determined that he should, and the new friends he'd made recently would almost certainly be a help to him. But another nine months was a long time to go on feeling the pinch.

He tramped on, looked idly into MacMurray's yard to see if any of them were about, and turned up the hill. A few minutes later, he walked through the front door, standing open in the midday sun. The big kitchen was quiet and full of sunlight. At the table, Sarah was making bread.

'Hullo, Sarah, what are you up to then?' he said brightly.

She glanced up at him, irritated and preoccupied.

'Were there no trains from Belfast?' she asked, as she looked him up and down, registered his town clothes and his dirty boots, which he'd forgotten to wipe outside.

'I didn't get Sam's message till this morning,' he said, shaking his head at her. 'Sarah, what's wrong ? Is Ma ill?'

'Ma nearly died,' said Sarah coldly.

'Oh now, surely not,' he said soothingly, looking round the tidy kitchen as if its order told him his little sister was exaggerating, as usual.

Sarah scowled and gave her full attention to the contents of her baking bowl.

'Where is everybody then?'

'Sam is sitting with Ma. Hannah and Elizabeth are lying down,' she began patiently, rather as if she were speaking to a small child. 'Da's gone up to Rathdrum to fetch things Elizabeth needs. She's staying here till Tuesday,' she ended, looking him full in the face.

'So what's wrong with Ma?' he asked, wary now, warned by her tone that something serious really had happened.

Sarah seemed to have grown taller since his last visit home. But perhaps it was just the apron, or the calm way she was making bread. It wasn't like her at all. She was usually in such a hurry to get on. Some things she did turned out well, others were just a mess. You could never tell with Sarah. But he could tell she was upset. Oh well, she'd get over it. There was nothing he could do about it.

'I'll go up and see Ma,' he said abruptly.

She glared at his dirty boots, but said nothing. He went upstairs, his steps loud and firm, fragments of drying mud dropping gently on each wooden stair as he went.

Sam had been brushing his mother's hair, but hearing Jamie arrive below he quickly put the brush away and took up her hand instead.

'Hullo, Sam.'

'Hullo, Jamie.'

In the strained silence that followed, Rose gasped and coughed. Jamie stared at her, his face a pale mask, his mouth falling open as he studied her closed eyes and heaving chest.

'She does that every so often,' Sam said, matter-of-factly. 'Her chest hurts, so she doesn't breath properly, then she gasps a bit to catch up.'

'Sarah said she nearly died,' Jamie said awkwardly, embarrassed now that he hadn't believed her.

'Aye,' said Sam, nodding. 'The doctor from Banbridge said to send for you. So I went up to Belfast. But you were out.'

'Well, what do you expect on a Friday night? Do you never go out?' Jamie came back at him crossly.

'I tell them where I'm going,' Sam replied, dropping his voice even further lest he disturb the sleeping figure. 'Would it be that hard to leave word?' Sam asked, looking away from his brother's face.

'Jamie, how good to see you.'

Jamie turned his head towards the cool, soft voice and saw Elizabeth Sinton standing in the doorway, a small tray in her hands.

'You mustn't worry about your mother,' she said reassuringly, as she noted the strained and anxious look on his face. 'There's every reason to hope she'll recover completely, even if it does take a long time,' she went on, as she put down her tray on the dressing table.

'Now, if you don't mind, Jamie, I think I must try to give your mother a little nourishment before we tell her you're here. She's been so looking forward to seeing you.'

Jamie got up and walked to the door. It had never occurred to him that the one person he'd always depended on might not be able to help anyone for quite some time. As for the other matter on his mind, he'd have to keep quiet about that. His father would not be well pleased at the best of times, but with all this anxiety about Ma he couldn't really expect him to understand. As Harry had said, if you want to be sure of a Manager's job, there are those that can help you and those that can't. That was why Jamie had joined the Lodge. Last night he'd become a full member of the Orange Order.

Nine

Some ten days after her close encounter with mortality, Rose woke in the early afternoon and blinked. Sunlight streamed into her bedroom. She ran her eyes over the familiar furniture, the quilt she and Elizabeth had sewn two summers previously, the chair where her warm dressing gown lay ready for her daily effort to stand by the side of the bed, the wardrobe which only just fitted under the sloping roof, its mirror reflecting back her own pale face and the neat arrangement of pillows that supported her. Her eyes rested on the rich colour of hothouse flowers on her dressing table and a jug of daffodils in the deep window-sill. For many minutes, she studied every small detail of the room as if she had been away for a long time and had only just returned home.

Then she listened to the stillness. Elizabeth had found someone to come and look after the household, a distant relative of her own Mrs Lappin, a worn, sad woman who fussed over her in a kindly way and moved about the house so quietly she never disturbed her sleep. She'd brought her soup some time ago, fed her patiently, encouraged her like a child when the effort of swallowing seemed almost too much. She'd slipped away with only a rustle of her skirt and left her to sleep.

Rose usually woke when she heard the sound of voices, the bang of the garden gate, the click of bicycles which told her Hannah and Sarah had arrived home from school. But today she'd woken of her own accord. For the first time in all these strange, confused days she felt she could see things clearly and recognize what she was seeing.

She lay very still, unwilling to set off the pain that would clasp at her chest if she moved without due caution, and gazed up at the fast-moving clouds driven by the brisk March wind. Some days previously she'd managed to ask Elizabeth if she'd nearly died. She was gentle, but honest, as she always was. Yes, indeed she had. Much earlier, one evening as John sat with her as she moved in and out of sleep, he'd confessed as much, but she couldn't hold on to it and kept having to ask him again.

She could remember nothing of the night when she'd been so ill except strange dreams of people long gone. She'd had a vague sense of hands touching. She knew she'd felt an exhaustion quite unlike anything she'd ever known before, however hard she'd worked.

The clouds closed over and the room grew dim, but her eyes remained wide open. For the first time since she'd staggered up the stairs, desperate to hide her aching head in a soft pillow, what she most wanted was not sleep, but just to lie in the quiet and watch the sky, the sudden swirl of gulls, white against the grey, now tumbling and crying.

She felt a sudden surge of excitement. She was alive. She was here in her own bed with the clouds racing and closing and darkening towards rain. She'd never thought of dying herself, always of losing her beloved John, or one of the children. It was a strange irony. After all her anxiety for them, she was the one who'd almost died.

'Almost,' she whispered to herself, her lips barely moving. *Sure a miss is as good as a mile.* The words were Granny Sarah's. They came unbidden and made her smile. There were no degrees about dying. You did, or you didn't. However close you came, you went or you stayed, and she had been allowed to stay.

Huge spots of rain drummed against the window. She heard its throb on the roof, its splash in the stone gutters below. What a comforting sound it was to those warm and dry indoors. *Listen, Ma, aren't we lucky we're not out in that.* To begin with, they'd been her own words, but the children picked them up and repeated them. And she had encouraged them. In the days when they had so little, it was proper to give thanks for warmth and shelter.

The sudden, scudding shower passed. The window still streamed with tiny rivulets as the sun broke through again. The last rolling drops caught the light and winked briefly with rainbow colours. The grey clouds had rolled away, the sun beamed down once more from a patch of flawless blue sky.

As she lay quiet, she thought of her dear friend Hugh. He had no patience with the murmured sympathy people showed when they observed his ungainly walk or caught the grimace that sometimes broke through as he mounted a horse or pulled himself up into the brougham. She understood now. Hugh had his life and he gave thanks. She had hers and so would she.

She turned her head cautiously, so she could make out the large hands on the alarm clock which John carried away with him each night and returned each morning when he came to look at her before he went downstairs. Three o'clock. An hour before the sound of voices disturbed the afternoon stillness on the hill, the cattle grazing peacefully across the road, Mrs Rea quietly ironing or baking downstairs.

She smiled and risked breathing a little more deeply. It was still very painful, but she'd promised Elizabeth to take deep breaths whenever she remembered. Her duty done, she returned her full attention to the sky and the continuous change of colour and shape of the clouds that gathered and dispersed and gathered again.

Within the hour they'd opened and closed again three times. The many weathers of a March day, as Thomas Scott would say. The rapid change comforted her. The energy of wind and rain was deeply reassuring, a continuity that would go on regardless of any human observer. Whether she was here or not, the sky would open and close, but she *was* here. She'd been spared to see the springtime come again. To go on caring for John and her children. Overwhelmed by gratitude, she felt tears trickle down her face. She ignored them, too tired to wipe them away and too happy to let them trouble her.

However many more weeks she would lie here, however many months it might be before she could sweep a floor or bake bread, however many years she might live, she knew she would never forget this moment of reawakening to life on a March day.

There were indeed times in the months that followed when Rose almost despaired of her progress. Day after day she would struggle to her feet only to collapse gratefully back on the bed again. But she never lacked encouragement. Elizabeth was a constant visitor and Richard Stewart came smiling to her bedside always ready to point out the progress she had made since his last visit.

To set against the tediousness of daily effort there were sudden moments of pleasure. There was the first time she managed to walk as far as the window. She stood triumphantly supporting herself on the sill and looked down on her garden, where Hannah and Sam had weeded and tidied and persuaded Sarah not to dig up the plants that still looked dead at the end of March.

A few weeks later, she'd alarmed poor Mrs Rea by turning round from her own window and setting off across the landing to Sarah's room, so she could look down on Dolly grazing peacefully on the new grass.

By the end of April, she finally managed the stairs, steep and awkward for her with a banister on one side only. She could now sit by the kitchen window, a piece of sewing on her knee. One warm, pleasant morning at the beginning of May she looked out longingly through the wide-open door and felt she could resist the freshness of spring no longer.

'Mrs Rea, do you think I could sit outside for a little while?'

'Oh, ma'am, would that be wise, do you think?' the older woman replied anxiously, her hands twisted together. 'What would Miss Sinton say if you were to catch cold?'

'Well, if I wrapped myself in an extra shawl . . .' Rose began, as if she were considering carefully. 'Which one do you think would be best?'

'Oh, the wool one, Mrs Hamilton. Definitely the wool one. I'll go and fetch it from your room.'

Mrs Rea was a dear, kind woman, a good worker and a reliable watcher, but, as well as being a rather sad soul, she was an innocent. It was Sarah who had discovered Mrs Rea was very easily distracted. She smiled to herself, amused she should be using her daughter's well-practised technique to such good effect.

'I'll take the other chair out and get it ready for you,' Mrs Rea said, coming back downstairs, the shawl over her arm. 'Now don't you move a step till I have it ready and can come and give you my arm,' she went on, picking up John's armchair and carrying it over the threshold as if it were a mere basket of vegetables.

'Thank you, Mrs Rea,' Rose said gratefully, as she settled herself. 'I'm sure the sunshine will be good for me.'

The sun was indeed warm and comforting. She could feel its soothing power through her blouse, bathing her chest and ribs where the pain still lurked. Three times a day when she did her breathing exercises, and in the evening when she was tired, it sprang to life, but mostly through the day it slept. She could forget it for the moment and give her entire attention to her new surroundings.

All around her there were signs of growth. The hawthorn hedge across the road was fully clad with tender leaves, though there was no sign of blossom yet. Bloom there was, though, in the flower bed alongside the garden path. Set against the turned earth and a background of flowering shrubs, there were spiky shoots and unfurling fronds of hosta and aquilegia. Then she spotted something she couldn't quite make out. Beyond her flourishing philadelphus and partly hidden by it, a splash of pink and a gleam of leaf.

Before she realized it, she had walked the length of the garden path and discovered the camellia John had bought the day he and Jamie went to the Horse Fair in Armagh. Despite the heavy frosts in February, the sheltered position they'd chosen had done its job. The exotic pink blossoms were as lovely as anything she'd ever seen.

Late that afternoon, when Mrs Rea told Hannah and Sarah what a fright she'd had, looking out and seeing an empty chair, she'd felt a kind of lightness, as if laughter was suddenly given back to her, even if it was a bit painful to begin with.

'Hello, Ma. How far today?' demanded Sarah, as she burst into the kitchen after school.

'Oh, I just strolled into Banbridge and back before lunch,' Rose replied, laughing, as Hannah followed more sedately.

'What about the play then? Did you both get parts?'

'Yes, we did,' Sarah nodded, her eyes sparkling, 'Hannah is Jane Bennet and I'm Darcy. Miss Clarke said my curls were just right if we smoothed them out a little, and I'm taller than Hettie Taylor, who's Elizabeth. So that's all right. But I have to learn to walk like a man and scowl. Arrogantly, but aristocratically,' she went on seriously, drawing herself to her full height and making a face.

Rose smiled and tried not to laugh. Miss Clarke clearly had an eye for character casting. She was about to ask Hannah how she felt about her part, *Pride and Prejudice* being one of Hannah's favourite novels, when she was startled by an unusual noise, a strange, wheezing sound, coming from the other side of the room. She looked towards the dairy. Mrs Rea was bringing in a tray with a pot of tea, one cup and saucer, two mugs and a plate of bread and jam, her face creased into a grimace, her arms shaking till she put the tray down safely on the kitchen table. She wiped her streaming eyes with the corner of her apron and went on laughing as if she would never stop.

'Can I come to your play, Miss Sarah?' she asked, recovering herself somewhat. 'I'd like real well to see you scowlin' at Hettie Taylor. A right saucy one she's been since ever I knew her poor mother,' she explained, as she poured a cup of tea for Rose.

'Of course you can come, Mrs Rea,' said Sarah firmly. I expect *all* my friends to come. You've got eight weeks, Ma. Will you be able to get into the trap by then?' she added, turning to her mother anxiously.

'I'm sure I shall, Sarah,' she reassured her. 'How could I miss seeing you both? And I went to the field gate three times today to look at MacMurray's calves. Mrs Rea will tell you.'

'Aye, there'll soon be no stoppin' her,' Mrs Rea agreed. 'Though she was glad enough to lie down to be ready for you pair comin' home, wi' all your news,' she added, as she stood watching them demolish the bread and jam. 'Missus dear, we need some more buttermilk. Can I go down to MacMurray's now the girls is home to keep ye comp'ny?'

'Shall I go?' Sarah offered.

'No, love,' said Rose gently. 'Mrs Rea has been busy all day. I'm sure she'd like the little walk,' she added, turning and smiling at the older woman. 'Take your time, Mrs Rea, and find us out all the news.

'Any letters today, Ma?' asked Hannah quietly, as she reached for her mother's empty teacup.

'Yes, there were. Why don't you change your pinafores and tidy up the tea things and then I'll tell you all about them.'

'Are you tired, Ma?' asked Hannah.

'Well, not exactly . . .'

'Yes you are,' burst out Sarah. 'I know by that piece of hair on the side of your cheek. You always push it back when you're *not* tired.'

Hannah exchanged glances with Rose.

'Why don't you close your eyes, Ma, while we tidy up.'

Grateful for Hannah's perceptiveness, Rose closed her eyes. She wasn't sleepy but she certainly did feel tired. Then she remembered that as today was Dramatic Society the girls were later than usual. As she always began to fade around five, it wasn't surprising she'd begun to find Sarah's liveliness a strain.

All had gone quiet, so she leant back in her chair. In the first week of her illness Hannah and Sarah had written to all the people in her address book. Letters had been flowing back ever since. They'd been such a joy. She hadn't realized how many good friends they had. Thomas Scott's letter was one of her favourites. He'd sat down right away to wish her a speedy recovery and tell her the news he hoped would please her.

His daughter Annie had just married the young farmer from Ballyards and they'd found a house in Annacramp, not far from where Rose and John had once lived. His eldest son had done well at school, but had taken a job with Robinson's next door to earn his passage money to Canada. He'd set off after his sister's wedding and was now in Toronto. On his very first day at work in the office of a big department store he'd met a man from Cabragh who'd once lived up on Church Hill. His youngest boy, Robert, had now joined him in the forge and was doing rightly. His wee daughter, Sophie, was walking and into everything, including the dirt of the forge if Selina took her eyes off her for a minute.

She could hardly believe *young* Robert was already at work. He was older than Sarah, but she remembered him as a sad child, cooped up in a horse collar to keep him out of the way while his mother did her work.

Thomas was too shy to say it, but what was so clear from his letter was his new wife's effect upon the whole family. Through her gentle care and kindness to them all she'd healed the worst effects of the old, hard life they'd suffered under Mary-Anne's rigid regime.

Suddenly, she caught the sound of wheels on the hill. It would be Elizabeth and Hugh coming back from Banbridge from one of the committees on which they served. She listened carefully, pleased and surprised as she heard the brougham come to rest by the garden gate. Elizabeth called every morning, but Hugh she'd not seen for some time.

As she opened her eyes, took some deep, painful breaths and waited to greet them, she heard Hannah's light footsteps on the stairs.

'Rose dear, are you too tired for visitors?' Elizabeth asked, coming straight over to kiss her. 'Hugh so wanted to see you and I promised we'd call, but our meeting dragged on and I know you get tired by this hour.'

'I'm delighted to see you, whatever my state,' she said beaming.

She turned to greet Hugh, who'd delayed long enough to tie his reins to the gatepost so Bess couldn't nibble any of her beloved flowers.

'Hugh, how lovely of you to call,' she said, as he moved awkwardly towards her.

She was surprised to see his handsome, tanned face seamed with lines of fatigue and anxiety. He took her hand and held it in his while he studied her carefully. 'You're mending, Rose. Thanks be to God,' he said quietly, before he dropped gratefully on to the kitchen chair.

'Where's Sarah?' he asked, after a few minutes talk with Hannah.

'She's started learning her lines,' Hannah said uneasily. 'She's got a part in the school play and it's only six weeks till the end of term, even though we've been practising different parts since January.'

'Didn't she hear Elizabeth and Hugh arrive?' Rose asked, puzzled.

'Oh yes, I think she did,' replied Hannah, dropping her eyes.

Rose and Elizabeth exchanged glances and Hugh's eyes moved uneasily round the room as if he was looking for something.

'Perhaps you'd ask Sarah to come down,' said Rose carefully.

Hannah rose to go, but cast an anxious look towards her.

She smiled encouragingly. 'Do what you can, Hannah. It's all right. I've had a little rest and I feel much better now.'

The three adults sat silently as Hannah ran lightly upstairs and tapped on Sarah's door. They heard the sound of voices. Hannah returned.

'Sarah begs to be excused Miss Sinton and Mr Sinton's visit as she is already behind with her commitments,' Hannah reported carefully, her own face reflecting what she thought of this extraordinary message.

Elizabeth and Rose glanced at each other and tried not to

smile, but any softening of their features disappeared when they saw how much Sarah's message had upset Hugh.

'I'm afraid this is my fault, Rose,' he began quietly. 'I was so concerned about you, I didn't deal with it at the time. She's been avoiding me for weeks, but I couldn't make up my mind what to do. I have asked for guidance but I fear I've failed to recognize any that has been given me,' he added sadly.

Rose looked from Hugh to Elizabeth and back again.

'We didn't want you upset,' said Elizabeth gently, 'but I think it's time Hugh and Sarah sorted out their differences.'

'But what differences? What have I been missing?'

'My dear Rose, the incident in question took place the day before you were ill. Elizabeth will tell you all about it,' said Hugh, continuing to look around him in an agitated way. 'Sarah blames me for the death of Maisie McKinley's child. She may also be blaming me for your illness. I've tried to talk, but she's refused to speak to me.'

'Oh, Hugh, this is too bad,' Rose responded gently. 'You should have told me sooner. I'm so sorry you've been upset.'

'Oh, it's of no great moment my being upset,' he said quickly, 'but she's young to bear the burden of her own perceptions, even if what she sees may be somewhat distorted at times.'

'I think we should resolve this as soon as we can,' said Rose firmly. 'If Elizabeth and I take ourselves into the parlour, Hannah will keep an eye open for Mrs Rea,' she went on. 'I'll insist she comes down and listens to what you say to her, but after that it's up to you. I really can't think how I would go about this one just at the moment.'

'I don't think I've much idea either, Rose, but I must try. I'd be grateful for the opportunity,' he said, as he watched her gather herself.

She nodded encouragingly, got cautiously to her feet and gripped the back of her chair quite firmly.

'Hannah, please tell Sarah I need her downstairs.'

She raised her eyebrows at Elizabeth, who smiled, pursed her lips, moved briskly across the room and up the step leading to the parlour.

Sarah came downstairs, her face grim, her lips pressed together in a firm line. She looked straight at her mother and ignored Hugh.

'Sarah, Elizabeth and I are going into the parlour for a little while. I want you to come and listen to what Hugh has to say. Properly listen. I'm sorry I didn't know you were upset, but then probably you kept it from me because you knew how tired I was, which was kind of you. But if you want to be kind to me now, you'll talk to Hugh and sort out whatever has come between you. Do you understand?'

Sarah nodded, her shoulders rigid with tension, her grim expression shifting towards a very presentable scowl.

'Then come and sit in my chair, so that Hugh doesn't have to stand.'

She waited till Sarah had seated herself on the edge of her armchair, her body held as far away from Hugh as was possible, before she released her grip and moved slowly across the room.

Hugh wasted no time. Sarah had been making sure she was only in his company when Elizabeth or her father was present. Recently, she'd even managed to avoid greetings and goodbyes. He guessed Hannah had spoken to her about her behaviour, but, wise and gentle as Hannah was, she was no match for Sarah's stubbornness when it got going.

'Sarah, I know you're upset with me and don't want to talk to me. Do you think, out of kindness, for your mother's sake if not for mine, you might answer Yes or No to my questions?'

She kicked the toe of her shoe on the flagged floor, looked away from him and inclined her head a fraction of an inch.

'Thank you,' he said, solemnly. 'You know, even in a court of law the defendant knows what crimes he has committed and has the opportunity to defend himself,' he said in a conversational tone. 'I can only guess at what I have done. Do you blame me, Sarah, for the child's death?'

She nodded vigorously.

'Do you blame me for your mother's illness?'

She stared at him, so shocked at what he'd said, it was some moments before she remembered to shake her head.

'Thank goodness for that,' said Hugh with a great sigh. 'That is a great relief to me,' he admitted, as he collected his thoughts again.

'Well then, on the count of the child's death, of which I stand charged. Was it because I did not drive faster on the icy road?'

A brief shake.

'Was it because I did not insist on the doctor coming out of his surgery immediately we arrived?'

Another shake.

'Was it because I gave the mother money to ensure a proper burial?'

Sarah tightened her lips and shook her head impatiently.

Hugh paused and looked at her attentive face, for she was now watching him carefully, her curiosity fully engaged.

'Oh dear,' he said, suddenly. 'I can't think what to ask next.'

'You know perfectly well why I blame you,' she burst out. 'That poor woman. All the way down from Lisnaree and all along the main road, and then up the hill. All that walk carrying the child to get a ticket from you. Why couldn't she just have gone to the dispensary in the morning when the little child took ill? It was nearly as far to walk, but the road's flatter and the snow hadn't started and the child wasn't so ill in the morning. It might have lived if it hadn't been for the stupid ticket,' she ended furiously, having completely run out of breath.

'Do you think it was my idea she come to Rathdrum for a ticket?'

'Well, who else?' she retorted furiously.

'The Dispensary System was set up many years ago. Someone in each area was given the task of holding tickets. My father was responsible until he died. Then it became my responsibility,' he explained quietly.

'Then it's a rotten system,' she said equally furiously.

'So would you be prepared to blame the system rather than the unfortunate man who has to work with it?'

She glared at him and said nothing.

'Has it occurred to you, Sarah, that if you blame me, or if you blame the system, another child might die?'

'That's why I'm so angry,' she shot back, her eyes widening every moment. 'Lots of other people might die, all because of a silly bit of paper. They have to have it because they're too poor to just send for the doctor. Why don't you pay them more? Then they could afford doctors.'

'Do you want an answer to that question, or are you too angry to listen? You can nod or shake.'

'Yes, I am angry, but I will listen. I can't think of any excuse, but I'm curious,' she said coldly.

'Workers in the linen industry are among the lowest paid of all textile workers,' he began coolly. 'Unless you have several members of a family working, there's seldom enough money going into a home to provide food and clothes, never mind doctors and medicine. Do you think I'm pleased about that?' he asked more sharply. 'Well I'm not,' he went on, before she had time to comment. 'But I'll tell you what the alternative is. Or one of them, anyway. You would say pay higher wages. But higher wages puts up the price of cloth and you run the risk of losing your share of the market. If orders stop coming in, then there's no work. Mills close and people starve, unless there's some provision made. And there's little enough of that,' he ended grimly.

Sarah said nothing. She sat staring at the toe of her shoe moving on the dark surface of the floor.

'Do you realize, Sarah, that blaming someone stops you doing anything about a problem?'

She looked at him and shook her head slowly.

'If you blame someone for something they've done, or something you think they've done, it makes an end of it. You just walk away from the problem. Blaming is easy. You don't have to do anything except be cross or angry. But is that going to help another child at another time?'

'No. No it's not,' she cried out in despair. 'That's what's so awful. It's because I can't *do* anything that I'm so angry. What can I do? What could I possibly do?'

'Well, you could talk to me,' he said promptly. 'You could

find out what the problems are and between us we might find some answers. It would be difficult, but it would be better than nothing, wouldn't it?'

'And you'd tell me things, like about the rates of pay for linen workers and why they're so low,' she said, turning towards him for the first time.

'Of course. I'll tell you anything you want to know.'

'And what about things *you* don't know about, like Managers who make stoppages in wages for singing at work?' she came back at him.

'Well then, you'll have to tell me. If you know something I don't know, you can explain it to me.'

'And you'll listen?'

'Of course I will. Have I ever not listened to what you tell me?'

She shook her head solemnly and then smiled.

'I'm sorry,' she said, holding out her hand. 'I've been horrible. I won't do it again . . . if I can help it,' she added quickly.

He bowed over her hand and kissed it in a rather exaggerated way. She giggled and then gave him a radiant smile.

'So we've agreed in principle?' he asked, his own face softening.

She nodded, mimicking her own cool responses, and laughed, her dark eyes sparkling with pleasure as she looked up at him.

'Yes, we've agreed,' she repeated firmly.

Ten

Rose watched John's face carefully as he read slowly down the last sheet of the long letter she'd handed him as soon as he'd finished his lunch. She waited patiently as he laid the folded sheets on the tablecloth. The hint of a smile touched his lips as he picked up his mug and drank deeply.

'Well, what do you think, love?

'What I think,' he said firmly, 'is that she's one great lady. An' she thinks the world of you,' he went on. 'Sure I cou'd love her for that, even if I diden know her from Adam. I think you shou'd go. Isn't it just what yer man Doctor Stewart recommended for you way back in March?'

'But two months, John,' she said uneasily. 'It's a long time.'

'Aye, it is,' he said, laughing wryly, 'For a couple never parted a night in twenty-two years, unless you count me sleepin' in Jamie's bed when you were so poorly,' he added, looking at her directly. 'But sure we might have been parted for good,' he said coolly. 'What's two months compared to that, an' me knowin' you're safe and well and has the best of everythin'? Wouldn't it put you rightly on your feet before the winter? Sure she's wanted to see you ever since our weddin' day.'

'Yes, it's true,' she replied, smiling suddenly.

She remembered the young woman whose knowledge of Irish geography was so vague she thought Armagh and Lord Harrington's estates in Sligo were within easy visiting distance of each other. Only an afternoon spent with an atlas had prepared her for his plans for their wedding journey. Before that France and Italy were all the same to her.

'We've had our plans often enough,' she agreed. 'But they never worked out. Like the plan you and I made for me to go and see my mother,' she added sadly. 'I really would love to see Lady Anne. She's my oldest friend, despite the relationship between us.'

'Sure what of that?' he said sharply. 'She knows if it hadn't been for you she'd never have married Harrington. You're more like sisters, the pair of you. D'ye not mind the state she was in when she got news of the rail disaster and didn't know you were safe? An' she was even worse when you took ill. It wasn't even a day after Hannah wrote before the flowers and the boxes of fruit started comin'. You go, love, and take the girls like she says. We can afford it well enough, thank God,' he said warmly. 'She's right, it'll be a new experience for them, leavin' Ireland for the first time, an' travellin' down England on the train. Aye and meetin' her boy and girl. What age are they now, I've forgot.'

'Young Lord Richard is just twenty-one this month. Do you not remember they were married at the end of August and he was born the following May?'

'Aye, an' we laughed and said there'd be some busy countin' on their fingers. There was a desperate amount of gossip went on in that place now I think back to it,' he said, a broad grin spreading across his face. 'Sure they gossiped about us as well. They had us married an' all from the first night we walked out.'

'Well, they weren't far wrong,' she came back at him, laughing gaily.

It was a long time since she and John had spoken of those glorious summer weeks of '75 in Kerry, when they'd walked in the evenings by Currane Lake and watched the water fowl sail across its calm surface, while Lady Anne in a green velvet dress was encouraging the shy and awkward Lord Harrington.

'Is there any more tea, love?' he asked, as he drained his mug. 'No, don't get up,' he added quickly, as he saw her begin to move. 'If there is, I'll pour it. An' if there's not I'll make some more, for I'm bone dry today, though it's not all that warm for the end of May.'

He picked up the teapot and glanced over his shoulder as he weighed it in his hand. 'Before you go, you'll have to practise being waited on and not hop up like you were about to a minit ago.'

'Do you not think I have had enough practice being waited on these last three months?' she said ruefully.

He laughed as he refilled their mugs, glanced up at the clock and put hers down in front of her.

'What time's Hugh picking you up?'

'It'll be well after two,' he said. 'They've a visitor for lunch, so he had to scrub off the grease. He was not well pleased, but it means I've another half-hour yet,' he said, settling himself. 'And what about the girl? Lady Marianne, isn't it? Wouldn't she be the same age as Hannah?'

'Not far off,' she agreed. 'They're both eighteen now, but Marianne will be nineteen in November. There's only six months in it.'

'They'll get on well enough, I'd think. Hannah has a nice way with her. An' any girl of Lady Anne's will know how to behave herself.'

They looked at each other across the lunch table, both silent, each suddenly aware of what the other was thinking.

'What about Sarah?' John asked cautiously. 'D'ye think she'll be agreeable to go?'

Rose raised her eyebrows.

'I really don't know what to expect,' she began. 'She usually jumps at any chance to be up and away, but she's not much enamoured of the "aristocracy", as she calls them. I'm not sure what Lord Harrington's proper title is now. Lady Anne still calls him Harrington, but I think it was an earldom he inherited. Whatever it was, Ashley Park is an enormous house. His great-grandfather owned half of Gloucestershire and he built it so he could entertain in the grand style and impress people. That may not go down too well,' she ended, even more doubtfully.

'Well, I still think you and Hannah should go,' said John firmly. 'I wouldn't want to force Sarah, but I don't want her to stop the two of you. You'll enjoy seein' Lady Anne and it'll do Hannah good to have a holiday. She's been that concerned about you she's had no chance to think what she wants when she leaves school,' he finished briskly as he caught the distant sound of the brougham on the hill.

'Ye needen' give a thought to Sam and me. Mrs Rea will see us right, but if Sarah's not for goin' maybe Elizabeth could help us out,' he said, bending down to kiss her. 'Between Elizabeth and Mrs Rea, we could manage Sarah rightly,' he assured her, pausing in the doorway as the brougham drew nearer. 'I don't want anythin' stoppin' you goin'. We'll just have to fit things in round that,' he said, turning away and striding down the garden path as Hugh drew up at the gate.

To Rose's amazement Sarah expressed great enthusiasm for spending two months with people of a social class and a level of affluence she had regularly described as indecent.

She puzzled over this sudden change of heart, but it was only by chance that some days after Sarah's declaration she overheard part of a conversation which went some way to explaining what had happened.

'You know, Hannah, it's very easy to blame people for the things they do,' began Sarah solemnly, as they wheeled their bicycles down the garden path. 'But I don't think you should make judgements until you know all the facts. You can't really blame Lady Anne for living in a huge place and having pots of money and dozens of servants. She didn't ask for it, it just happened. It's what she does with it that matters,' she announced firmly. 'Besides, blaming people doesn't get you very far.'

She was sorry not to hear Hannah's reply as they cycled off down the hill, but it was a real relief she need no longer be anxious about Sarah's behaviour when they actually got to Ashley Park. It was one less thing to think about in what looked like a very busy time.

This year the annual birthday celebration with the Sintons was due to be held at Ballydown, and although Mary Sinton had offered to have it in Armagh to spare Rose the effort, she'd decided that with the girls' and Mrs Rea's help she could manage. This year she would be forty-four and Sarah fourteen and she particularly wanted Elizabeth and Hugh to be there. If it wasn't for Elizabeth there might not be a party at all.

After the Annual Celebration, however, there were only two weeks to the end of June. Given the way her energy still ran out so quickly, she'd have to start preparations for the visit right away, if all three of them were to be properly provided with dresses and accessories.

Elizabeth was a real help and support. She brought the new season's pattern books and samples of fabric from Belfast, suggested a dressmaker in Banbridge who could make their best dresses, and came every day to help with the travelling dresses and everyday dresses they'd make at home. She also made sure Rose didn't over-tax herself.

Though Hannah loved sewing, trimming and embroidering, she was determined to do well in her Leaving Certificate, so she helped only when she could take a break from her revision. Sarah's sewing was perfectly competent and she did offer to help, but Rose decided it would be more peaceful if she and Elizabeth were left to themselves. Sarah was perfectly happy with this arrangement, especially as she had already begun her own preparations. While Rose and Elizabeth were at work in the parlour, she sat at the kitchen table and made copious notes from all the library books she could lay hands on that referred to either Gloucestershire or the Cotswolds. At regular intervals, she would favour the sewing party with the benefit of her studies.

First she dealt with the physical geography, then she turned her attention to the history of Ashley Park. Lord Harrington had indeed succeeded to an earldom and ought properly to be called Lord Ashley. She explained that while his son had been christened Richard Molyneux Harrington, he was now known as Lord Cleeve.

'Can you really imagine saying, "Lord Cleeve, would you please pass the butter?" she demanded, one afternoon, when

Hannah and Rose were fitting her with a new day dress in a fine, checked cotton.

'Keep still, love, or the pins will stab you,' said Rose patiently.

'Sorry,' she said, straightening up and holding her arms away from her sides. 'But, Ma, how will one know what to do?' she persisted.

'Hold on a moment till I've finished this bit,' her mother replied, suddenly weary as she pinned another tuck in the softly draped skirt. 'What do you think, Hannah? Have we tucked it enough?'

'Well, if we take it in any more she'll have to stop eating,' said Hannah lightly.

'Yes, but small waists are the fashion,' Sarah protested. 'I don't want to look like a country cousin.'

'Style is not a matter of clothes,' said Rose firmly. 'It's a matter of manner and behaviour. But if you're uncomfortable, it isn't easy to bc gracious. I think that'll be all right,' she added, walking round her.

'Can I take it off now?'

'Yes, and mind the pins.'

'I hate trying on clothes,' she said fiercely.

'So do we all,' said Rose sharply. 'The price of vanity is discomfort,' she added, as she sat down abruptly in the only chair not occupied by fabric or partly made dresses.

'What about the butter, Ma?' Sarah prompted, a few minutes later, when she'd climbed back into her school dress.

Rose hadn't the slightest idea what she was talking about.

'Would you be so exceedingly kind as to pass the butter, Lord Cleeve,' said Hannah, with a perfectly straight face.

Rose relaxed a little and sat back more comfortably. The parlour looked like a dressmaker's workroom, the mahogany table padded with an old blanket and a clean sheet. At one end the new Singer sewing machine sat waiting, at the other, a paper pattern already smoothed out ready to be pinned to the fabric Hannah had chosen for her travelling dress. Even the bookcases and window ledges had acquired a drapery of lace and pieces of ribbon waiting to be added to the finished garments.

'There are some rules, Sarah, you *can* learn from a book like that one you brought from the library, but many of the most important ones you can only learn by observation. You mustn't worry about it,' she went on reassuringly, when she saw Sarah's bright eyes had clouded over. 'You're both observant and this is a family visit, not a house party. What any family does when it's at home is different from what happens if there are guests. When in doubt, it's best to be more formal. There are some people who simply can't tolerate informality in young people, but I can't imagine Lady Anne's family being like that,' she said easily.

'Perhaps Lord Cleeve won't even appear,' said Hannah thoughtfully. 'He'll probably go off with his Cambridge friends when their term finishes.'

'It's certainly nothing to be anxious about,' Rose repeated firmly, concerned by the look on Sarah's face.

'You're quite right, Ma,' Sarah replied equally firmly. 'They're only ordinary human beings. And you're much cleverer than Lady Anne.'

'No, Sarah, I wasn't cleverer,' said Rose honestly. 'I just paid attention. Poor Lady Anne was too unhappy to think of anything but riding. She was very good at that. But she might have been good at French or watercolour or the piano if she'd been able to give her mind to it. You can't give your mind to things properly if you're unhappy.'

Sarah looked at her solemnly and nodded her agreement. 'Ma, d'you think we should call you Mama?'

She laughed and shook her head. 'I'll have to think about that one. Right now, I shall have to lie down for half an hour or I'll be too tired to eat my supper and you know your father will be upset if I don't.'

She left them to tidy up the room, went upstairs and lay on top of the bedclothes. The room was pleasantly cool, the scent of flowers carried on the light June breeze. Whenever she had to concentrate she still felt exhausted and had such an urge to go away and not have to make any more effort at all. She closed her eyes and whispered, 'Mama.' What *would* John say when she told him that?

The July evening was warm and rather humid, but a cool breeze from the lough blew in their faces as they leant over the rail of the ship, waving their handkerchiefs at John, Sam, Jamie, Hugh and Elizabeth.

Their journey so far had gone without a hitch. The train from Banbridge arrived on time, the baggage had been whisked away in a cab and was waiting in their cabins when they arrived on board ship. They'd had time enough to walk round the upper decks and look at the sights of the harbour before the warning bell rang for visitors to leave the ship. There were hugs and kisses and hurried last messages as a second bell rang, even more peremptory than the first.

The gangways were run back. The last hawsers cast off. The throb of the engines deepened as the gap between ship and quay widened minute by minute. Soon they were moving down channel and the small figures still waving vigorously grew smaller and smaller. Sarah could contain herself no longer. 'This is such an adventure, Ma. Aren't we lucky?' she said, her eyes sparkling as she turned towards her.

Rose stretched an arm round her and hugged her, but said nothing, her own eyes misted with the pain of parting. She'd promised herself not to cry, but for the last half-hour she'd been far from sure she'd manage it.

Yes, indeed, they were lucky. Very lucky to be able to afford the comfort of elegant travelling dresses, cabs and first class cabins, porters and stewards to spirit away their cases. It was a far cry from her only other crossing, a very young servant from Currane Lodge sleeping under a blanket in a communal dormitory far below the main deck.

She looked around at the berthed ships that lined the harbour, the tall construction of ladders and walkways surrounding the invisible shape of the *Oceanic*, the one they all referred to now as 'Jamie's ship'. Jamie, too, had been lucky, for James Sinton had made his apprenticeship possible long before his father could have afforded it.

But what was luck? Could they ever have accepted this invitation if John hadn't worked so hard, extending his knowledge and producing the improvements in textile machinery Hugh had then urged him to patent. The royalties from John's patents had paid all their expenses and ensured they would feel no unease at Ashley Park on account of dress.

So why was it people who worked just as hard were thrown out of work? Or struck down by illness? What would have happened to her and the family these last months if they hadn't had the money to pay Mrs Rea, or a good friend like Elizabeth to find her in the first place?

She sighed. Such questions were quite beyond her. Perhaps the only thing she could do was give thanks for her good fortune and make sure she never forget those that good fortune had passed by.

The figures on the dockside finally grew so small it was only an act of faith to continue to wave. She turned towards the bows. Ahead of them the red lights of the marker buoys winked along the deep-water channel as the vessel moved through calm water heading for the open sea.

On the northern shore of the lough the dark Antrim Hills raised their craggy summits above the steeply sloping fields. To the south, the softer shores of Down caught gleams of evening sunshine, the light picking out the ripening wheat, broad russet patches glinting in a green landscape. Beside them, fields of stubble lay like pale patches in a rich tapestry, still untouched by new growth after the hay harvest.

She turned her face towards the open sea, the breeze off the water a delight, the cry of seabirds an evocative sound, as haunting as the litany of names, the promontories and protrusions of the Antrim coast, Sarah was reciting with enthusiasm. Soon they would reach the open sea and their course would turn southwards, crossing the Irish Sea in the night to arrive at Liverpool in the early dawn.

'Ma, look, that must be it.'

Leaning back on the comfortable upholstery of the family coach, Rose glanced over her shoulder briefly.

'Yes, we're nearly there,' she said gratefully, wearied not so much by the journey, but by the continuous excitements of ship and train, docks and harbours, and the unknown English countryside with its villages, towns and cities.

'It's bigger than Buckingham Palace,' Sarah protested.

'No it's not,' said Hannah quietly. 'It's much wider than Buckingham Palace with those wings at both ends, but it's only two storeys in the middle, even if it does look like a Greek temple.'

Whether the coachman whipped up the horses to make a splendid arrival or whether the four matched greys scented home and the comfort of their own stable Rose didn't know, but the last mile or more through the park was accomplished in a very short time. The coach passed between formal gardens, rounded a huge fountain where mythical beasts supported a series of stone bowls surmounted by great jets of water arcing into the blue sky, and then halted in the shadow of a wall that concealed the sweep of stone steps leading up to the entrance in the pillared south front.

Hardly had the younger of the two coachmen opened the door, pulled down the step and offered his hand for Rose to alight, than a small, square figure came running across the gravel, the skirt and sleeves of her white gown flapping energetically round her.

'Rose, Rose, my dear. I'm so glad to see you,' Lady Anne exclaimed, as she threw her arms around her. 'Are you exhausted? I promise to let you go and rest the moment I've kissed you all. I've been watching with Teddy's binoculars for ages. Hannah, what a lovely dress,' she went on, embracing her vigorously. 'And, Sarah. Your mother was right, your curls are just perfect for Mr Darcy. You must scowl for me when you've all had a rest,' she said, hugging her.

'Rose dear, can you manage the steps if Huntley and I give you an arm each, or shall I send for a chair and two stout lads?' she asked, as a cluster of servants descended on the coach and disappeared with all the luggage.

Sarah and Hannah exchanged glances as they followed

Lady Anne and their mother up the long flight of shallow steps to the broad terrace that lay in front of the entrance hall.

'She's all right,' mouthed Sarah, as the sturdy figure ahead of her wrapped a protective arm round their mother.

'Who do you think Teddy is?' Hannah whispered, quite certain she would not be heard over the sound of her mother's laughter.

Whatever anxieties Sarah and Hannah might have had on their arrival at Ashley Park, many of them were immediately laid to rest. Lady Anne saw their mother quietly settled in her room to be left undisturbed until it was time to change for dinner, then took them to their own rooms.

'The grand visitors' rooms are all at the front,' she confided, as she marched them from Hannah's bedroom to Sarah's, then threw open the door of their own small, bright sitting room overlooking the gardens. 'They're huge and frightfully gloomy, so I've put you all on this side. I hope you won't be bored,' she went on anxiously. 'I haven't planned any outings until your mother is feeling better, but you can explore the house and the park. There's quite a lot of it. Go where you like and do ask for anything you need. I've left some things here for wet days, but I hope the weather is going to be lovely for you,' she said, pausing, as a housemaid approached and curtseyed to her and then to each of her guests.

Lady Anne introduced Betty, a sober girl with an unfortunate squint, who was to be shared between them.

'She's very strict,' she confided, when Betty went off to do their unpacking. 'She'll scold you if you get grass stains on your white muslins, but I'm hoping by the end of the summer you'll have taught her to laugh. Poor girl, she doesn't seem to know how.'

For a whole week, before any of Lady Anne's family arrived home, the two girls did exactly as she'd suggested. They explored the house, took long walks in the park and sought out all the tracks and trails where she still rode each morning.

Sarah made up her mind to find out everything she could about the running of such a huge establishment. She found her way to the kitchen, the stables, the bakehouse and the laundry rooms and was delighted to discover the servants were open and friendly. She interviewed them assiduously, asked dozens of questions and recorded her observations and discoveries in her diary.

She was thrilled to find so many new things to study. She walked the length of each of the greenhouses and discovered a special pit for raising melons. She found pineapples and peaches ripening and a huge old vine, so heavily laden it had been propped up with billets of wood to stop it bringing down the wall where it had flourished for over a century.

Beyond the house and stables lay the gas plant, which supplied the kitchens, and a newly installed electric generator. She made repeated visits to the laundry, the workshop and forge, the carpenter's shed and the kitchens, determined to miss out no part of this self-sufficient world.

As for Hannah, she'd found what she liked best at Ashley Park on their very first morning. A part of the flower garden had not yet been redeemed from decades of neglect, but Lady Anne had insisted that at least the former paths be reopened. There, Hannah had spent part of every morning with her sketch pad and watercolours.

The richness and profusion delighted her. She loved the roses and clematis that had run riot, climbed shrubs and trees and sent skywards great arching shoots laden with bloom, and the borders, once so carefully graded and pruned, which had long since broken all bounds. She found magnificent lilies towering over tiny seedlings that pushed out on to the paths, releasing their perfume at the merest touch of a passing dress.

'Well, what did you discover after you left me?' asked Hannah, as she set about stretching fresh sheets of paper for her watercolours one afternoon after lunch.

'Mangles,' said Sarah abruptly. 'Taller than I am. Made in Birmingham and specially designed for very large sheets. They come out so dry even in winter you can iron them and hang them over the ceiling airers to finish them off. You don't even have to hang them out,' she added, sitting down at the table and reaching for her notebook. 'Which is a good thing. After a house party, there might be as many as thirty pairs.'

'How did you find out all that?'

'I asked one of the laundry maids,' she replied abruptly.

'Do you like it here, Sarah?'

Sarah was frowning fiercely, but Hannah knew from long experience that neither frowns nor smiles were an accurate guide to what her sister was feeling. The only way to be sure was to ask.

'Yes,' she said quickly. 'But I couldn't live here,' she added after a long pause. 'Could you?'

Hannah laughed and put her brush down.

'I don't think Da is likely to inherit an earldom,' she said with a smile.

'Of course not,' Sarah retorted. 'But I asked if *you* could live here. Live this sort of life in a place like this.'

'Yes, I think I could,' said Hannah slowly. 'Why couldn't you live here?' she asked, watching her sister carefully.

'Too enclosed,' Sarah said, shaking her head vigorously. 'Shut off from the world. From ordinary everyday things.'

'But what's more ordinary than dirty sheets?'

'There's nothing ordinary about having thirty pairs and your own small laundry to deal with them,' she came back at her.

'But you do like being here, don't you?' Hannah asked again.

'Oh yes, it's great,' Sarah beamed unexpectedly. 'I love Lady Anne and she's so good to Ma. I'll come here anytime she asks us, but I couldn't *live* here.'

Hannah smiled, satisfied. Only Sarah would see the need to make such a distinction. She opened her paintbox and began to work on the morning's sketches while Sarah turned to writing up her notes.

For half an hour the silence was broken only by the scuffles of the gardeners who were hoeing the flower beds that lay on both sides of the terrace below the open windows.

'It's no use, Hannah,' Sarah said, throwing down her pencil in disgust. 'I can't get it all down. There's just too much detail. Too much to explain, even if I label all the sketches.'

'But you've got plenty of time, Sarah,' the older girl replied, soothingly. 'Look how much you've done in less than a week. Multiply by eight and think how much that will be. I'm sure you'll have covered everything about the house and garden by then,' she said encouragingly.

'Yes, I suppose you're right,' she said reluctantly. 'But words leave out so much. How would you like to have to describe just in words that lovely bit of garden you've found?' she demanded, getting up and peering over Hannah's shoulder at the pattern of colour taking shape on the page. 'I'm not as patient as you. I couldn't do proper sketches of *everything*.'

The answer to Sarah's problem came quite unexpectedly the following afternoon when Lady Anne sent Betty to ask the two girls to have tea with her and Rose in her own sitting room overlooking the park.

When they arrived, they found the conversation had moved once again to Kerry, a topic Sarah encouraged by every possible means, for she never tired of hearing about the summer of '75 and how Rose and Lady Anne had each found the love of their life.

'Do you remember that sweet little veil we ordered from Dublin?' Lady Anne demanded, looking up at Rose as she poured tea for them all.

'I don't have to remember it,' she replied smiling. 'I still have it. Very carefully wrapped in linen. It has only yellowed slightly and all the little pearls are still there.'

'Goodness, Rose, I can still see you in that veil. You looked lovely.'

'Yes, she did,' Sarah agreed. 'Could we possibly see your pictures of Ma and Da?' she asked politely. 'I'm sure Mr Blennerhasset took some for you as well as for them.'

'Mr Blennerhasset? My goodness, Sarah, I'd completely

forgotten him. He was one of my sister's admirers, but she turned him down. She turned all of them down,' she explained, with a wry look at Rose. 'I haven't thought of him for years.'

'Ma said I could bring his book with me. I thought perhaps you might like to see it,' said Sarah tentatively.

'How very thoughtful of you, my dear. I should *love* to see it. What a good idea. Do you like photographs?' Lady Anne asked, looking at her with a slight, puzzled frown.

'Oh yes,' she replied quickly, her eyes sparkling. 'I should love to take masses of photographs. Specially here. I could get so much more in than in a sketch but . . .'

'Well, if you haven't brought your Kodak, or if you haven't got one, we can soon put that right,' Lady Anne declared. 'Teddy must have three or four of them by now. He used to have a huge wooden contraption with brass handles and long legs,' she said laughing, 'but now they've got smaller, so he says. I'm sure you can have one he's not using, Sarah. He'll be *so* pleased you're interested.'

Sarah beamed with delight. She'd had no idea that photographic cameras had got smaller. The last time she'd seen one was when the school photographer came and his was just like the one Lady Anne described.

'Rose dear, a little piece of cake. Just a little piece,' she said coaxingly.

Rose laughed. 'I will if you want me to, but then I won't be able to eat any dinner,' she warned. 'You spoil us so.'

'I'm making up for all the years I had to do without you. I can hardly believe I've got you all to myself at last. Well, nearly all. I don't mind sharing you with Hannah and Sarah, and with Marianne and Teddy when they come,' she said honestly, as she put the cake back on the trolley.

'I warn you, Hannah,' she went on grimly, 'if Sarah wants to *take* pictures he'll have you dressed as a goddess or a nymph, or some other bizarre thing so they can practise upon you. Marianne and I have got so bored posing for him he doesn't dare ask us anymore,' she explained, turning to Rose with a broad grin. 'He has a studio in one of the attics and he develops in the knife room because it's got no windows. You can't imagine how horribly stuffy it is. Cook complains fearfully about the smell coming under the door. But Teddy can be very persistent,' she added, her tone unusually thoughtful.

She put down her teacup and smiled at Sarah.

'Sarah dear, if you've finished your tea, I'd love to see old Blennerhasset's book. Then, when Mama chases us away, we'll go down to the library together and I'll show you some of Teddy's stuff.'

'Right, won't be a moment,' said Sarah, as she popped up, shot across the room and disappeared at speed.

Rose and Hannah exchanged glances and grinned, while Lady Anne looked from one to the other and raised an enquiring eyebrow.

'Sarah is practising being ladylike,' Hannah explained, 'before Lady Marianne and Lord Cleeve arrive. But sometimes she forgets.'

Eleven

Ashley Park
July 1897

My dearest John,

I was amazed and delighted to get your letter this morning. I can hardly believe what you wrote yesterday, after lunch, should arrive this morning on my breakfast tray. Blessings on Mrs Rea for taking it into Banbridge when she went shopping.

It is very good news indeed about Hugh. I shall certainly be writing to Elizabeth and will ask her when they are going over to Manchester. I haven't mentioned it to the girls and would rather not until we see how things go. I do so wish him well.

Life here continues to be quite delightful, all the more so as Lady Marianne and Lord Cleeve have arrived for their summer holiday. There's still no date for Lord Harrington's arrival. Lady Anne says there's no hope at all before the recess, and with various controversial bills tabled no one knows when that might be.

I must say I had to smile when I saw her pair together for the first time. They are both so like her, not a bit like Harrington. It's hard on Marianne, for she has that same square, robust shape her mother has. As you'll remember when Sarah instructed you, the fashion these days is for tiny waists and a graceful, willowy look. The poor girl has neither, but she certainly makes up for it in liveliness and good nature.

She and Sarah took to each other immediately. She seems to make up her mind about people as quickly as

> Sarah does, but I admit I was pleased to see her walking with Hannah only a few days later. My window overlooks the garden and there they were, arms entwined, heads together. So that's good news.
>
> Lord Cleeve has been a bit more fortunate than his sister as regards looks. Some of his ancestors must have had long legs. He's a good head taller than either of his parents and it helps to offset his figure, which is just as unfashionable as Marianne's.

Rose put down her pen and leant back in her chair. She loved writing letters and her regular epistles to John were a pleasure, but unfortunately the effort of writing still tired her. She would set off in fine form, then find she was writing more and more slowly. If she persisted, first her shoulders would ache, and then, if she went on, the wretched pain in her chest would start up and leave her breathless.

Reluctantly, she went to the window and did her breathing exercises. The air was fresh and the gardens below a joy to behold. Every afternoon she and Lady Anne walked together as far as she could manage and then enjoyed a quiet hour or two before the young people joined them for tea. Sometimes they sat in one of the many shady arbours, sometimes in Lady Anne's sitting room, not even making a pretence of sewing.

Wondering how she might describe him to John, her thoughts went back to Lord Cleeve. While his height did offset his figure, there was nothing to mitigate the unyielding lines of his plain face. He was seldom animated and rarely revealed his feelings, so for most of the time his face appeared strangely immobile.

She'd watched him, puzzled, when they met at lunch, occasionally at tea, and always in Lady Anne's sitting room after dinner. He was an able young man, doing well at Cambridge, and sincerely fond of his mother and sister. She wondered if he'd inherited something of the shyness that had dogged his father for most of his life. Like him, he seldom initiated a conversation, but unlike the young Lord

Harrington, who had found *all* speech difficult, this young man was always able to respond .

It took her some days to realize that, although he appeared silent, just occasionally, in the midst of a conversation, he would suddenly speak out with unusual force and fluency, as he'd done the previous evening.

'My dear Miss Hamilton,' he said, bowing slightly to Hannah, who had just addressed a question to him. 'If I am to have the pleasure of calling you and your sister by your first names, then I insist you call me Teddy, except of course when we are in company, which I sincerely hope we will not be,' he added, glancing at his mother, 'or in front of the servants, a rule of my father's which we may not entirely understand, but which we all observe meticulously for his sake.'

Hannah smiled and blushed very slightly as she regarded him perfectly calmly.

'Then, perhaps, Teddy,' she said, with just the slightest hesitancy in using his familiar name, 'you might explain to Sarah and me, why, when you were christened Richard Molyneux, you ask us to call you Teddy.'

To Rose's surprise, he threw back his head and laughed, glanced from his mother to his sister and addressed himself entirely to Hannah.

'My nurse made great efforts to teach me the names of all the people with whom I came in contact,' he began calmly. 'Apart from Mama and Dada, she encouraged me to learn the names of all the servants and of all my toys. Unfortunately, I decided that, while everything had to have a name, any name would serve, so I selected from my list of names the one that took my fancy. As it happened, the one I learnt first and found easiest to say was Teddy, so when I was asked to produce a name for myself that was the one I always chose. So now you know one of the secrets of my early life,' he concluded.

Whatever Teddy's personal difficulties might be, Rose could not fault him in his kindness and courtesy to both Hannah and Sarah. Towards his sister, he showed real affection, but this was obvious only in the way he teased her with his ready wit. She went back to her table, took up her pen and described Teddy as coherently as she could before going on to tell John about Sarah's introduction to photography.

It seems that Eastman in America have produced a whole range of small cameras which everyone calls Kodaks. They're a far cry from that huge monster we met in Loudan's of Armagh back in '89. Do you remember how difficult Sarah was until the young man let her look through the lens? Well, Teddy, as I may now call him, thinks these old plate cameras very good, despite their limitations, and he has started teaching Sarah how to use one.

When she's mastered the principles of the plate camera, he's promised she can move to a Kodak and take pictures outdoors, and indoors, too, when there is sufficient light. But we did all have to laugh at Teddy's enthusiasm. So keen was he to get Sarah to practise up in the attic in what he calls his 'studio' he asked Hannah and Marianne to go and put on their best white muslin dresses. I haven't been up to the attic, but Lady Anne tells me it is thick with dust. The girls burst out laughing but Teddy was so focused on his programme he couldn't see what was so funny.

Sarah's first pictures are very good and Teddy is pleased. He says she has a good eye for composition and a marvellous knack of getting people to do what she wants. Poor Hannah and Marianne. Hannah tells me they spent hours sharing big books, admiring each other's embroidery and even playing with the cook's cat! Sarah is radiant and cannot wait to be allowed a Kodak to take outside.

Don't worry that they spend all their time indoors. The weather has been quite lovely, warm and sunny, and they go walking every morning after Sarah's lesson. There is a lake some mile or more from the house, and Marianne enjoys punting, though Teddy insists she has more energy than skill. I was a little anxious as neither of our girls can swim, but Anne says the lake is barely three feet deep. Apparently it was the fashion to have a lake when great-grandfather built the house. Teddy tells me the bird life round it is very interesting. When he spoke about it I remembered your Sir Capel and his bird sanctuary at Castledillon. Everyone thought he was mad in those days, but Anne tells me bird sanctuaries are now more common.

As you see, I have finally managed it. I still forget to call her Anne from time to time, but when we are alone together now I find it easy enough.

We talk of so many things but I must write about that another time. I promised I would not over tire myself, even by writing to you! Take care of yourself and give my love to Sam and Jamie, Elizabeth and Hugh, and my sincere thanks to Mrs Rea.

Rose added her signature and a row of kisses, folded up the stiff sheets of paper and put them in an envelope. She had just addressed it to *John Hamilton Esq., Ballydown, Corbet, Banbridge, Co. Down, Ireland*, when there was a knock at her door and Betty arrived carrying a salver.

'Come for your post, ma'am,' she said, curtseying, as she crossed the room and stood beside Rose's writing table in the window. 'And Her Ladyship sent you this.'

On the silver salver was a pretty china plate, a small fruit knife and a clean napkin. Beside them, in a tiny woven straw basket, sat a single peach, perfectly ripe and warm from the sun.

'Have you seen the latest prints, Rose?' asked Lady Anne, as they came back into her sitting room together after their afternoon stroll.

'More? Already?' she asked, a note of anxiety in her voice. 'Has poor Teddy been shut up in the knife room again?'

'No, dear, that's only for the big glass plates,' her friend replied reassuringly. 'With the Kodaks, you send the spools to the factory and the prints come in the post. Teddy says some of these are his. A few are Marianne's, but most are Sarah's. Shall we see what they've been up to?'

'This must be the lake,' said Rose, picking up the first one slowly. 'Oh dear. I think it's draining away,' she went on, beginning to laugh.

'That's Marianne's for sure. Yes, it must be. Look, Teddy has no feet,' she said matter-of-factly. 'What do you think this one is?' she went on, as she turned the next print upside down and then back again.

'That's better. My goodness that's good.'

Lady Anne held out a picture of an elderly gardener about to pick a peach.

'That must be one of Teddy's,' said Rose, looking at it closely.

'No, it's not. It's one of Sarah's,' her friend replied, beaming.

'How ever do you know?'

'Look! Look just there,' she said, pointing. 'She's caught Old Partridge picking a peach *and* she's caught reflections of Teddy and Hannah watching her. Isn't she clever?'

Rose looked more closely, and there, sure enough, were two figures standing close beside each other, intent upon Sarah taking her picture. She had to admit Sarah's pictures were rather good. So far there wasn't a fuzzy or lopsided one amongst them. There were lots of pictures of people working. A laundry maid ironing. Cook mixing something in a bowl. A groom throwing up a saddle on a pony. The postman arriving on his bicycle. The pictures all looked so natural, yet the people pictured must have seen her at work.

'They do seem to be enjoying themselves, Rose,' said Lady Anne happily, as they collected up the prints.

'Yes, Anne dear, you've all made the girls so welcome,' Rose said warmly. 'Teddy's spent hours teaching Sarah to use his cameras.'

She shook her head slowly. 'Sarah's grown up. I have to admit the young girl I brought with me has suddenly disappeared. Oh, I knew she'd already left girlhood behind. That happened one day when a poor woman with a sick child came to the door and Sarah simply took charge, but I could still see the young girl on the journey. She was still there when we first got here. Now, somehow, I just don't see that girl anymore.'

She paused and thought for a moment.

'Do you know, Anne, I think it's the photography that's done it.'

'Isn't that funny? Funny peculiar, I mean,' the younger woman replied. 'The very same thing happened to me last autumn. We went up to town for the season and Marianne had her ball. She took it all very casually. Paid no special attention to her dress. She wasn't awkward or anything like that, but she wasn't excited like most girls are. The morning after, she came and told me who she'd danced with and which of them she never wanted to dance with ever again. She was different. Just like that. Overnight.'

'So we neither of us have children anymore?' said Rose slowly.

'No, we don't. They may still be able to have fun like children, but even that's almost gone for mine. What about Jamie and Sam, Rose? Did they change quickly when they went to work?'

Rose paused a moment. She was seeing Sam's smile as he came and handed her his empty lunch box every evening. Then she thought of Jamie's infrequent and irregular visits.

'Jamie changed very quickly,' Rose began. 'Even the first time he came home, he was telling John and Sam things about his work as if they'd have difficulty understanding him. Yes, they were technical things, but even I could have managed them if I'd put my mind to it. But Sam didn't change. It's not that he's not growing up properly. Already he's a lot more mature than Jamie, but there's something about Sam that will always be childlike. He's so trusting, so good-natured. I'd almost say innocent. I used to worry about him so.'

'But you don't now?'

'Oh, I suppose I do in an everyday sort of way,' she admitted, 'but since I was ill I seem to see things differently.'

'Because you nearly died?'

'Probably,' she said, nodding. 'I try to think about it, but I can't make much sense of it yet. I feel even more grateful than I was before just to be alive, to have my family and my dear friends, but I accept now they could well manage without me were I not there.'

Rose paused, aware of the protest her friend was about to make.

'I don't mean my friends don't care about me, or wouldn't be grieved,' she said quickly, 'it's just . . . I know there's nothing I can do about living, or dying. It has to be accepted. So many things in life just have to be accepted,' she went on quietly. 'There's no use worrying about them. I'd never seen that before. And there's a strange kind of relief in knowing that there's no point in worrying.'

Lady Anne sat very still and said nothing. She waited to see if Rose would go on, and when she didn't she took her hand.

'You always were my teacher,' she said slowly. 'Don't go and die on me. I need you. I sometimes think you are the only person in the world who understands me. Harrington tries and I can forgive him almost anything because he loves me so, but you know what goes on in my mind in a way even the dearest man can't, especially when I don't know what's going on myself. Bless you, Rose. You're beginning to look tired and it's time you had a rest. I'll walk up to your room with you.'

As the weeks passed, the summer weather continued fine and dry. With Rose's progress obvious to everyone, only one thing marred Lady Anne's joy, the absence of her dear Harrington. Each morning at breakfast she would rifle through the envelopes by her plate, opening first the missive addressed in his familiar hand. Short and loving, with kindly queries about their guests and good wishes for all their activities, he could only say there was still no date to offer, although the recess had now begun.

The Prime Minister had asked for discussions with some

of his supporters from both houses. As the matter in hand was Ireland, and Harrington had been an Irish member for so long and still felt so strongly on matters Irish, he was an obvious choice. It was an honour and an opportunity which he couldn't turn down, but only Lady Anne knew how much he missed his family and how he longed for the peace of Gloucestershire after months of being in London.

'Oh, no,' said Lady Anne, with a long drawn-out sigh, as she scanned the familiar writing one delightful, sunlit Monday morning when, for the first time, a fresh breeze hinted at the possibility of autumn.

'Not bad news, Mama,' said Marianne quickly, as they all turned towards her and saw the troubled look on her face.

'No, not bad news,' she said quickly. 'Tiresome news. Irritating news,' she said, reassuring them. 'Your father will be able to come down on Friday,' she said briskly, 'but he has agreed to invite Lord Altrincham,' she added, with another heavy sigh. 'Oh, he's a sweet little man,' she went on hurriedly, glancing across at Rose, 'but his wife is just . . .' She raised her hands in the air, completely at a loss for words.

'And why is Lady Altrincham coming, Mama, if Father has business with His Lordship?' asked Teddy coolly.

'A good question, my dear Teddy,' she said, dropping the letter dispiritedly beside her plate. She looked around the table as every eye rested on her, with a mixture of sympathy and curiosity.

'At a guess the lady in question wishes to say she's stayed at Ashley Park,' she declared. 'In fact, I'm absolutely sure she'll indicate very cleverly that she is on intimate terms with each one of us whenever she's given the slightest opportunity. We shall all have to be on our best behaviour for your father's sake. She must have made it clear she wished to be invited,' she went on, waving a hand towards the abandoned letter. 'She knows perfectly well it's the recess and there's no real possibility of refusing her.'

'For how long, Mama?' asked Teddy, his face unmoved as he buttered another piece of toast.

'Oh, just the weekend,' she replied, wearily. 'But that's bad enough. Friday evening dinner. Entertainments laid on for Saturday. Church on Sunday morning. Perhaps they'll leave after lunch, if we're lucky. I'm so sorry, my dears, this will be a dreadful bore for you,' she said turning to Hannah and Sarah, who were listening quietly. 'At least Marianne and Teddy are used to it.'

'I think it might be rather interesting,' said Sarah promptly.

'Perhaps we could help in some way,' Hannah added, glancing at Teddy and Marianne.

'It's very sweet of you to think of that,' said Lady Anne, smiling for the first time. 'I'll give my mind to it. In the meantime, I want you young people to have a lovely week and try to forget all about it till the dressing bell rings on Friday evening. This is *your* holiday and I don't want it spoilt by a nasty, bossy lady.'

In the five days that followed, the dust sheets were removed from the handsome, elaborately decorated and gloomy guest suite that looked out over the fountain, the newly laid formal garden and the long gravel drive. The gardeners were much in evidence outdoors. Indoors, flowers blossomed in unexpected places. The housemaids were unusually visible during the day. Even the stables appeared to be having a spring clean.

Rose was surprised at the change in Lady Anne. Although they enjoyed each other's company, she found her friend very preoccupied. There was also a general air of tension that was quite new.

By the time the bell echoed through the house on Friday evening, family, guests and servants had all caught at least a glimpse of the very large coach with a newly painted coat of arms on its shiny door, drawn by six matched horses and attended by two coachmen and two grooms. Sarah, Marianne and Hannah, who'd shared Teddy's binoculars and then positioned themselves carefully in the upstairs linen room, had a good view of the visitors themselves. A small man in a top hat and morning coat, who smiled cheerfully at everyone in sight, and a taller, gaunt woman, grey haired, sharp faced and opulently dressed, who made up for her husband's amiability by not smiling at all.

'She hasn't improved any,' said Marianne, as they removed themselves from the linen room and made their way back to Sarah and Hannah's sitting room.

'Have you met her before?' Sarah asked, as they settled themselves comfortably.

'Oh yes,' she replied. 'She came to my ball. I didn't want to have them, but you have to do these things. If Mama hadn't invited her, it would have been a snub to Lord Altrincham, and, apart from the fact that he's really nice, he's a colleague of Father, so there wasn't much choice.'

'But I thought balls were for getting girls married off,' said Sarah abruptly. 'Why do older people get invited?'

Marianne laughed, her dark eyes shining with mirth. She waved her hands around helplessly as if Sarah had said the wittiest thing. In a few moments Hannah and Sarah were laughing too. Although they didn't quite see the joke, Marianne's laughter was quite irresistible.

'But, Sarah, you have to get them married to the right people,' she explained, still laughing. 'The parents come to make sure you don't dance with anyone unsuitable. At least most of them do. Mama hates balls, but she goes in case I need rescuing from someone awful. She doesn't interfere, but she's there if I need an excuse to get away from someone, like the Altrinchams' son. He is ghastly. He's smaller than I am and he thinks he's the catch of the season. And naturally his dear mama has her eye on me. You watch out for the way she says "dear Lady Marianne". She wouldn't say good morning to me if Father weren't an earl.'

'Now then, Miss Sarah, you've done your own hair as you wish, but let me settle your dress,' said Betty severely, as she came into her room, having left Hannah sitting by her window, her pale-green silk dress decorated with rosebuds, her long, fair hair piled up with ribbon to let her ringlets fall softly to her neck.

'Stand still then, Miss Sarah,' she went on, as she tweaked and smoothed with a practised hand. 'Are you wantin' a flower there at the neck like Miss Hamilton? It looks very well on her.'

'Yes, I'm sure it does,' Sarah agreed readily. 'Anything looks good on my sister. But no thank you, Betty. I'm sure if I wore a rose it would droop, or fall off and leave me with the leaf and the pin. Better without.'

'You look very nice, Miss Sarah,' said Betty softening, her good eye looking her up and down. 'That dark blue suits you fine, though I've never seen a *young* lady wear just that shade,' she added thoughtfully.

'How kind of you, Betty,' said Sarah, beaming with delight. 'My sister's the beauty in the family,' she said, striking a lively pose, her chin up, her arms elegantly outstretched, 'but I try not to let her down.'

She grinned at Betty as she pirouetted round the room in her first silk dress. To her further delight, she found she'd actually made her laugh.

There was a great deal of laughter over dinner, but not all of it was entirely comfortable. Lord Altrincham was exactly as Lady Anne had described him. Those who'd seen him arrive were not at all surprised to find he was lively, good-natured and a fund of amusing stories. His wife ignored most of them and certainly didn't join in the laughter they produced. Observing her across the table, Rose wondered if the lady had decided that laughter was ill-bred.

Lady Altrincham's sole contribution to the conversation was a detailed account of the recent Diamond Jubilee celebrations. She seemed to be exceedingly well informed about exactly what had happened in which location, what the Queen had worn, who had attended her and what magnificent decorations and arrangements had been made to add to the splendour of the occasion.

When her host and hostess failed to do more than listen with polite attention, it dawned on Rose that this was Lady Altrincham's strategy to draw out comments she could deploy on later occasions. To be able to quote Lord Ashley or his lady on the subject of the Jubilee would suggest a degree of intimacy very far from the true situation. She was not at all surprised when Teddy took up the conversation. With considerable skill he engaged her with a stream of civil questions about the details of all she had said. He showed great interest in her replies, but used them only to initiate further questions rather than respond with comments of his own.

Sarah was fascinated by Lady Altrincham. She could now see why Lady Anne had been so upset at the prospect of her visit. The woman was acting a part. She'd practised it well and was quite comfortable with her performance, but she was so busy thinking about herself, she'd no time for anyone else, particularly her rather nice husband beside whom she was sitting. Her Ladyship knew what she wanted and had a rather unpleasant, determined look which broke through her carefully composed expression from time to time, when other people were speaking and she was waiting for her next opportunity to respond.

Absorbed in her thoughts about what she had observed of the lady in action, Sarah was slow to react when the port came and the gentlemen rose to move back the chairs and let the ladies withdraw. Had she been on her feet already, she would not have seen the glance Teddy exchanged with Hannah as he leant towards her before stepping behind her chair, leaving the way free for her to follow the three older women. In the fleeting moment before she stood up herself, Sarah saw Hannah look up at Teddy and nod imperceptibly. His face softened and brightened, as he leant just close enough to her to brush her sleeve as she rose to her feet. He stood back and watched her as she followed Lady Anne, Lady Altrincham and her mother towards the double doors leading into the domed hall and the long, shallow staircase to the drawing room on the first floor.

For another moment her eyes followed her sister as she moved gracefully down the length of the long table. Then she collected herself, smiled warmly at Lord Altrincham, who was waiting patiently, bent over her chair, his whiskery face close to hers.

'Thank you,' she said softly.

'A pleasure, my dear.'

She moved steadily after the retreating figures, reminding herself not to hurry. Hannah and Marianne were now walking together, talking quietly, some distance behind the older women. Sarah took a deep breath to steady herself. She'd seen something no one else had seen nor was meant to see, and it had shaken her. Now she knew why Hannah was looking so lovely this evening. She was in love with Teddy and he with her. If they hadn't recognized the fact themselves, then it was only a matter of time before they found out, but she was pretty sure they knew.

As she made her way slowly upstairs to the great drawing room, she felt a great sadness come over her. Hannah was her dear sister, her only sister. They had always been so close, such good friends. They always would be, she was sure. But however close she and Hannah might have been in the past, the future would now be different.

Rose had explained to Sarah long ago the purpose of such very large rooms as the main drawing room of a big house, the opportunities it gave for private conversations, or for a little solitude, even when doing one's social duty. With her mind full of what she had seen, she longed to take advantage of the view from the window or the books of sketches laid out on little tables scattered about the room, but as she came into the room and saw the little group by the marble fireplace, she knew she must make an effort. Lady Altrincham had seated herself close by her mother, who looked composed, but not at all relaxed. Lady Anne was engaged in pouring coffee, which Marianne was handing round.

'My dear Mrs Hamilton,' Lady Altrincham began, with a wintry smile, 'I know so little about Ireland except what the dear countess has told me of the beauties of Kerry. I gather the Hamilton estates are in both Antrim and Down,' she said, leaning forward confidentially.

Sarah sat down promptly at the far end of the long settee on which her mother sat, a position from which she could face them both.

'Mama dear, do let me explain to Lady Altrincham about the Hamilton estates,' she said politely. 'You know you always get the dates wrong and the Johns and the Jameses mixed up,' she said helpfully.

'Willingly, Sarah,' Rose replied. 'I'm afraid, like my own mother, I have a memory for events, but not for their exact sequence,' she explained, smiling agreeably at Lady Altrincham.

'James Hamilton came to Ireland as an undertaker in 1606,' began Sarah, in a relaxed manner.

'What?' spluttered Lady Altrincham, putting her coffee cup down hastily.

'An undertaker, Lady Altrincham,' Sarah repeated clearly. 'He undertook to build a fortified house in each of his four territories in Antrim, which he'd received by grant together with two granges, one friary, the lands of Castle Toome and the fishing on the Bann from Lough Neagh to the salmon leap,' she continued fluently.

'And did he fulfil all his undertaking?' the older lady demanded, anxious their audience should put out of mind her unfortunate mistake.

'No, of course not. He was far too clever for that,' she replied cheerfully. 'A fortified house costs a fortune. No, what James did was dispose of his Antrim holdings so that he could concentrate on the Down properties. Somewhere around 1606 he persuaded his two brothers Gavin and John to become denizens.'

Lady Altrincham was not going to make a second mistake. If she was unfamiliar with denizens she was certainly not going to admit it. She looked at Sarah attentively and nodded at suitable intervals as she continued her narrative. Sarah knew she wasn't really listening, but everyone else was, so she warmed to her task and continued.

'His chief aim was to rearrange his holdings, so as to make the most of the fertile, well-wooded peninsula of Ards. He was very successful in attracting Scottish settlers to his lands and in 1608 he was knighted, though at that point he hadn't yet acquired Dufferin. But, of course, he managed that quite soon afterwards.'

Sarah paused to take her coffee from Marianne and then continued. She outlined the various manoeuvres, many of them distinctly dubious, by which James Hamilton and his brothers became the holders of enormous tracts of very productive land. She then proceeded to outline the activities of John Hamilton in Armagh, Robert Hamilton of Stanehous and their relationships with the Montgomerys, the Chichesters and the O'Neills.

Rose sat fascinated by the compelling tale Sarah was able to make out of the Hamilton machinations. However dubious their methods, they had certainly achieved King James's objective of re-settling the country with loyal subjects and developing its commercial potential.

'What an interesting history, my dear,' said Lady Altrincham sweetly when Sarah paused. 'As you say, Sarah, three centuries later it is such an extended family. And such a successful one,' she acknowledged, bowing slightly towards Rose. 'I presume your family are still mostly associated with Dufferin and Clandeboye?'

'Good heavens, no,' said Sarah sharply, before Rose could open her mouth to reply. 'We've been in Ireland *much* longer. We are the Hamiltons of Ballydown,' she announced proudly, as the drawing-room door opened and Lord Altrincham and Lord Ashley preceded Lord Cleeve across the wide spaces of carpet to where the ladies sat.

It was obvious next morning that Lady Anne had recovered her usual good spirits. After breakfast she offered Lady Altrincham a tour of the new formal gardens, the kitchen gardens and the greenhouses. There she explained to the staff what an experienced gardener Lady Altrincham was and how valuable her comments would be on their current projects.

After lunch Teddy insisted that Lady Altrincham be photographed with the family. When she agreed most readily, he and Sarah occupied her in the studio and the gardens for an hour or more until the whole family was available to pose for a long series of pictures. By the time they'd completed everything to their satisfaction, the lady in question felt the need to rest a little.

'Well, how did it go?' Hannah asked, as Sarah came into their sitting room and flopped down in a large, comfortable armchair.

'She's gone to have a rest,' she said thankfully. 'Teddy was great. He kept taking long exposures, so she had to keep still. There's only tonight to get through and Marianne says she'll do foreign travel. Ask her advice. She'll like that. She'll talk about anything so long as she's the centre of attention,' she said sharply.

'What will you do, Sarah? You were marvellous last night on the Hamiltons. Ma said this morning she'd no idea what she was going to say and you rescued her beautifully.'

'I really don't know,' Sarah replied, beaming with pleasure. 'I'll see how Marianne and Teddy get on. What's Teddy thinking of for tonight?'

To her amazement, Hannah blushed.

'He did very well last night, too,' Sarah said slowly. 'He just needs you to encourage him a little,' she went on with as much nonchalance as she could manage, her eyes averted as Hannah blushed even more deeply.

Ashley Park
August 1897

My dear Elizabeth,

What wonderful news about Hugh and what a relief for you that things have gone so well. I have thought about you both in Altrincham in this last week. By the strangest coincidence Lady Anne has been entertaining Lord and Lady Altrincham, though, of course, they live miles outside Manchester now, but each time Altrincham was mentioned I could think only of you. When do you think Hugh will be fit to travel?

How very quickly the weeks have flown. I can hardly believe how well I am. Walking every day. Yesterday, I managed it to the lake and back for the first time, which is about two miles, though it *was* on the flat. I have not yet tried a hill.

Do you remember the pale-green silk Hannah chose

and your dressmaker made up for us? She wore it for this visit of the Altrinchams, as we all had to be very elegant and proper. Elizabeth, she looked so lovely I couldn't quite believe it. Sarah's blue was a great success too. You will find her very much changed. Much more grown up. She will have so much to tell you, you'll need to be feeling strong.

Only two weeks now till our return. I long to see John and you and Hugh, but I shall be so sad to leave Anne. We seem to have caught up on twenty-two years of talk, but it will be hard to revert to letters.

Thank you again for writing so quickly. My fondest love to you and my loving good wishes to Hugh. I am so delighted for you both.

As always,

Rose

Twelve

The two summer months that had once seemed such an unlimited stretch of time now rapidly shrank to weeks and then to days. To everyone's surprise, the days themselves flew faster than ever. All three Hamiltons were overcome with such very mixed feelings of sadness at leaving Ashley Park and delight at the thought of being home again.

For Hannah, the feelings were particularly painful. Since the Altrinchams' visit, she'd found herself walking or riding with Teddy more and more. While they might well set out with Sarah and Marianne, sooner or later the two girls would ride ahead, or fall behind. Whether or not Hannah and Teddy sensed the opportunities being created for them, they were certainly aware of every moment they spent together.

One pleasant, sunny afternoon, a week before the Hamiltons were due to depart, the two of them sat together on a bench in the accessible part of the overgrown garden where Hannah had spent so much time sketching and painting. Yet once more, Sarah and Marianne were nowhere to be seen.

'I cannot bear the thought of your going,' said Teddy baldly.

'I'm trying not to think about it,' replied Hannah softly.

They sat in silence, staring out over the vibrant colours of the flower beds, the only sound the comfortable hum of myriads of small bees who disappeared bodily into the glowing interiors of large-throated blooms or swung perilously from the tiny ones.

'I *am* twenty-one, but I have another year to do at Cambridge,' he said soberly. 'I should like to take my degree,' he added, looking up into a nearby tree, smothered with late-flowering clematis.

'Of course you must take your degree.'

She glanced at him cautiously. His face gave not the slightest clue to his feelings, any more than it had done the evening he'd engaged Lady Altrincham. But she knew he was distressed. His whole body was alive with a tension he could control only by sitting bolt upright. Every few minutes he drew in a great, deep breath. Between times, he seemed hardly to breath at all.

'What can I do, Hannah? What can I do?' he said at last.

'About what, Teddy?' she said encouragingly.

'About not wanting to part with you ever again,' he burst out.

'According to Jane Austen's novels, at this point you are supposed to make me an offer,' she said steadily.

'And would you accept?'

'Yes, I would.'

'Truly?'

She nodded vigorously, as if only by some physical gesture could she persuade him she would.

'And would your father consent, do you think?' he persisted, a glimmer of hope softening his voice.

'I think he could be persuaded,' she said, smiling briefly. 'But I don't think my father is the problem. You must think of your parents, Teddy.' I have neither money nor title. I'm hardly a suitable match.'

'Hannah, my love, *you* don't need money or title. You can have mine. You can have everything I can give you, if you'll be my wife. But you'll have to help me, like you did when the Altrinchams came. I'd never have managed that evening but for you. How do I manage this?'

'Of course I'll help you. We'll help each other,' she said, putting out her hand and resting it on his. 'We must work out what it's best to do.'

He turned to her and smiled, a warm, glowing smile, such a rare thing with him she was quite overwhelmed.

'Can we seal our promise before we work out our strategy?' he asked softly, as he slipped his arm around her.

'Yes,' she whispered, as he drew her into his arms and kissed her.

Even if Sarah had not spotted Hannah and Teddy leaving the old garden hand in hand, she would have guessed something had happened from the sparkle in Hannah's eyes and the lightness of her step. She and Marianne had long ago shared their thoughts about Hannah and Teddy. They agreed something had happened, but before they could celebrate they had to find out exactly what.

Lady Anne was completely taken aback later that same afternoon when Teddy asked to speak to her alone. She'd never in her life seen Teddy so animated or so obviously and openly happy. She was even more amazed when he managed to tell her quite calmly that he wanted to marry Hannah. He'd asked her, he said, and she'd accepted him and now he'd like her advice about approaching his father.

'Teddy darling, I thought I was so old nothing would ever surprise me again, but you've managed it. Hannah is a dear girl and I'm sure we'll find a way, but do remember she *is* only eighteen . . .'

'And what age were you, Mama, when you said yes to Father?'

'I was *nearly* nineteen,' she said, trying to sound firm, 'and your father was much older than you are.' Then she laughed. 'Go away and let me think and don't say anything to your father yet. I want to talk to Mrs Hamilton before I speak to him,' she said, shooing him away. 'Send Betty up to ask her if she would come down to me now. If she's not too busy with her letters,' she added quickly.

Rose was equally surprised when Betty tapped her door and made her request. She'd left her friend not an hour earlier so they could both catch up on their correspondence, having spent the day on a most pleasant drive with Lord Harrington to the part of his estate nearest the Somerset border.

'I have a surprise for you,' Lady Anne said, as Rose crossed the room and came to sit beside her in the wide bay window.

'Nice, I hope?' she said, laughing.

'I hope you'll think so. I do. Or rather, I think it will be nice when you and I solve one or two little problems,' she added carefully.

'Now you're teasing me. I'm consumed by curiosity,' Rose responded, settling herself more comfortably. 'Now tell me, do.'

'My dear Teddy has had the great good sense to fall in love with your daughter,' said Lady Anne without more ado. 'She's only eighteen and he has a year to do at Cambridge, but it's perfectly clear they've made up their minds. I've never known Teddy so absolutely sure of what he wants. She's the only girl he's ever looked at. Three years of balls and house parties and he's never so much as remembered a girl's name when I've asked him. Will you and John give your blessing?'

Rose opened her mouth to speak and then closed it again. Now that Lady Anne had put it into words, she realized she'd been aware of something new in Hannah's behaviour, but Teddy had been so generous with the time he'd given to Sarah and her camera, she couldn't quite see how he'd come to know Hannah well enough to fall in love with her.

'I think the bigger question is what you and Harrington think,' she said slowly. 'It's hardly the match he might have had in mind, if he's thought about a match at all.'

'Oh, he's thought about it all right. Don't imagine we don't have to make our appearance at these wretched balls. I won't tell you what he says about some of the girls who think Teddy would be a good catch. Like Lady Altrincham's daughter. As great a charmer as her mother,' she added sharply. 'Besides, Harrington will ask me. And I'm asking you. What shall we do, Rose? Now we are old and wise,' she went on with a grin. 'Teddy did point out that I wasn't much older than Hannah when I said yes to Harrington. Though Harrington *was* twenty-five."

'If we're going to draw on our own experience, we can hardly object, can we?' said Rose, thoughtfully.

'Would you want to object?'

'No, I wouldn't,' said Rose, shaking her head vigorously. She paused before she continued more soberly. 'I'm only concerned at the question of status. Hannah's mother was a servant, if you remember,' she said, with a small, wry smile. 'Such things are important for their future, as you know only too well.'

'Yes, I suppose I do see what you mean, Rose,' she replied reluctantly. 'Hannah is prettier and better educated than most of these girls Teddy's been trying to avoid. She's very cool and steady, far more ladylike than Marianne. I can't imagine her having problems even if some stupid gossip found out how you and I became friends,' she went on more forcefully. 'But I expect you have a point. You usually do.'

Rose sat quite still, letting herself take in fully what had happened. With the wisdom of hindsight, she could see it all now quite plainly. It had been there in one of Sarah's first photographs. The gardener picking the peach. She'd seen something in the two reflected figures standing so close, so unselfconsciously watching Sarah take her picture. But only now could she make the connection.

'Don't forget now, Rose, thanks to Sarah, Lady Altrincham will be boasting in all the best places how she met the Ballydown Hamiltons at Ashley Park.'

They both laughed and put out their hands, each to the other.

'The same lady is more likely to go and look us up in *Burke's Peerage* before she does anything of the sort,' Rose retorted. 'I'm afraid she won't find us there.'

'It's none of her business,' said her friend fiercely. 'Teddy can marry whoever he wants and Hannah is a dear girl. I confess I've got to know Sarah better, but I can see why Hannah appeals so much to Teddy. She's just what he needs,' she added, thinking again of an assurance in Teddy's voice she'd never heard before.

'Oh, Rose, can you believe it?' she burst out suddenly. 'You and me, sitting here, discussing our children's marriage? It seems no time at all since we were discussing our own. You do realize, don't you, that if we can't be sisters, it looks as if we're going to be mothers-in-law to each other's children!'

They sat on, talking quietly, their laughter easing the tension as they gave their minds to the problems and difficulties they could foresee for the two young people. In the end, it was Lady Anne who hit upon a plan that might resolve Rose's unease about Hannah's status. Hannah should go with Marianne to finishing school in Switzerland.

'Marianne would love it and they get on so well together,' she said, enthusiastically. 'I'm sure Hannah will agree if she knows it will help Teddy. Switzerland is lovely, so I'm told. And I do know where it is,' she insisted, smiling. 'The school isn't far from Zurich. It's very expensive and quite international. A year there and Hannah would have no difficulties with the likes of Lady Altrincham or her daughter. It would be my engagement present to my future daughter-in-law. I'm sure your dear John wouldn't deny me that.'

From the hall below the dressing bell rang.

'Come, Rose, what do you say? Shall we put our plan to them after dinner? If they agree, I shall speak to Harrington tonight and you can write to John in the morning.'

'It's a very good idea, Anne,' she said warmly. 'You're very generous. The more Hannah can learn of the world she has to enter, the better it will be for both of them. I'm sure Teddy will understand.'

They kissed each other and parted. As Rose walked slowly along the wide landing towards her own room, quite suddenly she had an image of John on a hot day in Kerry, in a groom's coat that was too small for him, swinging her up into a Molyneux coach to keep an irritable old lady company. What was he going to say to his eldest daughter marrying Richard Molyneux Harrington and giving his blessing to Lord Cleeve, his prospective son-in-law?

Neither John Hamilton nor Lord Ashley raised any objection to the proposed marriage, none at least that stood up to the gentle and considered persuasion of their respective wives. John's immediate concern was a fear he might not see Hannah before she departed. As for Lord Ashley, his concern was that none of the manor houses on his estate might be available for the young couple in a year's time.

Rose and Anne agreed that Hannah must go home, however briefly. Her return journey to London to join Marianne would require an escort. With admirable timing, Anne's sister Lily, who still lived in the family house in Dublin, wrote to say she would be coming to London for her annual autumn visit, just when Marianne would be making her preparations for departure. John could take his daughter to Dublin by train and deliver her to a house he knew well enough, for he and Rose had spent part of the first week of their married life there.

As for a suitable home for the young couple, Anne simply assured her husband that something would turn up. She had been right so often in such circumstances, that Harrington forgot all about it and began to enjoy his summer break. He rode with his wife each morning, enjoyed the company of their guests in the afternoon and nodded off after dinner, overcome by much fresh air and two or three glasses of port with his son. To his great surprise and pleasure, his son seemed to have developed a firm grasp of the political situation in England, along with an awareness of the growing tension in South Africa, and Russian designs on the areas of China adjacent to their southern and eastern boundaries.

The last week was a happy one for everyone at Ashley Park. The engagement of Hannah and Teddy, symbolized by a pretty ring he'd recently inherited from his grandmother, was celebrated with outings and picnics, boating parties, and tea on the lawn. Sarah had the privilege of photographing the whole family, complete with staff, arranging them to her liking on the marble surround of the fountain.

Early that same morning she'd taken Teddy and Marianne on horseback. Now she posed Hannah and Teddy together, hand in hand, beneath a rose-covered arch in the garden. Finally, in the late afternoon, she tapped quietly at the door of Lady Anne's sitting room, knowing her mother was there.

She enquired politely if she might photograph them talking by the open window. It would only take a moment, she said.

She excused herself as soon as she'd taken her pictures and ran back upstairs to her own room. She pushed the door closed behind her, threw herself down on the window seat and wept. It had been a wonderful summer. She'd made such good friends with Marianne and Teddy. But now it was over. Hannah and Marianne would go off to Switzerland, Teddy back to Cambridge to take up lives utterly remote from hers. All she had to go back to was school in Banbridge. Boring old school. And no Hannah to share it with. Never again to cycle down the hill with her. Never again complain about the teachers they didn't like. Never again go sketching with her and Ma in the pony and trap. Soon Hannah would be Lady Cleeve, living in a big house somewhere in Gloucestershire.

She cried till she was exhausted, then she washed her face in cold water and carefully wrapped up her completed film ready to go to the post in the morning.

After the tears and kisses, the embraces and last-minute messages, the coach journey and the long hours in a stuffy train, all three Hamiltons were grateful for the cool and relative quiet of the ship. They ate supper silently and went to their cabins early, each of them absorbed in thoughts that arced backwards and forwards across the wide stretch of calm, grey sea that divided their lives from their own past, and now from another life in Gloucestershire.

In the early hours of the morning Sarah woke and lay listening to the unfamiliar noises of the ship, the slight creak of movement, the sudden muffled thumps and bangs from the decks below. A dim, misty dawn filtered through the salt-sprayed porthole of the cabin. She eyed it carefully. Even if the Irish coast were in sight, there wasn't enough light for what she wanted. She'd wait a while before she risked waking Hannah, who was fast asleep in the lower bunk.

Somewhere, miles away across the water, her father, Jamie and Sam would be getting up early to come and meet them.

She could imagine them standing on the quay at the very same spot from where they'd waved goodbye so many weeks ago. No Elizabeth and Hugh this time. Hugh had had his operation. Elizabeth had written to Ma some time ago and said it had been successful, but he'd been away four weeks already and they still didn't know when he'd be home. She wasn't sure Elizabeth had told them exactly what was happening.

Well, if Elizabeth and Hugh were to miss their homecoming, all the more reason to record it for them. She lay thinking about the pictures she might take as they came up the lough. She wondered if the throbbing of the ship would create camera shake. No Teddy to ask now, she thought, with a small stab of sadness. In a year's time, he would be her brother. She was going to miss him as much as she would miss Hannah and Marianne.

What she really wanted were the pictures of the harbour you could only get from the ship as she slowed right down to manoeuvre into her berth. But even if she were moving slowly, angles would change quickly, so she'd need to be in just the right place to catch the moment she wanted. She tried to remember exactly what she'd seen as they'd left and where on the deck she'd need to be. It was hard to recall the details of their departure now, it seemed such a long, long time ago. They'd walked round the upper decks with Elizabeth and Hugh, and Jamie had taken charge. She could hear his sharp, light tones.

'That's my drawing office down there,' he'd said, pointing to a one-storey building.

'And where's *your* ship, Jamie?' she'd asked.

'Over there,' he'd replied, not even bothering to look at her.

'So that's the *Oceanic,* is it?' Hugh had asked, gripping the rail, as he leant out for a better view of the forest of spars and planks that enfolded an invisible shape of enormous height and length.

'Well, it's the keel. That's where we start,' Jamie said, laughing. 'She's not due for launching till late '98 or early '99, you know.'

Jamie had got well into his stride then, telling them all the details of the ship. How long she was and how high. What engines she was going to have. He was not at all pleased when Hannah cried out suddenly.

'Look everyone. Look up there.'

She was pointing her finger towards the top of the central spine of a tall, three-masted barque berthed further down channel.

Sarah had spotted the small figure right away, but her mother couldn't see him until her father told her which mast Hannah was pointing at and whereabouts on it to look.

'My goodness, ye'd need to have a head for that, wou'dn't ye?' he said, as they all watched the lithe figure climbing steadily up the rigging.

'How high would that be, Jamie?' Sam asked thoughtfully, his eyes never leaving the small, dark shape.

'Probably about two hundred feet. They need a huge amount of sail to make any speed at all,' he said nonchalantly.

'But it would look magnificent under full sail,' said Elizabeth. 'It must carry a lot of canvas. I've never seen so much rigging before.'

'Oh, we see them all the time,' said Jamie, scarcely managing to show even a polite interest. 'They still bring grain from Australia and non-perishable stuff that doesn't need refrigerator ships. Anything so long as speed doesn't matter. But I can't see them surviving long myself.'

'A pity,' said Hugh, studying the tracery of ropes and rigging. 'They're very handsome, but I suspect the working conditions are very harsh compared with steamships.'

She'd smiled at Hugh then and he'd smiled back. Since they'd been friends again, they'd talked a great deal about working conditions in the mills and all sorts of other employments. He'd promised to lend her the Factory Inspector's Reports when she came back from Gloucestershire, so she could see for herself the problems that were known and being addressed and the ones that hadn't yet been picked up. Poor Hugh. Ma did say he'd been through a lot. But then so had Ma, and she was all right now.

She climbed down from her bunk, peered through the porthole and saw the solid grey line of the Down coast beyond the gleaming mass of gently oscillating water. She managed to dress without waking Hannah, picked up her camera and went up on deck.

There was no one else there, but as she leant over the rail she saw navy-clad figures moving on the deck below among barrels and boxes and huge coils of rope. She watched carefully, worked out what they were doing, framed them in her viewfinder. After ten minutes or so, she leant over the rail as far as she dared and shouted down to them.

'Excuse me. Please would you do that again, but a bit more slowly.'

'Aye, surely,' came the reply, as one of the two men caught sight of her. 'But watch out, Miss. Yer man Charlie's face might break yer wee box o' tricks,' he said, nodding his head at the older man.

She took her picture, thanked them, then peered into the mist ahead. Even as she watched, the muffling white presence began to disperse as the sun rose into a clear sky and laid a glittering golden swathe across the ruffled water in their wake. The distant shores had moved closer. Suddenly there were seagulls all around them, swooping and diving, their cries startling in the pearly quiet of the morning.

There was detail now, church spire and mill chimney, the white splashes of cottages amidst sloping fields on the Antrim side. On the Down side she picked out a lighthouse, a great mansion with gardens running down to the shore, a foundry with thick black smoke rising in the clear air and a train, close to the water's edge, its smoke floating upwards in white puffs like an Indian signal in a storybook.

'Hello, Sarah. You were up early,' Hannah said, slipping up to the rail beside her. 'Have you taken many pictures?'

'No, just a few. Not sure I won't get shake with the vibrations, but it's worth a try. It'll be better when we go into the lough. The ship has to slow down because of the erosion of the deep-water channel. That suits me,' she said grinning. 'I want a picture of that huge sailing ship we saw the night we left with the *Oceanic* behind her.'

'But won't she be gone?'

'Oh yes, I'm sure she will, but there'll probably be another one. Don't you remember Jamie said, "Oh, we see them all the time."' She caught his supercilious tone perfectly. 'He's got really pompous in the last year, but he's probably right about the sailing ships. *His* office *is* down on the quay near where they berth, so *he* should know.'

'Don't let him annoy you, Sarah,' Hannah said gently. 'He probably feels unsure of himself. When people aren't sure of themselves they often behave as if they know everything.'

Sarah stopped looking through her viewfinder and stared at her sister. She'd never heard her say anything like that before. Just the sort of thing their mother would say. Still, whatever the reason for Jamie's behaviour, she really couldn't stand him being so bossy.

There *was* a sailing ship berthed just where Sarah hoped it would be. Its deck was covered with small figures working with slings and ropes to hoist great loads of timber from deck to quay, while barrels and chests were being brought up from the hold in rope nets, swung like a shopping bag on a crooked finger. Sarah decided to forget about the *Oceanic*. She used up all her film on the sailing ship except for one last frame she was saving for Da and the boys waiting down on the quay.

'Did you get what you wanted, Sarah?' asked Rose, as she and Hannah came to join her where she was standing, camera in hand.

Their own vessel was much quieter now, the throb of the engines reduced to a distant hum, but seamen were still manhandling capstans and hawsers to secure her to the quay before the gangplank could be lowered.

'Yes, I did. But don't expect very much. We were juddering all the time,' she said, as they moved round the deck to watch the activity below and the people arriving to greet their friends and family.

'Still worth trying,' Rose said encouragingly. 'Teddy always said you had to make mistakes to see how to do it better.'

She ran her eye over the gathering crowd on the quay below her.

'I can't see Da and the boys anywhere,' she went on easily. 'Can either of you spot them? The stewardess told me the boat was very full last night. I suppose that's why there are so many people waiting.'

They watched as first one and then a second gangplank was rolled into place and two streams of people flowed steadily down to the quay to be greeted with hugs and kisses. In a surprisingly short time they dispersed and the quay was empty again, except for seamen and stewards going back and forth, up and down on the gangplanks.

'Perhaps Da and Sam have been delayed and Jamie's waiting for them at the Great Northern,' Rose said at last, when there was still no sign of them. 'I think we should go and have breakfast.'

'But would Da know where to find us?' asked Sarah, more than a hint of anxiety in her voice.

'Yes, of course. He'll come and ask the steward if we're still on board and we'll tell the steward that we'll be in the dining room.'

Breakfast was good and Sarah was ravenous. Rose did her best to eat, but she didn't feel very hungry. It was not like John to be late, however early the hour. He never minded getting up at six, or even five, if the job needed it, and he'd assured her he'd be waiting. Now she was about to come home, he'd owned up at last to how much he was missing her.

All the way through breakfast Sarah expected a familiar figure to appear in the doorway, speak a word to the steward and be directed towards their table. It would be wonderful if it was her father, or Sam, but even Jamie would do, though he was certainly not in her good books at the moment. But no one came.

By the time they finished breakfast, they were almost the

only people left in the dining room. They went back out on deck and looked around. The quay was empty of passengers and their families. The ship was settling to its morning routine, piles of sheets stacked in companionways, doors propped open for the cleaners. An hour had passed. There was now no question of lateness. Something had gone wrong. They would have to make their own way home.

'Right then,' said Rose. 'We'll need two porters and a cab to the Great Northern. Sarah, would you find the steward to deal with the cases while Hannah and I collect our hand luggage.'

They had to wait for a cab to be summoned to the quayside and then there was a long wait at the station for a train to Banbridge. The lovely morning that spilled its bright sunshine down on city streets and countryside just beginning to show the first hints of autumn did little to cheer them. Once they got to Banbridge, Sarah hurried across from the station to The Bunch of Grapes and found someone to collect up their luggage and drive them out to Ballydown. The last two miles of their long journey seemed the slowest of all, as they sat silent, all speculation pointless when the next mile would reveal all.

Rose found herself shaking with apprehension as she stepped down from the post chaise, leaving Hannah to pay the driver. She pushed open the gate and saw weeds poking out of her precious flower bed. The front door was open and a figure moved in the doorway. It was Sam. Sam with a bandage swathing his head, his leg in plaster, his arms gripping two crutches. He was smiling his usual warm, open smile as if nothing whatever were the matter.

'Sam dear, what *has* happened?' she cried, as he bent to kiss her.

'A bit of an accident, Ma. I'm none the worse,' he said reassuringly, as Sarah and Hannah came running up the path. 'Sorry I can't give Da and Jamie a hand with the luggage.'

He peered into the dazzling sunlight where the post-chaise stood at the gate, its driver beginning to unload the heavy cases.

'Sam dear, Da and Jamie aren't with us. We waited over an hour at the boat, but neither of them appeared. What time did Da leave to meet us?' asked Rose anxiously, as they all moved into the house.

Sarah wrinkled her nose. There was an unfamiliar smell and it wasn't very nice. She set down her small suitcase and saw the floor was covered with dust and crumbs.

'Da went off yesterday to Millbrook,' Sam explained, lowering himself cautiously into a chair and propping his crutches within reach. 'There was a bit of a fire. Not all that bad, I think. They got it in time, but he had to be there for the insurance people and the builders. He said he'd have to be there all evening to see to things so he'd stay overnight with the mill manager. Once he'd seen to the papers the manager needed, he'd get a bit of sleep and go up on the first train. Jamie was to meet him down on the quay. Sure, it's only a step from his office.'

Rose sighed. There was nothing they could do but wait. What had prevented John from getting to meet them could be anything from a rail delay to another outbreak of fire. As for Jamie, she had no idea what could have prevented him from meeting them, even if he had to go on to work immediately afterwards.

She took a deep breath, noticed an unpleasant smell that reminded her of unemptied chamber pots and wondered what had happened to Mrs Rea. She looked from Sarah to Hannah and towards the pile of suitcases now stacked by the front door.

'I think perhaps we should change our clothes and have a cup of tea while Sam tells us about his accident,' she began practically. 'I'm sure Da will be home as soon as he can manage it.'

Thirteen

'D'ye think I cou'd have a bite to eat, Ma?' Sam asked, hobbling after her into the dairy. 'I cou'den cut the bread standin' on my good leg.'

'How did you manage last night, Sam, when your father wasn't here?' she asked in turn, a look of horror on her face. 'If you couldn't cut bread on one leg you could hardly cook yourself bacon and eggs.'

'Ach, it was a bit of a joke,' he said, beaming at her. 'There was a big heel left in the bin, about two inches thick, and I found a lump of cheese. I cou'den carry it back into the kitchen, so I had to munch it leanin' against the sink,' he said, cheerfully.

Rose shook her head as another thought struck her.

'And how did you get upstairs on crutches, Sam?'

'Well, I thought about it,' he said with a soft laugh. 'An' I reckoned I stood a good chance of breakin' the other one, so I slept in the parlour,' he explained. 'I had a bit of luck, though. You'd left the sheet and blanket on the table, so I wrapped them round me an' stretched out on the couch.'

'The stove went out when the coal bucket was empty,' he went on. 'I can get about fine, but if I use my arms for the crutches, I've no hands for anythin' else. I never knew how handy legs were,' he laughed, as he eyed the plate of bread and jam Rose had made while he was talking.

They waited patiently while Sam devoured half the plateful and drank a full mug of tea.

'Well,' he said, sighing comfortably as Hannah refilled his mug, 'I can't tell you much. I was bendin' over the near-side wheel with an oil can an' I caught somethin' move in the corner of my eye. The next thing I knew I was lyin' on the ground bleedin', wi' m' leg broke. No one saw what happened 'cept wee Billy. You remember Billy, don't you, Ma? The wee lad usta be one of the flagmen?'

Rose nodded quickly, as his sisters urged him to go on.

'Well, he said one of the empty wagons started rollin' and I jumped outa the way, but it caught the back leg. He heard the crack, he says. He told the boss about my leg when he came out of his office, but the boss paid no attention till him. He just got out the kit and bandaged my head. But Billy ran away up the hill to Rathdrum for Da and he came an' took me straight over to yer man Stewart in Dromore,' he went on, pausing to lower half the contents of his mug. 'He said the leg was broke sure enough and he set it right away. We were powerful lucky he was there. He'd just come in to his dinner an' wou'da been away again in a few more minits. He asked after you, Ma, an' said Miss Sinton told him you were enjoyin' your holiday and feelin' better. He was real pleased about that,' he added, turning back to his bread and jam.

'But when did the accident happen, Sam?' Sarah burst out, her eyes grown wider as she listened to his story.

'The day's Saturday, isn't it? Well, then it was this day two weeks.'

'Two weeks ago,' Rose repeated, taken aback. 'And what have you been doing to amuse yourself when Da's been at work?' she asked, shocked at the thought of him hobbling around for that length of time.

'I've read every book in the parlour from the Bible to the *Children's Encyclopaedia* and half the novels forby,' he said, grinning. 'I liked *Pride and Prejudice* right well, but then I'd seen the play, so it was easier to get the hang of it than some of the others.'

Rose looked at Sam and smiled to herself. There was something about his irrepressible good humour that was utterly endearing. It wasn't every young man who would ask for so little attention.

'So why didn't you tell me what happened when you wrote?'

'Sure, I knew you'd worry,' he said promptly. 'Da and I discussed it and I said there was no need to trouble you, it was only a matter of weeks before I was back to work and none the worse. It mighta been different if it hadn't been for Doctor Stewart, but sure we knew not to go to the man in Banbridge,' he said, polishing off the last of his bread and jam.

Rose smiled and said nothing. He was quite right. Until she'd seen him for herself, she'd certainly have worried. The news would have cast a very different light on that last week when they'd celebrated Hannah and Teddy's engagement every day.

'Sam, dear,' she began, as one thought led to another. 'What's happened to Mrs Rea? Is she all right?'

'Aye, she's fine. She'd some relative ill, so she went to see to them. When she came back, she said she'd been offered a good place if she could take it right away. Da said she must go, for she'd been good to us an' we all knew she'd not be needed long once you were back.'

'And when was that, Sam?' asked Hannah, whose eye had been lingering on the cobwebs and the dark patina of the unwashed floor.

'About a month ago,' he said vaguely. 'It must have been just before Elizabeth and Hugh went off. Da and I managed fine until I broke the leg. We were going to have a good clean-up for you comin' home, but there's been one thing after another at the mills. Da's been back and forth every time anythin' goes wrong.'

'Sam, what about Dolly? Has she had breakfast?' Sarah demanded.

'Dolly's fine. Don't worry. The grass is good after all the rain and Da left her hay yesterday. She'll not go hungry. But she's lonely. She comes runnin' whenever she hears me clumpin' along,' he said, looking from one to the other. 'I think she's missed ye.'

'Could we go now, Ma? Just for a minute?' asked Sarah. 'Then we'll come back and see what jobs you want us to do.'

'All right. Don't be very long. I may need you to go down to MacMurray's or into town for some shopping,' warned Rose, whose first glance at the larder and store cupboards had not been encouraging.

A little later, when Sam had hobbled off to the privy, Rose heard footsteps at the door. Thinking it was the girls, she stepped back into the kitchen. She was just in time to see John come over the threshold.

'Ach, Rose dear,' he said, relief and joy written all over his face, as he strode across the room and put his arms round her.

'John dear, I'm so glad to see you,' she said, kissing him.

Only when he released her and held her at arm's length to look at her was she sure of what she'd glimpsed as he'd crossed the threshold, the worn and haggard look on his face.

'Why didn't you tell me, John, about Mrs Rea and then about Sam?' she asked gently.

His working trousers crinkled at the waist where he'd tightened his belt. He had most certainly lost weight.

'Aye, and that's not the half of it,' he said, sounding remarkably cheerful. 'Sure none of it matters now I have ye home an' ye lookin' so well. Where's all our family?' he went on, looking round the kitchen.

'Sam's in the privy after two mugs of tea,' she replied, laughing. 'Sarah and Hannah are away to say hello to Dolly.'

'And Jamie? Where's he?'

'I don't know, John,' she said slowly. 'He wasn't there to meet us. We waited an hour or more and then came on by ourselves.'

'Ach, Rose. Ach, Rose,' said John, his voice catching, 'what sort of a welcome home was that? When the fire sprung up again I thought to meself, well, at least Jamie's there to help them and warn them about Sam. Rose'll guess I coulden get away. Ach, Rose,' he repeated again, his face distraught.

'Never mind, love. I *was* worried when none of you were there, but I don't think we need be concerned about Jamie,' she said reassuringly. 'He might just have overslept if he was out on Friday night, or maybe he had some meeting first thing. He'd have known you and Sam were there.'

'But sure he knew about Sam,' replied John sharply. 'I told him about his accident when I wrote with the day and time to come to meet ye.'

Rose caught the look on John's face and was about to reply when two figures passed the front window.

'Da,' cried Sarah, flinging her arms round him as she and Hannah dashed into the kitchen. 'We didn't hear you,' she explained, breathless with excitement, as John hugged them both, 'but then Dolly whinnied and we heard Bess answer, so we knew it had to be you.'

'My goodness, yer both lookin' great,' said John. 'I suppose I'm lucky I amn't loosin' the both of you,' he said, slyly, as he glanced from one to the other, one daughter engaged to be married, the other no longer the lively schoolgirl he'd waved goodbye to two months ago.

'Sam, how are ye, son, did ye manage all right last night?' he asked anxiously, as Sam followed them more slowly. 'Sure I thought I'd have your mother and the girls back here in time to make your breakfast. But ye can never tell with fire,' he went on, shaking his head.

He sat down abruptly and pulled off his boots, which were spattered with ash and splashed with water.

'We all thought it was well doused, an' it was lookin' like rain forby. Then the next thing we know the nightwatchman was knockin' us up to tell us it had got goin' again.'

'What started it, Da?' asked Sam, as he lowered himself carefully into the other armchair.

'Oh, the usual,' John replied, the weariness obvious now in his voice. 'Always the same with an engine house. High temperature, dry air, fumes from the lubricating oils. A stray spark from somewhere. Possibly even spontaneous combustion. The afternoons have been hot even if the nights are gettin' cold, and the big double doors have to be kept closed at all times to stop the childer gettin' in,' he said, looking up at them, as he stretched his feet backwards and forwards to ease them.

'That's in the rules now, about the doors, an' right and proper too, for the sake of the wee lads and lasses that know no better than to sneak in for a look an' then get hurt. But closed doors means bad ventilation,' he summed up, as he got to his feet and hunted for a pair of shoes.

When Rose found out how few hours of sleep John had had the previous night she persuaded him to go and lie on the bed while she set about getting some lunch. With everyone already hungry from either a very early start or no breakfast, or both, she looked more carefully at the larder. Apart from half a baker's loaf that smelt mouldy, even if it didn't show any very obvious signs, the only other item in there was some bacon with a very strong smell and two eggs. She'd used the last of the milk when they'd made a fresh pot of tea for John.

She smiled to herself as she went out to the stable in search of potatoes, thinking of lunches at Ashley Park. Homely enough meals, a shepherd's pie or cold meats, but always beautifully served, with vegetables straight in from the garden and bowls of fresh fruit for dessert.

To her great relief there were potatoes in the sack, though some of them had sprouted in the heat. She gathered up what she needed, collected a handful of scallions from the patch by the back door and went back into the dairy where Sarah was scrubbing the stained Belfast sink.

'What next, Ma?' she asked, rinsing away the scouring powder.

'MacMurray's. You'd better both go. Three pints of milk, a dozen eggs, two pounds of butter, or whatever they can spare. Take my purse in case we owe them for what Young Bill's been delivering.'

By noon, Sam had peeled all the potatoes, Rose had fine-chopped the scallions and Sarah and Hannah had arrived back with everything she'd asked for together with the local news as well. When John tramped back downstairs in his socks, he sniffed appreciatively.

'Man, that smell's good. We made champ a couple o' times, diden we, Sam? But it diden smell as good as that.'

'Come on then, come to the table. I've made plenty, for there's no bread and no cheese. Does anyone want a glass of milk?'

She served a pale green mound, topped with a generous knob of butter, on to each plate. Silence reigned for some minutes until Hannah and Sarah paused to deliver the news from MacMurray's.

'Michael says the price of butter has dropped again,' said Sarah, between mouthfuls. 'There's so much coming in from New Zealand the packing station says they can't compete in price.'

'And he's worried about his potatoes,' added Hannah sympathetically. 'He says he's sprayed a second time, but he's heard rumours from the west coast they've had blight, but no one is letting on. If he loses his potatoes on top of the drop in his butter money . . .'

Hannah paused as a figure appeared in the doorway, knocking on it politely as if it were not wide open.

'Billy, how are ye?' called John. 'Come on in.'

'No, I'll no disturb ye at yer meal,' said Billy, coming in and handing Sam an envelope. 'Are ye doin' rightly, Sam?' he asked, as Sam put down his fork, took the large envelope and looked at it curiously.

'The best at all, Billy,' replied Sam promptly. 'Is this my pay?'

'Aye, I wou'd think so. I'll come up one evenin' in the week,' he said, nodding at Rose and John and shyly avoiding Hannah and Sarah. 'Be seein' ye,' he called cheerfully over his shoulder as he darted off.

'That was good of him to come up with yer pay, Sam,' said John warmly. 'An' he came last week as well.'

'He's a good sort, wee Billy, though he hasn't much hands for anythin',' said Sam, as he continued to stare at the unfamiliar envelope. 'He was lucky to get the job sweepin' up when the flagmen all went. His da wasn't so lucky, I hear he's lookin' for work yet.'

'That's near a year now,' said John, as he held out his plate for a second helping. 'Does his ma work?'

'Aye, she's in the bleach works with one of his sisters, but the wee sister's only a half-timer,' he said, as he finally tore open the envelope.

A small shower of coins fell on the table, some of them running on their edges till they encountered the milk jug. They collapsed with a small clatter as Sam drew out of the envelope some grubby banknotes and a battered brown card. He stared at the card open mouthed and then looked from John to Rose and back again.

'What's that, Sam?' Sarah burst out, staring at him across the table.

Sam looked inside the envelope again, but there was nothing there.

'Is that what I think it is?' he asked flatly, as he handed the brown card to his father.

John took it from his hand, glanced at it and pressed his lips together.

'Aye, it is,' he said, nodding grimly. 'I'd never have thought yer man Thompson capable of doin' that, an' you there from the minit ye left school,' he said quietly, as he pushed away his plate. 'I'm not sure he can do this to you, Sam, an' I'll make it my business to find out. Whatever happens we'll get over it somehow. Now finish your dinner like a good man. It's not the end of the world.'

Sam picked up his fork and made an attempt to finish his champ. Through no fault of his own, he had lost the job he'd dreamt of since he was a little boy. Sarah could see his eyes glittering with moisture as he bent over his plate. The look on his face she'd never forget.

However concerned she might be for Sam, Rose knew an immediate visit to Banbridge was essential. While John was saddling up Dolly and backing her between the shafts of the trap, she had a word with Sarah and Hannah in the dairy.

'Now, don't exhaust yourselves trying to do everything that needs doing,' she warned, as she saw them don aprons. 'The most important thing is the larder. It needs a good scrub before I get back. I don't think they've had clean sheets for about a month and there's a chamber pot somewhere. Don't start scrubbing the kitchen floor, just give it a sweep and we'll do it a bit at a time, and don't leave Sam on his own. Find him a job he can do sitting down. Poor love, I've never seen him so upset.'

'Ma, is Jamie coming tomorrow?' Hannah asked, as Rose collected her purse and shopping bags.

'Well, I'd have thought so, given he couldn't come this morning. Why, love?'

'Oh, it's just . . . I was thinking, if I'm off to Dublin next Saturday, I won't see him for nearly a year if he doesn't.'

'Gracious, Hannah, you're quite right. I think I've lost a weekend somewhere,' she said, peering at the calendar over the sink. 'Yes, next weekend is the *first* weekend in September. You leave London for Zurich the *second* weekend in September, but you've got to get to London first. What a good thing you reminded me.'

While Rose was reluctant to go shopping on her first afternoon at home, Dolly was quite delighted to be trotting along the main road on a fine, sunny afternoon. Already the lime trees were showing patches of pale, yellow leaves, the chestnuts had hints of pink, and the mountain ashes were hung with clumps of red berries, bright as beads.

'I didn't tell Jamie about Hannah and Teddy,' John said, turning to her as they bowled along. 'I thought she'd maybe like to tell him herself.'

'So he doesn't know she's going away again?' she said thoughtfully.

'No, but he knows his brother's in plaster, an' he hasn't been to see him,' he said, without taking his eyes off the road.

Rose sighed. Clearly Jamie's behaviour had not pleased his father while she'd been away, for almost everything John said about him was edged with sharpness. She could see he was still upset by Jamie's failure to turn up at the quay that morning. It was, after all, only a few hundred yards from where he worked and a mere hour before his usual time.

'Can we depend on him comin' tomorrow, d'you think?'

John asked, when Rose explained about Hannah's departure date.

'No, I don't think we can,' she said slowly. 'Maybe this was his Saturday morning off, the one he gets every two months or so. He might be away cycling with his friends over the weekend.'

'Then he might very well have let me know,' he retorted promptly. 'I wrote last Sunday tellin' him when ye'd be arrivin' and suggestin' where we'd meet, convenient for him. He had a whole week to drop me a line,' he said, his tone aggrieved.

'Would he get a telegram this late in the day if we sent it right away?'

'Ach, I couldn't rightly tell you. An' sure if he's not at his lodgings we'd still be none the wiser.'

They drove on, turning over the problem Jamie's silence had created for them.

'There's nothing for it,' said John, some time later, as he swung the heavy shopping baskets up into the trap. 'I may away up to Belfast meself an' see what's going on. Far better a couple of hours now than sittin' wonderin' tomorrow, is he or isn't he comin',' he went on, seeing her troubled look. 'Are ye sure ye'll be all right with Dolly. She's a bit fresh still.'

'I'll be fine,' Rose assured him, as he handed her the reins. 'Bring him back with you if you can. Sam could do with a bit of company.'

'Aye, I'll do that. Mind yerself now. I'll be back as soon as I can.'

She watched him stride away towards the station, turned Dolly in the busy street and wondered if it was really this morning she'd wakened up in a ship's cabin, a stewardess offering her a cup of tea. It seemed now almost as far away as the beginning of the summer.

John was no more successful in meeting up with Jamie than Sam had been on the February evening when Rose had taken ill, but in broad daylight, on a pleasant August day, he did succeed in gaining admission to the tall, red-brick house. The proprietress, a dignified woman who prided herself on the superiority of her establishment, ushered him into the young gentlemen's empty parlour, but did not invite him to be seated.

She confirmed that young Mr Hamilton had been out late on the previous evening and had not appeared at breakfast. He had been at lunch, however, and had then set off with some of the other young gentlemen for a tea party, to be followed by supper and dancing. Naturally, she had not enquired where this entertainment was to be held, but one of her staff had mentioned Helen's Bay, a favourite location for the senior management at Harlands.

She provided John with a pencil and a sheet of paper upon which to leave a message, after which she wished him good afternoon.

'What exactly did you say in your note, John?' Rose asked next morning, as she rubbed rosemary over a shoulder of lamb.

'Ach, I can't exactly mind,' he admitted, leaning against the wall of the dairy, watching her. 'I said you were sorry not to see him yesterday and we'd be expecting him for dinner. Something like that. With yer woman standin' over me as if I were goin' to pinch the silver, I had the dickens own job to think what to put. But I'd say he'll come.'

Jamie was angry his father's note mentioned his failure to turn up at the docks. As he read it over and over again, what made him angrier still was what he took to be an order to come home the following day because his mother and sisters wanted to see him. He was so furious at this intrusion into his weekend plans, he considered ignoring the note altogether. But by the time he'd finished breakfast he decided he'd have to go.

As every mile passed, he thought of the young managers he should have been meeting that afternoon at Waterside, the large, elegant home of his immediate superior. All he could think of was the wasted opportunity. He would be twenty-one in October, his apprenticeship complete. Now his whole attention was focused on the next critical step, Junior Manager. The warm sunshine of early autumn was lost on him as he strode out of the station, his resentment growing with every stride.

Rose was checking the table in the parlour when she heard footsteps on the garden path. She cast a final glance at the six places laid with the best china, the cutlery Sam had polished so devotedly and the small posy of flowers Hannah had made up from florets of delphinium. She paused, suddenly uneasy. Reverting to a habit out of the long past, she smoothed her skirt, as she'd done throughout all her years of service whenever she went to answer a bell.

'Jamie, how lovely to see you,' she said, crossing the kitchen and embracing him warmly.

'You're looking well, Ma,' he said, glancing round the room as she released him.

'And so are you, Jamie. Very smart indeed,' she said honestly.

Hannah was mending Sam's working trousers while Sarah had just finished peeling and slicing the apples for the pudding. Sam had put down his newspaper. The first greetings over, all three observed their brother as he stood awkwardly by the kitchen table.

'Where's Da?' he said casually, addressing his mother.

'He's just gone up to Rathdrum to see to Bess, he'll be back shortly,' she said, doing her best to make him feel easy. 'Would you like some lemonade, Jamie, it must have been warm walking out from the station?'

'No thanks, Ma, don't bother. I'm used to it. I do a lot of walking.'

Rose collected up the prepared apples and felt acutely the unease his presence had produced all around her. Apart from the hellos she'd half heard in the parlour, she hadn't registered another exchange between the four young people.

Sarah stood up and wiped her hands on her apron.

'Would you like to see the pictures we brought back from our visit?'

'Oh yes. What a good idea,' he said, a hint of humouring in his tone.

Rose wiped and dried the kitchen table and Sarah collected her precious album from the parlour and pulled up two chairs side by side. Jamie sat down and nodded as she turned the pages and explained who the people were and where each of the pictures had been taken. Sam watched them, listening attentively. Having spent much of the previous afternoon studying the photographs for himself, he knew exactly what Sarah was describing. Hannah appeared completely absorbed in her mending, the pretty ring on her engagement finger occasionally catching the light.

Jamie said very little. 'That's good of Ma,' he volunteered at one point. 'So that's Lady Anne, is it?' he added later. But mostly Sarah had to be content with nods and grunts.

She didn't tell him she'd taken the pictures herself, and he showed no curiosity whatever about them. Only when they came to the last pages and he spotted the picture of Hannah and Teddy under the rose-covered arch did he throw out a sudden sharp question.

'So, who's the boyfriend, Hannah?' he said, looking across at her.

'He's not a boyfriend, Jamie,' she answered quietly. 'He's my fiancé. We'll be getting married next year when I come back from Switzerland,' she added coolly, catching his eye for a brief moment.

'Switzerland?' he said, even more sharply. 'What on earth are you going there for?'

'You could call it job training, if you like,' she said steadily. 'You're learning to build ships, I'm going to learn how to run an establishment.'

'You mean a finishing school, don't you?' he retorted, an ill-suppressed sneer in his tone.

'If you like,' she said easily.

'Ach, hullo, Jamie,' said John, as he strode into the kitchen and saw the two figures seated side by side at the table. 'It's great to see you,' he added, as Jamie stood up and took his outstretched hand. 'I hope we're not puttin' out yer plans for today,' he went on agreeably, 'but we'd a bit o' news we thought we ought to celebrate.'

'So I've just heard,' said Jamie flatly, staring at Hannah, the tiny wink of diamonds catching his eye now he knew where to look.

Rose came in from the dairy with a pie dish in her hands. Hannah dropped her sewing to bend down and open the oven door for her. The smell of roasting lamb filled the kitchen.

'Not long now, everyone. Are you all hungry?' she asked, glad to see Sarah had managed to get Jamie to sit down.

She gave John a reassuring glance. Last night, in the privacy of their own bed, he'd admitted he never knew what to do to be right with young Jamie. He was doing his best now, but he wasn't getting a great deal of help from Jamie.

As she went back to the dairy, she heard John ask about the production schedule on the *Oceanic.* Whipping cream for the apple pie, she learnt that a launch date had been proposed for January '99, by which time Jamie hoped to be a Junior Manager. There was another silence and then she heard Jamie asking Sam when he hoped to be back at work. She caught the sharp note in Sarah's voice as she asked Jamie about compensation for injury in the shipyards. At least twelve men a year died in accidents and dozens were injured, particularly by falling rivets, she said. But Jamie didn't appear to know anything about such matters.

It was a relief to everyone when Rose called them to the table and she and Hannah set about serving the sizzling roast with a rich gravy and fresh vegetables from the garden.

'Nothin' like your mother's good home cookin',' eh, Jamie?' said John pleasantly, as he observed how quickly he cleared his plate.

'No, not on an apprentice's wage,' he replied, coolly.

'Well, you won't be on that for much longer, will you, love?' Rose offered, aware of John's uneasy movement by her side.

'No, thank goodness. It's only two months now till I'm twenty-one.'

'And a year and five months till *your* ship is launched,' said Sarah abruptly.

'All being well,' he replied dubiously. 'Assuming your friend Lord Ashley and his like don't manage to sell us out to Dublin with another Home Rule Bill. If he does, I can tell you it'll be the end of the yards in Belfast. Harlands looked for space on the Mersey the last time there was one and they'd do the same again. But what would he care if ten thousand loyal Protestants lost their jobs?'

There was a moment's stunned silence.

'And what about the five hundred Catholics that do most of the dirty work?' Sarah demanded promptly.

'That's their lookout,' he said turning and facing her. 'Ulster is Protestant and we don't need idle Catholics to take up jobs when we could find better men to do them.'

'Are you suggestin', Jamie,' said John slowly and carefully, 'that a Catholic worker is not the equal of a Protestant?'

'Yes, I am,' he replied quickly. 'There's nothing but trouble with the Catholics in the yard. We'd be far better off without them.'

'Do you not think some of the trouble might arise from the way they're treated?' demanded Sarah, turning in her seat to stare at him.

Rose looked across the table and saw the determined look on Jamie's face. If he'd set out deliberately to provoke his father he couldn't have made a better start. She moved her knee cautiously to touch John's, hoping a gentle reminder of her presence would steady him.

'Is that what they teach you in the Lodge, Jamie?' said Sam in a conversational tone as he finished up the last morsel on his plate.

Rose and John stared at Sam in amazement.

'Lodge?' Rose repeated incredulously. 'Have *you* joined a Lodge, Jamie?' she asked, looking at him directly.

'Yes, I have,' he replied firmly. 'The Orange Order is the only organization with any sense. They see the way the wind's blowing. If we loyal Protestants don't look out for ourselves, you'll have a bunch of Catholic farmers in power in Dublin with no knowledge of industry and no interest in anything but their own problems,' he went on, addressing himself to John and Sam and pointedly ignoring everyone else.

'Did you tell them your grandfather was a Catholic when they made you a member, Jamie?' Hannah asked quietly. 'Did you mention that your uncles and aunts are Catholic? And all your cousins? That some of them are even farmers who do happen to be poor however hard they work?' she went on, her tone growing ever colder.

'That's hardly going to bother you, Hannah,' Jamie burst out. 'You're making sure *you'll* never be poor. Da puts you in a silk dress and Ma gets you a rich husband and they leave me to walk to my work, with not enough money to buy a round of drinks.'

'That's enough, Jamie,' John shouted, getting to his feet. 'You'll apologize to your sister for what you've just said. If you're short of money, it's your own fault. Haven't I asked you every time you've come home if you needed anythin', forby payin' your lodgin's and the bill for the suits, and the shoes and so on? What you get for your pocket from Harlands is more than I earned when your mother and I had you and Hannah and your Granny to keep. How wou'd I know it wasn't enough, unless you tell me?' he asked, sitting down as Rose put a hand on his.

'I shouldn't have to come begging,' he shot back. 'Did Sarah and Hannah have to come crawling to you for all their smart dresses?'

'No, Jamie, they didn't,' Rose said quietly. 'But it was clear what was needed and we did make most of them ourselves. If you'd told us what *you* needed, you could have had it. Have we ever refused you anything if we could give it to you?' she asked, trying to keep her voice calm and steady.

'No, you haven't,' he said grudgingly. 'But you don't seem very interested in *my* well-being and my career. All I hear about when I come home is your grand friends up the hill and across the water.'

'We don't need to ask about *your* career, Jamie,' said Sarah furiously, 'you tell us about it all the time. All you can think of is Junior Manager,' she went on, 'and who's useful and who's not. I suppose you joined the Lodge to get in with the right people.'

Rose shot her a warning glance, but the idea that Ma had got Hannah a rich husband had made Sarah hopping mad and she wasn't finished yet.

'You haven't apologized to Hannah,' she said, her eyes flashing with fury. 'Or to Ma or Da. You've said horrible things about Da putting her in a silk dress and Ma getting her a husband. As if Ma would do such a thing even if Hannah needed her to. Come on, Jamie, we're all waiting,' she insisted, fastening her two bright eyes upon him.

'Why should I apologize to anyone? I'm entitled to my own opinions,' he said, glaring round the table. 'You're all so comfortable, living out here in the countryside, eating good dinners and going away on holidays to these English aristocrats that don't give tuppence for us here in the north. Where would the province be without the hard work of people in industry to prop up agriculture in places like this?' he demanded, his voice hectoring and bitter. 'Where will you all be if the likes of me and my friends don't try to hold on to our Protestant birthright? You'll not be so comfortable, or have life so easy, if we end up with Home Rule. You're just sitting back leaving the struggle to someone else,' he said, glaring from Sam to his father, and back again, ignoring the fact that it was Sarah who had challenged him.

'You and Sam ought to be standing up for what Protestants have achieved in the north and not sitting back taking your ease.'

'Does it ever occur to you, Jamie, there might be some other way of lookin' at things?' said John, with an effort of control.

'No, it doesn't. There's no two ways of looking at what's happening in this province. There's only those who see the truth and those who can't or won't take the trouble to see for themselves. You've only to read your newspaper to see Redmond getting in with the likes of Ashley and Altrincham, and Salisbury no match whatever for their manoeuvring.'

'What do you know about Lord Ashley, Jamie, except what you want to think?' Sarah demanded witheringly. 'He's been working half the summer with the Congested Districts Board to help poor people in the west, people like Ma's parents, who haven't enough land to make a living, who starve when there's blight and get evicted if there's no one to stand up for them. Do you care nothing about anyone else but yourself? You've been lucky. You wouldn't even have survived to be in Harlands if it wasn't for Ma and Da working to keep you fed and James Sinton paying your apprenticeship money when Ma and Da hadn't got it. But you've forgotten that, haven't you? We'd still be living in a two-roomed cottage opposite the forge if it wasn't for Ma and Da. We were *poor*, Jamie. *Poor.* Have you forgotten that?'

'Well, we'll all be poor again if your fine friends get their way with all of you to encourage them,' he said, springing to his feet so violently he knocked his chair over. 'And I'm not staying here to be lectured by a chit of a schoolgirl. Catch yourselves on, for God's sake, before it's too late,' he said, as he shoved the fallen chair out of his way, pushed past behind Hannah and Sam and banged the parlour door as he left.

There was a moment's silence before they heard his feet on the road.

Sarah looked from Rose to John, unrepentant, but distressed by the look on their faces.

'Sarah, would you run after him with the cake?' Rose said, abruptly.

'Where is it?'

'Wrapped up ready in the larder.'

Sarah picked up Jamie's fallen chair, slipped behind Hannah and Sam and out into the kitchen. A few moments later they caught a glimpse of her flying past the parlour window.

Rose studied the floral border on her dinner plate and knew there was nothing she could have done, even without Sarah's intervention. John might have tried to argue. He might have told the story of the Orange intimidation that took away his job with Thomas Scott and forced him to look for any work that would keep them fed. He might have recalled the violence in Belfast when Mary Wylie's sister, Peggy, saw her young husband killed outside their own front door.

There would have been no point in any of it. He would have dismissed his father's views as old-fashioned. Only *he* had the true story, the real insight into the affairs of the day. She thought of the twelve-year-old who'd got them out of a runaway train, carried his little sister when she was exhausted and pumped spring water so vigorously for his thirsty family he'd splashed them all. That was another Jamie in another life. That Jamie was as dead as if he were buried in Grange churchyard.

Hannah was stacking the dinner plates and John was still staring at the empty place when they heard Sarah come back. They waited silently until she came into the parlour.

'I'll never speak to him again,' she burst out, tears streaming down her face, as she put a well-wrapped package in front of her mother. 'He didn't want to take it, and when I said you'd got up early to bake it for him before the roast went in, he took it from me and threw it in the ditch.'

Fourteen

'What are we gonna do, Rose?'

Standing with her arms round Sarah, steadier now but still crying, she heard John's voice as if from a long way away. She gave Sarah a kiss, asked her to go and make a cup of tea and suddenly found herself back in her childhood, the noise and smell of demolished cottages all around her, her father's voice echoing in her ears. Whenever her father couldn't solve his problem by hard work or devotion to his family, when all else failed him, he had always turned to her mother with those very words.

Now it was her turn to find an answer for her man. They were not being evicted from their home, but suddenly, out of the blue, they were facing hurt and loss. She knew now Jamie had come home unwillingly and, having come, he'd been confronted by a decision. His family and its history was an embarrassment to him, so he had rejected them. Whatever the future might open, here on this sunlit August afternoon, Jamie, who had been dear to them, had been lost, not through death, which had its proper rituals of mourning, but by a deliberate rejection that left a bitter, private grief to be made known only to the closest of friends.

'First, we're going to have a quick cup of tea,' she began with an encouraging smile as she looked down at him in the chair beside her. 'Then we're all going to go down to Corbet Lough while the sun's out. We'll see if the swans are there. I've a bit of stale bread for them,' she said, dropping a hand on his shoulder and squeezing it.

It was difficult getting Sam up into the trap, and once he was safely settled there wasn't much room left, so Sarah and

Hannah went for their bicycles. They rode down the hill behind the trap, with sunlight firing the red of the berries in the hedgerows.

The air was warm but there was a hint of the freshness of autumn. The light had that particular clarity they'd not see again till the spring. For the first time in her life Sarah asked herself how an afternoon could be so lovely when they were all so unhappy. When Da was at work, Hannah on her way to London and Sam standing on his crutches looking across at MacMurray's cattle, she'd ask her mother and see what she said.

Meantime, the swans had appeared accompanied by a number of dirty-looking cygnets. She watched the slow, stately glide of the adult birds and wondered whether she could get a picture if she brought her camera down to the shore one day after school.

Rose woke early next morning and couldn't go back to sleep. She lay with her eyes closed, her mind already running through the list of things she ought to get started on immediately after breakfast. There were Thank You letters to be written by each of them to Lady Anne. A stack of sheets that would need bleaching before they could be washed. Hannah hadn't nearly enough underwear for ten months in Switzerland and it looked as if she'd need at least three more everyday dresses. Sarah would certainly have to have a new school pinafore before school started, for she'd grown taller and more shapely in the last months. The whole house needed cleaning and the garden was full of weeds.

She went through the list again and wondered whether Elizabeth and Hugh might arrive home this week. At the thought of Elizabeth, Rose opened her eyes. She'd have to be told about Jamie. Like a dark cloud blotting out the sun, the memory of yesterday's spoilt celebration moved across her mind and swallowed up her energy and her enthusiasm.

'Is there nothin' we can do, Rose?' John had said the previous evening, staring into the fire, after he'd helped Sam negotiate the stairs and Sarah and Hannah had both said goodnight.

'Well, we could try writing to him.'

'What would we say?'

'We could say that many a family has had to cope with strongly differing viewpoints,' she began sadly. 'It's hardly a new problem in this part of the world. It's not impossible to agree to differ,' she continued. 'There were times when Sam and I nearly fell out over the Land League, especially when Harrington got shot at. But we managed to stay friends.'

'Aye, I remember you were hard enough on him in some of your letters,' he said, nodding. 'What else would we say to Jamie?'

'Well, we could reassure him he's just as valued as the other three,' she said slowly. 'He seemed to me to be jealous of Hannah and Sarah, and even poor old Sam in some way. It's as if they have something he wants and can't have, and he resents them for it.'

'He was powerful angry about the girls' dresses,' said John abruptly. 'Am I mistaken, or did his last two suits not cost more than the dresses?'

'A great deal more,' she agreed easily. 'Tailoring is far more expensive than needlework. Besides, we made all but the best dresses at home and pretty fabric is nothing compared to broadcloth or tweed.'

'So it's not just about money, d'you think?'

'No, I think that's just something he's hanging on to,' she said, shaking her head sadly. 'But we could try to put that right if you like. We could say we were sorry there'd been a misunderstanding and send him money for the next two months. See what he says. If we apologize for our part, it would give him the chance to apologize for his.'

'Could we do that now? Then it could go back into Banbridge with the postman in the mornin'.'

'Would you sleep better if we wrote tonight?' she asked, glancing at the clock and looking at him.

When he nodded sheepishly, she went to the dresser and took out her writing materials. By the time she'd written and rewritten the letter and he'd drafted a cheque for fifty pounds, it was long past midnight and they were both grey with tiredness.

It was Sarah who solved the problem of Hannah's everyday dresses.

'Ma, why doesn't she have *my* new dresses?' she asked, when Rose spoke of shopping on Monday morning. 'I've not torn them or anything, and they'll only need the hems taken up a bit,' she said reasonably. 'We chose the material together, so you won't *hate* them, will you, Hannah?'

'No, of course not, they're all very pretty. I could just as easily have chosen them myself, but what about you, Sarah?'

'I won't need anything much once school starts,' she replied dismissively. 'I've got my blue silk in case the Queen invites me to go to one more of her Jubilee parties,' she said, grinning, 'but she must be fed up with them by now. If she gets any fatter, she'll burst.'

'Poor old Queen Victoria,' said Rose smiling. 'Some people can't help getting fatter as they get older,' she said gently. 'Do you really think your dresses will fit Hannah? If they do, we can replace them easily enough. It's being so short of time is the problem. We might manage one or two, but we just can't make three by Friday night.'

The dresses were duly tried on. For two girls who looked so very different, they fitted remarkably well, apart from the odd tuck and some extra turn-up on the hems. They were ready to pack by the end of the day.

On Tuesday, when they arrived home with Hannah's underwear and Sarah's new uniform, they found a letter from Elizabeth sitting on the table. She and Hugh would be arriving on Friday morning and would certainly be able to come and see them and wish Hannah well sometime later in the day. Rose put the letter down, breathed a sigh of relief and began to feel distinctly easier.

The first shock of Jamie's departure now behind her, John's mind eased by the letter they'd written together, and the prospect of being able to talk to her dear Elizabeth once more, Rose began to feel her spirits rise. With his sisters for company and all the sitting-down jobs she could find him, Sam, too, had begun to look more like his old self. Not surprisingly, she slept better on Tuesday night than on any night since she'd arrived home. She came downstairs on Wednesday morning ready to scrub the dairy, bake bread, help Hannah go through her clothes list in Jamie's empty room and weed the garden.

'Here ye are, Ma. Post,' said Sam, swinging expertly over the threshold and pausing by the table.

He fished down the front of his shirt and brought out a small pile of envelopes the postman had given him when he found him leaning on the field gate gazing at the misty blue outline of the mountains.

Only as he dropped them on the table did he see beneath a long, blue airmail a small, regular envelope with the thin black border that meant bad news.

'Oh, Sam, such very bad news,' she said, looking up at him, tears in her eyes. 'Thomas and Selina's wee girl. The poor little creature.'

'What's happened her, Ma?' he asked, his eyes wide with concern.

'She was playing outside the forge and a dog came up the lane,' she began, steadily enough. 'She put out her hand and it bit her. Sure, the bite was nothing and she was soon comforted, but when Thomas heard her cry and came and chased the dog away, he saw the foam around its jaws. He'd read in the paper about a rabid dog down at Annacramp, but he thought it had been reported to the police and shot. But it hadn't. So he knew the worst. She took three days to die,' she said, sitting down abruptly and bursting into tears.

'Ach Ma, that's desperate,' he said, dropping one hand awkwardly on her shoulder. 'An' Thomas dyin' about the wee thing. Sure he mentions her every time he writes.'

She nodded and wiped her tears on a corner of her apron.

'Your Granny Hannah used to say that children are only lent to you,' she said looking up at him. 'You have to give them back sooner or later, but two is much too soon. They'll be in a bad way,' she said, taking out her handkerchief. 'I'll have to write to them this afternoon.'

'Maybe there's better news from my uncle,' Sam said, nodding towards the familiar airmail envelope with its brightly coloured stamps.

Without considering at all, Rose reached for her brother's letter. As she lifted it, the remaining envelope lay revealed, smaller and squarer than the airmail, but more substantial than the delicate, black-edged missive. Her first glance told her it was addressed in her own hand to Mr Jamie Hamilton. She stared at it, puzzled by the strong, dark lines that had been drawn firmly through the Belfast address. To the right of the deleted address in a small, well-shaped hand she read: *Mr and Mrs John Hamilton, Ballydown, Corbet, Banbridge, County Down.*

Jamie had returned their letter unopened.

Rose decided that the very worst thing about bad news was having to pass it on. They were all sitting at lunch when John asked about the morning post. There was nothing for it but to tell him what everyone else already knew. Over little Sophie Scott he was upset and angry. He said a few harsh things about a police force that didn't know when to use a gun and neighbours who hadn't paid proper attention to such a real danger.

It was harder for her to see just how Jamie's returning their letter affected him. When she told him, he said nothing, but there was a tightening of the lips and the whites of his eyes seemed suddenly more obvious. She wondered if she detected even a hint of relief, as if, having made the effort, he need struggle no more. As he picked up his cap and headed back to Rathdrum without a word, she decided that only time, or the quiet of the night, would reveal what John really thought.

'Ma, are Elizabeth and Hugh coming for a meal on Friday?' Hannah asked, as they cleared the table after lunch.

'Well, I hadn't thought that far, Hannah,' she said honestly. 'I expect they'll be tired and Mrs Lappin will be expecting them. But it's a nice idea. Would you like them to come?'

she asked, as she filled the washing-up bowl at the stove. 'It's your last evening at home, remember.'

'Ma, they can't come for a meal,' said Sarah urgently. 'I've nothing to wear except what I've on and I cleaned out the stable this morning.'

'Oh, we could shake lavender water over you,' said Hannah laughing. 'You look all right to me.'

'Would you really like us to have them for a meal in the evening, Hannah?' Rose continued. 'They'll have had a rest by then and we could do a cold supper with roast chicken and ham, or something like that.'

'Yes, I really would, Ma,' said Hannah nodding. 'But only if you let us do the work. You've had enough to do this week and you still haven't got out to weed your border.'

'Oh, Hannah, we can't do a special meal and me turn up in my oldest dress,' protested Sarah.

'Well, I'll lend you one of your own back,' said Hannah soothingly. 'I can pack it again before we go to bed.'

'I think I've got a better idea,' said Rose, smiling, as inspiration came to her. 'Why don't you *both* wear your best dresses? Elizabeth was away the day they came, and they were packed the next day when she came to say goodbye. Why don't we leave her a note and tell her we're dressing up as it's Hannah's last night, so she can do the same,' Rose went on enthusiastically. 'We'll make it a proper double celebration, a "welcome home" for Elizabeth and Hugh and a "bon voyage" for Hannah.'

Sarah's eyes lit up at the thought of wearing her blue silk dress.

'What about Sam? What can he wear?' she demanded.

'A nice clean shirt is all he needs, his trouser and a half won't show when he's sitting down,' said Rose laughing. 'You could always put bows on his crutches.'

There wasn't any possibility of forgetting what had happened at their last celebration, but on Friday afternoon at least Rose could be sure everyone who would sit round the table in the parlour would behave properly. The guests were bidden for six o'clock, an unusually early hour for an evening party, but Hannah and John had to make an early start for Dublin the following morning.

All but one of Hannah's cases were closed and left ready in Jamie's room. Beside them sat John's overnight case, the outcome of an unexpected but most courteous letter from Lady Anne's sister, Lily. The journey was tiring, she said, far too much to have to return on the same day. She would be pleased if John would stay the night in Dublin. Besides, as they were so soon to be so closely related, she would like to renew her acquaintance with him, as well as meeting his daughter.

John himself arrived home earlier than usual on Friday evening and offered to don his best coat for the occasion. He was much relieved when Hannah pointed out that if he wore his coat then Hugh wouldn't be able to remove his. On such a pleasant, warm evening with seven people round the table, they'd both be far too hot.

Just before six o'clock, Sam was seated by the stove with his newspaper, looking as if he had polished his large, squarish face, his clean shirt gleaming from Hannah's careful ironing. As his sisters came downstairs one after the other, he eyed them, looked them up and down and nodded his vigorous approval. A little later, Rose appeared in her wine-coloured silk, her hair expertly piled up by Sarah, who'd never let Betty do her hair, but watched most carefully each time she'd dressed Hannah's long, fair tresses. When Sam caught sight of her, his eyes filled with such tenderness he could think of nothing whatever to say.

Watching him from the kitchen table, where she was adding a handful of newly arrived pictures to her album, Sarah suddenly thought of Jamie. If she had to lose a brother, she could much better spare Jamie. Sam was far too dear to her.

John appeared last, freshly shaved and very tidy, and stood with his back to the stove where he could admire the rest of his family. The clock now pointed to six.

'It's not like Hugh to be a moment late,' he commented, as he cocked his ear for the sound of the brougham.

At that very moment, Elizabeth appeared in the doorway

wearing an elegant grey silk dress with a flower pinned to her shoulder.

'Elizabeth, come in, come in,' Rose cried. 'Welcome home.'

She crossed the room and hugged her, followed by Hannah and John.

Sarah prepared to follow after, but stopped dead as she stood up. Behind Elizabeth appeared a tall, handsome man, waiting courteously till she moved further into the room.

His face was bronzed and he held a walking stick in his right hand. It was only as Elizabeth moved away to bend down and kiss Sam that the unfamiliar figure smiled warmly at her and she found her tongue.

'Hello, Hugh,' she said shyly. 'Welcome back. Did it hurt?' she added after a tiny pause.

'My dear Rose, I think your daughter is trying to embarrass you again,' he declared, as he turned to greet her, 'just as she did the very first time we met.'

'How so, Hugh?' she asked, as he kissed her cheek.

'She's just asked me if it hurt.'

She laughed in her turn, remembering how very awkward she'd felt that first evening when Sarah had thrown out her questions in her usual direct way.

'And did it?' she asked, more soberly, glancing at Sarah, whose eyes were shining with delight.

'Yes, it did. It still does,' he said cheerfully. 'But if I'm a good boy and walk every day, it will stop. Then maybe Sam and I can start kicking a football,' he said, clasping Sam's hand and shaking it vigorously.

The meal was a great success. Everyone was hungry and Rose was amused as the platters of cold meat, so prettily arranged by Hannah, were soon reduced to fragments of parsley and sprigs of mint. Extra bowls of potato salad, chopped beetroot and apple in raspberry jelly, and marinaded mushrooms had to be fetched from the larder.

By the time they reached dessert and John fetched glasses to sample the bottle of Elizabeth's pear wine she'd brought for them, everyone was in the best of spirits. Even the anxieties and troubles of the last two months past were recounted with a certain humour.

'My dears, when he started getting these dreadful pains in the chest I thought all was lost,' said Elizabeth gazing round the table. 'They were dreadful, weren't they, Hugh?'

'Yes, I'll admit to that,' said Hugh, beaming.

'They thought his heart was about to fail after the strain of surgery,' she went on. 'One of his nurses more or less told me I ought to see about mourning. She was quite upset when I told her Quakers don't wear mourning. She seemed more upset over my failure to buy a black dress than about her patient expiring,' she said, shaking her head helplessly.

'So what happened then, Elizabeth dear,' Rose asked, reassured by Hugh's lively presence and the fact she had never seen him in such good spirits before.

'Well, fortunately, the surgeon who had done the work on his leg observed that the pain went away when Hugh bent over. Provided he walked crabwise, there was no pain at all,' she said, laughing wryly.

'So it wasn't the heart?' said John thankfully.

'No, it was the muscles in his shoulders and upper back,' she continued reassuringly. 'They'd adapted to the way Hugh walked and they complained when he stood up straight. What I didn't know is that if the muscles in the back are upset the pain frequently comes out round the front. Quite a useful thing to know, isn't it?'

'So how did they get you straightened out?' Sarah demanded, as she moved her empty plate and leant on her elbows to study him carefully.

'Well, first they rubbed me with something that smelt like axle oil, then they took it in turns chopping me in slices with the sides of their hands. After a few days chopping, they found an ancient instrument of torture and tied me to that. Bit like being on the rack, I imagine,' he said, laughing. 'I was waiting for the thumbscrews, but they didn't have any in stock. So they made me do more exercises instead.'

'Oh, poor Hugh,' said Hannah, smiling at him sympathetically.

'No, Hannah dear. Rich Hugh. All that care, all those people doing their best for me. And your good father here carrying all my problems on *his* shoulders for five weeks, when I'd only asked him for two. He and I have a bit of settling up to do next week,' he said cheerfully.

'Ach, not at all, man,' said John dismissively. 'Amn't I only too glad to be of use?'

'Rather more than that, John, if I hear rightly. Has he told you all about the singing doffer crisis?' he asked, looking round the table.

'Was there a stoppage?' asked Sarah, promptly.

'There would have been if it hadn't been for your father,' he said, nodding to her. 'I had a report from the Manager waiting for me when I got back,' he went on, smiling across at John. 'Apparently, one of the doffers was told off for singing. She goes on singing and gets a warning she's to be laid off. Whereupon all the other doffers start singing. Unfortunately, they're not so competent, they couldn't both sing and doff, so there's a sudden shortfall in the spindles going over to Lenaderg for weaving. So they send for the boss. And the boss is John, poor man. And away he goes and in a twinkling he's got it sorted out.'

'How did you do that, Da?' Sarah asked, as John looked sheepish.

'He'll not tell you, Sarah, so I will,' said Hugh, cheerfully. 'First he goes and talks to the Manager whose getting all the complaints from Lenaderg and he asks why the girl was told off in the first place. Because you can't sing and work, says he. So your Da asks to see the production schedule and finds out that this wee singing lassie is one of the best workers. Production only dropped when she was warned and the *other* lassies started singing. The Manager takes the point well enough, but now he wants to know what he's supposed to do when the minute he appears all the doffers start singing at him.'

Everyone laughed as Hugh mimicked the face of the unfortunate Manager who couldn't make himself heard over machinery and singing.

John was now blushing slightly.

'So what did John do, Hugh?' Rose asked.

'Well, I can only tell you what I've been told,' he replied, grinning. 'It seems this man of yours went into Banbridge and bought a songbook and came back and gave it to the wee singer. He said there'd be no more objections to her singing, but maybe she'd have a word with her friends who didn't sing quite as nicely as she did.'

'And did they stop their singin' at the Manager?' asked Sam.

'They did indeed, and production is back to normal. I doubt if we've ever had a labour dispute solved for the price of a songbook. I'll have to see he actually claimed the cost of it from the petty cash. I wouldn't put it past him not to bother,' said Hugh, with a shake of his head.

The glasses were filled and Elizabeth's pear wine raised. Hannah was toasted for her journey and her engagement, Sam for a speedy return to the use of both of his legs. Then a toast was drunk to old friends and new. The wine was delicious and somewhat more powerful than anyone quite expected.

'Would you like to see the pictures we brought back from our holiday, Hugh?' Sarah asked, as Hannah helped Rose to carry the small remains of the feast back to the dairy and Elizabeth settled herself with John and Sam to hear about his accident.

'Did you take these, Sarah?' Hugh asked soberly, as she turned the first two pages.

'Yes, I did. Teddy showed me how on his big plate camera and then he gave me one of his Kodaks.'

'These are very, very good,' he said slowly. 'No, no. Stop. You're going too fast. I want to look at each one,' he protested. 'You've just caught the right moment,' he went on, 'that old gardener picking the peach. And isn't that Hannah with someone reflected in the glass.'

'Yes, that's Teddy. You'll see more of him later,' she said, blushing with pleasure at the concentration with which he studied each page.

'Did you keep that diary you were planning when you went?'

'Yes, but I gave it up when I started to take pictures. The pictures say so much more.'

'Yes, of course they do,' he agreed. 'To you. Even to me, perhaps, but that's because I know about this place and these people. How would it be if I were a stranger and didn't know England or the life of a big house? What then? You need words as well, Sarah. Just think how much more the two together would say.'

Sarah paused and looked up from the pictures to regard him directly. She couldn't help but remember sitting here only last Sunday with Jamie, who could only mutter and grunt, his only comment to ask Hannah who her *boyfriend* was. How very silly he'd been, she thought now. How childish and immature.

'I did think, Hugh,' she said soberly, 'that I might take some pictures in the mills.'

'That's an excellent idea,' he responded promptly. It's just possible pictures might reveal things I don't know about,' he went on thoughtfully. 'But you must write down your own impressions to complement them. You've given me an idea, Sarah, but we must wait and talk about it more next week,' he said, smiling as he stood up. 'Right now, I must give this seat to Elizabeth. I want her to see what a marvellous job you've done.

Fifteen

'You won't be lonely, will you, Sam?' Rose said, as she put her sewing things in her basket. 'I'll be back by twelve to lay the table for Da coming in to his lunch,' she added, as Sam emerged from his newspaper to watch her. 'Is there anything I can fetch for you before I go?'

Sam shook his head at the idea of his being lonely, thought for a moment and made up his mind.

'Would you leave me out some writing things?' he said slowly. 'There's a job here in the paper I might write about. I think they want someone older, but there's no harm in tryin'.'

'None at all, Sam,' she said encouragingly, as she went to the drawer in the dresser. 'You might write a few lines to Hannah while you're at it, you'll have to keep your hand in now,' she said lightly, as she dropped a kiss on his shiny forehead.

'Rose, my dear, come in and sit down,' said Elizabeth warmly as she heard her friend's step and pulled open the back door. 'How lovely to have you here again.'

She sat down and ran her eyes round the bright, plant-filled conservatory that was Elizabeth's pride and joy. Only when she saw a row of flourishing pelargoniums, tiny cuttings when she'd last come, did she recall the February morning she'd packed her basket but couldn't get further than the chair by the stove.

'It's been quite a year, hasn't it?' said Elizabeth, seeing the look that crossed her face as she settled herself in the chair opposite.

'And it's not over yet,' Rose said, laughing ruefully.

'Goodness knows what's in store for us next,' she went on, unrolling her sewing from its cover. 'But I can't complain at what life throws at me, can I? You know better than anyone that I've been given back life itself.'

'You had a close call, Rose,' her friend replied. 'Do you think it's changed you?'

'Lady Anne asked me that about a month ago and I wasn't sure what to say then. I'm still not sure, but I get closer,' she began quietly. 'I must tell you about this business over Jamie. It's really set me thinking. I hope you'll tell me if you think we've done right.'

Elizabeth sighed and shook her head.

'I knew something must be badly wrong when you said not to ask about him in your note. We guessed you didn't want to spoil Hannah's last evening.'

'I knew I could depend on you,' Rose said warmly. 'Friday evening really did make up for the previous Sunday.'

She fell silent for a little as she collected her thoughts and then told her friend as clearly as she could what had happened over Sunday lunch.

'And you've not had a letter from him?' Elizabeth asked, the strong lines of her face making her look severe as she listened intently.

'Only the one John and I wrote that evening with the cheque. He returned it unopened.'

'That *was* hard on you both,' she said coolly, her clear grey eyes full of sympathy.

'Yes, it was *awful*, Elizabeth. My stomach turned over when I saw our address in his handwriting, but maybe that's where I've changed. I *was* hurt. I was even more hurt for John. But then I began to think. We did all we could for Jamie. We loved him and cared for him. He's reached manhood, which many a poor child never does. If he has to go his own way, then we've got to accept it. I'm sad. Of course, I'm sad. But I won't let it bring the world down round me. There are others who need my love and care. Jamie has walked away. If he comes back, he'll be made welcome, but if he chooses not to, life must go on without him.'

Elizabeth nodded, reassured that Rose had been able to reach beyond the pain and disappointment.

'Did John take it hard?'

'He did at first. But the night after he came back from leaving Hannah in Dublin, he suddenly said to me, "Jamie's alive. He has all we gave him. It's in God's hands whether he comes back or not. We mustn't grieve for what is his own choice."'

'I think John is right. I think you both are. It is very sad. But how much sadder if Jamie had been killed in the yard. Or if Sam hadn't been so quick on his feet, when that wagon started to roll,' she said, dropping her work in her lap. 'You've had quite a homecoming, Rose.'

Rose smiled ruefully.

'If anyone had told me in February that Jamie would have taken himself off in a huff, that Sam would be unemployed, Hannah engaged and in Switzerland, I really couldn't have believed it,' she declared. 'And I certainly wouldn't have thought I had the strength to cope with it. Perhaps that's the gift of my illness. I know I gave thanks for all the good things in my life, but I hadn't given thanks for life itself.'

Elizabeth nodded slowly and said nothing. She'd had a great deal to give thanks for herself in these last demanding months, but her story would keep. She was more concerned about the burdens Rose had shouldered the moment she arrived home.

'How do you think Sam is?' Elizabeth asked quietly. 'He was being quite philosophical about it when we talked to him on Friday, but there was hurt there as well.'

'He's fine physically. He couldn't have had a better doctor. But I can see he's worried about getting a job. He reads every newspaper he can lay hands on and asks for more. John thinks he shouldn't even consider going back to Thompson's, even if they did offer to re-employ him when the leg's mended.'

'Yes, I agree with John,' replied Elizabeth, nodding vigorously. 'Hugh was absolutely furious when he heard what had happened. He thinks Sam wouldn't have got his cards if he'd been a member of the Lodge. Thompson became Master this year, and by a remarkable coincidence most of the lads who work for him join as soon as they're seventeen,' she said sharply.

Rose sighed and put down her work.

'Oh, Elizabeth, how stupid of me. I never thought of that. I should have guessed. When Jamie made his disparaging remarks about Catholics, it was Sam who asked him if that was what they taught him at the Lodge. I suppose he'd heard that kind of talk at work. Knowing Sam, he'd just set it aside in his own quiet way, but it looks as if the accident was an opportunity to get rid of him, doesn't it?'

'I'm afraid it does. But you mustn't worry,' Elizabeth went on quickly. 'Hugh said I was to tell you he's found something that might suit him. A cousin of mine, one of the Pearsons, has started up a new haulage business. They're a Quaker family, too, so there'd be no nonsense about joining the Lodge. There is one problem, however,' she added. 'That's why he asked me to tell you before he spoke to Sam.'

'What's that then?'

'It's in Portadown, Rose,' she said steadily. 'Sam would have to live in digs like Jamie. Do you think he could manage that? He seems so happy at home. And what about you?' she went on, looking hard at her friend. 'Jamie, Hannah and Sam, all gone in the course of one summer?'

Rose smiled reassuringly.

'I told Sam the other day that his Granny Hannah always used to say your children are only lent to you. It looks like we're handing them all back. Except for Sarah. And even she's growing up fast,' she added, as she held up the bodice of the dress she was making for her.

Elizabeth nodded and grinned broadly, her whole face transformed, her grey eyes twinkling.

'Oh, Rose dear, I did have to laugh on Saturday morning. Poor old Hugh,' she went on, smiling. 'He looked over my shoulder on Friday night as we walked into your kitchen and he thought, "Oh, a visitor, I wonder who she is," and the next moment Sarah smiled at him and he couldn't believe his eyes,' she went on. 'And all day Saturday he kept saying to me, "Hasn't Sarah grown over the summer? Weren't those pictures she took remarkable?" I think he still hasn't got over the shock.'

'Then that makes two of them,' said Rose, laughing happily. 'Sarah told me she wondered who the tall man was. She says she didn't recognize him till he smiled at her. Can you believe it, Elizabeth, him walking properly again after all these years? John said he looked ten years younger, more like twenty-two than thirty-two. I don't think I've ever seen him laugh so much as he did on Friday night. I began to think it was your lovely pear wine,' she said, dropping her work in her lap and studying her friend's face.

'It *was* a splendid evening, Rose. I hope Hannah enjoyed it,' Elizabeth said, a hint of sadness in her voice.

'Yes, she did. She said it really made up for the way Jamie spoilt Sunday's celebration. It's not like Hannah to be so forthright, but she was really angry at Jamie for forgetting who his grandparents were and how many of his uncles and aunts are Catholic.'

'Will Hannah be happy, Rose?'

'With Teddy?'

Elizabeth nodded silently.

'Yes,' she said simply. 'There was something between them from the beginning, but I missed it because Teddy spent so much time teaching Sarah photography. I didn't realize Hannah was always there in the background encouraging him. Anne told me she's the only girl Teddy's ever looked at. She said when they went to a ball and she asked him the name of the last girl he'd danced with he could never remember,' she added, grinning.

'So you think we'll have a wedding next year?'

'Setting aside illness and accident, I can't see anything else coming between them. They're totally committed to each other.'

'I thought we might make them a quilt . . .'

Rose glanced up and saw a small, awkward smile on her friend's face. She looked at her more closely and recalled the unusual radiance about her last Friday evening. This morning, too, there was an air of excitement that hadn't totally vanished as they'd spoken of Jamie and Sam and Hannah.

'Elizabeth,' she began firmly, 'we've gone through my entire family and not said a word about you. There's something you're not telling me, isn't there?'

To her absolute amazement, Elizabeth blushed.

'I don't know when it will be possible,' she began awkwardly. 'I can't leave Hugh till he's properly recovered, but I *have* promised to marry someone.'

'Someone!' exclaimed Rose. 'Do I know this extremely fortunate individual?'

'Yes, you do. In fact, it's all your doing,' she replied shyly. 'It's Richard Stewart from Dromore. He says he knew he wanted me to be his wife when he looked at me across your bed. He asked me to think about it before we went to Manchester. After his visit to Sam on Monday he came up here and asked me what I'd decided.'

'And you said "yes" to Richard Stewart on Monday and didn't tell me,' said Rose, with a feeble attempt at outrage.

'It's taken me till today to believe it,' admitted Elizabeth honestly.

'Then I forgive you,' said Rose, beaming with delight, as she got up to kiss her friend. 'I think we'd better start on a quilt for you. You'll be married long before Hannah, if Hugh and John and I have anything to do with it,' she said, glancing at the clock.

'Goodness,' said Elizabeth, 'it's almost twelve. I don't know where the morning's gone. I've missed you so, Rose dear. Suddenly, there seems so much to catch up on. Can we meet again soon?'

'As soon as you like. I've missed you just as much. And I want to hear a great deal more about Richard Stewart of Dromore. Oh, Elizabeth, I'm so pleased. It makes up for so much,' she said, standing up. 'What about Tuesday? If you come to me, I can cut out on the parlour table and you can have a look at Sam for yourself. He always loves seeing you.'

'Yes, let's make it Tuesday,' said Elizabeth promptly. 'I'll see you before, I'm sure, but Tuesday will give us time to talk.'

Rose collected up her sewing and they said a hurried goodbye. She walked briskly down the lime avenue, her eye picking out the first yellow leaves lodged in the longer grass. At its end, away from the arching canopy of the trees, she stared up at acres of bright blue sky piled high with masses of cloud. She loved this walk from Rathdrum to Ballydown, less than a quarter of a mile, but so varied, each handful of yards revealing a different perspective, green fields, ploughed earth, the sharp outline of the Mournes, so close in the bright light.

After their quiet period in late summer the birds were active again. Everywhere there were scuffles and flutterings in the hedgerows and ditches. A whole flock of sparrows rose protesting as she walked towards the bush where they sat. Cheeping furiously, they flew off, wheeled and came back, settling almost exactly where they had been.

'Hello, Sam. Have you had a walk?'

'Aye, I've been to the gate a couple of times between visitors.'

'Visitors? So who did you have?' Rose asked, delighted that he'd had company while she'd been away.

'Michael MacMurray said he'd like a word with Da. He came to ask when was a good time to catch him. He stayed a while. He says they've settled on Canada. It's been a bad year for him. He says another like that and he'd not be able to pay the mortgage on the bit of land he owns.'

'Oh dear,' said Rose, as she began laying the table. 'I'll be very sad to lose such good neighbours, but he's spoken about Canada more than once recently. What about his potatoes?'

'They're all right, he says. No blight, but a poor yield. I've a feelin' he can't pay Da the rent of our field. That's why he wants to see him.'

'Oh well,' said Rose, pulling the kettle forward and preparing to make tea, 'Da'll not be hard on him. Sure what's a few pounds from a neighbour when things are so bad with him.'

She went out into the dairy for cheese and cold meat. It was only as she brought it back to the table she remembered Sam had said 'visitors'.

'Who else did you have, Sam?'

'I had a visit from my boss, as was.'

'Thompson?'

'Aye,' he replied, nodding at her, as she paused, teapot in hand, a look of amazement on her face.

'What did he want?' she asked shortly.

'He said I could have my job back, provided I joined the Lodge.'

'And what did you say?' Rose asked, wide eyed.

'I said that unfortunately I had something else in mind.'

'And have you?'

'No. But I intend to see that I have, as soon as the plaster's off,' he replied, with a cool determination she'd never heard before.

'Well, John, that's got that sorted out,' Hugh said, putting down the oil can and wiping his hands on a piece of cotton waste. 'There's something I want to talk to you about,' he continued. 'Why don't we go and sit in comfort in the conservatory and I'll ask Mrs Lappin to bring us a mug of tea. The ladies are at your house this morning, I'm told.'

'Aye, so I hear,' replied John, as he turned off the lights over the work bench and parked a hammer on the drawings he'd been working from, so they wouldn't blow away in the draught. 'I think there's a bit of talk to be caught up on after the summer, so Rose says.'

'They're not the only ones have some catching up to do,' Hugh replied, as he picked up his stick, pulled back his shoulders and took a deep breath before he strode out and headed for the back door.

'I can't get over how well y'are walkin' Hugh,' said John, catching up with him. 'I still have to remind m'self what ye've went through, because it looks so easy now.'

'Even better when I get rid of the stick,' he replied, grinning, as Mrs Lappin appeared and they sat themselves down to wait for their tea.

'How long does Doctor Stewart think that'll be?'

'Depends on me. If I do all the exercises regularly to build up the muscles and keep walking every day, it could be as little as a year.'

'Man, that's great,' said John warmly. 'And so's this,' he added, nodding his thanks to the older woman as she put a mug of tea in his hand and set down a plate of homemade biscuits between them.

'John, my friend, I had a lot of time to think when I was away in Manchester. After the operation, I was quite helpless for a week or more. I couldn't do anything at all for myself. Real disability concentrates the mind,' he said soberly. ' I'm truly sorry you had such a hard time of it here all those weeks, but something good will come out of it.'

John looked across at him, a slightly puzzled look on his face.

'If I'd asked you to go and do all the things you did in those five weeks I was away you'd have said, quite rightly, that it was *my* job. You committed yourself to working on machinery, not sorting out disputes and management problems and dealing with a fire. You might also have told me you couldn't do them, mightn't you?' he added, with a slight grin, a note of question in his voice.

'You're right there,' John responded vigorously. 'It wasn't my line of country at all, but sure there was nothin' else for it, was there?'

Hugh laughed heartily.

'John, you know they did tell me two to three weeks. I had no idea of landing you with five. But an ill wind sometimes blows in something good,' he went on, pausing to drink from his mug. 'What your five weeks showed me was something I'd not have seen otherwise. I couldn't have managed as well these last years if you hadn't been here to help me. Oh yes,' he said, raising a hand to stop John's protest, 'I know what you're going to say. You were only doing your job. Nonsense, man. You were making it possible for me to do mine as well. If I hadn't had you backing me up and listening to me when I was at my wits' end what to do for the best, the Sinton mills wouldn't be as well off now as they are.'

He paused and John fidgeted awkwardly.

'Now, John, plain speaking is the Quaker rule as you well know, so let me be plain. I want you to come into partnership with me. Now, don't start objecting till you've heard me out,' he went on quickly. 'When I was lying in bandages, I saw clearly that you already were my partner. You just weren't getting the credit for it. Nor were you getting paid for it. I want that put right immediately,' he said coolly, naming a figure that left John speechless.

'I've been remiss, John. I've never paid much attention to money beyond looking at the balance sheet each year. I've never actually drawn a salary from the business myself, just taken enough from the profits to cover our expenses living here. I talked to a textile finance expert in Manchester, and when I told him that, he just laughed at me. He pointed out that the money I didn't take simply increased the company's tax bill. He then went on to tell me how firms went broke.'

John sat wide eyed, listening carefully. He'd always left the running of the household money to Rose, assuming he wouldn't be any good at something she did so well. It had never struck him that, for years now, he and Hugh had been discussing expenditure of all kinds. Whether to repair looms or change them. Whether to extend the weaving sheds to cope with big orders that might only be temporary. Which contractor to employ for repairs after a storm or a flood. Which insurance company offered the best rates for the critical fire policies.

'Did he now?' he said, putting his empty mug down without taking his eyes from Hugh's face.

'Yes, he did,' Hugh replied, nodding cheerfully. 'It might surprise you to know, John, we've been on the right track, for all we didn't know it. Apparently, the main cause of mills going down is that they don't keep up with changing technology. And when they do see they're being left behind, they panic and bring in a whole lot of new machinery, all in one go. They clean forget they have to train up staff to use it, so their production drops and the quality too. Consequently, they lose orders just when they've big bank borrowings. Then it only needs one more thing to go wrong, a change in fashion, a lift in the exchange rate, higher shipping costs, or a rise in the price of steam coal, and that's it. The straw that breaks the camel's back. Receivership. As easy as that, John,' he said, spreading his hands out in a sweeping gesture.

'If I hadn't had your reports in Manchester about what you'd done and what you thought needed doing, I might not have started thinking, and I certainly wouldn't have asked around and found a specialist in textile finance. We've done very well despite our ignorance, John. I think we must make changes to secure the future, but I can't do it on my own.'

He paused and looked steadily at his friend.

'Now say you'll be my partner and give me your hand on it.'

'But, Hugh dear, I'm not an educated man,' said John awkwardly.

'You can read and write can't you? You can draw plans. You can invent useful things. What more do you need?' retorted Hugh crisply.

'But sure don't partners have to put a pile of money into a company?' he replied uneasily, his eyes focused entirely upon one of Elizabeth's flourishing fuchsias.

'Not unless it's going public. And even if it was, it's been known for a partner to put in a pound note.'

John stared at him and could think of nothing whatever to say.

'I do intend to find us some more partners,' Hugh went on conversationally, giving his friend time to recover himself, 'but they'll not be working partners. They'll be advisors. They'll get a fee for attending Board Meetings, but not a salary. Richard Stewart might be one, if you agree. Sprott of Dromore, the JP, might be another. You don't know him yet but he's a good man. Very shrewd, and very successful in the hemstitching business,' he explained. 'I also have in mind a certain young woman, when she reaches the age of twenty-one,' he went on with a half-smile.

'Who would that be?'

'Your younger daughter. Miss Sarah Hamilton,' said Hugh, grinning.

'Sarah? Why Sarah?' John exclaimed, entirely confused by this new line of thinking.

'Because, John, with her on the Board, we need never have the slightest worry about Factory Inspectors. Sarah will give us a far worse time on behalf of the staff than *any* of them will ever do.'

Hugh grinned more broadly as John shook his head and laughed. John knew his own daughter well enough to see that Hugh was perfectly right.

'Come on, John,' Hugh said encouragingly as he stretched out his hand. 'It's a family business. Yours as well as mine. Or do I have to go to Rose and get her to make you see sense? All I'm asking is that you do what you've done for years, but accept a proper appreciation and recompense for it. You wouldn't say no to me, would you?'

'Ach, no. I couldn't do that.'

Smiling sheepishly, he put out his hand and shook Hugh's firmly.

Sixteen

On a mild, late September morning, a hint of mist still lying in the valley bottoms, Sam Hamilton got off the train at Richhill Station. He made his way up a long lane, crossed the broad track used by the road vehicles delivering to the furniture and jam manufactories, and walked on to the village itself. Much to his mother's apparent delight and amusement, his father had explained that Richhill Station was about a mile from Richhill. He'd then added that though Pearson's Haulage was Pearson's of Portadown, their premises were about a mile on the Portadown side of Richhill in a townland called Ballyleny.

The distance was immaterial to Sam. Since Doctor Stewart had taken his plaster off two weeks earlier, he'd been walking miles every day for the sheer joy of it. Dressed in his second best coat and trousers, carefully shaved, with his boots polished till they gleamed, he strode out, noting as he went the wheel marks of the various engines that had passed earlier in the day. He found Pearson's with no difficulty whatever, the smell of hot engine oil borne on the breeze alerting him before he was anywhere near the wide space with its large, newly built engine sheds.

'And what age are you, Mr Hamilton?' said the overseer, a man in his fifties, wearing working clothes and a hard hat.

'I'll be seventeen in October,' said Sam steadily.

'And you say you've been drivin' for three years?' he asked doubtfully, his eyes narrowing.

'That's right,' said Sam, pricking up his ears and casting a quick glance out of the window.

'Have you ever driven a Fowler?'

'Like the one that's comin' into the yard, or the newer one?' Sam asked promptly.

To Sam's surprise, the overseer hurried to the window and stood there for several minutes looking out. Only when a cloud of smoke and steam blew through the open door as the engine crossed the yard did he turn round and face Sam again.

'How did you know it was the Fowler was comin'?' he demanded.

'Sure, I heard her out on the road,' Sam said easily. 'She's the only engine makes that sound. She tends to run a wee bit high in damp weather and there was mist about this mornin'.'

The overseer looked at him more closely, asked him where he'd look for a cross head and what he'd do if there was steam coming out of the fusible plug.

Sam answered him cheerfully, taking the odd glance out the window where the well-maintained machine was now at rest, steaming gently.

'Would ye like to drive her into Portadown and back with Sammy?' the older man asked, a slight easing in his somewhat hostile manner.

'Aye, I'd like that fine,' he replied, beaming.

An hour later Sam met Harry Pearson, who asked courteously about Hugh Sinton and his sister and then enquired if Sam would like him to find lodgings for him. He hoped he could start the following Monday.

Sam tramped back to the station, a grin on his face and a cheery greeting for everyone he met. Not only had he got a new job, but Harry Pearson had told him he was hoping to expand his business and move into road vehicles of all kinds. He'd ordered a Siddley for himself and he wanted a lad who'd be interested in all the new motor vehicles, not just the haulage engines that made up their present business.

As he passed the last farm before the station, a low, thatched dwelling with blue-painted window frames, he suddenly remembered something Thomas Scott had said to him when he was a wee boy. 'One of these days, Sam, you'll be comin' to see me in yer motor car.' Well, indeed, it might not be long before he had a chance to prove him right.

By the end of the first week in October, Sam was comfortably lodged in Richhill. On his weekly visits home it was clear he was thoroughly enjoying his job and was already making friends. Hannah, too, was writing lively letters from the enormous castle-like building that had been converted to create her finishing school. The best news of all was that Elizabeth had yielded to considerable pressure from Rose and Hugh and agreed to a wedding date in early April.

As the weather grew colder and the first autumnal storms began to strip both trees and hedgerows, Sarah cycled to and from school with less and less enthusiasm each day.

'But why do I have to stay on at school?' she demanded one Thursday evening, as she banged her books shut and pushed them back into her satchel.

Rose put her library book down, but John went on reading.

'Sarah, it's very important to have a good education. You know that,' she said soothingly.

'But Sam left school at fourteen. Look how well he's doing. He loves his work,' she retorted sharply.

As John shuffled his newspaper and folded it up, he caught Rose's warning look.

'Sarah, if we were all the same, it wouldn't be good, would it?' he said agreeably.

He noticed the dark shadows under her eyes and remembered what her mother had said about how tired she got towards the end of the week. Every afternoon after school there was something on. Choir or Dramatic Society, hockey or Debating Society. Like all young women there were times when she got very short tempered. He knew that well enough by now. Take her the wrong way when she was tired as well and you'd get the kind of storm they used to have when she was a child.

'Sam's a great practical man, God bless him,' said John as calmly as he could manage, 'but you're a clever girl, Sarah. You could do things Sam or Hannah could never do.

That's not just what Ma and I think, it's what better educated people like James Sinton and Hugh and Elizabeth think too. They say you could go to college, now that there's places for women. Would that not be a great thing?'

'No, it wouldn't. It would be just awful,' she spat out fiercely. 'It's bad enough being stuck at school, but then to get out of that and go into Queen's College for three or four more years. I'd go mad. I'd do something desperate,' she said, her voice rising ominously. 'I can't stand being cooped up day after day with the same boring old teachers and the same boring old lessons and not even Hannah to share it with,' she said, bursting into tears and sobbing as if her heart would break.

John looked at Rose helplessly as she stood up and put her arms round Sarah. She held her close, feeling the narrow shoulders shaking, the warm tears soaking through the light fabric of her own blouse.

Over the dark, ruffled curls, they exchanged glances. Rose knew he would back her up as best he could, but she would have to find a way. He'd never had much idea what to do when any of his children was in distress, but Sarah always defeated him completely.

'Things always look grim when you're tired, Sarah,' her mother said softly, stroking her curls. 'How would it be if we had a talk about it after school tomorrow or on Saturday afternoon, when we're all fresher? If you're not happy, we'll find some way to make it better. Didn't we find a way for Sam when he was so upset loosing his job?'

'Yes, but we didn't find a way for Jamie,' she sobbed.

'Sarah dear, Jamie didn't let us try, did he? You'd give us a chance, wouldn't you?'

'Yes,' she mumbled, rubbing her eyes with her knuckles.

'How about some cocoa and a nice hot-water bottle?'

Sarah shivered, suddenly cold with tiredness and tears. She nodded. She was sure they'd try to help her, but she couldn't see what they could do. She was fourteen. She was a girl. No going off like Sam at fourteen to find a real job in the real world. Three or four more years of Banbridge

Academy lay in front of her before she could have any life of her own.

At this moment, the enormity of the acres of boredom to be endured was so appalling she thought she'd rather be dead.

Rose did her best. She talked to Elizabeth and went to see the only one of her teachers Sarah seemed to like. They both said wise things about the adjustments Sarah was making in her life. In the course of the summer, she'd grown up and she'd lost a beloved sister whose constant companionship she'd never questioned. Her favourite brother no longer lived at home. Sarah's teacher didn't know about Jamie, so it was Elizabeth who suggested she might be blaming herself for his absence.

'Why can't I just leave and get a job in the mill, Ma? That's what other girls have to do. Why do I have to be coddled up at school?' she demanded one wet October afternoon when she arrived home soaking.

'Sarah dear, if you just went into the mill, how would you ever do the things you want to do?'

'What things? What things do I want to do?' she shouted.

'Well, you want to take pictures, don't you?'

'Yes. And I don't need to go to school for that. What use is school to me?' she demanded.

'It's a good way of using time till you're older, Sarah. You can't just go off like Sam, you know that. After all, he had to do the equivalent of another three years at school when he went to Tullyconnaught as an apprentice.'

'Yes, but that's what he wanted. I don't want any of what they're teaching me. Nor all those boys being silly and the girls giggling in corners. I can't stand it, Ma, I can't stand it.'

She searched vainly for words of comfort, but nothing she said seemed to touch Sarah's distress. She was forced to watch her dragging herself from day to day, weighed down by a burden of frustration, her discontent floating round her like a cloud.

It had been agreed there'd be no question of her going to Queen's College. They'd also gone as far as saying she could leave at seventeen, but, for Sarah, the gap between these last months of 1897 and the longed-for freedom the summer of 1900 would bring was still an eternity of time almost impossible to visualize and equally impossible to survive.

Rose tried everything she could think of to cheer and encourage her, but her intuition told her so much depends upon the way we see things for ourselves. Searching back through her own early years, she remembered times when she too had been dogged by the same weariness. She too had blamed the slow passage of the days and weeks for her frustrations.

'But is it really time, or is it circumstance?' she asked aloud, one dim December morning as she looked round the tidy, well-swept kitchen and thought how she'd spend her own solitary day.

John would not be coming in to lunch and Sarah had a rehearsal after school. Nothing to prevent her doing whatever she chose.

'Is today a wonderful opportunity to do what I want to do?' she asked herself, 'or a miserable piece of time to be filled as best I can?'

She made up the fire and settled in her chair to watch the leaping flames. She smiled to herself. She felt well, there was no immediate problem or weight of sadness to press upon her. She had books from the library. Sewing and embroidery under way. Letters to write to family and friends. If it stayed dry, she could dig up some of her perennials that needed splitting.

She sat on quietly, thinking of Sarah, and suddenly she saw herself sitting on a hillside, her sleeves rolled up, the top buttons of her blouse undone, a soft breeze stirring the tassels on the fuchsia and cooling her warm skin. She was in Kerry, on her one afternoon off, the only time in her busy life as a servant at Currane Lodge that was really hers. Time was only your friend when you were free to act as you wished.

She thought of the early months of the year and shivered

slightly, thinking of the weeks after her illness when time was a blur, the days slipping into weeks as she slept and rested. Then came the months when she was well enough to know what she wanted to do, but not well enough to do any of it.

Perhaps that was Sarah's real problem. She could see so clearly what she wanted to do, but present circumstances would not let her do it. She was simply not old enough and the waiting was intolerable.

Even with all the reassurances she'd had from Elizabeth and Doctor Stewart, it hadn't been easy to believe health and strength would be returned to her, if only she waited patiently. How much worse it must be for Sarah. There was no way of reassuring her that what she knew she wanted would come to her if only she could be patient.

Of course the months and years would pass. This long century of dramatic change would end, and with it her schooldays. But what comfort was that when the burden of the time ahead lay so heavy upon her?

So far, she'd discovered it was not school work in itself which bored Sarah, but the fact that school stood between her and making her own life. Twice recently, she'd seen the old sparkle return and both times it was school work that had done the trick. A history project on the Great Famine set her reading every book and paper she could lay her hands on. She'd talked about it at great length to anyone who would listen. An essay on the Industrial Revolution had the same effect. She'd filled notebook after notebook with the plight of the rural unemployed as they flocked to the towns to be herded into miserable little houses in the shadow of mills.

'But what do I do for her now?' Rose asked herself, gazing out at the damp, uninviting day.

She thought of her Quaker friends waiting patiently on guidance. She'd tried that, but nothing had come to help her. She sat on quietly, her mind moving to the affairs of her friends and family. Elizabeth's marriage plans. Hugh and John working yet more closely in their partnership. Hannah and Sam, each happy with the future they'd chosen. And Jamie?

To her great surprise, it was thinking of him that finally gave her an answer to her question. Obvious, once you saw it. There was nothing she could *do* for Sarah, any more than there was anything she could *do* for Jamie. She could love them, cherish them, think of them, but what was ultimately important to them, they had to find out for themselves.

It was only as spring came with flickers of dazzling light and lengthening days that unexpected hope and possibilities began to diminish Sarah's sadness and frustration and restore Rose to her happier self.

Elizabeth had been granted permission to marry by their local Monthly Meeting, but there couldn't be a Quaker marriage as Richard Stewart was a Presbyterian. As a Quaker, Elizabeth couldn't be married by an ordained minister of any other church. The only solution was for Elizabeth and Richard to be married in a Registry Office. To make up for this loss of a ceremony they decided to have a small celebration afterwards in Richard's house in Dromore where they were to live after their marriage. Elizabeth came down from Rathdrum especially to ask Sarah if she would take some pictures for them.

Sarah was delighted. She hadn't touched her camera since she'd taken a picture of Sam on crutches, to use the one remaining exposure on the roll for the journey home from Ashley Park. Now, she took it out again, loaded it up and began to practise. She wanted to be sure her hand was steady and her eye was in, for she'd decided she would make an album for Elizabeth and Richard. Just like Mr Blennerhasset had for Ma and Da all those years ago.

Ballydown
May 1898

My dear Hannah,

Thank you for your lovely long letter. It was great! It wasn't quite as funny as your account of learning to ski, but now I shall always think of you whenever I see someone wearing a cap and apron. I cannot imagine

ANYONE wanting to measure the exact angle of a cap, or the distance from apron to floor. I really can't see you spending your time bossing your servants round like that, but it *was* funny. Especially as you had to practise on Marianne, who was being 'pert'.

Elizabeth's wedding was lovely. You knew she wouldn't be having a wedding dress, because Quakers don't, but she did wear a most lovely new gown. It was perfectly plain as always, but it was silver-grey. I never realized what wonderful grey eyes she has until I saw her standing looking at Doctor Stewart, though she says I must call him Richard now. She looked quite beautiful and I so wished I could catch the exact colour of her eyes and the dress.

Hugh says one day there'll be colour film, but in the meantime he was going to see if he could have some of my pictures hand-tinted. A few days ago he showed me one of his mother, very delicately done, like one of your best watercolours.

I was so busy taking pictures I didn't get anything to eat, but when I stopped Hugh appeared with a huge plate of all my favourite things and a glass of wine. He said if I wanted to take more pictures I was to sip it slowly with the food. A good thing he said that. I was terribly thirsty by then. I could easily have drunk it all up. What would your dear Teddy say if I had camera shake from drinking wine?

I took pictures of everybody, but no big groups. One of Ma, straightening Elizabeth's dress, one of Richard talking to Da and Hugh. That sort of thing. Not those awful groups that get made into postcards. I'd hate to be stamped on the back and dropped through a letter box.

Sam is well and still loves his new job. Da bought him a bicycle for getting to work and last time he came home he asked me to go over some weekend, so we could go riding round that part of the world. I didn't know I could take my bicycle on the train, but I can.

Now the weather is so much better I can start taking pictures again.

I also must tell you that I have been offered a job! I am *so* delighted. I don't get any pay, but I'll have all my expenses plus a small fee. Hugh wants me to start work on the four mills, building up a picture of each of them. Not just the machinery and the buildings themselves, but the people and the things they do.

He keeps mentioning that picture I took at Ashley Hall of the oldest gardener picking the peach. He says he wants the equivalent with all the different processes. Unfortunately, he also wants written notes to accompany the pictures, which is a bit too much like school, but never mind. It means I can have all the film I need and lots of practice. Do tell Teddy I'm going to save up for a plate camera. He is quite right, there are some things it does very well that you can't manage with a Kodak.

I can hardly believe it's only six weeks till you set out for home. I'm longing to see you, even if it is for such a short time. Will Teddy be able to come and meet you in London before you come on here? And have you finally fixed the date? If it has to be September, I shall play truant. I simply cannot miss your wedding. Give my love to Marianne. I owe her a letter. I've ordered extra prints of Elizabeth's wedding. If they arrive soon, I'll put them into her letter and you can share them. Write soon,

Fondest love from us all, but especially from me, to both of you,

Sarah

Hannah arrived home via London, glowing and self-possessed, and for most of July gathered Sarah up into their old habits of riding and walking, before going back to Ashley Park to prepare for her wedding in late August. Sam appeared frequently on Saturday afternoons, bringing his bicycle so he could swoop off early on Monday morning and get back to Richhill in time for work.

Throughout the fine weather there were visits to Elizabeth and Richard in Dromore, John driving Rose in the trap and Sarah keeping Hugh company in the brougham. Hugh himself became a much more frequent visitor at Ballydown, walking down the hill several evenings in the week after his solitary supper. Sometimes, on a Saturday afternoon, he'd ask Sarah if she'd like to drive over to one of the mills instead of going on her bicycle. While she was taking her pictures, he said, he could cast his own eye around without being very much noticed.

Long before Hannah's visit, Sarah had drawn up a list of what she wanted to photograph in and around the four mills. But it was only when she got started, after Hannah's departure, that she discovered it wasn't as simple as she thought it would be. Before you can choose what you need to record, you have to make yourself familiar with the whole set of processes involved in production, from the growing of the flax right through to the boxing up of the finished linen for export round the world. With her usual enthusiasm, she began questioning both Hugh and her father. She spent yet more time in the local library and poring over prints spread out on the kitchen table for minute and critical study.

Rose breathed a sigh of relief as the characteristic frown reappeared. In another person a sign of irritability or bad temper, with Sarah a sure sign of complete absorption and the surest sign of all that she was happy.

'I think maybe we're over the worst with Sarah,' Rose said to John one warm August evening when they walked out along the Katesbridge road.

'Aye, she seems more settled,' he said easily. 'Are ye not afeerd that wi' the excitement of the weddin' she'll find it hard back at school?'

'There's bound to be a bit of a come down, but she'll have her pictures to work on,' she replied reassuringly. 'She's so delighted that Hannah and Teddy want her to take their wedding pictures when they could've had a society photographer down from London,' she went on. 'I daresay they'll go and have portraits done when they're up in town, but when you look at Elizabeth and Richard's pictures, you can see why Hannah was so keen. I think she has real talent, John.'

'Aye, so does Hugh,' he responded promptly. 'He says you should just see the way she goes about things when she gets on to the weaving floor or down with the beetlers, eyeing things up from all angles. What gets him is the way she goes up to people and says, "Will you do this, will you do that?" with that big smile of hers. He says he's waitin' for the day anyone has the heart to say no to her.'

She laughed and they walked on in silence, the evening quiet but for the distant noise of a cow lowing, a dog barking at a passing stranger.

'Do you think Hugh is missing Elizabeth?' she asked quietly.

'Not as bad as I thought he would,' he answered after a moment's thought. 'But he said he'd think of movin' into town if it weren't for us. Dromore most likely, to be near Elizabeth and Richard. But he says he never feels lonesome knowing we're just down the hill.'

'He's been a great encouragement to Sarah. Do you think it's just his kindness, or does he really want to collect up all these pictures?'

'I think maybe it's a bit a both. He says he's foun' out more about workin' practices since Sarah was walkin' about with her camera than he's ever learnt from the Mill Managers. She doesn't miss much, an' she tells him everythin'. I'm amazed at what he comes out with sometimes. She's been at him to start a co-operative shop. He'd bring in the stuff in bulk an' the workers wou'd get it near cost. Any profit goes back into stock for parcels at Christmas or when people are sick.'

'Sounds like a very good idea,' said Rose enthusiastically.

'Aye, so Hugh thinks,' John replied, nodding. 'But he's a crafty one. He's goin' to pursue it, but he's not told her that. He's told her he has a problem and he wants to know what he's goin' to do about it. So she's away to work that out.'

'So what's the problem?' asked Rose, intrigued.

'What he does about the shopkeepers who'll complain he's takin' away their livelihood.'

'But he's not taking away their livelihood,' protested Rose.

'No, I know that and you know that, but the shopkeepers will probably have a go at him anyways. Hugh wants to test her out to see if she can come up with somethin'. He's serious you know about her comin' on the Board when she's twenty-one,' he added suddenly.

'My goodness, love, can you remember her tramping up the path at Ballydown with Ganny under her arm?'

'Ach, it seems no time ago. It moves so fast these days and there's so much change goin' on ye can hardly keep up with it, what with things so bad in South Africa and the Russians eyeing up China and all this disturbance here with the anniversary of 1798, forby our own family . . .'

He broke off suddenly. She knew at once he was thinking of Jamie.

'D'you think we'll ever see him again, Rose?'

'I don't know,' she said honestly. 'I sometimes think he'll come to his senses and remember he has a family. And then I think, if he does, he'll be so ashamed at what he said and what he's done, he'll be too proud to come back. Sometimes I try to imagine what it might take to bring him back, but I don't expect anything. I try to accept he's gone, as they'll all go. I don't dwell on the manner of his going.'

'Ach, you're wiser nor me, Rose. Ye take that from your mother. Aye an' ye've passed it on to Hannah. It takes a lot to ruffle our Hannah. Sarah's different, now. I don't know where she comes from at all.'

She laughed as they turned at their usual spot. Down here on the road, the sun was already hidden behind the trees, but as they went back up the hill it would re-appear. They'd pause at their own gate and watch it sink. In June it had been light till well after ten, but by the time they came back from Ashley Park it would be September and the evenings would have shrunk enough for neighbours to say, 'The nights are drawing in,' a phrase that always made Rose feel sad.

Ultimately, life drew in, like the days from June to December. It became shorter, more limited, until it finally disappeared altogether.

She took John's arm as they began the steep part of the climb and pushed away such sombre thoughts. A week today, they'd be travelling with Sarah and Sam to Hannah's wedding. Surely that event would be joy enough to sustain them through the dark of winter.

Sarah opened her eyes in the darkened room, jumped out of bed and stuck her head between the nearest set of heavy curtains.

'Oh, no,' she cried. 'It can't. Not today of all days.'

Her eyes filled with tears as she threw them back and gazed out at the rich colours of late summer transformed into a blur by the raindrops pouring down the windowpanes and the heavy swags of cloud lying low over the parkland beyond. After days of sunshine and warmth, she could hardly believe what she saw.

Furious with herself, she wiped her tears on the back of her hand and peered at the dim face of the tiny clock by her bed. It was half past six. She hauled off her nightgown, dressed quickly and ran down through the empty house and out into the garden. She ignored the driving rain as she splashed her way to the main greenhouse. A familiar figure sat in his usual place, a minute pair of scissors in his knobbly fingers. Bent over and rigid with concentration, he was removing tiny thorns from the long stems of yellow rosebuds he'd picked the night before.

'Oh, Mr Partridge, isn't this awful?' Sarah cried, as he caught sight of her.

His face crinkled into a wise smile.

'Ah, never worry, Miss Sarah. I heard it plumpin' down two hour ago whin I was still in me bed. It'll be clear by eleven, an' the service not till twelve. Your sister'll not get wet. Were ye worryin' about takin' the pictures?' he added slyly, as she began to smile.

'Yes, I was,' she admitted, 'but mostly I was thinking of

it pouring down on Hannah's lovely dress and not being able to have the buffet in the garden and everyone worrying about their best clothes.'

'Aye, I have a new coat meself, thanks to the master,' he said proudly. 'Every one of us had a gift from him. Did ye know that?'

She shook her head slowly as he added another stem to the green enamelled bucket.

'Even if it did rain, isn't your sister sunshine enough for any man, eh?'

Sarah beamed at him. A year ago she'd met him for the first time, picking a peach to send up to her mother. She'd never known anything trouble him. Even when his arthritis was so bad he couldn't bend, he'd wait patiently till one of the boys fetched him all he needed, then go on with his work, as steadily as if he were a hale young man.

'Yes, she is,' she agreed vigorously. 'Just wait till you see her dress, Mr Partridge. It's a most wonderful gold brocade. When they come back, she'll have to wear it for the ball in London with all the jewels Lord Cleeve has given her.'

She paused and went on, a puzzled tone in her voice.

'She's not wearing any of them today, though. Just these roses and a little veil that my mother wore at her wedding.'

'Ah, she'll have her reason,' he offered, as he put the last rosebud in the green bucket. 'She'll maybe tell ye whin ye take them to her.'

Mr Partridge was right about the day. By the time Hannah had made a corsage for her dress and a matching bouquet to carry, the clouds were rolling away. A stiff breeze followed the rain. A little later, as Rose pinned the veil in place, even the puddles had disappeared, the flowers had shed their burden of raindrops and the garden paths were almost dry.

Hannah's dress shone in the sunlight as she drove with her father to the village church on the edge of the estate. The massed crowds of guests and tenants, far too many for its tiny nave, cheered as she passed between them, and crowded round the west door, opened especially for this great occasion, to get a closer look.

Between helping Hannah and Marianne, her bridesmaid, and taking her pictures, Sarah had such a busy time through the long, exciting day, that it was only weeks later she found out how important a part she had played.

Capri
18th September 1898

My dearest Sarah,

I hope you have at least had some postcards from us, but I'm sorry this letter has been so long delayed. Between the excitements of travelling and the wonderful places we have stayed and Teddy's reluctance to leave me alone to write letters, I have not had an opportunity to say Thank You for all you did for our wedding.

I have to confess when I woke and saw what a dreadful day it was, I was quite overcome. I know it was silly, but it seemed such a bad omen, as if, after all my efforts to be a proper Lady for Teddy, it was all going to go wrong. And then you came in with the bucket of roses and were so certain the rain would stop. Do you remember you asked me, 'Why yellow roses?' and I confessed they were for Teddy, a remembrance of the night he knew for sure he wanted me to be his wife. After that, my courage came back and it all went as wonderfully as we had hoped.

Thank you, Sarah, dearest. The day was unforgettable and I long to see the pictures you took. I'm wondering which of Teddy's best friends you favour most. I have seldom seen two young men more willing to be your faithful servants when you were working or more attentive when the dancing began.

One day, my dear, I am sure you will be as happy as I am now.

For the moment we both send our fondest love and most sincere thanks.

Hannah

The days shortened, but the weather stayed remarkably mild. Life settled back to its autumn routine as Hannah and Teddy turned towards home from Naples, the most southerly point of their journey. Sarah was so absorbed by her work on their pictures she had difficulty fitting in the visits to the mills she'd promised herself. Then there was schoolwork, and when there was not, she read volumes from Hugh's library on the complexities of spinning and weaving, because she was determined her notes for the pictures she'd already taken should be as accurate as possible.

As long as Sarah was complaining of not having enough time for all she wanted to do, Rose could relax and enjoy the extra hours she had for herself now she'd but two to look after. She took up her reading and sewing gratefully and made Sarah a new dress for her first school dance.

So long awaited and so much anticipated by the other girls in Sarah's year, this great occasion came and went in early December. Clearly she enjoyed the dressing up, being bowed to by Hugh, when he chanced to call just before she departed, being driven down in the trap by her father, and listening to the very good band, but the opportunity to dance with her contemporaries filled her with no great enthusiasm.

'Most of them can't think of two words to say to you,' she summed up next morning, when she came down to a late breakfast. 'The best thing was the supper,' she added, as she buttered more toast.

Rose enquired about one or two boys she'd mentioned occasionally and the handsome, red-headed lad, eldest son of the Jacksons, who'd recently moved into MacMurray's empty farmhouse at the foot of the hill.

'Oh yes, I danced with all of them. I danced with nearly everyone. Peter Jackson's not a bad dancer, but the only one I like dancing with is Kenny Taylor and he's stupid.'

'So why do you like dancing with him?'

'He's a marvellous dancer,' she said coolly, as she munched steadily. 'He's so light on his feet, I sometimes think we'll take off and fly,' she said, her eyes lighting up. 'And I don't have to bother talking to him. He's so lost in the music, it puts him off his step if I say anything.'

'What's Kenny going to do when he leaves school?' Rose asked casually, wondering what she really meant by 'stupid'.

'Oh, he'll be a solicitor like his father,' she replied, indifferently.

'You have to be quite clever to be a solicitor.'

'I suppose so. That sort of clever he can manage, but he says such stupid things. He keeps asking me to go for walks with him. Honestly, as if I hadn't better things to do,' she added, as Rose turned away towards the stove to hide her smile.

It was later that same morning when the postman delivered an invitation to Hugh which he certainly had not been expecting. Standing in the kitchen finishing a quick mug of tea with John, he flicked through the handful of envelopes parked on the table. Out of pure curiosity, he opened the only one he couldn't immediately identify.

'Good gracious,' he said, as he drew an elegant card from its equally elegant envelope.

John glanced across at him, caught sight of the stiff, gold-rimmed communication and laughed.

'Are ye for London or Dublin, then?'

'Neither,' said Hugh, his tone strangely sad as he examined the printed text with greater care. 'It's an invitation to the launch of the *Oceanic,*' he said awkwardly, as he dropped card and envelope on the table.

'Aye, it's due, from the last I heerd of it,' John replied steadily.

'"Jamie's ship", I've always called it,' Hugh said, tightening his lips.

He remembered the summer day in '96 when they'd all climbed the wall to watch Sam steaming past in the new Fowler. Delighted by Sam's achievement, he'd thought immediately of Jamie. 'We'll have to do better than a wall to stand on when they launch Jamie's ship,' he'd said then.

'Maybe there'll be one waiting for you at lunchtime,' he went on quickly.

John shook his head.

'Ach, I don't think it's very likely, Hugh. Sure it's sixteen months now since we last saw him. We've had no word at all. Not so much as a wee note to his mother for the Christmas present and the two birthday presents she's sent him. Even if there were an invitation, I wouldn't have the heart to go, unless there were a letter from Jamie himself alongside of it.'

'I really can't think why I've been invited.'

'Sure all the big manufacturers has likely been asked,' John replied. 'There'll be a lot of publicity for it, an' people over from England and abroad. Ye ought to go, Hugh,' he added more firmly. 'It's a historic occasion. She's a fine ship and a credit to Ulster. Don't let our sorrow put you off. Sure life has to go on,' he said, getting up from his chair and heading back for the workshop.

'John, it says "and party, maximum four",' Hugh added, as he caught up with him. 'Would you and Rose, and Sarah, not come with me if you don't get an invitation of your own. You're quite right, it *is* a historic occasion. It would be something for Sarah to tell her grandchildren about. See what Rose says and I'll maybe walk down tonight to see what you've decided,' he ended, as he took up his drawings and collected his thoughts.

There was no launch invitation among the morning's post at Ballydown, just a postcard from Hannah, a note from Elizabeth and a letter for Sarah from Marianne.

'Well, what do you think?' John asked, as they sat down together.

'I don't think we should go,' Rose said quietly. ' It wouldn't do any of us any good if we met up by accident,' she went on, shaking her head. 'But it'd be a pity if Hugh doesn't go. He's quite right about it being an important occasion. It's the world's biggest ship, isn't it?'

'Aye, it is. They say she'll beat the German one on the Atlantic run when she's finished. And there's others comin' on behind her. D'ye think Sarah wou'd enjoy that?'

'Well, there's no harm in asking, as the saying is,' said

Rose laughing. 'Maybe we should let Hugh ask her himself, if he has a mind to. Will he be down tonight?'

'He said he might, but I'll have to walk up this afternoon some time. I left my spectacles on the work bench. Sure I can't read the newspaper now wi'out them,' he added ruefully. 'I'll tell him what ye've said and leave it up to him.'

The first week of January 1899 was wild and stormy but not particularly cold, but the following week the storms died down and on the second Saturday in the month, the day of the launch, the air was bright and dry with hints of sun and no threat of rain.

Hugh had asked Sarah if she would like to go and Sarah had jumped at the chance. Rose noted that she was looking forward to the outing with a great deal more anticipation than she had to the school dance.

As Hugh had lost no time at all in claiming his tickets, they were directed to seats halfway up the specially constructed grandstand alongside the Victoria channel. From where they sat, not only could they see the huge, elegant shape of the ship almost directly in front of them, but also the smaller, beflagged and bedecked pavilion a little distance away, where the lords and ladies, distinguished guests and foreign visitors would take their seats.

'Hugh, isn't this exciting?' Sarah exclaimed, as they sat down and she took in the scene with one long, sweeping glance.

'Yes, I have to admit it is,' he replied, laughing. 'There's an extraordinary atmosphere. I must say I hadn't expected so many people. No wonder we had to wait so long for a cab at the station.'

'Special trains from all over Ulster,' she replied promptly, running her eyes over the gleaming hull. 'What time does it happen?' she went on as she studied the tiny figures on the deck above.

'Eleven, I think. But nothing will happen till all those seats are full,' he said, smiling and nodding towards the pavilion.

'I don't think I can do much in the way of a picture,' she

said, opening up her camera. 'She's too big. But I'd like to take some pictures of the crowd and I might just catch the wave. Do you know about displacement waves?'

'No,' said Hugh grinning. 'But I'm sure you do. I'm listening,' he said, as he sat back in his seat and waited.

She laughed up at him, thinking what a lovely smile he had when he was happy. She'd observed that Hugh wasn't always happy. In fact, she had come to the conclusion that he was often rather unhappy, though he concealed it awfully well. If ever she dropped into the workshop unexpectedly she'd catch a look in his eyes that made her wonder if he was as bored with machines and running mills as she was with school. She also noticed how quickly the look disappeared, because he seemed always so pleased to see her. Which was nice. But it didn't mean that the sad look wasn't there when there was no one to distract him.

On the still air, voices carried long distances. They heard instructions being given to the shipwrights by megaphone and picked up the witty comments of those in the crowd who were impatient for proceedings to begin. At regular intervals, there were great booming explosions which turned out to be salutes in honour of the small parties of distinguished guests arriving at the pavilion to their left.

'Them bangs wou'd do ye no good if ye'd a bad heart,' said a man, seated a row in front of them.

A section of the huge crowd on the terrace below them had begun to sing 'Go on the blues.' Other sections took it up and, either by accident or by design, it proceeded antiphonally with great gusto, until another series of explosions suggested that something might really be about to happen.

Silence descended once again. From where Sarah and Hugh sat they could see it was a salute to a final party of guests, whether the most important or the least important they couldn't tell, as they watched yet more bejewelled ladies accompanied by men in top hats and morning dress being led to the few remaining seats under the canopy.

'Do you recognize any of them?' she enquired, as she

surveyed the pavilion through her viewfinder and decided that it was too far away.

'I don't exactly move in those circles, do I?' he said, with a slight disapproving look.

She laughed, knowing he was teasing her.

'There'll be some of the top men at Harlands. You might know them. Ismay or Pirrie or Gustav Wolff,' she offered. 'And the Marquis of Dufferin and Ava, he's our local bigwig isn't he? I heard there are some Americans have come over especially. Why do you think they like things just because they're big?'

Hugh laughed. Before she could continue, he put his hands on her shoulders and turned her round to face the pavilion.

'Is that Jamie?' he said quietly.

'Yes, it is,' she replied, her voice tight with tension the moment she caught sight of the tall, lithe figure who ran up the steps of the marquee and handed a note to a seated dignitary, before bowing and withdrawing out of sight.

'It's his big day too, remember.'

'It should have been a big day for all of us,' she came back at him, unable to keep the bitterness out of her voice. 'You really mean I should forgive him, don't you?' she went on, glaring at him.

'You could give it a try. We all make mistakes and hurt people.'

'Even you?'

'Of course. Perhaps particularly me. Or so I sometimes think.'

She looked at him in silence, wondering how he could ever have hurt anyone.

'Look,' he said urgently. 'They're waving a flag. I think that's for the launch.'

His words were drowned by another barrage of explosions. Sarah swung round and glued her eyes to the ship. For what seemed like an age, there was neither movement nor sound. Then, quite suddenly, she heard the snap and crack of the timbers that had stood against her sides. Like matchsticks, the huge, tree-sized wedges were thrown in the air, as ropes ran out and hawsers gave way. She began to move.

'Oh, Hugh, look!' she cried.

Down on the promenade below, the displacement wave had soaked some of the photographers and all of the people standing close to the dock. Even more unexpectedly, the force of its movement under the lower part of the grandstand pushed up fountains of dirty water among those seated immediately below them. There was laughter and cheering, even among the unfortunates who had been soaked, as the *Oceanic* settled with grace and equilibrium in the placid waters of the Lagan.

Above the roar of the crowd and the cheers of those who had worked upon her, an incredible symphony of sound erupted into the air. The ringing of ships' bells and sirens, foghorns and hooters, rang out in peal after peal of joyous celebration.

Suddenly she felt tears pouring down her cheeks.

'Are you all right, Sarah?' Hugh asked, his face full of concern.

She nodded fiercely and rubbed her eyes.

'Yes,' she said, taking his hand. 'Thank you for bringing me. I don't think I shall ever forget today, however long I live.'

Seventeen

'Here y'ar, miss. Ye've got a lovely day for your outin'.'
The guard on the Armagh train lifted down Sarah's bicycle and glanced from her to the young man waiting at the foot of the lane. He winked at her as he waved his flag and blew his whistle.

'He's a good-lookin' fella,' he said, nodding down at her when he'd climbed back up again into his van.

'He is indeed,' she agreed, beaming at him. 'Pity he's my brother.'

'Aye, but sure there's one around somewhere just waitin' for you,' he said laughing, as the train creaked, lurched and moved forward.

She waved to him gaily and wheeled her bicycle along the platform to where Sam stood watching, a broad smile on his face.

'Was the guard givin' you the eye?' he said, teasing her.

'No, the poor man's not quite right in his head,' she said, her face perfectly straight. 'He said you were good-looking.'

Sam laughed and reached out for the shopping bag she was carrying.

'What's this?'

'Food,' she said, shaking her head. 'Ma must think they starve you in Richhill, though I see no signs of it myself,' she went on, looking him up and down. 'There's sandwiches and things for today and a cake for next week,' she explained, as he secured the contents in his saddlebag.

'Where do you want to go?'

'Everywhere,' she said happily. 'I've brought the camera,' she went on. 'Somewhere high with a view. And then, after lunch, I want to go and visit Thomas Scott. I've been wanting to do it for *years*, but we mustn't arrive at lunch-time. Anyway, this light might not hold, so let's find a hill first. I haven't done anything yet about landscape.'

Sam laughed to himself as he pedalled off.

'I'll find you a hill all right,' he threw back over his shoulder. 'An' you won't go up it on a bicycle.'

A few minutes later she saw what he meant. Having crossed the railway, the lane ran uphill and soon became so steep they had to get off and push. Sam kept up a vigorous pace and she was soon out of breath.

'Are you puffed?' he asked, a twinkle in his eye, as he paused by a field gate and lowered his bicycle against the hedge.

'No, I'm not. You have longer legs than I have,' she retorted, gasping, as she took out the camera and handed it to him, so she could prop her own bicycle up against his. 'Why have we stopped here?' she asked, wiping her damp forehead with a bare arm.

'You said you wanted a hill,' he said easily, as he opened the field gate and closed it carefully behind them.

Sam nodded towards a grey stone obelisk topping the field that sloped steeply upwards from where they stood.

As they climbed, the grass became progressively shorter. By the time they stood at the foot of the tall stone finger, it had disappeared altogether, leaving the earth surrounding it bare and tramped. They leant against the rough, cut stone and looked about them.

'There's Armagh,' said Sam, turning his back on the slope. 'Ye can see the cathedrals plain. An' the Observatory with the green domes. D'you remember Armagh from when you were wee?' he asked suddenly.

'I remember the Library on the Mall,' she said after a moment's thought. 'Ma and I used to sit under the trees outside after we'd collected the books. It was an awfully long walk home.'

'Aye, I suppose it was. Sure you were only six when we left Armagh.'

'And you were only nine,' she said, mimicking his dismissive tone. 'What do *you* remember best?'

'The engine sheds at Armagh Station.'

'I don't know why I bothered to ask,' she said, shaking her head as she drew her camera from its case and opened its front.

Sam settled himself on a nearby patch of grass and lay looking out over the rich green landscape. Last Saturday he'd had to drive to Newry so he'd not been able to go home as usual. On Sunday he'd come up here with some of the lads from work and a crowd of girls. It had taken a while, but eventually he'd got Martha Loney to himself. He knew her well enough by now, meeting her every morning and evening going to and from his work, but he'd never yet talked to her.

'Martha, will you come for a walk one evening next week?' he said, guessing correctly there was no use being shy with the same girl.

'What would I do that for?' she came back at him.

'Ach, sure exercise is good for you,' he said slowly. 'You can't always be walkin' out with that horse of your Da's.'

She'd laughed and said she'd think about it. She told him she was saving up to go to Canada. She had an uncle there with a big job and a big house. His wife needed help. She'd no notion of being a skivvy, she said, but it would do for a start. If you paid your own fare you could go where you like, but you needed an address so as to get your papers.

'Sa-am, Sa-aam.'

He turned round and saw his sister gazing at a short concrete pillar a few yards from the obelisk. He smiled, got up and went over to her.

'Sam, give me a leg up, will you?'

'There's not much room with that pointy thing sticking out of it,' he said, looking at the pillar doubtfully. 'What is it anyway?'

'It's a meridian of Armagh Observatory,' she answered absently. 'If I stand on it, it will give me a better angle. You didn't tell me you could see Lough Neagh from here,' she said, as he put his hands round her waist and swung her up to perch precariously on the narrow surface.

'Can you?' he asked, not recollecting anything at all about Lough Neagh from the time he'd spent sitting on the grass with Martha.

He hung on to the waistband of her skirt in case she fell off. He'd never be able to face his mother if she hurt herself and her out with him.

'Fine, great,' she said, handing him the camera and jumping down beside him. 'Where will we go to eat our sandwiches?'

'We could head for Annacramp and find a nice spot by the roadside.'

'Great, let's go. I'm starving. Must be the fresh air up here,' she said, as she took her camera back, closed it up and tramped off ahead of him.

'Ma was right,' she declared, as she gathered up the empty brown paper bags that had held their lunch. 'She said we'd probably find an appetite if we were cycling.'

She folded them up, put them back in the shopping bag and brushed a few crumbs from her skirt.

'Do you miss home, Sam?'

'I might of a Sunday if I diden go over home, but durin' the week I'm too busy to think long,' he said directly, as he polished off the last of the sandwiches. 'We're powerful busy with furniture goin' out and stuff for the jam factory comin' in, forby the linen comin' and goin'. There's plenty o' work to keep us goin' till we start on the motor carriages.'

'Hugh said he was hoping to have his in a month or two,' she replied. 'He's had it ordered for ages.'

'Aye, I remember him sayin' he'd written for it when we got the trap, but they're desperate slow to make. It's not the engines, it's the bodywork. It's easy enough to build an engine and put it on a chassis, but what do ye do about the driver and the passengers? You need coach builders, but they haven't got the right equipment,' he went on, shaking his head. 'They're havin' to make the machinery for the bodywork while turnin' out the motor itself. There's one in Armagh. I saw it in the paper.'

'So maybe Hugh's will turn up soon.'

'I'd say it wou'd. He got his name down brave an' early. I was askin' Da did he want one, now he's a Director, but he didn't seem too keen.'

'Didn't he? Why do you think that is?'

Sam laughed.

'Ach, Da's kinda cautious. I reckon he'll wait t'see how Hugh's goes and how much work they'll have to do till get it to climb our hill. I think Da feels Dolly might be more reliable for a while,' he added, as they got to their feet, leaving two flat patches in the long grass of the hedge bank.

Sam pointed out Granny Sarah's house at Annacramp, which he remembered but Sarah didn't, then they cycled on till they came to the main road from Armagh to Loughgall. Together, they braked and stopped. There was no vehicle of any kind to be seen, neither motor vehicle nor farm cart, not even a straying cow or chicken. What had stopped them was a familiar sound. Borne on the gentle breeze came the rhythmic dance of a hammer on the anvil.

'I remember that,' said Sarah abruptly. 'And I remember Da and Thomas rimming the cartwheels with the fire in a circle.'

'Aye,' Sam nodded, as they set off up the hill. 'At least we know he's at home.'

They wheeled their bicycles carefully up the rutted lane, avoiding the stray horseshoe nails and bits of metal filings, and parked them against the low bank beyond the shoeing shed.

'Hello, Thomas,' said Sarah quietly, as the hammering stopped and the figure at the anvil caught sight of her in the doorway.

He put down the hammer and came forward to meet her, his eyes gleaming white against the dark cave of the forge.

'You've maybe forgotten me, Thomas,' she said, beaming at him.

'Ach, how wou'd I an' you the image of your mother?' he said, looking her up and down. 'Wee Sarah, an' you a lady grown.'

He laughed and glanced up at Sam, who had hung back, overcome with a sudden shyness.

'Hullo, Thomas,' Sam said, shooting out his hand.

'Sam! Ach dear, your mother said you'd got awful like your Da. You'd make a good smith with those shoulders of yours, but I hear it's all engines with you, an' you're not that far away now. Over beyond Richhill I heer tell.'

From the deep shadow beyond the hearth, a young man appeared and leant against the doorway. Not as tall as Thomas, but with the same muscular arms and grimy, soot-streaked face, young Robert Scott glanced shyly at Sarah and offered his hand to Sam.

'You'd hardly remember our Robert, Sarah, and you only a wee thing when you moved to Banbridge,' said Thomas, drawing Robert into the conversation, as he waved them all over to the bench beneath the pear tree where once they'd sat waiting for Sinton's dray.

'Now, tell us all your news and then we'll away up and make a pot of tea. Selina is away over to Annie an' she'll be right sorry she missed you, but now you're so close, Sam, sure ye'll come again, won't you?'

The talk was lively and even young Robert, so shy to begin with, began to offer his own small memories of the Hamiltons at Salter's Grange. What he remembered best, he said, was Mrs Hamilton singing at her work and speaking Irish to the two girls from Donegal who worked at Robinsons.

'Ach it must be ten years since ye left us.' declared Thomas, with a long glance down the lane as if he were seeing some event in the past. 'But at least you were still here to leave,' he said, turning towards his son. 'Sarah and Sam were on that excursion train with their mother and James and Hannah. We tried to keep it from you, for you were only a year older than Sarah, but sure there was dozens killed and hundreds wounded,' he explained. 'Their mother always said it was James who saved them. He and Sam were great men for engines, even then, but James understood air brakes forby, and when he heard them go, he knew the train would run back. An' it did. But he told his mother and she had them out double quick, aye, an' all the others in the carriage, as well, James Sinton and his family and a couple of girls in service with their sweethearts.'

'Do ye mind it at all, the pair of you?' he said, his eyes wide, as he looked them full in the face.

'I remember goin' to look at the engine and thinkin' it was not near big enough to pull the train,' said Sam thoughtfully.

'I only remember the long walk home,' said Sarah. 'We had to go across fields and they were muddy in places. And I remember stopping at the pump and James splashing us with water, he was so keen to get us a drink. It was *so* hot.'

'Aye, it was,' Thomas agreed, wondering how it was they were talking about something so sad on this lovely summer day.

'Will you drink a cup of tea?' he asked abruptly. 'Selina has us well taught how to make tea for visitors, hasn't she, Robert?'

'Aye, she has,' replied Robert ruefully. 'She came home one day and found us with no saucers and the cake on the lid o' the tin and we got told off, the pair of us,' he said, with a smile that even included Sarah.

'Tea would be lovely,' said Sarah warmly, 'but there are two things I'd like to do first. I'd like to go and look at our old home and then I'd like to take some pictures of the two of you working in the forge. Is it safe to go into the house, do you think?'

'Ach yes. It's safe enough,' he said reassuringly. 'Just don't stand under where the thatch is bulging. It'll give way one of these days, but it's still dry. I keep some wood and iron in there, but the door's not locked. The weeds has grown up something powerful the last two weeks. Let Sam go first, Sarah, or you'll spoil your nice clothes.'

Sam pushed the door open and stooped under the lintel. Sarah followed close behind and they stood together in the middle of the kitchen, looking at the dusty hearth, the iron crane still in its place. The windows were partly covered with ivy. Pale, greenish light filtered through the fluttering leaves and made dappled patterns on the floor.

Sarah turned towards the bedroom, pushed open the door and walked across to one of the two small wooden cubicles, the bedroom she'd shared with Hannah. Her walking boots echoed on the bare boards.

'Sam, I can't believe it. It's so small,' she said, whispering. 'Six people in this room. How on earth did we manage?'

'Aye. It's a good thing we were all so wee then.'

'Yes, but lots of people live in houses smaller than this. And there were only four of us. Some families have six, or seven, or even more. Some of the spinners and weavers at the mills have eight, or nine, of a family in houses no bigger than this,' she said, her voice rising.

She looked around her for several minutes, then, pulling the door shut behind her, she made her way round a pile of wood, crossed the kitchen and pushed open the door of the wash house. Still hanging from its nail on the wall was the calendar for 1889, marked off with a pencil all through the month of July down to the day of their departure. The last reminder of the life that had once flourished in this small cottage.

Sam moved past her as she stood staring at the crossed-off squares. She turned to watch him go, tramping cautiously between the abandoned spade rigs where their father had grown potatoes and vegetables for the family. She watched him head for the broad outer wall of the garden and suddenly remembered what he was looking for. He stopped, took out his knife and bent down. A few moments later, he came back into the house and handed her a long stem covered with dozens of tiny pink roses.

'You won't remember I'm sure, but we used to play weddings. Hannah was the bride and one of the wee Wylies cut her a bouquet of those same roses. And then we took them to the station, because they were goin' to emigrate. I can't remember the name of the wee lassie. I think she died of TB,' he said slowly.

'Yes, she did. And her mother was killed in the rail disaster. It was Thomas found her body. Ma told me about it once.'

They fell silent and walked back into the kitchen side by side.

'Nice bit of iron work,' Sam said, swinging the crane out over the empty hearth and looking up at the dark crust of soot inside the chimney.

'Of course it is. Da made it,' she replied sharply.

He glanced at her and saw she was upset. He sighed to himself. You could never tell what was going to upset Sarah. He moved the crane carefully back against the chimney stack till it rested exactly where it had been for the last ten years and stood waiting till she made a move.

Sarah was so preoccupied with her thoughts on her homeward journey she almost forgot to collect her bicycle from the guard when she changed trains at Portadown. Sitting by the window of the Banbridge train, she watched the familiar countryside flow past, the evening light casting long shadows, summer flowers picked out in pools of sunlight, couples walking out, enjoying the first real warmth of summer.

Sam had asked her to go over to Richhill soon after he got his new job in the autumn of '97 and they'd spoken of going to visit Thomas many times, but she'd never quite got round to it. Almost two years later, she asked herself why she'd left it so long.

She could think of no reason that satisfied her, but she was sure the delay had made the day even more important. This month was the tenth anniversary of the disaster. It was now ten years since they'd moved to Ballydown. She'd been six, a child with a beloved companion under her arm. Next week, at the Annual Celebration, she would be sixteen. Six to sixteen. Could any decade in one's life bring so much change?

The thoughts and images swirled in her mind like the smoke and steam blown back from the engine as it puffed southwards. She saw Thomas's face, bent over a piece of metal on the blackened workbench at the back of the forge where dancing sunlight gleamed through the dusty windows. A strong, kind face, marked by sorrow and joy, the scar of his injury faded, the comfort of Selina a palpable presence after the hard, loveless years with the unlamented Mary-Anne, and the more recent loss of little Sophie, which none of them could bring themselves to mention.

How vulnerable men were, she thought, the ones who were supposed to be so strong and so capable. They were the ones who went out to work, who ran the business of the world, sat in Parliament, governed the country. Good men like her father and Thomas, James Sinton and Richard Stewart. But where would they be without the women beside them, keeping up comfort and hope against all the hurt of the world?

Her mother had spoken often enough of Granny Sarah and the house at Annacramp. She'd explained why they'd had to leave. But only today, standing in that derelict house, had she begun to guess what it must have cost to make a life there after the loss that had come upon them.

She leant her head back on the lumpy upholstery of the carriage and studied the wide, faded prints of Irish beauty spots above the empty seats opposite. The Lakes of Killarney. The Glens of Antrim. The Giant's Causeway. She was tired and her mind was racing. She knew what her mother would say; 'Let it settle, Sarah. Give it time.'

She stepped down on to the platform, collected her bicycle, put the bag with her camera carefully into the front basket and freewheeled out of the station. The main road was crowded, as it always was on a Saturday evening. She turned down the hill and pedalled past the Crozier Monument. Couples were meeting below it, or waiting beside the polar bears who'd seen his ship trapped in the ice. They greeted each other, strolled off along the pavement outside the handsome house where Crozier himself had once lived, or turned back up the hill to a dance. Poor man, despite his monument, his heroic effort had no part in the thoughts of the Saturday night pleasure-seekers. What he had achieved was soon forgotten. Like the efforts of so many good men and women with no monument except a derelict house or a heap of tumbled stones.

The sun had disappeared behind the trees as she followed the main road home, but it re-emerged as she wheeled her bicycle up the hill. She was tired now, and so aware of being alone. Not anxious, or afraid, in this familiar place on such a lovely evening, but alone. Very much alone. A figure surrounded by space.

She paused to unlatch the garden gate and wondered if in the end the problem was the same for women as it was for men. They too could only manage their very best if they had someone to help them bear whatever life asked of them. Like Ma and Da at Salter's Grange.

Sunday promised to be as bright and sunny as Saturday had been. The front door was propped open at breakfast time and throughout the morning sunlight spilled into the kitchen as Sarah and Rose made preparations for midday dinner.

'Four plates, Ma?' Sarah asked, as she put them on the rack above the stove to warm. 'Is Hugh coming down?'

'Yes. He gave Mrs Lappin the weekend to go and see her sister. I only found out yesterday. He won't have had a hot meal since Friday night,' she said, smiling, as she dropped down into the armchair for a rest.

'Ma, Thomas said yesterday that you'd "saved his life more than the once". What did he mean?'

Rose looked thoughtful. She brushed some crumbs from the skirt of her second best dress and glanced across at her daughter.

'Well, he probably didn't mean it literally,' she began. 'He's always insisted I saved his life when George Robinson and I took him to the hospital after his accident. But if he says I saved him more than once, he must be thinking of some of his bad times when Da and I maybe helped him to keep his spirits up,' she said slowly.

'But he said *you,* Ma. I know he thinks the world of Da and it's so obvious they got on well, but it's you who *saved his life.* I think I know what he means, but I'm not sure.'

'I'm not sure either, Sarah. Do you really want to know?'

'Yes. I do. I'm trying to work something out for myself and I can't get the bits to fit,' she admitted.

'All right then,' her mother said, nodding and taking a deep breath. 'Sometimes one loses hope. It happens to everyone sooner or later. You lose someone you love, a home, a job, a dream you had, your well-being, your health. When that happens, you need someone to encourage you. Not directly, perhaps. Sometimes it can happen just because someone is there, a friendly presence. Maybe what Thomas means is that when life was hard on him, somehow I cheered him.'

'Young Robert says what he remembers is you singing. And speaking Irish to the girls from Robinsons. And laughing.'

Rose smiled.

'We can't always tell what we mean for others, Sarah. Poor little Robert had a hard time of it with his mother. Sometimes I wept when I heard her shouting at him for some wee thing any child might do. I hope maybe he's forgotten, for he was very young. Mary-Anne was very hard on them. But I know Selina loves them as if they were her own.'

'And she lost her own little Sophie?'

'She did,' said Rose slowly. 'Like I nearly lost you.'

'Ma! You never told me.'

'You never asked,' Rose replied, laughing. 'There's so much to talk about in the present, the past sometimes gets forgotten. Sometimes that's a good thing. Sometimes it's not.'

'Thomas said it was Jamie who told you we had to get out of the train,' Sarah went on, her mind following its own logic.

'Yes, it was. Didn't you know that?'

'Maybe I did.'

Sarah looked down at her hands and studied the deeply etched lines as if she were expecting to find an answer to her question there.

'Ma, it was so strange standing in that old house yesterday, trying to imagine what life was like for all of us. Were we very poor?'

'It depends what you call poor. We never starved, though

we were very short of money. The worst time was when the Orangemen boycotted the forge because Thomas and Da wouldn't join the Lodge. We ended up with me earning more from sewing than Da earned in a long week. That's when he had to take the job in the mill. You know about that.'

'Yes,' she replied, sharply. 'I've put him over it many times. I'm so very grateful he got out, but I just can't forget about all those who are still in there. Getting lung diseases. Becoming deaf. Dying in what is supposed to be the prime of life. The figures are grim.'

She fidgeted restlessly, the light suddenly gone out of her eyes.

'At least Hugh agrees with me,' she said at last.

Rose looked across at the slim figure of her youngest daughter, the soft curls framing her creamy skin, her dark eyes clouded and sad. She could not tell what was going on in her mind. So often she could only sense a struggle, an effort to resolve something she felt would have been beyond her, even if Sarah had been able to put it into words.

'Ma, when we came back from Ashley Park, two years ago, I was absolutely horrible, wasn't I?'

Rose had to laugh.

'You were very unhappy. And lonely. I know you missed Hannah badly,' she said gently.

'And Jamie,' she added abruptly.

'Jamie? Did you really miss Jamie?'

She blushed slightly and looked away.

'No. I was glad he was gone. I was so angry with him I thought I hated him. But I felt guilty because you and Da were so sad.'

'Oh, Sarah dear, I am *so* sorry.'

'You're sorry?'

'Yes, of course I'm sorry,' said Rose warmly. 'You had quite enough to bear without feeling guilty about Jamie. It wasn't your fault. Did you think it was?'

'Yes, I did.'

'Oh dear. Elizabeth did say that might be part of the problem. I wish I'd paid more attention to her at the time,' she confessed. 'But it's easy to be wise after the event. I thought it was mostly that you wanted your own life and that just wasn't possible for a girl of fourteen. Not for the kind of things I think you'll want to do.'

'What do you think I want to do, Ma?'

'I think you want to make changes,' she replied promptly. 'You see things you think aren't right. You're concerned about people being poor and overworked and underfed. You'll want to find a way to make life better for people. I've no idea how you'll do it, but I'm sure you'll try.'

'I haven't any idea either.'

'Don't let that worry you,' she said strongly. 'You're sixteen, not twenty-six or thirty-six. You've got plenty of time,' she added as she bent down to make sure the roast was sizzling merrily.

'Ma, before we do the next bit, I want to say sorry,' Sarah said, as Rose got to her feet.

'But sorry what for?' Rose asked, sitting down again.

'I gave you and Da a really bad time over school,' she said sadly. 'I promise I'll not say another word about it. It's only another year now, but I promise I'll make the best of it and not moan, and try to get a really good certificate,' she declared, her eyes lighting up for the first time. 'I can at least do that, even if I can do nothing about Jamie. I'm *so* sorry.'

'Don't dwell on it, love. Maybe Jamie will come back to us. If he does, we give thanks. If he doesn't, we give thanks he's alive and well and can make his own decisions. Don't waste any time on regrets. You have far too much else to do. And now we must make a move, or there'll be no lunch for two hungry men.'

Eighteen

Sarah was as good as her word, though she admitted often enough she found her last year at school no great hardship. Everything seemed easier when she knew the summer would finally bring her freedom. In the darkest days of winter she read widely, wrote to Hannah and Marianne, rehearsed for the Dramatic Society, worked on her pictures of the mills and the commentaries that went with them, and played hockey, all with the same vigour and energy.

As the worst of the winter weather passed and the first signs of spring became obvious, a long awaited event occurred to delight everyone. Hugh's motor carriage finally arrived, polished and gleaming and smelling of new leather. It was hard to tell whether he or John was more excited by the prospects it opened up.

Sam had been spending more of his weekends in Richhill, but he promptly asked for a day off and arrived home one Friday night to study the specifications and the 'instructions for your chauffeur'. The following morning, a mild April Saturday, the first trial runs were made, Sarah sitting beside Hugh in the front seat, Sam and John listening for trouble, ready for action, in the back. They drove from the temporary motor house down at Jackson's farm to Katesbridge and back with no worse mishap than frightening a few chickens and amazing two old men sitting dreamily in the morning sun.

By the time the elegant new vehicle was tuned and modified to cope with the steepest part of Rathdrum Hill, summer was on the way and Sarah was already making plans for her future.

'Hello, Mrs Jackson,' she said cheerfully, as she came into the kitchen by way of the dairy, her arms full of the contents of her school locker on the last day of June.

'Hello, Sarah,' said the older woman, getting to her feet. 'You've caught me gossiping to your mother and I only came in to rest my legs for five minutes when I brought the eggs.'

'Don't run away, Mrs Jackson. Help me celebrate. I was thinking of burning my school dress on a bonfire, but the trouble is I'm too sensible,' she said laughing, as she leant over the table and allowed the top layers of her assorted possessions to slide across its bare surface.

'We could always chop it up and use the pieces for quilting, if that would give you any satisfaction,' Rose offered, as she came over and kissed her cheek.

'Before I forget,' said Mrs Jackson, shaking her head to an offer of tea, 'Congratulations. Peter told us you'd won Artist of the Year.'

She blushed and looked pleased.

'I'm not sure I deserve it,' she said honestly. 'They created a special category for photography and I was the only one in it.'

'Ah now, that's not fair,' said the older woman, waving a finger at her. 'My Peter says she was far and away top in the voting,' she went on, turning to Rose. 'It was the others who were lucky they made a special prize. He says every lunchtime there was a crowd in the Art Room looking at her pictures. You know, Mrs Hamilton,' she added, in a confidential tone, 'some of them at that school don't know what the inside of a mill looks like. No, nor the wee cottages the workers live in.'

She paused, as if about to say more, then changed her mind abruptly.

'I must away,' she declared. 'If those two boys of mine are back and I don't go and keep an eye on them, the cake tin'll be empty. I'll take a wee run up again next week, Mrs Hamilton. Cheerio now.'

'I'd planned to have our tea all ready today,' said Rose, smiling ruefully, as their neighbour disappeared in a flurry of skirts beyond the garden gate. 'Best cups and a plate of cake.'

'She's a bit of a gossip, isn't she?'

'Yes, she is,' Rose agreed. 'But she's never malicious. I think she gets lonely in a house full of men,' she went on, as she pulled the kettle forward on the stove and warmed the teapot. 'There are times it's good to have another woman to talk to.'

'Do you miss Elizabeth?'

'Yes, I do,' replied Rose honestly. 'It's not that I don't see her almost as much, but it was so comforting having her just up the hill. I'm lucky to have you around for a wee while longer,' she admitted, laughing, as Sarah pushed at her spreading possessions to leave a space for the cake tin she'd brought out from the dresser.

'Mmm, this is good, Ma. I was thinking about it all the way up the hill,' she confessed, munching her fruit cake devotedly.

The late afternoon sun threw shadows diagonally across the floor as it moved westwards. There was silence in the room for a long moment.

'Did you ever used to feel, Ma, that time would never pass?' asked Sarah, at last.

'Oh yes. Waiting is one of the hardest things we ever do. Especially when you're young. And I don't think it gets that much easier as you get older,' Rose went on, putting out her hand to refill Sarah's cup. 'You become more reconciled to the need for it, but it's still hard.'

'Was being poor hard?' Sarah asked, as she helped herself to a another piece of cake.

'Whatever made you think of that?' Rose replied, laughing at the unexpectedness of her daughter's question.

'The cake,' she mumbled, having just taken a bite. 'Mrs Jackson mentioned her cake tin and then I brought out ours. And I'm having a second piece, which is a bit greedy,' she went on, with a slightly sheepish look. 'I always think of Marie Antoinette when they told her the people had no bread. "Then let them eat cake," she said. Do you remember?'

'Yes, I remember.'

'So when I eat cake, I always think of people who are poor. But I've never been poor. I try to understand what it might be like.'

Rose sat and thought how she might explain. She saw herself standing in the bedroom of the old house, counting shillings into her purse. She had always given thanks for having her own purse and money to put in it.

'There was one very bad winter when I had to keep buying more turf,' she began. 'I'd saved up a little during the summer for clothes for the boys and boots for your father, but the weather was so bad I had to use it all up on fuel. There was only a shilling left in the account and that was just to keep it open. We had almost nothing coming in except for what my sewing made. In the deep winter weeks, sometimes the forge hardly paid for the milk and eggs.'

Sarah finished her cake and sat silent, listening intently.

'Being poor is tiring. It's exhausting,' Rose continued with a great, heaving sigh. 'Because you have to think about everything. Nothing is simple. And all the time you wonder if you're going to fail, because if life should deal you one more blow you'll find yourself without food, or fire, or shelter. I used to think I could bear being poor if it were just me, or just Da and me. What I couldn't bear was you children going short.'

'We never did,' said Sarah, slowly shaking her head.

'No, thank God,' Rose said, smiling. 'But there were times when it came too close for comfort.'

Sarah hung her school dress in the wardrobe. Even if she wasn't keen on the style and was heartily pleased to be rid of it, she could imagine many a young woman who would be glad of something so well made.

'No need to think about that now,' she said aloud, as she worked her way through the pile of things she'd carried upstairs.

There were some books she'd chosen to keep, her indoor shoes, her sketchbook and the portfolio she'd made to hold her best prints, especially enlarged for the end of year exhibition. By the time she'd found a place for everything, she heard water running in the dairy. Her mother was washing the vegetables for supper.

'Any post this morning, Ma?' she asked, as she came behind her to take a peeling knife from the rack on the wall.

'Goodness, yes. I'm sorry, I forgot,' she replied, smiling. 'There's one from Marianne. I could tell that handwriting anywhere. The other is local. Go and have a look if you want, there's only the potatoes to do. I made a stew this morning.'

Sarah left her peeling knife on the draining board, went and lifted down her letters from the mantelpiece, put Marianne's in her pocket to read later and tore open the other one.

'Ma,' she called out. 'I've got a job.'

She ran back to the door of the dairy and leant against the doorpost as she read.

'What? Already? I didn't know you'd applied for any.'

'I hadn't. I just had an idea and went in to see them after school one day. It's the new photographic studio. I asked the boss if he needed any help and he said yes, they needed someone downstairs in the shop and upstairs in the darkroom, but they hadn't advertised it yet.'

'So he's offered it to you?'

'Yes.'

'Do you think you'll like being in a shop?' enquired Rose cautiously.

'No, not much,' Sarah replied. 'But I need to learn developing and printing and enlarging. If I'm good enough at it, perhaps they'll let me do more of it. Anyway, it's a start.'

'When *do* you start?'

'Monday next, 8 a.m. to 6 p.m.,' she read out quickly. 'One week's holiday with pay after one year's service. Bank Holidays. Half day off on Wednesday and Saturday alternately.'

'And how much do they pay you, if it's not a rude question?'

Sarah laughed and told her.

'Not a lot, is it?' Rose said quietly.

'I'd say it was a pittance myself. How much would you like for my keep, Ma?'

'Sarah!' she expostulated. 'As if I'd want anything when you're earning so little. Don't be silly,' she said laughing.

'But Sam paid for his keep when he stopped being an apprentice,' she protested.

'Of course he did, but he did have a decent income then,' she replied. 'Besides,' she went on gently, 'it made him feel good. I used it to open a bank account for him. It's all there for him when he needs it. What you're earning won't keep you in stockings.'

'Do you mind, Ma? Do you think I'm being silly?'

'No, I don't,' Rose said firmly. 'I think you know exactly what you're doing. I'm just so glad the money doesn't matter. Your father will be pleased you've got something you want. In fact, he's going to be delighted, given the little surprise he has for you. But I mustn't say another word and spoil it,' she added hurriedly. 'Now go and find a clean tablecloth, will you, while I get these potatoes going.'

When John came in, they could see how tired he was by the way he hung up his hat and dropped his jacket over the back of his chair.

'Sometimes I think a day's work at the anvil is far easier than an afternoon sittin' roun' a table,' he said, as he came to the table, picked up his knife and fork gratefully and began his meal.

'Ventilation again?' asked Sarah quietly.

'Aye,' he said, nodding at her. 'The people from Belfast specialize in drying equipment,' he explained, turning to Rose. 'Their big blowers are great if ye want to dry tons of tea in India, but we need to clean the air as well as move it. An' there's the problem of the heat generated as well. They're comin' again next week,' he said with a wry laugh. 'Remind me, Friday is the suit, not the corduroys.'

Rose laughed and was pleased to see him look easier.

'Ach, sure I forgot,' he said suddenly. 'Haven't we got a lady of leisure dinin' with us tonight. So you're all finished, Sarah?'

'Yes. But I start work on Monday,' she replied promptly.

'You're jokin',' he said, the lines of tension disappearing from his face.

'No. No joke.'

'Well you don't let the grass grow under your feet,' he said, shaking his head. 'Come on then, tell us all. Ma and I have a wee surprise for you and you're definitely not havin' it till you tell us what you've been up to. Isn't she the sly one?' he added, smiling across at Rose.

Sarah told her story and John nodded, as aware as Rose how useful this modest beginning would be. It was when Sarah mentioned the very small weekly wage that the lines of tiredness reappeared in his face.

'I hope ye'll not try to keep yourself on that, Sarah. Don't for any sakes do what Jamie did, when you know there's money in the bank.'

'John,' Rose said quietly, a note of warning in her voice.

'Ach, I'm sorry. I shou'den have mentioned Jamie,' he replied wearily. 'Sure it wasn't all about money, but that's the part that sticks in my throat. An' you'd never be like that, Sarah,' he said, looking at her directly. 'You're as different from Jamie as chalk and cheese.'

'Will we tell Sarah where her wee surprise is?' prompted Rose, as she took his plate away and stacked it.

'Aye,' he said, brightening visibly. 'It's in the parlour, under the table, with the chenille cloth pulled down over it. A right big box, quite heavy. It says Fragile on it. Mind it doesn't bite you,' he added, winking at Rose, as Sarah hurried off to find it.

'Put it down here, love,' Rose said, folding the tablecloth back from the unoccupied end of the table.

John offered his penknife and she cut her way through the knotted string and the flaps of the substantial cardboard box. The top was full of squeezed-up newspaper. She paused and moved more slowly when she met long pieces of clean rag and the gleam of well-polished wood showed amidst the generous packing. Only when she removed the fabric that swathed the sides and revealed brass fittings and catches did she begin to suspect what it was.

With a final effort to free the beautiful object, she thrust her hands underneath it and drew it out. Rose reached over and lifted the empty box on to the floor so Sarah could put her present on the table. She set it down gently, a few tatters of rag still clinging on to its grained surface, and stared at it.

'My goodness,' she whispered, suddenly afraid she was going to cry. 'A plate camera. Isn't it beautiful?'

She came round the table to kiss her mother and then her father, tried to find words to thank them and failed completely.

'I know they cost a fortune,' she said anxiously.

'Aye, they do,' said John laughing. 'But your ma says we can afford it. Sure it's now ye need it, not when ye've saved up for ten years,' he said, beaming with delight, as she opened the front, drew out the bellows and adjusted the polished brass rim of the lens.

'If it's any help to you, love, we've put the same amount of money in Sam's bank account,' her mother said softly. 'Da thinks a plate camera mightn't do him much good, but he'll be thinking of a motor in a few years when they come down in price.'

Rose and John exchanged glances as they watched her search in the bottom of the box for the accessories and the book of instructions.

'My goodness,' she said, reading the cover quickly. 'How did you know I wanted one of these?' she demanded, looking from one to another. 'Teddy says they're better than the one he had at Ashley Park.'

'All your father's work, love,' her mother admitted easily.

'So how did you know, Da?' she asked, staring at him intently.

'Ach, it was Hugh. I never thought of him knowing anything about photography, but the minute I said "plate camera" he was away,' he said, shaking his head. 'He'd all the details. Where to get it. What the different models were. What it would cost. I've no idea where he foun' it all out.'

Rose nodded agreeably and glanced sideways at Sarah, who'd disappeared into the bottom of the box to make sure there was nothing she'd missed. Perhaps it was just the effort of bending over immediately after supper, but she was almost sure Sarah was blushing.

Ballydown
August 1900

My dearest Anne,

Yes, of course we are delighted. Such wonderful news. We had a letter from Hannah earlier this week and I must say she does sound extraordinarily composed. Were you as confident about your first child? I certainly wasn't. I do so hope all goes well with her. I did miscarry twice myself, much to John's distress, but I'm hoping that Hannah may be more fortunate.

That's the second baby we've heard of this week. My dear friend Elizabeth is also expecting. I'm so glad she's married to a doctor, for she is rather old for a first child. On the other hand she's is a very fit and healthy woman and she has a strong personal faith, something for which I have had cause to be grateful. From everything John and Sarah have told me, I doubt if many other women could have kept me in the land of the living the night I was so desperately ill.

I'm glad you've been able to have a proper summer's rest at Ashley Park. It's such a joy to me to be able to imagine you sitting by your window, or walking in the gardens, or out riding in the park. Of course I will come again, with or without John, but you'll understand why I didn't feel I could come this year.

Sarah has now been working for six weeks. The first three weeks were dreadful and I was so concerned about her. She came home every night pale with fatigue, almost too tired to eat. Of course, she'd been used to sitting all day in school, not standing behind a counter or in a darkroom, or running up and down the stairs in between. She's getting used to that now. She admits freely that much of what she has to do is boring, apart from the darkroom work. What has been a surprise to her is how much she's learnt from just being at work in the town, observing customers in the shop and in the studio. I've seen the notebooks come out again on a Sunday afternoon if we're at home.

Now that Hugh's motor is properly run in and both he and John can drive it, we've had some splendid outings. I'm sure you know the song: 'Where the Mountains of Mourne Sweep Down to the Sea'. Well, last Sunday we went to Newcastle with a picnic lunch. How strange to see 'our' mountains in this different setting. From the field gate across the road they're misty blue shapes that seem close, or far, depending on the weather. But in Newcastle, the little watering place at their foot, they are green and have shady paths where one can walk up to various viewpoints, though I preferred to sit on the beach with John listening to the sound of the sea. Last Sunday we spoke of Kerry and thought of you and Harrington while Hugh and Sarah climbed up the lower slopes of Slieve Donard.

My dear, I have written enough for one letter, but I shall write again soon. Give my love to all our young ones and to Harrington and please do not exhaust yourself when you go back up to town, or I shall have to scold you as you would scold me.

As always, your loving friend,
Rose

'There's a letter for you today, Sarah,' announced John, one Wednesday lunch-time, some weeks later, as she stepped into the kitchen dripping puddles on the floor, having cycled through the grey, misting rain that had swept in during the late morning.

Rose got up from the table where she and John had finished

their meal and handed her a warm towel from the rack over the stove.

'Thanks, Ma,' she said, hanging her sodden cape on a hook and burying her wet face in the warm fabric.

'Should you change that skirt?' she asked, as Sarah wiped her wet face and towelled her hair vigorously.

'No, it's only the skirt, Ma, my petticoat isn't wet at all,' she said as she sat down and blew her nose. 'Oh, that's better. Rain is so tickly running down your face,' she went on as Rose brought her a bowl of champ from the oven.

'Your ma looked for a silver salver to put it on,' her father continued, grinning cheerfully, 'but she couldn't seem to find one.'

'Maybe you should eat a bite first, Sarah. You don't often get letters from Westminster,' added Rose.

'Ma, this is wonderful,' Sarah said, as she breached the pale-green mound on her plate and watched the melted butter trickle out. 'I wasn't expecting anything hot.'

She munched vigorously as she looked from one to the other. 'Now what's all this about a letter?'

By way of answer, Rose reached down a long, stiff envelope from the mantelpiece and placed it beside her plate.

'House of Lords,' said John, as she examined the embossed seal on the reverse. 'Maybe they want you to go and take their picture.'

Sarah put down her fork, picked up a clean knife and opened it.

'It's from Lord Altrincham,' she said, beaming, as she drew out two thick, folded sheets and glanced at the small, well-formed hand that covered the pages.

'The man ye met at Ashley Park? Ye liked him but ye didn't think much of the wife, did ye?'

'That's putting it politely, Da,' she replied, taking up her fork again. 'She was awful. But he and I talked a lot. That's why I wrote to him.'

'You wrote to him?' he exclaimed, his eyes wide, as he glanced at the clock and stood up. 'And now he's written back?'

She nodded, her mouth full, as she scanned the closely written pages.

'I'll maybe walk up later,' she said, as John reached for his coat and cap. 'I think Hugh might be interested. It's a bit tricky to make out but I'll read it to you later when I've figured it out myself.'

'Aye well, I'll leave you to it.'

He bent to kiss Rose and then Sarah.

'We don't hear from the Houses of Parliament every day,' he added, smiling to himself as he stepped out into the rain.

House of Lords

25th September 1900

My dear Miss Sarah,

I was delighted to receive your interesting and informative letter. Our acquaintance may have been brief but I remember it with great pleasure and most certainly do not consider it impertinent that you should write to me.

On the contrary, I am honoured that you should confide in me and go to so much trouble to inform me of the improvements that your father and his partner, Mr Sinton, have been making towards the health and safety of the workers in the four mills for which they hold themselves responsible.

Would there were many more to take such a view of their responsibility. As we agreed at Ashley Park, questions of safety are seldom uppermost in the minds of those who see manufacturing merely as a source of profit for themselves and not as a means of livelihood for large numbers of workers, all of whom have families to support.

I must congratulate you on the photographs which you sent to me. My wife treasures the pictures that you and young Lord Cleeve took when we first met, but you have turned what many see as a pleasant hobby into a very effective tool. It doesn't surprise me, but it pleases me greatly. With your pictures I can argue more specifically. It is not that my colleagues on the Factory Health and Safety Standing Committee are entirely ignorant of conditions in mills. Some of them have gone to considerable pains to educate themselves, but time is of the essence. Your pictures and annotations sum up the situation so clearly. Rest assured I shall make good use of them.

I would very much like to be kept informed of the progress of the innovations you have spoken of. I am familiar with the co-operative movement, but not of the particular application of which you speak. Similarly, the ticket system has long been overdue for reform. It seems you are already several steps ahead with your card system and in your plan for regular medical examinations and seaside holidays.

What you say of your own present employment is somewhat alarming. You, who are campaigning for shorter hours, are working very long hours yourself. I know your dear mother will be taking great care of you, but may I, as someone who sees the potential of your future work, beg you not to exhaust yourself.

I have no doubt that you will be visiting your sister at some future date. Should it be convenient for you to visit while they are in London, I would be very pleased to entertain you in the House and to accompany you to the Stranger's Gallery should you wish to observe a debate.

Please convey my good wishes to your dear mother and to your sister.

I remain,
Yours faithfully,
Altrincham

'Well,' said Rose, with a great, deep breath, as Sarah finished reading the letter to her, 'you've begun. I said you'd change things and it looks as if Lord Altrincham thinks so too. Congratulations, love. I think you should be pleased.'

She smiled awkwardly.

'Yes, I am pleased,' she admitted, leaning back comfortably in her father's armchair. 'But I couldn't have done anything if you and Da and Hugh hadn't helped me. It's their work I've written about . . .'

'And your pictures you sent.'

'And some of the best were taken on the plate camera you and Da gave me,' she continued, not to be deflected from expressing her sense of fairness.

Rose laughed.

'I highly approve of modesty in a young woman. It is very becoming,' she said in a teasing tone, 'but I will not let you diminish what you've achieved. Take it, treasure it, build on it. There will always be disappointments enough you'll have to carry. If you don't take the goodness of what you achieve you won't have the strength of spirit to weather the bad bits.'

She nodded and stretched her legs out in front of the stove. A faint mist of steam drifted upwards from the damp hem of her dress.

'Oh, it is lovely to sit and talk, Ma,' she said suddenly. 'That's what I miss most as a working girl. All our cups of tea after school and on Saturdays if there wasn't a hockey match. Now it's Wednesday or Saturday afternoon, and that's only when I don't go to one of the mills.'

'Yes, I miss you too. But one day you'll be gone altogether, so I'm enjoying what I have,' she replied quite calmly.

'Oh, Ma, don't be daft. I'm not going to marry an English Lord like Hannah. Ireland is my place and Down is my corner. I won't be far away. There's work enough to do here without me emigrating,' she declared. 'I'll maybe be one of these fierce old spinsters who are doing such good work for Womens' Rights. Could you see me in the Suffrage Movement?'

'Goodness knows what you'll get up to, but there is something I want you to think about.'

'What's that?'

'A blessing on Lord Altrincham for paving the way for me,' she said sighing. 'I know you'll say that other girls have to work even longer hours than you, Sarah, but other girls may not have the gifts you have,' she began cautiously. 'If you exhaust yourself out of sympathy for them, you won't be able to do much to help anyone.'

She nodded and admitted that sometimes she was so tired by Saturday she just wanted to sit by the fire and read a novel.

'What I want you to do is see this job as a temporary thing. Give it up when you've learnt all you can. Take some months off. Go and visit Hannah. I'd love you to come with me to Donegal to visit your Aunt Mary. It would be marvellous for your landscape work. Then, when you're ready, look for something different. You don't have to earn a living. That's a real gift, but it's you who must take it.'

Sarah beamed at her.

'Am I easier to talk to than I was when I was at school?' she asked, her eyes sparkling with amusement.

'Yes, you are. They say girls in their teens go through a rebellious phase. They always hate their mothers. You didn't do that, thank goodness, but you did do some hating. I used to feel I was treading on eggshells when I tried to help you.'

'Isn't it nice to be old, Ma. One's got past all that.'

'Old?' Rose retorted. 'Do you mean me, or you?'

'Both of us. We're both so old we can talk to each other like friends. I'm so happy about that.'

Rose looked across at her, as she bounced up from her chair and looked out of the window to see if the rain had stopped.

'Yes, I'm happy about it too. It's much more restful,' she said, laughing gaily.

Nineteen

The last week of January 1901 brought with it two memorable events, the long-awaited departure of Queen Victoria and the anxiously awaited arrival of Elizabeth Stewart's first child. While the country went through the rituals of mourning for a Queen who had mourned for most of her long life, Elizabeth, after a long and difficult labour, borne with her customary calm, gave birth to a robust baby boy who already had a cap of the same fine dark hair as his father. Elizabeth and Richard were relieved and delighted. Every moment they could spend together with their child was a kind of celebration.

Visiting in the evenings after work, when Hugh drove her over to spend a few hours with the new parents and her mother, who was looking after Elizabeth, Sarah was overwhelmed by their joy. She held the very new baby, was amazed at its smallness and its perfection, totally entranced by the curling and uncurling of its fingers and amused by his name. James Richard Pearson Stewart seemed such a big name for such a very small creature.

It was only when Elizabeth was on her feet again and Rose safely back home that Sarah admitted she was so exhausted she felt she could sleep for a week. She wondered how women who worked all day in shops and factories could manage to buy food in their brief midday break, cook an evening meal, keep up with the laundry and housework and be up early enough to get to work by eight o'clock the next day. She'd done it willingly enough for three weeks, but she wasn't sure she could have kept it up much longer.

With Rose's encouragement and the knowledge that her

mother would be away again quite soon, she gave up her job gratefully in the middle of March and spent her first week of freedom having breakfast in bed and getting up very late indeed.

'Are you sure you'll be all right?' Rose asked, the morning her sailing tickets arrived.

'But of course, Ma. I'm absolutely fine now,' she reassured her. 'If it weren't for looking after Da while you're with Hannah, I'd be thinking of a new job. But I won't even look at Situations Vacant until you're back.'

'You won't get bored?' asked Rose cautiously.

'No. I've got lots of plans,' she said quickly. 'I'm going to work out how I can use my old bedroom as a darkroom. Da says he can fit a frame over the window and I've found a filter I can use on a torch to make a dark light. That'll keep me busy when I'm not cooking and cleaning.'

'You will get out in the fresh air, won't you?' Rose went on, suddenly remembering what Lady Anne had said about the smell from the knife room at Ashley Park when Teddy had used it as a darkroom.

'Yes, I will. Hugh's offered to help me with my landscapes,' she explained. 'He got me to admit you can't carry a plate camera and a tripod on a bicycle. He says the motor needs regular outings to keep it running sweetly, so he might as well drive me around the countryside rather than just take it out for the sake of keeping it ticking over.'

Rose looked at her carefully. Her daughter's eyes were bright, her usual good spirits completely restored. Clearly, she was looking forward to the next month, her plans already made. She wondered what changes might occur in her absence. A month was a long time. Only a week earlier, Lady Anne had enquired if Sarah had any admirers.

'She is such an attractive, lively girl,' she'd written, 'I can't imagine she hasn't her admirers.'

She'd sat for a while thinking about it, her regular letter already half written.

> I hardly know how to answer your question about Sarah, Anne dear. I sometimes think of what you said about

Teddy, that he couldn't even remember the names of the girls he danced with. Sarah's a bit like that. Quite disparaging about most of the boys she was at school with. Occasionally, I mention a name, like Peter Jackson, our new neighbour's son, who is a nice lad and distinctly good looking, but Sarah just laughs.

I sometimes wonder if it's because she's always had such a good friend in Hugh that she finds boys of her own age so very young and unappealing. I must say I'm surprised Hugh has never married. He's an attractive man, and although he does still have a scar, the damage of that terrible fall seems to have been completely corrected. He hasn't even got a limp now. What marvellous things they can do these days to mend damaged bodies, though I must say Hugh worked terribly hard himself and suffered a great deal to get his muscles working again. I really did think when Elizabeth got engaged to Richard Stewart, Hugh would look around him.

But speaking of looking around, Anne, I've remembered something else I must tell you. Sam arrived last Saturday afternoon looking smarter than ever. I've never know anyone who could get such a shine on their boots! Sarah began teasing him right away. Sam, of course, said nothing. He has a way of just smiling. But John and I both think there's a girl in it somewhere. Sarah is perfectly certain there is. She says he may not be saying anything, but she won't be one bit surprised when he does.

So much happening, my dear, babies and engagements. I'm so much looking forward to seeing you next week when I come over for Hannah's confinement. What a mercy she is so well and has you at hand. I am so grateful for that. Love and kisses to you both,

Rose

Francis John Molyneux Harrington was born at Cleeve Hall, one of the manor houses on the Ashley estates, on the last day of March 1901, arriving just before midnight in the midst of an equinoctial gale that felled timber in the park and disrupted sailings to and from Ireland. But within the comfortable old manor, all remained calm and quiet. Shortly after the birth, Rose and Anne retreated to the sitting room to drink tea, leaving Hannah holding her child as if she'd spent her young womanhood caring for babies, while Teddy sat beside her, unable to take his eyes from her face and the fall of her hair.

Rushed to the nearest Post Office by one of the younger servants, the expected telegram arrived at Ballydown next morning. Sarah heard the scrape of handlebars against the garden wall and hurried to the door.

'Here y'are. I hope it's not bad news,' said the telegraph boy, as she flew down the garden path, grabbed the envelope he held out to her and ripped it open.

'Lovely boy. Hannah well. Letter follows. Love, Ma,' she read, her stomach doing a double somersault before it settled back into its normal position.

'No, it's not. It's good news,' she said beaming. 'My sister's had her baby. All's well. Isn't that wonderful?'

'Ach aye. That's great. An' how's Sam?'

Sarah paused, confused and somewhat taken aback. She looked more closely at the young man in his smart uniform.

'Billy?' she said, still a little uncertain, 'Of course it's Billy. 'I didn't recognize you for a minute. You were Sam's flagman.'

'Aye, till I got abolished in '96,' he said wryly.

'But you went on working at Tullyconnaught, didn't you? It was you went for Da when Sam broke his leg. Thank goodness you did.'

'Aye,' he replied, lifting up his bicycle and preparing to mount. 'But when I came up to see Sam an' he told me he'd got his cards, I thought to meself, that's that. And I started to look about. I'm a lot better off where I am. And I'm learning the telegraph forby. As long as they don't invent somethin' else for sendin' messages quicker, I'll do rightly,' he declared, as he got into the saddle. 'Tell Sam I was askin' for him,' he called over his shoulder as he pushed off down the hill.

'I will indeed, Billy. Thanks a lot.'

She read the telegram three times more as if it still had something new to tell her. Laughing at herself, she pulled on her cape and set off up the hill, the bright, torn envelope in her pocket.

The stiff, chill breeze from the north-east almost took her breath away, but it was powerful enough to blow holes in the clouded sky. By the time she got to the top of the hill, great patches of blue sky had already appeared. Against them, the still-bare branches of the limes swayed back and forth, the light picking out the pale, swollen buds that would break into leaf as soon as they felt the touch of some real warmth.

She made her way to the workshop, but, finding it empty and silent, she proceeded to the conservatory. It was Hugh who saw her first and sprang to his feet, setting aside a pile of papers.

'Sarah,' he said, beaming.

'Hello, Hugh,' she replied. 'Sorry to interrupt the work. I have a message for Granda Hamilton,' she continued, almost managing to keep her face straight.

'Ach dear,' said the man himself, looking up at her, his eyes suspiciously damp. 'When did you hear?'

She pulled out the crumpled telegram, put it in his hand and dropped down gratefully in the chair Hugh brought for her.

'And all well?' Hugh said softly, meeting her eyes, as John read and reread the brief message just as she'd done.

She nodded happily.

'About ten minutes ago,' she said, answering her father's question as Hugh disappeared in search of Mrs Lappin and a pot of tea.

'I can't rightly take it in,' he said, blowing his nose and glancing again at the insignificant piece of beige paper.

'Tea in a couple of minutes,' Hugh said, coming back into the sun-filled conservatory. 'Mrs Lappin says congratulations,

John. This makes you an aunt, Sarah. How do you like the idea?' he asked, his sober, grey eyes unusually bright.

'I hadn't thought about that,' she replied, laughing. 'I hope he's as lovely as Elizabeth's baby. What does it feel like to be an uncle?' she demanded in return.

Tea arrived. Mrs Lappin was not noted for her enthusiasm or her smiles but even she seemed delighted. What was it, Sarah wondered, that brought such joy? A child born in another place, to a girl once known, a neighbour's daughter, no relation or close friend. She'd never seen her look so cheerful.

'We must go to Dromore and tell Elizabeth and Richard this evening,' said Hugh, as he finished his tea. 'What time can I pick you up?' he asked, looking from Sarah to John and back again.

'I think maybe I'll write Rose and Hannah a few lines this evenin',' he answered thoughtfully. 'But you and Sarah away over an' see them. They'll be powerful pleased to hear the news.'

'Did you get what you wanted?' enquired Hugh, one calm April evening two weeks later, as he reached out to take the camera and tripod from her. He waited while she climbed over a stone wall.

'I think so,' said Sarah slowly. 'I have a feeling the light level dropped just as I was ready to take it. But I couldn't work any faster. There are so many pitfalls with landscape,' she explained solemnly. 'One wobbly tripod leg and that lake drains out down the main road.'

He studied her closely, surprised to hear her tone so flat.

'You look tired.'

'Do I?'

'You often do when you take pictures. I think it's because you concentrate so hard.'

'I never thought of that,' she said honestly.

'Come and sit in the motor. It's better padded than this wall.'

She laughed and climbed up gratefully into the parked

motor. Behind her, she heard Hugh make sure her equipment was safely wedged on the back seat.

'That sky just gets more beautiful,' she exclaimed, as he got in beside her. 'But I can't do anything about it till they invent the colour film we talked about after Elizabeth's wedding.'

'Probably won't be all that long before they do,' he said thoughtfully. 'I'm not sure I can keep up with the rate things change at these days. Probably a sign of advancing age,' he added, with a slight, wry laugh.

She looked at him and grinned.

'Da says it's all the fault of the change of century,' she declared, leaning back comfortably. 'Making him feel old, that is. Francis and James will be twentieth-century men, but all the rest of us span two centuries. And two reigns,' she added, as the thought struck her.

'Yes, we're Victorians and the babies will be Edwardians,' he mused. 'Just think what they'll live to see. More radical things than colour film, I suspect. What do you think?'

'Moving pictures, certainly,' she replied, as she watched fragments of tinted cloud move across the paling sky. 'Marianne persuaded Lady Anne to go to the cinematograph in London. They do marvellous things with horses. She said some people screamed when they came racing towards them and flew over their heads on the screen,' she went on, laughing. 'But I expect that's only a beginning, like me using a plate camera and a Kodak.'

He smiled at her and gazed out over the broad prospect below them, the calm surface of a small lake perfectly reflecting the low hills that surrounded it, a solitary fisherman standing thigh deep in water, creating ripples that vibrated outwards into the still water.

'So what's your next project, Sarah, now you've got your darkroom going?'

'Belfast,' she said promptly. 'I want to learn portraiture and I need a big studio for that.'

He glanced away and for a moment Sarah wondered what had caught his eye. A blackbird in the hedgerow or a patch of light on a distant field.

'You'd go into lodgings?' he said, matter-of-factly.

'Yes,' she nodded, not looking at him. 'I thought I'd have a word with Elizabeth. She always knows people who know people,' she said, smiling.

But, to her surprise, Hugh didn't smile at all. He just looked thoughtful and rather sad and said it was time they were getting back.

Sarah stood on the shallow steps of the Great Northern Railway Station and looked up and down Great Victoria Street. It was full of vehicles of all kinds coming and going, the noise of hooves and wheels on the cobbles, the cries of carriers and street sellers loud in her ears. There was no sign at all of a cab, but Hugh had insisted she would need one. The Abercorn Studio was in Anne Street, he'd said, studying the street plan in his Trade Directory. It was too far to walk through crowded streets carrying the albums of work she'd decided to take.

It was much warmer in the city than in Banbridge and her smart straw bonnet seemed to make her head hotter rather than keep her cool. She patted her face with her handkerchief. It was much noisier too. She'd have to get used to that. But the thought of getting used to this continuous noise oppressed her.

'It's just a question of giving it time,' she said to herself, thinking of what her mother would say.

She'd got used to standing all day and running up and down that steep staircase in the tall, narrow building looking out over The Cut, when she first started work. Other girls did it. So could she. She spotted a cab, waved her handkerchief and was grateful when the driver tipped his whip in acknowledgement and manoeuvred his way towards her.

The Abercorn Studio comprised two floors above a chemist's shop and wasn't nearly as elegant as it claimed to be in its advertisement. But it did have its own entrance, a familiar steep, narrow staircase. Clutching the bag with her albums in one hand and picking up her skirt with the other, she climbed up to a landing where she was greeted by the unmistakable smell of fixer.

A number of doors opened out from the landing. None of them was labelled and it was not immediately clear where someone coming for interview should apply. Knowing she was early, she sat down on a hard wooden chair to consider her next move. Hugh had been quite right. The albums were heavy. She'd never noticed that before, but then, she'd never before carried them around all at once.

As she sat collecting herself, a woman emerged from one of the adjoining rooms. She swept past without taking the slightest notice of her. On her return, Sarah stood up.

'Excuse me. I've come to see Mr Abernethy. I have an appointment at three o'clock.'

'He doesn't see sales people in the afternoon,' she said disagreeably, her eye lighting on the albums as she looked her up and down.

'I'm not a sales person,' she replied coldly. 'My name is Sarah Hamilton. Perhaps you'd be so kind as to tell Mr Abernethy I'm here.'

The superior being moved on with a swish of skirts, the only acknowledgement of her words a slight tilt of the chin. Some minutes later Mr Abernethy himself appeared.

'Ah, Miss Hamilton,' he boomed jovially, as he extended his hand. 'Please come into my office.'

He waved her into a large room filled with heavy furniture, bookcases full of ledgers, large pot plants with very shiny leaves, a collection of plaster pillars, cherubs' heads and velvet drapes.

'Do sit down,' he said charmingly, as he retreated behind his desk and took up the letter she had written in reply to his advertisement.

'You are eighteen, Miss Hamilton,' he said, looking at her sharply with small, dark eyes.

'Yes,' she said, looking straight back at him.

Her birthday wasn't for another two weeks, but she was determined not to miss this opportunity for the sake of a fortnight.

'You say you have quite a lot of experience, though your last employment was only some eight months,' he continued, his joviality beginning to grate, his manner wearing rather than pleasant.

'I've been taking pictures for almost four years. I've brought some of my work to show you.'

'Ah, excellent. Excellent,' he said, as she took the albums out of her bag and placed them in front of him.

He flicked through the pages of the first one.

'Of course, we seldom have much need of landscape pictures,' he said in the same genial manner. 'We don't do picture postcards,' he added, by way of explanation as he slid the album aside and began on the next.

'Hmm, most interesting,' he said, leafing through marginally more slowly. 'We *do* sometimes have commissions from manufacturers, but more often for exterior pictures. For advertising, you understand,' he said, nodding to her.

She watched him closely. For all his avuncular manner, there was something unpleasantly calculating about him. He knew exactly what he wanted, and if he didn't think she could provide it he'd escort her to the door within the next three minutes, still as charming as ever, and forget her before she'd even set foot on the stairs.

He'd reached the third album now. She knew by the cover it was her first one, the pictures from the summer of '97 at Ashley Park.

'And what did you use to take this one?' he asked, smiling at her over the first double page.

'That's the only one I *didn't* take,' she said steadily. 'I got that from a friend who borrowed a rotating camera. I wanted it as an introduction to the rest of the pictures. I took all of them.'

Mr Abernethy peered at the panoramic picture Teddy had taken and turned the pages more slowly. He came to an abrupt halt at the study of Hannah and Teddy under the rose arch.

'And these pictures were taken at . . .'?

'Ashley Park, in Gloucestershire.'

'And how, may I ask, did you gain access there?' he enquired with a confidential bow.

'My mother and Lady Anne, the countess, that is, are old friends.'

'Ahh,' he said, nodding vigorously, as if that fact explained the quality of the pictures. 'We do a lot of portraiture for the gentry. In fact, we rather specialize in engagements and wedding photography. Such interesting work, don't you think?'

'I'm very interested in portraiture, that's why I applied to you. There are some wedding portraits in the fourth album, but they're only first attempts with a Kodak. I didn't have my plate camera then,' she added slyly, as she saw the way his mind was working.

'Charming. Quite charming,' he said. 'May I ask who this beautiful young woman is?'

Sarah could see exactly what he was thinking. With her face as straight as she could manage and a cool, slightly offhand tone, she replied to his question.

'Oh, that's my sister Hannah, Lady Cleeve.'

'Delightful picture,' he enthused. 'But, as you say, a first attempt with a Kodak. I'm sure you'll find our resources will give you much more scope. Now, about your hours and remuneration . . .'

'So you said yes,' Rose asked uneasily, as Sarah finished her story some hours later.

'I did,' she replied, drinking her mug of tea gratefully. 'The hours are just as long, 8. a.m. to 6 p.m.,' she went on. 'But the wages are *much* better. Stockings *and* tram fares,' she said laughing. 'They are well equipped, though. They've got stuff I've never even heard of.'

'I don't much like the sound of the boss.'

'I probably won't see much of him,' she responded cheerfully. 'I think he does the money. It's Mrs Cheesman is the real horror. "How do you do, Miss Hamilton,"' she went on, mimicking the over polite tones of the woman who had previously swept past her on the landing. 'She's the kind of woman who gives you her hand and it feels like a dead fish.'

Her mother laughed and shook her head.

'Honestly, love, I *cannot* see much to recommend this job, I really can't. Are you sure you're doing the right thing?' she said, trying not to sound anxious.

'No, I'm not sure,' she said honestly. 'But there are things I want to find out. I know nothing about living in a city, or being a working girl in lodgings, or being away from home and family. Jamie did it. Hannah did it. Then Sam did it. I feel I have to do it too. If it's awful I won't pretend it's not, but I think I can learn a lot at the studio. Abernethy is a real snob,' she continued, her tone contemptuous. 'I could see his mind working. If he gave me the job he could put big enlargements of Hannah and Teddy in the studio and just casually refer to them when he's showing customers in. I agreed, of course. It won't do them any harm and I'll get a close look at what he calls "gentry". All part of my education, Ma,' she ended with a sigh.

'Yes, I can see that side of it,' Rose replied, looking at her carefully. 'I admire your courage, to be honest. I'm just thinking how much Da and I will miss you. And so will Hugh, I'm sure.'

'But I'll be home every week,' Sarah protested.

'Well, perhaps,' replied Rose, thinking of Sam.

'Of course I will. Saturday afternoon, by the first train. You just wait and see,' said Sarah firmly.

The first weeks of the new job went well. Despite the long hours and the fact that Mrs Cheesman treated her like a servant, she was so intrigued by the work she simply didn't allow her behaviour to upset her. The other assistants, all young men in their twenties, were friendly enough, given to silly practical jokes, but good-natured and otherwise harmless.

Her lodgings, run by a vigorous, middle-aged Quaker lady, were clean, old-fashioned and mercifully quiet. In a tree-lined street near Queen's College, the tall brick house was inhabited mostly by single ladies who worked in offices. In the evenings, if she stayed in, reading in the sombre sitting room, or writing letters in her small bedroom, she did feel lonely, but, encouraged by the long, warm evenings, she began to go for walks, sometimes going so far across the city she had to take a tram to bring her part of the way back.

With the light lingering till after ten, she would take pictures of people strolling in the parks or looking in shop windows. Having something to do kept her from thinking longingly of the countryside round Ballydown and the evenings she'd spent with Hugh visiting local beauty spots. But she couldn't always keep herself busy. Sometimes, after a long, difficult day with tiresome customers or when things went wrong in the darkroom, she was too tired to go out. She lay on her narrow bed looking up at the small patch of sky in the single window and thought of what her mother had said about Hugh missing her.

She knew she missed him. She thought of him often, storing up things to tell him, wondering what he would say when she described a particular person, or explained the problems she'd had with a particular picture. But then, she remembered, Hugh had been part of her life since the very first day they'd arrived in Ballydown. She'd always talked to him, asked him questions and told him what she thought. Even when she was only a little girl he'd listened to her and considered her words as seriously as if she were a grown-up. For years now, he'd asked her what she thought about the changes he wanted to make at the mills.

June passed and the heavy, thundery weather of July made the city even less appealing than usual. She longed for Saturday and counted the hours till she stepped into the Banbridge train. As she felt the miles diminish between her and Ballydown, she stared out at the familiar, green countryside as if she were afraid it had somehow disappeared while she'd been closed up indoors all week.

Although Saturday afternoon was supposed to be her half holiday, there were occasions in the summer months when she was obliged to work, because all the young men were out photographing cycling clubs or field clubs, church outings or wedding receptions. She hated it when that happened, but, while she had no choice in the matter of working, she could at least choose to have time off in lieu of the extra hours. That meant she was sometimes able to be free on Friday afternoons and then the weekend beckoned invitingly, for it seemed almost twice as long.

It was on one of these Friday afternoons in early August she found herself walking along the platform in Banbridge with Peter Jackson.

'Hello, Sarah. I thought you didn't get home till Saturday?' he said, greeting her with a cheerful smile.

'Don't usually. Had to work *all* last Saturday. I've got time off for good behaviour,' she said laughing. 'What about you?'

'Been for an interview,' he said, as they handed in their tickets and came through the barrier into the gloomy entrance hall. 'Don't think I can stand cows all my life. Shipping Office and Travel Agents. Pay is poor, but it goes up when I'm twenty and I've an aunt I can lodge with. How's photography?' he asked, nodding at the camera slung over her shoulder.

'Very mixed,' she said honestly. 'I've actually got to missing cows,' she went on, grinning, as they paused by the bicycle park.

She watched him as he unlocked his chain and wheeled his bicycle back to where she stood.

'Haven't you got yours?' he asked.

'No. Da leaves me down in the trap on Sunday nights. Anyway, I'm looking forward to the walk. Don't let me keep you back, Peter. I'll probably see you tomorrow if Ma wants eggs or milk. We get through twice as much when Sam comes home,' she said, laughing.

'I'll walk as far as the Memorial with you,' he said easily. How *is* Sam? I hear he has a girl.'

'How did you hear that?' she asked, curious, as they stepped out of the station yard into the sunlight of the warm August afternoon.

'Busy as ever,' Peter commented, looking up and down the main street, crowded with randomly parked carts and drays.

As Sarah followed his gaze, her eye was suddenly caught by a figure on a bicycle weaving expertly at speed between the pedestrians and parked vehicles.

'Billy,' she called, as she recognized his trim uniform.

He spotted her and skidded to a halt beside them.

'There's a fire at Millbrook,' he gasped. 'I'm away up for your da and Mr Sinton. The manager telegraphed us. Must go,' he added, whizzing off without a backward glance.

'Peter, could I ask you a great favour?' Sarah said carefully.

'What?' he asked, looking at her in surprise.

'Would you lend me your bicycle?' she said promptly. 'I wasn't planning to take pictures of a fire, but they could be useful, especially if I can get there quickly.'

'Yes, of course. Can you manage the bar?' he asked, handing it over. 'Can I take your bag? It'll be safer with me.'

She handed him her overnight bag, moved her camera from her shoulder to lie diagonally across her chest and caught up her skirts with a practised hand.

'Thanks, Peter. You're a real friend,' she said warmly. 'Don't worry, I'll take great care of your bike. See you later.'

'Just take care of yourself,' he called after her as she pushed off and wove her way into the middle of the road.

Twenty

Millbrook was located near the river Bann, a tall, solid, four-storey brick building. Unlike the other three mills, it was sited a few hundred yards back from the river itself, but close to a small tributary which provided water for the steam that powered the spinning frames. For some reason which no one could explain, it had a worse record for fires than any of the other mills, a problem which had absorbed much time, energy and money over the last years without a satisfactory solution being found.

Sarah pedalled hard, her skirt well bundled up on the bar of Peter's bicycle in case the breeze should catch it and ruin both skirt and wheel by flapping it between the spokes, or, worse still, wrapping it around the chain and landing her in the ditch.

In a very short time she was freewheeling down the last hill to the waterside site. She could see the smoke pouring out from the ground floor at one end of the long building. She slowed down and ran right up to the main entrance, where she'd spotted the manager directing operations.

'What's happening, Tom? No Fire Brigade yet?

'No, miss. We've got two pumps of our own going and the men are using buckets,' he said promptly. 'With a bit of luck, we'll get it out ourselves, if this damn breeze, beg your pardon, miss, would die down.'

Sarah smiled, as much from relief as from the manager's sensitivity to her delicate ears.

'And everyone out?' she added, looking across at a long line of women and children. A supervisor and an assistant sat at a small wooden table in the cool shadow of the far end of the long building handing over money and taking signatures, or witnessing marks, on their record sheets.

'Oh yes,' he said, nodding confidently. 'It was just like one of the fire drills we'd had. There was hardly any smoke till a few minutes ago,' he explained, with an uneasy look towards the increasing volume now rising into the summer sky.

'I'm going to take some pictures, Tom,' she said briskly. 'They might be useful. I saw the telegraph boy in Banbridge. He'll be up at Mr Sinton's by now. He and my father should be here soon.'

She wheeled Peter's bicycle back up the slope towards the road, parked it carefully against the stone wall of the night-watchman's hut, then hurried down towards the stream, where a line of men were passing buckets from hand to hand. A single jet of water was being directed into the ground-floor room where the fire had started. There were ladders against the adjoining walls and buckets of water were being passed up to men who were soaking the floors of the rooms above and beside the source of the smoke.

She took four pictures, then looked round, considering what best to take next. Two men were dismantling a hand-pump.

'What's the trouble?' she asked.

'Dirt,' replied the older man. 'The stream's low wi' the good weather an' this hose doesn't reach as far as the river. If there'd been more water we'd a had it out by now.'

She shaded her eyes from the glare and gazed up the slope towards the main road. Surely the Fire Brigade would be here soon. Their hoses should reach the river and their pump ought to be more powerful. As she watched, the fine jet being played through a broken window into the billowing smoke faltered and failed. A few moments, later she saw the first flames. Licking outwards, they rapidly consumed the window frames of the ground floor room where the fire had started.

There was still no sign of the Fire Brigade or Hugh's motor. Already it was becoming dangerous for the men on ladders to go on trying to damp down the wooden floors adjacent to the room. She was not surprised when the Works Foreman gave orders for the bucket chain to stop. Hugh had given the strictest instructions that no employee was ever to be put at risk.

The men who had been forced to pull back from the end of the building were now walking down to the river to wash dirty arms and splash water on hot, sweaty faces. Four men were now dismantling filters and reassembling metal parts, trying desperately to get the two pumps going again, but nothing could be done directly to check the flames.

Thinking anxiously about the insurance claim, Sarah walked down to the end of the building, the smell of linseed oil strong on the breeze, and made her way across to the engine house which backed on to the stream, its doors some twenty yards or so from the main building itself.

The engines had been turned off and the ventilators closed to keep out smoke. With the strengthening breeze behind her, she climbed up a grassy mound behind the low building and clambered on to its shallow-pitched slate roof. Steadying herself, she took two more pictures of the mill from this new angle. Between one exposure and the next, to her dismay, the flames reached the second storey and she heard the crack and tinkle of glass as the heat shattered the lower panes of the large windows.

From where she'd perched on the roof ridge, she could see up to the main road but not into the area immediately in front of the main entrance. Above the roar of flames she might not have heard the horses pulling the fire engine or Hugh's motor. She had just decided to climb down and go and see if there was any sign of them, when a small movement caught her eye. High above her head, on the top floor of the mill, she caught sight of something white.

She stared up at the window, sure it must be a reflection of the small white clouds moving quickly across the blue sky, or a fragment of cleaning rag hanging on a nearby hook. But the more she looked, the more convinced she became that it had to be a face, a child's face, for it appeared through the haze of smoke only in the lowest pane of the window. Often enough she had braced herself against those window ledges taking pictures of the girls at the spinning frames. She knew well enough they were only three feet above the floor.

With the heat and smoke now making her eyes water, she

stood up carefully astride the roof ridge, as if the change of angle might make the pale, smudged image clearer. She waved her hand and was convinced that the white smudge moved in reply.

She folded up her camera, pushed it back into its case, secured it across her body and slid down the roof, jumping the last few feet on to the convenient grassy mound, part of the winter flood defence. She ran past a group of men who'd managed to get one of the pumps going again, round to the main door where Tom was making a record of events and cursing the Fire Brigade.

'Tom, keep this safe for me,' she said, hauling off her camera. 'There's a child up on the top floor. I'll have to get to it before the smoke does,' she cried, dashing past him and up the main stairway that led to all four floors.

She was breathless by the time she got to the top, but there was no smoke yet at the top of the stairway, only the familiar, thick, dusty air of the spinning floor. The silence was strange, almost eerie, as she ran along the bare boards between the windows and the tall, metal frames, the motes of dust dancing in the sunlight. She'd never been in the mill before with all the spindles still. Halfway along, she began to hear the roar of flames and saw smoke and sparks shooting upwards outside. Then she spotted a small figure. It was crouched by a window, exactly where she had seen it, its back to her, still staring down at the scene below.

As she bent down to pick up the child, it turned towards her, eyes wide with fear. At the same moment, she heard glass in the windows below crack and tinkle as the flames got to them. Smoke billowed up more densely outside.

'Come on, we must run,' she said, taking the little girl's hand.

'Can't run,' said the child. 'Bad leg.'

'Right then, piggy back,' she said quickly, not stopping to wonder how the child had got there in the first place.

She lifted her up on to the window sill, bent down and felt the small arms clutch her neck.

'It is getting very hot up here,' she said to herself, as she straightened up and began to run back towards the distant stairwell. She had to pause to persuade the child to grip her blouse and not throttle her by clutching her tightly round the neck.

She made good speed to the staircase, but going down was far more difficult than she could have imagined, her skirt threatening to trip her at every step because she had no hand free to hitch it up. As they came down to the third floor, they met the first wisps of smoke. Pouring along between the idle machinery from the burning end of the building, it had already reached the stairway.

The child was clinging like a limpet, its small weight increasing every moment, as she hurried down the next flight, knowing that each lower floor would be worse than the last, and that smoke, not fire, was the real danger. Her eyes were streaming and she and the child were coughing repeatedly. Had she not known the building so well she would have been thoroughly confused by the turns and landings she had to negotiate. Halfway down the last flight, she found her way blocked by a dark figure.

'Sarah. Thank God.'

She couldn't see who it was and she was coughing so hard she couldn't manage a reply, but suddenly an arm was round her, the child lifted from her back. Moments later, they burst out into the sunshine and a woman, held back forcibly by the manager, broke free and called blessings upon her.

'Sarah, come over here into the shade. Just a little further,' Hugh said as she bent over still coughing, her eyes streaming.

She sat down gratefully on the supervisor's chair and felt the bliss of a damp handkerchief wiping her face. She rubbed her eyes and was able to open them at last as the irritation eased. Hugh was kneeling beside her on the dusty cobbles with a look of such anxious concern and tenderness on his face, she knew she would never forget.

A short time later pumps arrived from the Lenaderg and Seapatrick mills. The stream had now been dammed and men were taking it in turns to stand in the small reservoir of water and hold the hoses just under the surface where the water was cleanest. A handkerchief had been tied over each hose-end to filter the water as it was pumped up. For half an hour, the entire contents of the stream were directed into the burning building without any visible effect on the flames. The afternoon grew heavier and more humid. The heat and smoke swirled so much there was now no place free of it.

Hugh came up to the nightwatchman's hut where he'd left Sarah gratefully sipping a mug of tea one of the women had brought from the nearby cottages.

'Sarah, I can't leave to take you home. Will you let me send you with Tom on one of the small drays?'

'No thank you, I'm staying,' she said, shaking her head emphatically. 'I'll be perfectly all right when I've drunk this. I want to finish what I started,' she insisted, touching the camera on the seat beside her. 'Are they making any progress? '

'No, it's a losing battle,' he replied, matter-of-factly. 'The breeze gets stronger all the time and now it's gusting. We'll run out of water shortly unless the Fire Brigade show up.'

'Hugh, why isn't Da with you?'

'They had a problem down at Ballievy. His department, not mine,' he said shortly. 'I asked Billy to tell him on his way back to town. I'm sure he'll come when he can.'

They walked back down to the main forecourt together. The women and children had all gone, but a small crowd of watchers sat on the grassy slopes nearby. The two hoses from the neighbouring mills appeared to have failed and efforts were being made to get them going again. As they walked, they felt a sudden gust of wind in their backs. Immediately, they saw the flames bend back upon themselves. The other hose bearers adjusted their position. A few moments later a great jet of water, far more powerful than either of the two that had failed, began to play upon the flames as they retreated in the direction they'd come, their strength diminished by the lack of fresh fuel in the area they'd already devastated.

As they registered the diminishing flames and the power of the new jet of water, there was a warning cry. The fierce gust that had blown the flames back on themselves had also sent a raft of burning material across the narrow space from the main building to the engine house. Flames rose from the roof as slates cracked with the heat. The wooden doors flared up before their eyes and the foreman leading the firefighters shouted for everyone to get well back as the roof dipped under its burden and collapsed on to the well-greased machinery below. There was a flash and a roar as the flames reached the tins of lubricant that had been removed from a storeroom on the ground floor and put there for safety, well away from the original source of the fire.

Apart from the men playing the single, powerful jet on the retreating flames of the main building, everyone just watched from a safe distance. The engine house disappeared behind a wall of flame from which missiles flew into the darkening sky as tins of lubricant detonated with a series of explosions that sounded like a Jubilee firework display.

Sarah looked at Hugh, his face damp with sweat, his expression inscrutable. She would have liked to take his hand and comfort him, but she couldn't do that in such a public place. All she could do was stand close to him and let him sense how fully she shared the frustration and anxiety she knew he was feeling.

Before the flames had quite spent themselves, leaving the twisted and burnt remnants of the engines smoking in the ruins, they heard the wheels of the brougham behind them. It was her father arriving. Following him closely was another pump from Ballievy with four volunteers ready to use it. As they swept down the slope, they heard in the distance the clanging of a bell. The Fire Brigade was approaching, at last.

'I need to take some more pictures,' Sarah said quickly. 'I'll be perfectly safe. You can watch me from here.'

She left Hugh to direct the men from Ballievy and greet her father. She waved to him as she tramped off to where she could take a picture of the smoking ruins of the engine house.

Behind her the Fire Brigade had stopped by the main entrance to consult Hugh and her father. She saw the Fire Chief shake his head. He was waving his arm at the distance between the river and the still-burning mill. Even from where she stood, she could guess what was going on. Their hoses were even shorter than the ones in use at Millbrook.

She took two pictures of the engine house, now a smouldering ruin after the conflagration. As she was selecting the best angle to photograph the still-burning remains of the west end of the mill, she felt something brush her cheek. For most of the afternoon flakes of ash had filled the air with flying fragments, fine as early snow, catching in her hair and clothes and sticking to her damp skin, but she was surprised there should be any left. The sudden stiffening of the breeze and its change of direction had swept all the floating debris away, wafting it across the river and into the surrounding pastures, leaving the air cleaner and cooler.

She took one picture. Then another. As she lined up a third, to show the west end of the mill in relation to the burnt-out engine shed, she felt the same tickling sensation. She managed to ignore it until she'd pressed the shutter. Then she put her hand up to her cheek. To her great surprise she found that it was damp.

Only then did she look up at the sky. The drop in the light level was not due to the smoke, as she'd thought, but to a great mass of dark, threatening clouds. They'd crept up the sky and now entirely shut out the sun. They had just released the first large drops of rain.

She hurried back to the main entrance and arrived just in time to avoid getting soaked. The conference with the Fire Brigade was coming to an end. The Fire Chief, his polished helmet splashed with huge drops, went to view the damage, his firemen standing around their shiny new pump from which the hoses had not even been unrolled.

The heavy rain saturated the blackened brickwork round the empty, gaping windows, poured down through the burnt-out floors and filled up the temporary reservoir created by damming the stream. By splicing two hoses together and running it back to the river, the Millbrook firefighters had created one powerful jet. Now their colleagues from the other mills created another in the same manner. The short hoses brought by the volunteers from Ballievy were quite adequate to tap the overflowing reservoir, their hand pump manned in turn by many willing men from Millbrook. They worked on, soaked to the skin by the pouring rain, until the last pockets of flame were doused and only great columns of steam rose from the damaged building.

The Fire Brigade left without a mark on their new uniforms or a speck of ash on their well-polished pump, the Fire Chief's report promised for Monday morning. As the rain eased, a group of women came down from the nearby cottages carrying kettles of tea and jugs of milk and took over the sodden table where earlier that afternoon they'd queued up for their wages.

A young lad brought Sarah a steaming mugful as she stood patiently in the shelter of the main entrance, knowing well she would only add to Hugh's worries if she got wet. From her vantage point, she watched the women quietly serve the small groups of men who came up in turn from the pumps and hoses. Some men exchanged a word or two with a wife, or a sister, but most remained silent. Not so much exhaustion as apprehension, she thought, as she studied the faces.

She had no idea how long it might take to restore the buildings, refit them and get back into production. They knew no better than she did. But for them every week's delay raised the question of survival. No wages, no food. It was a brutally simple equation. For families whose only breadwinners worked in the mill, today had been a disaster.

However sodden the blackened remains might look, pumps and hoses would be kept in readiness all through the night, for everyone knew the danger of hot spots surviving, even after such a soaking, under the burnt wreckage of floor girders and scorched machinery. The exhausted Millbrook firefighters were sent home, while the fresher team from Ballievy and the recently arrived men from the other two mills volunteered to be on hand till morning.

Suddenly there was nothing more to be done, except remove the tarpaulins Tom had hastily over thrown both Hugh's motor and the brougham.

'Da, I'll keep Hugh company. Is that all right?' Sarah whispered to her father, as a young man brought Bess back from the nearby meadow where all the mill's working horses had been led.

'Aye, do that,' he said, as the young man manoeuvred Bess between the shafts. 'Ye might raise his spirits a bit, more than I can,' he said wearily, his face streaked with soot and ash.

'Tell Ma I'll be a wee while yet,' he said, as he prepared to leave. 'I have to call in at Ballievy on the way home to see if we've solved our other problem. We had the beetles jammed this morning.'

'Right, I'll tell her. I'll see you later,' she said, kissing his cheek, as Hugh came up to them, grey with exhaustion.

'If we wrap Peter's bicycle in the tarpaulin and put it in the back seat, I wouldn't have to cycle home,' she said thoughtfully, looking him straight in the eye.

'Peter's bicycle?' he repeated, baffled.

'I met him at the station and borrowed it when I heard about the fire. How did you think I got here?' she asked, teasing him gently.

'I never quite thought,' he said honestly. 'Not when I heard you'd gone into the mill,' he added, shaking his head, as the memory came back to him. 'Where is it?'

'Where is what?' she echoed, confused by his obvious distress.

'The bicycle.'

'Oh yes. I'll fetch it,' she said quickly. 'I parked it up by the nightwatchman's hut.'

'No, you won't,' he said firmly. 'Get in and sit down. I'll see to it.'

They said little to each other as he drove up the slope and turned right on to the main road. The sky had cleared and the air was fresh again after the rain. Huge, spinning globes of water fell from the trees, showering them as the breeze freshened again. A stream of carts and wagons came towards them as they drove into Banbridge. The Post Office clock said it was ten to six.

'It's been a long afternoon,' she said quietly.

She found herself almost unable to think back to the

moment when she'd met Billy outside the station and learnt of the fire.

'Are you exhausted?' he asked, after a moment.

'No, I'm not as tired as you are,' she replied, turning to register the grim set of his face. 'But I haven't the burden of responsibility that you have. What happens next?'

'Fire Chief's report. Insurance assessor's valuation. A greater or lesser degree of haggling, which they like to call negotiating. Meantime, we must start the rebuilding just as soon as we can. If I wait till the claim is settled we could lose months of production. And I'll have to find a new source of spun thread, otherwise the weavers go out of production, followed by the hemstitchers and the finishers,' he said calmly.

'What will you do in your spare time?' she asked, as he stopped on the road just beyond Ballievy Mill to let a herd of cattle make their leisurely way across the road ahead of them.

He looked at her in surprise. Seeing her smile, he managed a little laugh.

'If you were at home, I'd ask you to let me come and carry your camera,' he replied, picking up her light tone. 'Perhaps we might manage an hour on Sunday and go and feed the swans.'

'That would be lovely, Hugh,' she said, beaming at him. 'Is there anything I can do to help in the meantime?'

'I think you've already done it,' he confessed, smiling, as they drew to a halt outside Jackson's farm. 'I shall think of the swans all day tomorrow when I'm tramping round the debris with your father, thinking of empty pockets and purses,' he added, as he raised a hand in greeting to Peter Jackson and his father, who'd come out to greet them and now stood staring at their smirched faces and dishevelled dress.

'Thank you so much, Peter,' Sarah said politely, as they moved to extract the bicycle from the back seat.

'She won't tell you if I don't,' said Hugh, looking from father to son. 'Thanks to your bicycle, Peter, she got to Millbrook twenty minutes before I did. She spotted a child way up on the fourth floor. God knows how she got into the mill, or how she got up to the fourth floor, but she owes her life to Sarah,' he said, shaking his head slowly. 'Sarah went and got her out,' he ended, matter-of-factly.

'Much damage?' Tommy Jackson asked abruptly

'About a third of the main building and the entire engine house. Bad enough,' Hugh nodded, as he got back into the driver's seat. 'But no one hurt, thank God,' he added, as he reversed back down the yard to give him more momentum for the hill.

The Jacksons watched till they were out of sight and went back indoors to tell the story to Mrs Jackson and a former neighbour from Lenaderg who had come to visit them. By the next day, everyone in the district would know all the details of the fire at Millbrook, probably somewhat enlarged in the telling.

Hugh stopped outside Ballydown, but kept the engine running.

'I'd be poor company tonight, Sarah,' he said wearily. 'Tell your mother I'll see her tomorrow and I'll expect Sam up later,' he went on, as she picked up her camera.

'Sam?' she repeated, puzzled.

'Yes, he's home this weekend and he needs a bed for the night,' he replied, all the life gone out of his voice.

'Goodnight, Hugh,' she said quickly, baffled by the reference to Sam, but concerned by the exhaustion she saw written all over his face. 'Thank you for bringing me home. Please try not to worry. I'll see you tomorrow.'

Rose glanced up from her chair by the fire when she heard the engine. She recognized the familiar footstep on the garden path.

'Sarah!' she exclaimed, completely taken aback by the apparition who appeared in the doorway.

Her dark hair was threaded with grey, her working dress streaked with dust, her white blouse creased and crumpled and smudged with soot, but she herself seemed entirely composed, unaware of the slightest disarrangement of her dress.

Rose got to her feet and checked her impulse to go and put her arms round her.

'Sarah love, Peter Jackson told us you'd gone to Millbrook. Are you all right?' she asked, as coolly as she could manage.

Sarah made no answer. She moved over the threshold and stood looking absently from Sam to the other figure who sat by the fire.

'Yes, yes, I'm fine,' she replied after a pause, her eyes fixed on an unknown young woman.

'Come and meet your new sister-in-law,' Rose said, slipping an arm round her waist and drawing her forward. 'Martha, this is Sarah, Sam's younger sister. Sarah, Sam and Martha are going to be married in October, on Sam's twenty-first birthday. October the 24th. Isn't that a lovely idea?'

She offered her hand to the red-headed girl and registered at last the uneasy, puzzled glances she and Sam were giving her.

'Martha, I'm sorry. I've just realized how dirty I am,' she said easily. 'Ma, do I smell of smoke?'

'Yes, you do. Very strongly. And machine oil. And you have dark circles under your eyes. I can't tell whether its soot or tiredness.'

Sam came forward to give her a hug. As she felt his soft, warm arms close around her, she suddenly felt tears spring to her eyes. She had no idea why she should cry. Perhaps it was tears of joy, because he looked so happy. Perhaps tears of sorrow for all the poor people who'd been made jobless by today's fire. Or perhaps she was just tired out. Tired beyond politeness. Quite beyond saying friendly things to this unknown and rather unprepossessing girl.

'Martha, if you'll excuse me. I think perhaps Sarah could do with a hand to get washed and changed.'

Rose picked up a kettle of water from the stove and gently propelled her towards the stairs.

'Sam dear, would you like to take Martha out to see Dolly,' she suggested, over her shoulder. 'Maybe you'd have a wee walk perhaps, till your father gets back. I'm sure he'll be here as soon as he can.'

Twenty-one

Neither Rose nor Sarah quite knew what to make of Martha Loney. A plain girl with rather sharp features and small bright eyes, she laughed a great deal and, like many plain girls, managed to look appealing enough. She appeared to have no strong likes or dislikes, accepted the preoccupations of the household and said little about herself.

The questions Rose put to her, designed to show interest rather than curiosity, she answered politely enough. But beyond the bare facts that her father farmed near Richhill Station, she had an uncle a grocer in the village itself and two other uncles and an older brother in America, they were left to guess what so appealed to Sam he wanted to marry the moment he reached twenty-one.

Late on Saturday afternoon, Sam explained they had to go back to Richhill to share their news with some friends and to visit an old aunt of Martha's on the following day. Rose was relieved to see them go. She had found Martha's presence curiously depressing and she was concerned she'd had no chance to talk to Sarah about the fire.

'Now, love, I want to hear about yesterday,' she said, as she pulled forward the kettle on the stove. 'I hadn't the heart to ask you when you were so tired and there hasn't been much chance since,' she went on, sitting down gratefully in her own chair to wait for the kettle to boil.

Sarah, too, breathed a sigh of relief. Apart from the small murmurings of the kettle the only other sound to be heard in the big kitchen was the soothing tick of the American wall clock.

'It's a long time since you've had to wash my face for me,' Sarah said, grinning broadly.

As Rose made tea, she glanced up at the small and much quieter clock on the mantelpiece and thought of John. Hugh had collected him at eight o'clock and now it was nearly five. She wished she'd made sandwiches for the pair of them. But then they might have had lunch in Banbridge. Much of the morning would be spent there, talking to the Bank Manager and the local representative of the insurance company.

'Ma,' began Sarah thoughtfully, her mind still full of the recently departed couple rather than her own adventures. 'Did you notice that Martha never looks at Sam, except in the ordinary way?'

'Yes, I did notice,' she replied, nodding, as she fetched mugs from the dresser. 'But I thought maybe she was avoiding being too affectionate. Someone may have told her mothers are always jealous.'

'I don't think so,' Sarah retorted, her brow furrowed in a familiar frown. 'I can't imagine Martha listening to *anything* anyone told her. She seems to shake everything off. Nothing reaches her.'

'"Like water off a duck's back," my mother used to say,' Rose offered promptly, Sarah's words bringing into focus something she'd been puzzling over since Martha's arrival.

They sat in silence for a little while, Rose wondering if perhaps the events at Millbrook were too distressing, or too recent for Sarah to want to speak of them yet, while Sarah was actually asking herself if Martha Loney really loved Sam or was just pleased to have such a good-natured and successful young man to show off to her relations.

'Ma, how did you know Da was the man for you?'

The question was so unexpected, Rose hardly knew what to say.

'Oh dear, now you've got me. It was rather a long time ago,' she said, pausing. 'I suppose there's no use telling you I just knew?'

'No,' said Sarah, shaking her head. 'I need to know *how* you knew.'

'All right. I promise I'll give my mind to it and give you a proper answer as soon as I can.'

Walking up the slope to the motor, parked by the roadside at Corbet Lough that Sunday afternoon, Sarah looked back over her shoulder and saw the two adult swans moving slowly away across the calm water.

'I wish I could be here to help you, Hugh,' she began. 'Not shut up in the studio all week.'

He smiled and followed her gaze out across the blue-grey, shimmering expanse.

'You've been a great help already,' he said, as they climbed into the motor and sat watching the family of grubby looking cygnets following behind their elegant parents.

'Your idea of relocating the engine house at the other end of the building and starting with half a mill is well worth looking into,' he continued. 'Your father says the machines have taken no harm at all. Every door was properly closed, so the smoke didn't get across the stairwell. That's something to be pleased about.'

She'd left her departure to the last possible moment, utterly reluctant to go back to the city, and now sat in the slow-moving train, moodily watching the dusk gather over the countryside. She asked herself why she'd found it so very hard to leave this particular time. She kept coming up with the same answer.

All afternoon, she'd been so aware of the lines of strain in his face. She smiled ruefully to herself. It wasn't surprising she knew all the telltale signs of weariness and anxiety, was it? After all, she'd known him since she was six years old.

'That's the problem,' she exclaimed, alone in the rattling carriage, the lights of scattered farms now blossoming like starflowers in the folds of dark fields and on the sides of the little hills. 'He's been my best friend for so long now I can't tell whether I love him or not.'

With her mind so preoccupied by Millbrook, Rathdrum and Ballydown, Monday's work at the studio was a real burden.

She had to force herself to concentrate. Anything less than her total attention would produce the sort of error that would bring Mrs Cheesman down on her like a ton of bricks. She ended the day exhausted, too weary even to ask for permission to print the roll of film she'd developed at the weekend.

Even when one paid for the printing paper and used chemicals about to be thrown away, Mrs Cheesman managed to make her permission into a grand concession. On this occasion, Sarah felt she couldn't trust her temper. Had she not wanted to study the pictures as soon as possible, she'd have sent them away to be done.

When the lady in question failed to turn up for work on Tuesday morning, she was relieved and delighted. Not only was the atmosphere more relaxed, but when she had a word with Harry Carroll, the senior darkroom assistant, he offered to print her pictures and give her a lesson in enlarging using her own negatives.

A kindly man, with no great love for Mrs Cheesman, Harry watched as the images came up in the developer and listened to her story of the fire. He nodded gravely when she spoke of the number of people who might be put out of work. They printed all the pictures on Tuesday morning, leaving them to wash and dry while they processed the previous day's work. Then, late in the day, when they'd studied the prints in good light, Harry made a second set of enlargements himself showing her how to pull out detail by 'shading in and dodging out' as he called it. She went home from work delighted with what she'd learnt and well pleased with the folder of carefully selected enlargements under her arm. She spent the evening writing to Hannah and Teddy about the fire and ended up feeling a lot easier in her mind, once she'd set it all down on paper.

But her good spirits did not last. Coming down to breakfast next morning, she found a letter from her mother. Unable to bear the thought of a whole week without news, she'd asked her mother to write if there was any significant progress on the insurance claim, or if the Belfast firm responsible for replacing the engines had given any delivery date.

She tore open the letter and read, her heart sinking with each paragraph.

Ballydown
Tuesday

My dearest Sarah,

I am keeping my promise, but with such a heavy heart. All my news is bad and while I hope things may seem lighter by the time you come home on Saturday, I can't depend on it. It's better that I warn you.

It seems the Fire Chief has presented his report to the Insurance Company and told them that the fire started in the engine house and spread to the mill. He says the engine house was already burnt out when he and his men arrived, but the mill was still burning. I know this isn't true because both you and Hugh have told me what happened, but apparently the Fire Chief's report is accepted by the Insurance Company in preference to the report from the Mill Manager, for obvious reasons.

I couldn't understand what difference it made where the fire started, providing all the premiums were paid up. They were, and they are huge. I had no idea how enormous. But it seems that, in order to keep the premiums as low as possible, there are exclusion clauses concerning engine houses, the chief source of fires. That is why Da and Hugh have worked so hard on ventilation systems for them. Apparently, the fire in the mill was discovered *during the hourly inspection of the engine house* when one of the foremen smelt something on the air outside and went searching for it.

If it cannot be proved that the fire started *in the mill building itself* the compensation is reduced to twenty-five per cent, a sum that will not even cover the new engines. Hugh's accountant is hard at work trying to find money for rebuilding, but although interest rates are steady and Hugh's credit is good, it is a desperate risk to take. Da is in a bad way as you would expect.

As Hugh's partner, he feels our savings should be set alongside his, as they have almost all come from the success of the mills. Hugh has said a firm no.

I know this will distress you very much and I pray there will be better news soon.

As I sat down to write, I remembered the question you asked me on Saturday after Martha and Sam had left. This is perhaps not the best time to answer it, but I shall, because I cannot bear to end this letter on such an unhappy note.

The reason I knew that your father was the man for me was that, apart from liking him and enjoying being with him, I felt *most myself* in his company. Sometimes, as I look back on the bad times, and I have been reminded of them today, I am amazed at the things I managed, the courage that came to me, the hope I had the strength to generate. I feel sure these things came to me because I had a man with whom I could be *most myself.*

I'll write again as soon as I have any news whatever. I know how upset you must be.

Keep up your spirits. I am thinking of you,
Your loving
Ma

It was all Sarah could do to stop herself packing a bag, collecting up her pictures and getting the first train home. The thought was so tempting, she knew it must be wrong, so she put a few things together with her pictures, went in to work early, waited for Mr Abernethy and asked if she could have the day off, unpaid, or even the half day, to attend to a family matter.

Mr Abernethy was his usual avuncular self. Full of sympathy, he went immediately to consult Mrs Cheesman. He returned in a matter of moments full of apologies. It was simply not possible given the high level of bookings for the day. He was sure she would understand.

Knowing perfectly well what the bookings were for the day and that it would have been perfectly possible to let her go, she was hardly able to contain her fury. As there was nowhere else to go, she went and sat in the lavatory adjoining the stuffy cubicle laughingly called the staff cloakroom. It was still only ten to eight, and in there even Mrs Cheesman couldn't follow her. She tried to think clearly. She *could* just walk out, here and now, but how would that look if she applied for another job?

As she heard footsteps on the stairs and her colleagues' voices, she made up her mind. It wasn't what she wanted, but it was better than nothing. She'd get the first possible train to Banbridge after six o'clock and the last one back. She'd have nearly an hour at Ballydown.

Rose sprang to her feet, dropping her book, as she walked into the kitchen.

'Sarah love, how did you get here? Is anything wrong?'

'No. Nothing more than we know, that is,' she replied, swinging off her cape gratefully, for she'd walked quickly from the station on a damp, humid evening and was now thoroughly hot and bothered.

'Hullo, Sarah,' said John, getting up to kiss her. 'What brings you?' he said, puzzled, his face traced with weary lines.

'Photographs, Da,' she said, still out of breath. 'Ma wrote and told me about the insurance. I think you and Hugh need to see these pictures,' she went on, taking a bright, yellow envelope from her bag, laying it on the table and dropping gratefully onto one of the kitchen chairs beside it.

'Have you had any supper?' Rose asked, looking at her pale face.

'No, I hadn't time. I only just made the train. But I'm more thirsty than hungry.'

'Ach, sit down and let your mother get you a bite,' said her father briskly, as he picked up his cap. 'I'll away and fetch Hugh down here. Sure the poor man's only sittin' up there with his papers on his own. We asked him for supper, but he said he was no company for anyone,' he explained as he paused in the doorway before striding off.

'Would you like bacon and eggs, Sarah?'

Sarah shook her head.

'What I'd really like is bread and jam,' she said honestly. 'And a whole pot of tea,' she added, laughing.

'You've brought good news?' Rose declared, studying her closely, as she followed her into the dairy and stood watching her cutting bread. 'Damson?' she asked, as she reached up into the cupboard.

'You must have known I was coming if there's damson,' she replied happily. 'It's been an awful day, Ma,' she confessed, as Rose boiled water on the gas. 'I asked for the day off without pay, or a half day, but that old So-and-So Cheesman said no. She could have spared me perfectly well. I nearly walked out.'

'I couldn't have blamed you for that. Why didn't you?'

'I don't know. Perhaps I need a little longer.'

Rose was about to ask what she needed a little longer for when they heard the sound of Hugh's motor outside.

'How thoughtful,' she said. 'He'll run you back to the station for the last train far quicker than Dolly. It'll give you longer.

'Sarah,' said Hugh, coming into the kitchen behind her father. 'I hear you know what's happened.'

'Mmm,' she said, smiling at him, her mouth full. 'I *hope* I've got good news. Let me go and wipe my fingers.'

As Rose lit the gas lamp Sarah spread out the pictures on the table. Hugh and John stared at them unblinking.

'They're very clear, Sarah, but I'm afraid I can't see how they help,' said Hugh steadily. 'Especially the two of the burnt-out engine house with the mill still burning.'

Sarah nodded and drank gratefully from her mug of tea.

'Those aren't the useful ones. These are,' she declared, moving to one end of the kitchen table, where she'd lined up the pictures in the order in which she'd taken them.

'This is the west end of the mill, before either of you got there, when the fire was just getting going and the first hose had failed.'

'Look,' she said, pointing to a fuzzy object in the foreground. 'That's the little decorative bit on the gable of the engine house. I was so busy making sure I didn't fall off the roof, I just didn't notice it in the picture. If the fire *had* started in the engine house, I couldn't have taken these pictures standing on its roof, could I?'

The two men looked at each other and then at Sarah.

'I can't see any two ways about that, Hugh. Can you?' said her father, a slow smile spreading across his face.

'I've had another thought,' said Hugh quickly. 'If the engine house *had* been on fire, the men would never have let Sarah anywhere near that end of the mill. How then could she have seen the wee lassie she brought out, if she hadn't been able to look up at those end windows?'

'Aye, now yer talking,' said John gleefully. 'We'll away in an' see yer man again in the mornin'.'

Rose and Sarah exchanged looks as Hugh sat down at the table and peered at the photographs again, his face slowly shedding its anxiety.

'Well done, Sarah,' he said quietly, looking up at her. 'I know your mother's been praying for a miracle, but I wasn't expecting it so soon,' he said, finally managing to smile.

It was almost dark as he drove her back to the station, the untried headlights of the motor creating a strange tunnel effect on the familiar road. She knew he was exhausted and finding the road difficult in the dusk, but she suddenly felt shy of offering words of comfort and encouragement.

'Shall I see you on Saturday?' he asked calmly, as they stood on the platform, the train already approaching.

'Yes, I'll be home as usual.'

'Can I pick you up?'

'It's too uncertain, Hugh. I may have to work all afternoon. Could we go and see the swans?' she asked quickly, as the train stopped beside them and doors flung open around them.

'Any time you want,' he said, as she stepped in and he shut the door behind her.

She watched him standing under the yellowish light of the station lamps, a tall, composed figure, solitary now the platform had cleared of the new arrivals. She sat back in her seat when she could no longer wave to him and felt tears trickle down her face. In the empty carriage she didn't even bother to wipe them away.

The only good thing about the days that followed Sarah's hasty visit to Ballydown was the smile on Harry Carroll's face when she told him that his enlargements might well resolve the insurance claim.

Harry wanted to hear the whole story and nodded his head vigorously when she told him about the pictures taken from the engine-house roof. He added to the argument by reminding her that if anyone tried to argue about the sequence in which she'd taken her pictures she had the evidence of the negatives. She was not to let them out of her sight, he insisted, but she could show them the tiny numbers at the edge of the film that could in no way be interfered with.

The days were wearying, the effort of keeping her mind on her work a strain, the evenings were too short now to walk far and she was sleeping badly. All the time, she felt she was trying to resolve something that refused to shape itself. If only she knew what the problem was, she might have some chance of solving it.

Since the moment she'd emerged from the burning mill, she'd been sure Hugh loved her. Now she was equally sure she loved him. She loved him. Wanted to be with him. Wanted to share his life and whatever it might bring. As her mother had said, she felt *most herself* when she was with him. She was sure he would never own up to his feelings for her unless she made her feelings clear. But that seemed so difficult.

The only person who might be able to help her was her mother, but there was nothing to be done about that until she went home again. She would simply have to be patient. To make matters worse she found out that Mrs Cheesman was attending a gala on Saturday afternoon and she would have to take charge of the bookings for portraits in her place.

'Miss Hamilton, a moment, if you please.'

Sarah looked up from inserting a fresh plate into the main

studio camera and found Mr Abernethy beaming down at her.

'Ah, I see you are getting ready in good time,' he said approvingly. 'Miss Slater is not due till two o'clock, but it is always good to be well prepared. You are aware who Miss Slater is, I am sure?' he said, with that tone which made Sarah wish she never had to see the awful man again.

'Miss Slater?' she repeated calmly.

'Yes, indeed. Her father is one of our best customers. *Alderman* Slater,' he went on, clear now that further instruction was necessary. 'A very flourishing provisions business. Opening new branches all the time. I wouldn't be at all surprised if he was to be our next Lord Mayor,' he added gleefully, the pictures on the studio walls already rearranged in his head to accommodate this new and very prestigious portrait.

Sarah nodded and looked attentive. She wondered why he didn't go away now he'd made it clear this young woman was to be treated with special attention. No mistakes with spotlights to turn her into a witch, as Harry Carroll would say.

'You appreciate, of course, by now the significance of the double booking,' he continued, his eyes narrowing just a little.

'Personal portrait, plus engagement portrait,' she replied promptly.

The smile broadened.

'Good. I shall bring Miss Slater up myself,' he went on. 'Then, at half past two, I shall send one of the young men up with her fiancé.'

To Sarah's great relief he left, and she was able to go on making her preparations at her own speed, a part of her mind already counting the hours till she could get on that train and feel the miles begin to diminish between her and home.

'Miss Slater, let me introduce Miss Hamilton,' said Abernethy, with a bow to the skinny, but elegantly dressed, young woman he was escorting. 'You may be a little surprised that I am not allowing myself the great privilege of taking your portrait myself, but, alas, times move on,' he said, laughing jovially. 'I have had to admit that this young lady is more up to date than I. You may see for yourself what splendid portraits she produces. Like this one of Lady Cleeve. Charming, isn't it?' he said, sweeping a hand towards one of Harry Carroll's splendid enlargements, double mounted and hung in an ornate gold frame.

Miss Slater nodded, mollified. Abernethy retreated and Sarah began work. Once she got behind a camera it wasn't so bad. This was the part of the job she enjoyed, attempting to catch something of the person beyond the lens. Miss Slater did as she was asked and knew what she wanted when Sarah consulted her about angles and backgrounds. Beyond a habit of looking down her rather unfortunate nose, she behaved quite correctly. She saved her smiles for the camera, but did manage a 'Thank you' when Sarah excused herself to take the plates to the darkroom and return with a fresh supply.

When she came back into the studio, Miss Slater's fiancé had arrived. With his back to her, he was looking down at his intended, who still sat on the carved wooden chair on which she'd chosen to be photographed.

The young man turned as he heard the rustle of her skirt.

'Jamie,' she cried, her heart leaping to her mouth.

'Sarah.'

He stared at her in amazement while Miss Slater, her smile vanished, looked from one to the other.

'James, you know this young woman?' she asked sharply.

'She's my sister,' he said, as he looked around desperately for some way out of the situation.

'But you told me your sister was married to someone in England, some Lord or other,' she exclaimed, a horrified look on her face.

'That's quite true, Miss Slater,' said Sarah quickly. 'Lady Cleeve is James's sister and mine. He hasn't misinformed you. But it's some time since James and I have seen each other,' she said soothingly. 'All families have their upsets,' she went on, amazed at her own calmness. 'I'm afraid I badly upset James when I was *much* younger and he hasn't been to see us since. I hoped he'd forgive me one day, but I never dreamed of meeting like this. I do apologize, it must be so upsetting for you,' Sarah ended, smiling at them both.

Jamie managed a frosty smile and looked enormously relieved.

'I must congratulate you, James,' she said, beaming at him. 'Now, I insist that you help me produce my best ever engagement portraits.'

Without waiting for further agreement, Sarah started work. She took her time with the settings, consulted them jointly about the backgrounds, took great pains to arrange Miss Slater's hands to reveal becomingly the ring which James had brought with him. But under cover of her activity, she was thinking what she would do. By the time she'd finished she'd made up her mind.

'There now, I think we have some good pictures,' she said easily. 'You do make a very nice couple,' she added, as warmly as she could manage. 'Miss Slater, could I beg a small favour? I should like to apologize to my brother for all the upset I've caused, but I'm somewhat embarrassed. Would you be so kind as to allow us a few minutes together?'

Put so graciously, Miss Slater could hardly refuse. She picked up her skirts, moved cautiously between the lamps and cables, paused at the door and said, 'I shall wait in the ladies' reception room. Five minutes only, James, we *do* have another engagement,' she said, as she shut the door behind her.

Now that she'd achieved her objective, Sarah hadn't the slightest idea what she was going to say. The thought that she had a mere five minutes to try to resolve a situation that had existed for four years almost overwhelmed her.

'When are you getting married, Jamie?'

'James,' he said, automatically.

'I always did prefer James. Ma will be pleased. She's always been so sorry they gave you a name you didn't like.'

'October,' he said, ignoring her remark.

'Goodness, so soon. Sam's getting married in October as well. Two Hamiltons in one month,' she went on, not knowing where she was going.

'Are Ma and Da well?' he asked, looking uncomfortable.

'Yes, they're well. Da's a partner now and there was a big fire at Millbrook last week. It was a great anxiety, but it's been sorted out now,' she went on, studying his face.

He had looked pale and uneasy most of the time, except when he managed a determined smile for the camera, but behind the unease there was a unbendingness she'd not seen in him before.

'Perhaps you could come and see them, James,' she said quietly. 'It was my fault you were so upset, but it's they who have suffered. You'd be so welcome. And Miss Slater, too.'

He shook his head.

'No, Sarah, it wasn't your fault,' he said coolly. 'If it was anyone's fault that day it was Hannah's. She wouldn't stop rubbing it in about our Catholic relatives. Da was bad enough but she was worse. It's not Da and Ma in themselves. There's no way up the ladder for a man with handfuls of Catholic relatives, Land Leaguers and Redmondites. I made up my mind when I got my managership there'd be no going back.'

He took out his fob watch and looking at it meaningfully.

'What about Ma?' Sarah asked. 'She loved you so.'

'Long ago, Sarah, long ago. The world moves on. You'll understand better when you're older,' he said, his tone insufferably condescending as he moved towards the door.

'Would you like me to say thank you for the shirts?'

'What shirts?'

'The ones she made for you and sent every Christmas until you moved and she had no address,' she explained, her voice rising with her distress.

'I'd forgotten,' he said, his hand on the doorknob. 'Yes, do that for me, Sarah. And good luck with the photography,' he added, as he slipped through and closed it firmly behind him.

Twenty-two

The evening train was crowded. There were many people like Sarah herself, going home to farmhouses in the countryside after a long working week in the city. There were others, too, already free from their week's work, heading for Hillsborough, or Dromore, or Banbridge, for some Saturday night entertainment. Couples sat together close enough to hold hands without being observed. Young men in stiff collars, like Peter Jackson, put down their newspapers and thought about a home-cooked supper, a Sunday lie-in, a walk in the lanes, listening to news of animals and fields, weather and prices, in the different world to which they were returning.

Sitting by a window, she stared unseeing at the passing landscape and saw no one in the crowded carriage. Her thoughts were all of Jamie. She turned over and over in her mind the brief conversation Miss Slater had granted. It didn't give much hope. In fact, the more she considered it, the more sure she was it didn't give any hope at all. Jamie had shut the door of the studio behind him, just as he had shut the door on the Hamiltons of Ballydown, when he got his long-awaited managership.

'He'd forgotten Ma's lovely shirts,' she said to herself, torn between sadness that her mother's loving gesture could be so rejected and her own anger that he'd become a person who could do such a thing.

She recalled the way he had stood behind Miss Slater's chair, his carefully assumed posture both protective and possessive. The picture she'd composed for the camera lens was a picture of what he wanted. His every word, his every move, made it clear he had indeed made up his mind long ago and he had not the slightest intention of changing it. His final words to her, 'Good luck with the photography,' were said with a particular dismissiveness that told her he never wished, or expected, to lay eyes on her ever again.

She pulled out her bag from under her seat and took out a bright, yellow envelope. Another bright, yellow envelope. Only four days ago, she'd journeyed home on this same early evening train with just such an envelope, but that one had held a cluster of pictures that brought hope and promised an end to anxiety.

She slid out the single print of the happy couple Harry had made for her. It was a good picture. Neither Mrs Cheesman nor Mr Abernethy would be able to find fault with it. Miss Slater seated, Jamie standing erect, the sharp figures nicely offset against the drapes they'd chosen. She studied it carefully, pretending she herself had not taken it. What did it tell her about this couple and about this young man in particular? What could she guess at from Jamie's poised, immaculate dress, his confident smile, his hand placed casually, but proprietorially, on the back of the carved chair.

She gazed at it for a long time in the golden light reflecting through the dust-streaked windows of the train. It confirmed all she'd read when she was face-to-face with her brother. She pushed it back into the black-lined envelope and into her bag. The question now was what she did about it.

The station was crowded, but the moment she emerged from the booking hall she spotted Hugh's motor. Her father and Hugh himself were sitting watching the crowds that spilt out from the Belfast train. Hugh was the first to spot her and wave.

'Hello, Hugh. Hello, Da. I wasn't expecting to see either of you,' she said, smiling up at them.

'Hop up there beside Hugh,' said her father, getting down and taking her bag from her. 'We were out at Millbrook and Hugh remembered the time. When you weren't home by three, we knew you'd had to work on. We thought we'd save you a walk,' he explained, as he settled himself in the back seat.

She sat back gratefully. The walk would have been pleasant on such a fine evening, but suddenly she felt very tired and very grateful to be riding home. Hugh smiled at her, then gave his attention to weaving his way through the usual Saturday evening throng of carts and traps parked at random between the station and the Crozier Monument.

'Well,' she said, as they cleared the town and the road opened before them. 'What news? It can't be bad, for Ma promised to write if it was.'

'No, it's not bad, Sarah. It's as good as it can be,' Hugh began. 'They're paying up. We've employed all our own men to clear the debris and the builders are starting on Monday. It'll take Mackies six weeks to build and install the engines, but we're going to hire portable ones for the east end and work half the mill on a double shift system,' he said, smiling broadly and looking pleased with himself. 'Not my idea,' he added, 'but I do listen to my friends.'

'So most families will have wages coming in,' she replied, breathing a great sigh of relief.

'All families,' he declared, nodding, without taking his eyes from the road. 'When the men finish clearing the debris, those still not needed in the mill are starting work on a small reservoir on the brook so we'll never be short of water again. We might even attract a pair of swans, like Corbet Lough,' he added, a strange, wistful note in his voice offsetting her pleasure in what he was saying.

'Are ye sure ye won't come in for a bite of supper, Hugh?' John asked, as they stopped outside Ballydown.

Sarah smiled encouragingly. After this long, hard week, it would be so good to share the whole story of the claim and the plans they'd made as soon as it was clear the worst was over, but she saw a look pass across Hugh's face which meant he would not come. She felt sad, disappointed. Once more, after a short and happy meeting, she was to be deprived of his company.

'Thank you, John, that would be very pleasant, but I've some contracts to go through, so they can be delivered by hand first thing on Monday.'

Suddenly, she remembered she had a job of her own to do this evening. With luck, when she and Hugh went down to look for the swans tomorrow her mind would be clearer.

* * *

'Well, well, so that's the way of it, is it,' John stated flatly.

Sarah looked from her father to her mother and wondered yet again if she'd done the right thing.

'He didn't ask for Sam or for Hannah, did he?' said Rose, already turning over her careful account of the brief conversation in the studio.

Sarah shook her head.

'And he's James now again, is he?' John asked, an edge of irritation in his voice.

'Yes. Miss Slater didn't seem to like Jamie at all from the look on her face, so I called him James. But when we were alone I called him Jamie and he corrected me.'

'Did you not find out her first name, Sarah?' her mother asked in turn. 'Surely he didn't call her Miss Slater?'

'He didn't call her anything. Not in front of me. I've a feeling he didn't want me to know, now I come to think of it. He really didn't want to give away anything. I'm sure if I'd had longer and asked more questions he'd just have put me off.'

They sat in silence in front of the stove, the big kitchen filling with shadow though the light was still golden across the road in the field the Jacksons had rented for their cattle.

She searched her mind for any word or detail she might have missed, but there was nothing really to add to the simple account she'd given.

'I do have one of the pictures I took of them. Harry did an extra one by mistake and I asked him for it. I'm not sure now whether it makes matters better or worse. I can't throw it away till I've asked you.'

John said nothing and Rose studied his downcast face for many minutes before she replied.

'Oh, I think we should see it, Sarah,' she said quietly, giving her a reassuring glance which he failed to see.

She fetched the envelope from her bag, drew out the picture and handed it to her mother. She studied it coolly for a long minute and then passed it across to John without comment.

'A well set up young man,' he said, sharply. 'If you diden know you'd never guess his Granda laboured tossing sheaves on a Galloway farm and went to Mass on Sunday,' he went on bitterly. 'Indeed, you'd hardly think his mother sewed wee babies' dresses till her eyes ran red to keep him fed, and his wicked oul' Uncle Sam that helped keep poor, evicted people from starvin' spent a week's wage to buy him an' his brother the first books they iver had about steam engines.'

He handed the photograph back to Rose.

'Aye, maybe he'll end up a big man,' he said nodding. 'He has the brains for it. An' he's picked a girl to get him inta the right places. Sure he might end up on the Board of Harlands and be Sir James.'

He paused, a strange, grim expression on his face, so unlike him.

'Wasn't he lucky he had a good Ulster name like Hamilton?' he continued at last. 'Sure can't he pretend he's one of the Hamiltons of Clandeboye or Dufferin. He need never let on he's only one of the Hamiltons of Ballydown.'

He got up and marched across the floor.

'I'll just away out an' see to Dolly. I can't mind if I left her any oats earlier,' he announced, as he picked up his cap and disappeared round the side of the house.

'Da's very upset,' said Sarah sadly.

'Yes, he is. But he'll be all right given a bit of time,' her mother replied calmly.

'Do you think I should just have torn up the photograph?' she asked, still utterly distressed by the bleak look on her father's face.

'No, I think you did right,' she replied firmly. 'The only thing to do with a hurt is to face it. I faced my loss some time back when there was no word after the second Christmas. But your father has no way of coming to terms with something unless he can see it and touch it. It has to be there in front of him. It's often that way with men. The photograph was a gift. It helped him do what I've already done,' she ended, with a great sigh.

'So you've really accepted it, Ma?' Sarah asked gently.

'Yes, love. There's never any use wasting time on regrets. There's so much else more worth doing. But perhaps it's easy for me. Remember, Sarah, I might not have been here to see Jamie turn his back on us. Death would have spared me the hurt. But I'd rather have life. I'm so grateful for all I've got.'

Sarah got up and moved restlessly to look out of the open door.

'Will Da really be all right?'

'Yes, he will. He's hurt, but he knows he's loved. Once the sharp sting passes, he'll remember that and he'll be fine again. Don't worry, Sarah, he's got over worse than this.'

Sarah glanced up at the clock on the mantelpiece. It was only just after eight o'clock.

'Ma, there's something I need to say to Hugh,' she said quickly. 'I know I'll see him tomorrow, but I'm afraid of losing hold of it. Do you mind if I leave you for half an hour or so?'

To her great surprise, her mother smiled, her dark eyes springing back to life.

'No time like the present, Sarah. I'll see you later,' she said encouragingly, as Sarah caught up her cape from the hooks by the door.

At the bottom of the hill, Peter Jackson and his father were driving the cows back up to their pasture. She waved, but called no greeting, the quiet in her head was so fragile she felt she dare not risk disturbing it.

She walked quickly up the hill and down the avenue to Rathdrum, more aware of the scatter of yellowed leaves at her feet than of the clear sky now paling as the sun went west. There was no sign of Mrs Lappin in the kitchen or in her sitting room nearby, so she went down the hall to the dining room where the long, polished table was usually three-quarters covered with paper. She knocked gently.

'Come in.'

Hugh was bent over his documents. He glanced up and looked startled, but reassured by her smile, he stood up and came towards her.

'Sarah, what a nice surprise,' he managed, recovering himself.

'There was something I needed to ask you, Hugh.'

He brought her a chair and placed it near to his own. She sat down without taking her eyes from his face.

'I wanted to ask you if you ever feel lonely,' she said, matter-of-factly.

'Well, yes. Yes, of course I do.'

'I've been wondering why you haven't done anything about it.'

'Should I have?'

'No. There's no requirement. But it's a pity to be lonely if it's not necessary.'

He looked around him awkwardly, surveying the piled-up pieces of paper as if one of them might just contain the answer. They had always been direct with each other. Candour had come to Hugh from his Quaker upbringing. It had been a characteristic of Sarah ever since he had known her.

'If I were twenty-six and not thirty-six, there might be a possibility of a solution,' he said with an effort, the struggle to choose his words drawing out the lines of weariness the last anxious week had brought.

'You'd marry?'

'I'd risk a proposal.'

'So why would it be a risk?'

'Because I feel old and tired and the woman in question is young and energetic and has infinite possibilities in front of her. Besides, were I to propose and be rejected I would lose what is precious to me. It's not worth that risk,' he said, dropping his face in his hands.

'Oh dear, you have had a bad week, haven't you?'

He looked up and saw her smiling, her eyes sparkling with laughter.

He managed a feeble smile in response but said nothing.

'I've had a rotten week too,' she said softly. 'I missed you. I wanted to be with you. I longed to be here helping you. I've been just as lonely. So what are we going to do about it?'

'Sarah, are you saying you'd be willing to marry me?'

'Yes, I think that's the general drift of my thinking,' she

replied, in a light, teasing tone. 'It might be a good idea if you forgot about age, yours or mine, and just concentrated on friendship and love.'

'And cherishing whatever time we have?' he said, reaching for her hand.

His eyes wide with surprise, he found at last the words he needed.

'Sarah, my dear love, will you marry me?'

'Yes.'

'As soon as possible?'

'I have a half day next Friday,' she said, her face straight for a few moments before she dissolved into laughter.

He stood up, gathered her into his arms and kissed her.

'I really ought to ask your father's permission,' he said, hesitantly.

'We could go and do that now, couldn't we?' she said, releasing him. 'No time like the present, as the saying is,' she added, thinking of her mother, who had finally shown her what she needed to do.

Sunday afternoon was fine and warm when they drove off down to Corbet Lough with two bags of crusts for the swans. Back at Ballydown, Rose and John sat by the stove reading the Sunday papers.

'Did you know this was goin' to happen?' he said suddenly, his paper lowered to his knees.

'Yes, I did,' she replied, dropping hers on her lap.

'Well, if it's not a rude question, how did ye know?'

'John dear, he's been fond of Sarah since she was a wee girl,' she said, laughing.

'Aye, ah know that. I'm not completely blind. But how did ye know Sarah was fond of him?'

'I knew from the questions she was asking me. Only a week or so ago, she asked me how I knew you were the man for me.'

'An' you told her?'

'Of course I did,' she replied. 'That's what mothers are for.'

'But why last night, Rose?' he persisted. 'Why did she suddenly away off when I was out seein' to Dolly and the next thing we knew Hugh was askin' my permission to marry her? My goodness, I've never seen a man shed the years like our Hugh last night. Sure, he cou'da been in his twenties and the sight o' the pair o' them standin' there did my heart good.'

'They say love does that to people, John. Had you forgotten that in your old age?' she asked, teasing him.

'Aye, well,' he said sheepishly. 'I am gettin' old, I suppose, but I haven't forgotten that,' he went on. 'But ye haven't answered me. Why last night, after all that talk about Jamie?'

'I'm not *sure,* love, but I think suddenly Sarah saw her way. Maybe it was the contrast between her and Jamie. Jamie is ambitious, he has a plan and marriage is a part of that. Sarah has great hope. She wants to do things, but she could never use someone like Jamie could. With Sarah love must come first. She just had to be sure of herself. She may be young, but she wasn't hasty.'

'No, I can see that. Hugh wouldn't let her do something that wasn't the right thing for her. That's why he's never spoken.'

He paused, staring at the flames through the open doors of the stove.

'Do you think they'll be as happy as we are, Rose?'

She smiled and looked across at him, smartly dressed, with his Sunday coat hung over the back of his chair, his dark hair well dusted with grey at the temples. There were times when she felt such an overwhelming tenderness for this man with whom she had shared so much, she hardly knew what to do about it.

'Yes, I think they'll be happy. If they're as happy as we've been, they'll do well,' she said, getting up and bending her face close to his to brush a kiss against his wind-roughened cheeks. 'Sarah told me Hugh said they should cherish the time they had. Good advice, don't you think, love?' she asked gently.

'Aye,' he replied. 'Cherish the time *an'* cherish the ones that love you. We've got so much, Rose, we'll waste no time on regrets,' he said, with an air of finality.